JERSEY BRIDES

THREE-IN-ONE COLLECTION

LAURIE ALICE EAKES

BARBOUR
PUBLISHING

Cover design: Kirk DouPonce, DogEared Design

Published by Barbour Publishing, Inc., P.O. Box 719, Uhrichsville, Ohio 44683, www.barbourbooks.com

Our mission is to publish and distribute inspirational products offering exceptional value and biblical encouragement to the masses.

ecpa Member of the
Evangelical Christian
Publishers Association

Printed in the United States of America.

Dear Readers,

My first job out of college introduced me to New Jersey. I worked in the US headquarters of an international mission. Although I was only there for a few months, something about this state with its settings from quiet rural, to frantic urban, and its fascinating history as one of the original thirteen colonies, got into my blood. I returned several times for various reasons.

After spending several weeks in Morristown, where George Washington spent some time during the American Revolution, I picked up a couple of books on New Jersey history and began to read. In those books, I learned so much that I could write ten books set in New Jersey.

One item jumped out at me and set my imagination spinning—the glassblowing industry. I researched glassblowing, learned Scotland was one of the primary glassmaking countries in the world, and thus my Scottish glassblower hero, Colin, was born. I paired him with Meg, the boss's daughter, raised the stakes so that loving one another could ruin not only their lives, but the lives of others dependent on them, and wrote *The Glassblower*.

Then I couldn't let the Grassick family go, so I wondered what would happen to Colin and Meg's children, perhaps grandchildren. Daire, like his grandmother, is a bit of a rebel against his family and the Lord, and causes trouble mostly for himself because of it. He sells a family heirloom—of glass—to Susan. The heirloom is more valuable than Daire realized, and he needs it back. But Susan, in her chaotic life, has lost it. They set out on a quest together and find more than the heirloom. Thus *The Heiress* finds herself a part of the Grassick family.

To say much about *The Newcomer* gives away the ending of *The Heiress*, so I'll simply say that I paired Marigold, with her generous heart, and Gordon, with his empty heart, and gave them a mission that brings joy and love and danger into their lives in the resort town of Cape May.

In each story, my characters are on a quest to find where they are supposed to be in their lives. What they find is the love between a man and a woman, the greater love of God, and how He has a purpose for each of their lives, as He does for ours. My prayer is that you are not only entertained by these stories, but also grow closer to the Lord as you read.

Sincerely,
Laurie Alice Eakes

THE GLASSBLOWER

Dedication

To my agent, who wouldn't let me give up.

Chapter 1

Children's laughter rang through the trees. Her heart leaping to the playful sound, Meg Jordan increased her pace.

She wanted to tell everyone about her school. In less than two months, she would open the doors of the old building, and every child in Salem County, New Jersey, could learn to read and write, not just those whose parents hired a governess or sent their offspring to boarding schools. Any child wishing to do so would sit before her while she instructed them on the alphabet and sums. If all went well, she would add lessons on the history of the United States of America. For years to come, children in her district of Salem County would enjoy an education. In time all young people could remain home while they learned instead of being sent away from their families as she had been, despite her protests.

She would start her school, fulfill her promise to her dying mother, as long as her father didn't make her marry before she was ready to do so.

"Dear Lord, please let Father change his mind." Her voice rose above the hilarity of the children and sigh of smoke-laden breeze through the bare branches of oaks and conifers. "Please don't let Mr. Pyle ask for my hand. The children need me."

And she didn't like Joseph Pyle, owner of the farm next to her father's. He was young enough at three and thirty, the same age as the United States and only a dozen years older than Meg. He was certainly handsome with his blond hair and blue eyes. His farm was prosperous. But his smile never reached his eyes, and he always took the most succulent slice of meat off the serving dish.

Meg laughed at herself for assessing a respected man on such flimsy details. Joseph Pyle would make a fine husband. She simply found her school more important to her than getting married. No fourteen-year-old daughter, the age Meg had been, should have to be away while her mother was ill, was dying. . . .

She mustn't dwell on that. She should be hunting up whoever had dumped a load of soot in the middle of the one-room building. Without windows to the building and both glassworks and charcoal burners plentiful in the area, she could expect some soot to dirty the floor. This, however, was far more than a dusting of grime. This was a mound, as though someone had removed the grate beneath a glasshouse furnace and emptied the contents of the bin in the middle of her floor. Nonsensical mischief, plain and simple, but she didn't know how she was going to clean it or stop it from happening again if someone was set on tomfoolery around the as yet unused building.

"I need windows," she declared aloud. "They can even be crown glass."

Most houses had crown glass. It was thick in the middle, and though one could only see clearly through it on the edges, it let in light and kept out the elements. It would keep out undesirable persons who sabotaged a mostly unused building, since she would be able to lock the door.

Ahead of her, the laughter of the young people shifted to yells and shrieks. Meg slowed. If the game they were playing was boisterous, she didn't want to charge into the midst of it.

She reached the bend in the road, where a lightning-struck pine leaned over the burbling creek like an old woman drawing water. The lane widened there with a narrow track leading to several small farms and the furnaces of the charcoal burners. In the midst of the Y-shaped intersection, half a dozen boys raced from corner to corner in pursuit of several kittens.

"You're herding cats?" Meg stopped to stare at the game.

If it was a game. It appeared more like chaos with each youth—from the youngest of perhaps five years to the eldest of somewhere around twelve—diving, ducking, and careening into one another as they charged after tiny balls of black-and-white fur. The felines also lacked a plan for their escape. They darted one way, lashed out needlelike claws to fend off a reaching hand, then sprang in the opposite direction. Boys yelled over scratches and laughed at cats somersaulting over one another.

"If you just stand still—"

Two boys no older than five or six streaked past her, jostling her to the edge of the road, and dove onto one of the kittens.

"Bring it here," an older child called.

Meg glanced his way and caught her breath. "No, you can't."

The boy held up a burlap bag that bulged and wriggled, proclaiming that the cat now on its way to the sack was not going to be the first occupant.

"Let them go," Meg cried.

The boys swung toward her and froze. The still-free cats vanished from sight.

"Now look what you've done." The boy with the bag glared at Meg. "They're gettin' away."

"Of course they are." Meg stared right back at him. "Would you want someone to put you in a sack?"

"I'm not a cat." The youth of perhaps twelve years shook the bag.

A pitiful yowling rose from inside the rough fabric.

"Let them go." Meg threw back her shoulders—in an effort to make herself appear taller, more authoritative, more menacing if possible—and narrowed her eyes. "You must never harm an animal."

"But Pa said we was to get rid of them." One of the younger boys stuck out his lower lip. "We can't disobey Pa."

Meg winced. The child was right. If their father told them to do something, then they should do it. But stuffing kittens into a sack was unacceptable.

"Did he say how"—she swallowed—"you should get rid of them?"

"Nope." The eldest boy ground the toe of his clog into the sand. "He just gave us the bag of kittens and said to take 'em away."

"But Davy dropped the bag and they got away," another boy said.

"Then you should have left it at that." Meg crossed her arms. "Indeed, set the bag down and let the others go free."

"Can't," the eldest boy insisted. "It's too close to home, and they'll just go back."

"Pa says they're a menace," another youth piped up. "He tripped over one and burned his arm on the charcoal burner."

"Dear me." Meg tapped her foot.

From the corner of her eye, she caught movement in the lightning-struck tree. Gray wings blended into cloudy sky as a dove took flight. In response, a plaintive *ma–row* drifted from the branches.

Meg's heart sank. No doubt the kitten didn't know how to get down from the tree or would slip and fall into the foaming water. It was so tiny it couldn't possibly survive on its own.

None of them appeared old enough to survive on their own. Even if the boys let them go and the cats didn't get back home, they probably wouldn't live.

"All right." Meg took a deep breath. "Round up the kittens, and I'll take them to my father's farm. We have so many—"

The boys' shouts drowned out her claim that her father wouldn't notice more cats in the barn or stable. Rough shoe-clad feet thumping and white paws flashing, boys and cats set up their game of tag. Meg watched, half amused, half concerned. Kittens scratched, and two of the boys cried out in protest then held up bleeding hands. Shortly, however, far faster than their earlier efforts, the children held all but one kitten inside the bag.

That bag pulsed and writhed in the eldest child's hand. The *me–ew*s emanating from it were enough to break Meg's heart, and she began to wonder just how she was going to get the sack home.

"How will we get the last kitten?" the youngest boy asked, pointing to the lightning-shot pine.

Meg followed the direction of the jabbing finger and drew her brows together. The tiny cat still clung to a sturdy branch, well out over the rushing waters of the creek.

"One of you will have to climb up and get him?" The statement came out as a question and not as the suggestion she intended.

The children met it with blank faces and shakes of their identical blond heads.

"No miss," the eldest one finally said. "Pa don't allow us to climb that tree."

"Father *doesn't* let you," Meg said, correcting his grammar.

"That's right, miss." The boy nodded. "He don't."

Meg tightened the corners of her mouth to keep herself from smiling at his impudence. But her amusement died with a plaintive *me–ew* from the tree.

"We can't leave him there." She sounded about as mournful as the cat. "Please—" She snapped her lips together.

She couldn't ask the boys to disobey their father. Nor could she let the kitten remain in the tree. It was so small an owl might get it after dark, or if it grew tired and fell, it would drown in the creek.

She glanced down at her muslin skirt. The gown was an old one she'd worn to inspect the progress of the work on the school. She could do it little harm. And what was a gown or her dignity in comparison to the life of a cat?

"I suppose there's no help for it." She glanced at the boys, the eldest one still holding the sack. "Leave the kittens on the edge of the road and run along home."

At least they didn't need to watch her make a fool of herself, and the narrowness and remoteness of the road assured her no one else would come along to witness it either. The hour was still too early for one of the Jordan or Pyle farmworkers or men from her father's glassworks to travel home that way.

"You can assure your father the cats are gone."

"Yes miss." The eldest youth drew the drawstring tight around the neck of the bag and laid it on the grassy verge of the road. Then, with shouts rather like victory cries, he raced up the track to the charcoal burners. His brothers followed. Just as they disappeared through the trees, the youngest one paused, turned back, and waved.

Meg waved back, thinking how much the children needed her school.

Yowls from the sack and a piteous squeal from the tree reminded her she'd better hurry if she intended to rescue the last kitten. First reassuring herself no one was coming along the road, she dropped her cloak next to the bag of kittens then drew the back of her skirt between her ankles up to the front and tucked it into the ribbon tied around the high waist of her gown. Shivering in the chilly October wind, she headed for the tree.

The pine was dead, seared by lightning from the previous summer. Most of the needles had long since swirled away down the stream, but the remaining branches appeared sturdy and close enough together for easy climbing. She simply hadn't climbed a tree since she and her dearest friend, Sarah, had been fourteen. They'd hidden from some boy who wanted to cut off their plaits. Meg had climbed plenty of trees before that day when she'd decided if she was old enough for boys to flirt with her, however roughly, she was too old for hoydenish antics. She supposed no one truly forgot how to climb, except she'd never climbed a tree leaning precariously over foaming water and sharp rocks.

"Please don't let me fall." She sent up a murmured prayer and stepped on the lowest branch she could reach.

The limb held firm. It didn't even bow under her slight weight. She caught hold of higher branches and drew herself up another level. Despite appearing as though it would tumble into the creek with the first winter storm, the tree remained strong. Half a dozen more sets of limbs took her over the water. It bubbled and splashed, sending up white plumes where it broke at the rocks. Meg's head spun, and she lifted her gaze to the kitten not more than a yard away.

The poor creature clung with paws no bigger than her pinky fingernail. Its emerald green eyes took up half of its face, and its pink mouth opened and closed in constant cries for help.

"I'm—coming, baby. Hang—"

Her foot slipped off the branch. She let out her own howl for aid.

"Hang on, lass, I'll be right there."

The voice, deep and masculine, slammed against Meg's ears like a blow, and she jumped, losing her grip with one hand. She glanced to the road to make certain she wasn't hearing things. Unfortunately, she wasn't. A man sprinted around the bend in the lane, long legs making short work of the distance, bright hair glowing like a sunset.

Meg wondered what would happen if she let herself fall into the creek. She supposed she'd be badly hurt instead of merely sinking far enough into the water to swim away and come up out of the man's sight.

"All for a silly kitten," she grumbled.

"Ma–row?" that silly kitten responded.

Meg narrowed her eyes to glare at him. She may as well rescue him. If she couldn't go down, down, down into the water, she may as well go up, up, up to the cat.

She reached up and grasped the next higher branch. Her left foot snagged near the trunk of the tree. She raised her right foot for the next stair-step limb.

"Do not—" the man called.

Too late. Meg stepped onto the branch. A crack like a rifle shot echoed through the trees, and the limb gave way.

Chapter 2

Nothing but thin air lay between Meg's right foot and the creek twenty feet below. Her left foot began to slip.

"Ahh—ahh—ahh!" she shrieked.

Nubs of pine needles dug into her palms. Her arms ached with the strain of keeping herself from falling.

"Hold on, lass, I'm here now."

And he was. A firm hand grasped her right foot, set it on a sturdy toehold, then repeated the process with the left.

"You can move your left hand to the lower branch, can you now?"

With him so close to her, she noticed his accent, a rolling burr of the *r*'s and musical cadence. She wondered who he was. She hadn't heard of any newcomers.

How mortifying to have a stranger see her in such an ignominious position. Nearly as embarrassing as having someone she knew see her acting in so unwomanly a manner.

"Are you too frightened to move then?" The man's tone was gentle. "Come now, it's not so far down."

It sounded like "doon."

"Lass?" He tapped her foot.

Her foot was encased in a sturdy leather boot but was far too exposed with her skirt kilted up into her sash. Her stomach felt as though it dropped into those boots. Her face burned despite the cold. Perhaps if she scrambled down the tree, she could run off before he discovered her identity. The deep brim of her hat should obscure her features from his position behind and below her.

"Let go of the branch with your left hand." The command was firm but calm. "Place it on the branch below it."

The kitten yowled.

Meg managed to release her left hand from the limb and reach for the little creature. With her feet now on a lower branch, she fell far short of the feline. Her outstretched hand flailed in the air. She teetered on her perch.

"Do not tumble into the burn, lass," the man admonished her. "I doubt I can catch you. Just grab the branch below where your right hand is."

"But the kitten. . ." At last she managed a squeaky explanation.

"Do not fash yourself about the wee beastie. I'll fetch her down. But first I must get you on the ground."

"All right then." Meg took a deep, steadying breath.

14

The faster she got down, the faster she could get herself away from this stranger who was seeing her ankles. Even if her boots covered those ankles, for anyone to see the tops of her boots was improper.

"I can do it," she added.

"I have no doubt of it."

With the cat staring at her with wide, accusing eyes, Meg curled the fingers of her left hand around the lower branch. She managed to release the grip of her right hand enough to move it below. Her balance improved at once, and she made the slanting descent with ease and speed if not grace. Always she knew the stranger moved ahead of her, watching her, ready to steady her if she slipped again.

By the time she attained the ground, her heart beat so hard she could scarcely breathe. Her hands shook as she tugged her skirt free from her sash, her legs trembled, and she hugged herself against the cold blast of the wind and to stop the shivers coursing through her body.

"Your cloak?" He picked up the garment and draped it around her shoulders.

"Thank you." She caught hold of the collar before he let go.

Their fingers grazed, and a shiver different than those produced by the cold air raced through her. She looked up to his face, more than a head above hers, and her mouth went dry.

He had the greenest eyes she'd ever seen—eyes as green as grass before the summer heat turned it brown. Eyes as green as the emerald in her mother's betrothal ring but much warmer. Eyes as green as the kittens', though certainly not frightened. The thought made her smile.

He smiled in return. "There now, was that so bad?"

"Yes." She glanced toward the tree and up to where she'd dangled. "Quite dreadful."

The man laughed. "Then you're a braw lass to climb a half-dead tree after a wee kitten." He glanced at the more subdued but still squirming bag of cats. "You were rescuing them, I presume?"

"Certainly." She stiffened. "Did you think I risked my life so I could toss them into the creek?"

"Nay lass, nothing so unkind." His fair skin tinged a fiery red that clashed with his hair. "I'll be fetching the wee thing down."

He swung around and climbed the tree with the agility of a feline. In moments he was reaching his hand toward the kitten. The ungrateful little beast darted away, dug its claws into the trunk, and streaked to the ground.

Meg snatched it up and hastened for the sack of its relatives. The others protested and writhed, jabbing claws through the sacking and setting up a cater-wauling loud enough to be heard across Delaware Bay. She could scarcely hold on to her burden.

"Allow me." The stranger appeared beside her, holding out a broad, long-fingered hand with several white scars crisscrossing the back of it. "I'll take care of the wee thing."

"Thank you." She relinquished the kitten into his hold. The tiny feline nestled into the palm of his hand, and he stroked its soft fur with a forefinger before lifting the burlap bag and tucking the kitten into the mouth.

"They don't much like it." He cradled the bag in the crook of his arm. "I can carry it for you if you don't have far to go."

"No, not far." Meg lowered her gaze to the toes of her boots and gestured down the road. "It's no more than half a mile."

"Then, if you'll give me a moment to fetch my bag, I'll accompany you. I'm heading that way as well."

"I'd best not."

Father didn't care so much if she walked the half mile to the school building on her own, but if she returned home in the company of a stranger—a male stranger—Father would likely insist she go nowhere without someone accompanying her. That was never a difficulty when her friend Sarah was well, though once Sarah married, she would be too occupied with her husband to join Meg in her projects, and Meg didn't want to be thwarted because Father placed restrictions on her movements.

"I don't think I should." She glanced up the track toward the charcoal burners, wondering if she dared cut through the trees to her house. "I can manage."

"Perhaps you can, but—ah." He grinned. "I beg your pardon. I am forgetting my manners." He set down the bag and removed the small round cap from his head. "My name is Colin Grassick, newly arrived in New Jersey from Edinburgh—Scotland."

"How do you do?" She bobbed a curtsy and posed a question so he wouldn't notice she had no intention of giving him her name—so he could tell no one he had rescued Miss Jordan from a tree. "What brings you so far from home?"

"My profession." He indicated the leather bag he carried, which was at least a yard long and clanked metallically.

"Your profession?"

Meg feared she sounded astounded, but he didn't look like a professional man. He wore simple dark wool breeches and worsted stockings, brogans, and a plain wool jacket. Doctors and lawyers wore finer suits and top hats; light leather shoes with buckles; and showed snowy shirts with cravats. Maybe they did things differently in Scotland. She hoped so—not that what he did for a living made any difference to her.

He gave her a gentle smile as though understanding what she was thinking of his appearance. Or maybe she was staring too long.

"I'm a glassblower," he told her.

She gave him an overly bright smile to mask the unreasonable stab of disappointment in her middle. "Then I assume you're heading for the Jordan glassworks?"

"Aye, that I am." His face lit as though the prospect of working in the hot, noisome glassworks made him happy. "Shall I carry the kittens until our paths part?"

"Thank you." She nodded then set out along the road, telling herself he wouldn't find out anything. The glassworks came before the entrance to the farm.

He fell into step beside her, hefting his bag of tools and the sack of kittens, the latter squalling with every step. He didn't say anything, and she strove for a conversational gambit. Walking beside a stranger, one doing her a favor, without speaking felt uncomfortable.

"No one's mentioned Mr. Jordan hired another glassblower," she blurted out.

"I expect no one thought it important to you." His long legs set a fast pace for her to keep up with. "Ladies don't usually take an interest in business matters."

"Not usually, no." She pattered along beside him as they stepped beneath the trees. "But we don't get a lot of newcomers here, especially not ones from Great Britain. Are you meeting Mr. Jordan at the glassworks?"

"Aye, he told me to come straightaway for the introductions and to get the key to my room."

"Room?" Meg couldn't stop herself from letting out a breathless laugh. "Mr. Grassick, you get a whole cottage if you're a master glassblower."

"Truly?" He slowed and gazed down at her. "I never expected so much."

"It's the only way Fa—Mr. Jordan can lure qualified glassmakers here, providing them with housing big enough for a family." She peeked at him from beneath her hat brim. "Do you have a family coming?"

"If all works out here, aye." He gazed up at the bare branches of the oaks stretching above them, thick enough with the accompanying pines to darken the lane in broad daylight. "My mother and the bairns."

"You have children?"

He hadn't mentioned a wife, just his mother.

"Nay, my younger brothers and sisters."

"How young?" Meg's tone grew excited. "Young enough for school?"

"Aye. Five of them."

"Five pupils for my school." Meg let out a contented sigh.

"A school?" He stopped in the middle of the road. "The sort any bairns can attend? I mean—" His face colored.

Meg smiled. "Yes, a school for all children. At least I will soon."

"Seems an odd thing for a young lady to do." He resumed walking too quickly again.

"Not for me." Meg nearly skipped to keep up with him. "Father asked me what gift I would like for Christmas last year, and I told him I wanted to open a school for the children who don't have the means or time to go to the city for boarding school. There are quite a lot of them, like the boys who had the kittens. So he gave me permission to clean out an old, abandoned cottage and repair it a bit so I can teach there. It's taken awhile, but soon the children can at least learn to read and write. Maybe it'll help them get a trade. We have so much need for skilled craftsmen here in America, but we don't have many schools out here in the countryside." She stopped walking at the end of a lane guarded by wooden gates. "This is the glassworks. If you pull that rope by the gate, someone will let you in."

"Thank you." He looked toward the gates but didn't make any move toward them. "Can you manage the kittens, then?"

"Yes, I don't have much farther to go."

"I'd be pleased to carry them to your destination for you." He didn't look at her.

She kept her gaze on the road and building beyond the gates, certain someone stood before the glassworks door returning their regard. Her nose tickled with the strong scent of charcoal from the chimneys sending smoke from the great furnaces into the cloudy sky. She'd love to keep his company a bit longer, love to have more time to learn about his family and why he came all the way to America when the United States and Britain weren't getting along all that well. But if she let him walk her home, he would know who she was.

"Thank you, but you've done quite enough for me already, and you mustn't keep Mr. Jordan waiting."

"True, but I'd be that honored to serve you."

"Serve me?" She laughed. "I feel like I should be doing something wonderful for you. Your coming is such an answer to prayer for me. I can't open the school until I have glass in the windows. It's simply too cold."

"Does Mr. Jordan not have the window glassmakers already?" He glanced at her, his arched brows drawn together.

"He has window glassmakers and men who make drinking glasses. But people want more and more glass for their windows, and with the embargo last year, not much is getting imported from England or France." She wrinkled her nose. "Mr. Jordan says he'd give me the glass, but he needs to fulfill orders from paying customers first."

"Aye, 'tis the way of businessmen." He handed her the sack of now-quiet kittens. "Someone's coming to the gate now, so I'd best go in. Perhaps we will meet again." With a courtly bow, he headed for the gate.

Meg trotted off before anyone from the glassworks reached the gate and recognized her. Once headed up the drive to the Jordan farm, with majestic oaks and pines keeping her out of sight from the road, she began to skip—for about ten steps. The kittens set up such a commotion she had to slow to a sedate walk. Her heart, however, felt as though it skipped along ahead of her, and she clamped her lips together to stop from singing.

She couldn't wait to tell Sarah about meeting Colin Grassick. Besides his being the most interesting man she'd met in too long to remember, he was also another glassmaker who would surely get the window glass done now. And he had brothers and sisters for her school. And she had more kittens for the stable and barns. And—and—

She skidded to a halt halfway between house and stable. Her heart dropped to the pit of her belly, and she heaved a huge sigh.

Father wasn't about to let her make friends with one of the glassblowers, let alone one from Great Britain. He might be willing to hire a Scotsman for his skill, but he'd not let an employee befriend his daughter. He thought it unseemly for a worker to fraternize with his employer. It might give the man notions of slacking off in his duties. So even less would he like the man talking to Miss Meg Jordan.

Had she been ten years younger, Meg thought she would have stamped her foot in frustration. This was America. Weren't men all to be equal? And surely Colin Grassick was special. Father must be paying him a great deal to come all this way. A skilled craftsman was far different from just anyone.

Resuming her walk to the stable, she resolved to talk more with Mr. Grassick.

Chapter 3

She had the bonniest eyes Colin had ever seen. He held the memory of them as he tugged the rope by the gates and a tuneless bell clanged a hundred yards away. They were wide, round eyes of a golden brown hue like the finest amber glass, framed in extraordinary black lashes. He could gaze into those eyes for hours while listening to her sparkling voice.

If only he knew who she was so he could find her again.

He was smiling when a fair-haired man, in shirtsleeves despite the cold October day, pushed open the gate.

"Yes?" the man clipped out.

Until that moment Colin had forgotten to be anxious about beginning work at a new glasshouse in a strange country. Perhaps the Lord had sent the young lady along to distract him from his previous worries that the men might resent his arrival as a craftsman intended to produce the finer pieces Jordan wished to sell.

Inclining his head in greeting, Colin reminded himself he wasn't supposed to be anxious about anything. The Lord was supposed to take care of it all.

Except when His servants forgot to take care of their own, a little voice reminded Colin.

He swallowed before he could find his voice. "Colin Grassick reporting my arrival to Mr. Jordan."

"Grassick, am I ever glad to see you." The man's face lit up with a wide grin, and he thrust out a broad, scarred hand. "Thaddeus Dalbow at your service."

"My service?" Colin welcomed the man's firm handshake and warm greeting, but he wasn't certain how to proceed after such an effusive greeting. "You were expecting me then?"

He grimaced at such an absurd comment.

"Expecting your arrival?" Dalbow laughed and pushed the gate wider. "We've been praying for it. If you hadn't come now, we all would be trying to make the glassware for Mr. Jordan's daughter's wedding chest, among other fancy things."

"You don't already make the fancy things here?" Colin followed Dalbow into the tree-lined lane leading to the glassworks.

"Not often." Dalbow set a brisk pace past the tree line to where the lane opened into a yard stacked with charcoal.

The sharp scent of smoke and molten glass permeated the air, offensive to some, perfume to Colin.

"What do you make then?" he asked.

"Windows mostly. We've got a lot of need for windows, especially now that everyone wants just the clear glass." Dalbow grimaced. "Jordan finally hired an apprentice to do the cutting."

Colin understood that the man meant the process of cutting the thinner, clear glass away from the thick, gray, and nearly opaque glass from the center. He'd heard the French were working on a way to avoid that thick center altogether, using a process other than blowing and spinning the glass against a metal plate until it flattened out, but he didn't know if they were successful and never much liked making windows enough to care.

"Do you fit the pieces into the frames here then?" Colin glanced around, seeing no evidence of woodworking.

"No, they go to a carpenter in Salem City." Dalbow strode up to the door of a long brick building with two chimneys jutting into the sky. "You may wish to take your coat off. It's hot in here with both furnaces going."

"Aye, that it would be." Colin set down his tools with a clink of metal and took off his coat.

Removing it would also protect it from any flying sparks. A shirtsleeve he could afford to replace but not an entire coat.

Dalbow opened the door. Heat and the odors of hot iron and sodium blasted out with strength enough to taste. But the long room, brightly lit from several clear windows and the two great fires, lay quiet save for the crackle of the charcoal in the furnaces, the occasional clank of a metal tool set on one of the iron gratings, and sighing breaths of the two men on their stools engaged in spinning out the sheets of glass for windows.

"Mr. Jordan?" Thaddeus Dalbow called. "Grassick is finally here."

From a desk at one end of the factory, a tall, thin man with hair nearly the same dull gray as the center of the crown glass windows rose. Despite the heat, he wore a coat and cravat, and Colin wished he hadn't removed his outer garment.

"I wasn't expecting you until tomorrow." Jordan smiled, drawing out crinkles at the corners of wide, dark brown eyes. "I'd heard you just got here this morning."

"Aye sir." Colin strode forward as did Jordan, and they met behind one of the men perched on his bench, blowing gently and steadily into a long pipe, while the parison spun into a flat panel. "The ship docked in Philadelphia yesterday, and I found transport here straightaway."

"Good. Good." Jordan shook his hand. "With your country and France at war, I always worry about ships crossing the Atlantic."

"Not to mention the limited number of English ships allowed to come here," Dalbow added.

"I had to come on an American ship from the West Indies." Colin shuddered involuntarily. "Two extra weeks at sea was not much to my liking."

"That'll keep him here." Dalbow laughed.

"We hope so, if you are as good as my agent in Edinburgh says you are." Jordan turned back toward his desk. "Let's talk about your work and your accommodations. But I don't expect you to get started until tomorrow unless you want to."

Colin felt his lungs expanding as though he were about to breathe life into the molten silica. "I'd like to begin, sir."

"Good." Jordan nodded. "A man eager to work. I like that." He gave Dalbow a pointed glance. "If you please, Thad? I did promise Margaret she would have her windows before the first snowfall. And we have to fulfill that order for the new town hall before she can have the glass."

"Yes, sir." Dalbow trotted to one of the workbenches.

Colin's stomach tightened. Margaret, the young lady's name. A fine, noble name. The name of a lass of whom Jordan must think highly, likely making her too high for him.

Not that he should even think in that direction after so short an acquaintance—or at all.

". . .if you like," Jordan was saying.

"I beg your pardon, sir?" Colin's neck heated from more than the fires. "I was distracted."

"I said you can work on windows for a day or two to get back into your work, if you like." Jordan's tone showed no impatience, but the corners of his mouth tightened.

Margaret could get her windows faster that way.

"I would like to, sir. Thank you."

"I'll show you your quarters now." Jordan moved around his desk and opened a rear door.

They exited to another yard, this one with small outbuildings filled, Colin presumed, with supplies, the sodium and lime and other elements necessary for making glass. Beyond a wooden fence lay half a dozen cottages: neat, wooden structures with small windows and gardens that would be fine in the summer. Trees shaded the houses, and a petite woman hung laundry outside one of them.

"I built these so I could bring in skilled craftsmen, and they could bring their families." Jordan headed in the direction of an end cottage with two floors. "This one is big for a single man, but I understand you have a family."

"Aye, that I do."

And the cottage into which Jordan led him was twice the size of the croft his family lived in now.

"This is fine indeed," he added.

Though it was damp and dim, and holland cloth covered the furniture, it looked like a palace to Colin.

"You have a kitchen," Jordan explained, shoving open a door into a stone-floored room with a fireplace at one end. "But if you don't cook, Thad Dalbow's wife is good at it and happy to earn a few extra pennies making meals for you bachelors."

"I'll keep that in mind."

The tour continued for a few more minutes; then Jordan led the way back to the glassworks and stopped at his desk.

"My daughter is getting married in a few months," he explained. "I'd like her to have some fine glassware to take to her new home. On Monday you can start working on these." He pulled some sketches from a stack of papers on his desk.

They were for drinking goblets, objects that required skill and experience without being difficult.

"Aye sir. How many and what color?"

"Purple. I have a good supply of manganese."

"That'll look grand on a dining table."

"I thought as much." Jordan smiled. "Now, if you'd like to work for the two hours left to the day, I'll have Thad show you where you'll be working and introduce you to your assistant."

Jordan wove his way past furnaces and workbenches, racks of finished glass plates, and stacks of charcoal fuel to where Thad was just finishing up the first stage of a window. Thad let his assistant, a youth of fifteen or so years, carry the panel to the lehr for its gradual cooling, and he turned his attention to Colin.

"Help him with everything he needs." Direction given, Jordan returned to his desk.

"He's a generous and fair employer." Dalbow jutted his chin in Jordan's direction. "Better than some of the other glasshouses. What's he have you working on?"

"Windows, to start with." Colin began to unpack his tools: the blowpipe, the tongs, various cutting tools. "Then I'm to make some goblets for his daughter. He wants them purple, but I'd rather be asking her what she wants for herself."

"Jordan doesn't like us talking to his precious daughter, but if you can persuade him to let you discuss the glassware with her, that's a fine idea." Dalbow grinned. "She's as strong-willed as she is pretty and kind, but you probably already figured that out."

"I beg your pardon?" Colin raised his brows. "How would I be knowing that?"

"You've met her." Now Dalbow was the one to look surprised. "At least you were talking to her outside the gate."

"I didn't ken she was Jordan's daughter." He felt a twist in his middle that she had avoided telling him of her parentage, after knowing he worked for her father. "She's a bonnie wee thing."

"The most eligible female in the county, now that Sarah Thompson is engaged. That is"—Dalbow grimaced—"as long as the interested party owns land. For any tradesman it's as much as his job is worth to speak to her without permission."

<hr/>

"But I always help with dinner." Meg frowned at Ilse Weber, the housekeeper, wife to one of the glassblowers and surrogate mother to Meg since her mother's death seven years earlier. "No one expects you to cook and serve."

"It's what Mr. Jordan told me." Ilse spoke in a musical cadence, her lips curved in a perpetual and genuine smile. "It's not trouble to let you be extra pretty for your guest." Her smile broadened. "Especially not when it's such a fine gentleman."

"Mr. Pyle." Meg's stomach felt as though she'd swallowed a lump of under-baked bread dough. "I'd rather you sat at the table and let me do all the work."

"Now, Miss Margaret." Ilse laughed. "Mr. Pyle is the most eligible bachelor in the county. He could be dining with any number of girls, but he comes here."

"Because his farm adjoins ours." Meg sighed. "He and Father want it to be the biggest farm in the county."

"You shouldn't talk to me about these things." Gently spoken, the scold nonetheless hit its mark.

Meg apologized immediately. "I'd better go change my gown."

Feet still dragging, she climbed the steps to her bedchamber on the second floor. It was one of five bedrooms and overlooked a garden on the side of the house away from the glassworks. Most of the time she didn't smell the smoke from the factory. Beyond the garden, her view gave her a vista of trees and fields, bare now after the harvest, and, seeming to protrude through the branches of a massive oak, one of Joseph Pyle's chimneys.

One of the chimneys. Unlike the Jordan house, which boasted four, Mr. Pyle's dwelling possessed seven, as he had even more rooms.

Meg thought having so many rooms for an unmarried man was silly. But she didn't want to be the lady who made the huge, nearly empty building a home. She wanted to get married, just not to him. Or anyone else she'd met since she'd been of courting age. The difficulty was, she'd known all the eligible men since she was a child. If they were her age, they'd pulled her hair and played games with her. If they were older, they seemed like her father's friends and just too dull.

Father, however, insisted she wed soon. He wanted grandchildren before he was too old to enjoy them. He wanted a son.

Mr. Pyle made a perfect son. He'd turned to Father for guidance on business and other matters since his own parents died when he was Meg's age. A union between the two families, what was left of them, made sense even to Meg.

"But I want someone I choose." She spoke aloud as she drew a blue muslin gown over her head. "I want someone who will let me have my school and my cats and maybe a dog." She yanked tight the ties under her bust. "Please, Lord, don't let Father make me marry anyone I don't want to."

An image of the glassblower flashed through her mind, that strong-boned face with his frame of sunset red hair. He would let her keep her school.

He wasn't considered eligible—alas. She may as well greet the dinner guest.

With her dark hair brushed and pinned up so a few curls fell on either side of her face, she waited until she heard first Father arrive home then Mr. Pyle enter the front door a few minutes later. Then she waited for a few more minutes before making her descent to the parlor.

"Margaret, there you are at last." Father rose and came forward to lead her into the room. "You're looking well."

"Thank you." She smiled at her father and then Joseph Pyle.

He bowed and returned her affable expression, except for his eyes. They were so cold, like the bay on a clear January day: a lovely pale blue but not welcoming.

She couldn't help herself from comparing those icy azure eyes to eyes the color of spring grass. Eyes like emeralds with the warmth of a flame burning inside them. Eyes that belonged to a man who had stepped beyond the gates of the glassworks and, in belonging there, stepped out of her world, as her father and friends defined it.

She had to force her smile to remain on her lips.

"I concur with your father's assessment, Miss Jordan," Mr. Pyle said.

Meg repeated "Thank you," like a sailor's parrot. She didn't want to say she was pleased he could join them, as she knew she should. It seemed too close to lying.

"I believe dinner is ready," she said instead. "May I assist Ilse in bringing dishes to the table, Father?"

"No no, she can manage on her own." Father shook his head. "Joseph, why don't you escort Margaret into the dining room."

"With pleasure." Mr. Pyle strode forward and offered her his arm.

Meg rested the mere tips of her fingers against the crook of his elbow and allowed him to lead the way across the entryway and into the dining room. A fire blazed on the hearth, warming the chamber and reflecting in the ruby glasses on the table. Those glasses had come from England with her great-great-grandmother, who had sailed across the ocean to marry a man she had never met—a colonial at that—because her father had lost all his money. Meg wanted not merely to know but to love the man she married.

She released Mr. Pyle's arm as soon as politeness allowed.

"This is so much nicer than dining alone." Mr. Pyle drew out Meg's chair. "I eat in the kitchen or at a table in the parlor more than in my dining room." He waited for Meg to seat herself; then he nudged the chair closer to the table before taking his own seat across from her and on her father's left.

"Company always makes a meal more pleasant." Father sat at the head of the table and nodded to Meg to direct dinner to be served.

She knew that many of the wives and daughters of the successful farmers, the ones like her father and Joseph Pyle, who could afford servants rarely lifted a finger with meal preparation or serving. Perhaps because Ilse had taught Meg about running a household after she returned from boarding school, she didn't like the older woman waiting on her. She rang the bell then clasped her hands around the edge of the table in an effort to hold herself in place and not jump up to snatch serving bowls from the housekeeper the instant she pushed through the swinging door from kitchen to dining room.

The aromas of roast pork and vegetables wafted along with her. Across the table, Mr. Pyle's eyes lit with pleasure, and he licked his lips.

"The pork is fresh, not cured," Meg told him. "And no one cooks it better than Ilse."

"Ach, child, you flatter me." Ilse blushed as she set the steaming dishes on the table. "I went ahead and carved the roast in the kitchen, Mr. Jordan. This is easier, ya?"

"Much, thank you." Father nodded his approval. "And bread rolls?"

"I am forgetting them." Coloring nearly as deep a red as the goblets, Ilse scurried from the room.

Meg bit her lip. The poor woman couldn't carry everything at once. But she tried. In her next entrance she balanced plates of bread rolls, butter, and fresh apple slices.

"That is everything until the sweet." She bobbed a curtsy and scurried from the room.

"Joseph," Father said, "do ask the blessing."

Mr. Pyle prayed a brief but sincere-sounding message of thanks for the food and company. Father passed the dishes to Mr. Pyle first then Meg, admonishing her about how little she ate.

"You were out for quite a while today, Margaret. You need to keep up your strength."

"This is—" Meg stopped arguing and took another spoonful of stewed carrots.

"So where were you out to today?" Mr. Pyle asked. "Visiting Miss Thompson?"

"No, Sarah is ill. I was visiting the school." She turned to Father. "Now that you have a new glassblower, will I get my windows? I'd like to be able to protect the school from vandals."

"Vandals?" Father and Mr. Pyle said together.

She nodded. "Someone dumped a load of soot in the middle of the floor."

"Disgraceful." Mr. Pyle scowled over a forkful of roasted potatoes glistening with butter. "I'll send two of my men over to clean it up for you."

"That's very thoughtful of you, Mr. Pyle." Instantly, Meg warmed toward him. "But you needn't go to such trouble. I can clean it."

"Never. It's no trouble. They're laborers I keep on all winter, but they haven't much to do." He set down his fork with the food untouched. "But do, please, call me Joseph. We are such old friends that we needn't stand on formality."

"Well, um. . ." Meg glanced toward Father.

"I think it quite appropriate to use Christian names"—Father gave them each a benevolent grin—"considering you'll be married in the spring."

Chapter 4

Meg buried her fingers in the pale pink velvet of Sarah's wedding dress. The plush fabric reminded her of the furry kittens she had rescued from the rowdy boys and who now lived in the stable, adopted by a motherly feline. And inevitably thoughts of the cats reminded Meg of Colin Grassick.

She'd seen him twice in the past week. Neither time had they been close enough to so much as exchange polite greetings. The first time she caught sight of him on the far side of the glassworks gate, he'd smiled then avoided her eyes. The second time she lifted her hand and waved. He'd nodded in response but hurried away to the door of the glasshouse.

"The new glassblower is a fast and skilled worker," Father had told her. "He'll get you your windows straightaway."

The joy of that knowledge fell under the shadow of her father's announcement that she would marry Joseph Pyle on April 28, the Saturday after Easter and at least a week before any planting would commence, even if the spring proved to be a warm one. She had sat at the table stunned into silence, her insides feeling punched and unable to accept food. She would rather go to bed without supper for a week, like a recalcitrant child, than comply with her father's wishes. She had never outright disobeyed him in her life. Reaching her majority at one and twenty changed none of that. He was her father, and she lived in his household. But she couldn't do it, simply could not marry that man.

Not when nothing more than the sight of the near stranger, the new glassblower, made her heart skip a beat or two.

"If you're going to cry all over my dress," Sarah said in a light tone, "I won't let you help me with the embroidery."

"I'm not crying." Meg blinked rapidly and dislodged a tear from her lashes. "Or not much."

"Don't you like the color?" Sarah's porcelain-perfect face glowed with amusement. "Perhaps I should be getting married in red to match my hair?"

Meg laughed. "You'd look a fright. This pink is perfect and so soft."

"So expensive." Sarah knit her brows as she bent toward the minute stitches of silver embroidery around the square neckline. "It came all the way from Paris. Daddy does spoil me."

Mr. Thompson could afford to spoil Sarah. He owned a large farm, as well as a lumber mill near the coast and most of the charcoal burners.

"He loves having a girl after four boys," Meg said with complete truth, "and he wants your wedding to stand out."

"I know." The crease between Sarah's auburn brows grew deeper. "It's just so ostentatious when most girls get married in their Sunday best. But don't think I'm ungrateful." Her head shot up, and she grinned. "I'll just have to have several parties to have an excuse to wear it."

"That's right, and you'll be going to Philadelphia with Peter several times a year."

"Then maybe Daddy should have brought me more fabric." Sarah giggled.

Meg smiled, but this special gown for Sarah's wedding to Peter Strawn no longer made her as happy as her friend. Side by side with Sarah, she set aside the sleeve she was hemming with nearly invisible stitches. "I need a rest, or I'll strain my eyes. Do you want me to make us some tea or coffee?"

"Coffee would be lovely if you have some of those cookies of Ilse's." Sarah knotted her thread. "But I'll come with you. You're right about straining our eyes. It's awfully gray today."

"It's been gray for a week." Meg led the way from the dining room, where they had spread the gown across the table, to the kitchen.

Ilse stood at the worktable grating sugar from a fat, conical loaf. Cinnamon permeated the kitchen air, and Meg and Sarah sighed with pleasure.

"You are like my children." Ilse laughed. "You want coffee and cookies, I know. I have just taken them from the oven and am now grating the sugar for your coffee. Miss Meg, you run out to the springhouse and fetch the cream, but take your cloak. It's raining." She turned to Sarah. "You should not have come out in this weather with you being sick so recently."

"It wasn't raining when I left." Sarah looked as chagrined as a scolded child. "I'll just have to stay until it stops."

"You certainly can't take your dress out in the rain." Meg snatched her cloak off a hook.

A blast of icy wind hit her the instant she opened the door. Her nostrils flared, picking up the sharpness of snow amid the faint odor of charcoal from the glassworks. Cold moisture struck her face and pinged off a metal bucket by the door.

"Sleet," she called out and slammed the door.

She dashed through the half frozen rain, grabbed a pitcher of cream from the springhouse, and ran back. Her feet and hands were numb by the time she slipped into the warmth of the kitchen.

"You might need to stay all night." Meg set the cream on the table. "It's awful out there."

"Maybe I should go home now." Sarah stood by the door to the dining room, her posture stiff. "I could leave my dress here so it doesn't get ruined."

"Of course you can leave it here. I'll put it in one of the spare rooms, but—" Sarah narrowed her eyes at her friend. "What's wrong?"

"It is my fault." Ilse twisted her hands in her apron. "I didn't know you didn't tell Miss Sarah that you were getting married."

"Oh." Meg pressed her cold hands to her now hot cheeks. "I thought—I didn't think—Sarah, please don't be angry with me. You must understand—" She glanced at Ilse.

"You'd think you would tell me something so important." Sarah's lower lip quivered. "We've been friends since we were in the cradle."

"Yes, but..." Meg sighed. "Let's clear your gown off the table so we can have our snack in there by the fire."

Without a word, Sarah spun on her heel and pushed through the swinging door.

In silence Meg prepared a tray with coffee, cream, and sugar, while Ilse stacked several cookies on a plate. Meg nodded her thanks and carried the tray into the dining room. Sarah had packed her gown and the special embroidery threads into its canvas bag and added wood to the fire.

"I am sorry," Ilse murmured as she set the plate on the table.

"It's all right." Meg gave the housekeeper a smile. "She's just hurt."

"No, I'm not hurt." Sarah yanked out a chair. "I'm angry."

"Of course you are." Meg spoke in a soothing tone. "Then you'll be hurt; then you'll laugh at yourself."

Sarah chuckled. "You know too much about me." She sat and reached for a cookie redolent of cinnamon and butter. "So why did you think I wouldn't be upset about your not telling me about your getting married?"

"Because I want it to go away." Meg dropped onto her chair and poured them both coffee, adding large dollops of cream and pinches of sugar to both cups. "I don't want to marry him."

"You don't want to marry Joseph?" Sarah's hazel eyes widened. "Why not? He's handsome. He's amazingly blessed in his farm, and he's nice. If I hadn't met Peter, I'd have set my cap for Joseph."

"His eyes are cold." Meg wrapped her hands around her coffee cup, savoring the warmth seeping through the china. "And what about the school? I can't bear the thought of other girls being away while their mothers are dying, as I was. And if I can get it started and popular in the county, even girls like I was can stay home."

"He'll let you teach the children for those reasons." Sarah laid her hand on Meg's arm. "It's honorable, generous work, and any man would be proud to have a wife doing something like that. Peter said he's happy to let me help you"—her cheeks grew pink—"until we have children, of course."

"I don't know if Joseph will feel that way." Meg sipped at her coffee, reveling in the heat going down her throat. "He kept talking about how he needs a wife to make his house beautiful."

"Does he mean new furnishings or just by your being in it?" Sarah grinned. "I'll say it's you he thinks will make the house beautiful and that he's smitten."

"Maybe, but he's never acted smitten. Father's just mentioned he thinks a match would be a fine idea." She sighed. "For all I know, he asked Joseph to marry me."

Sarah laughed. "I can't believe that. But about the school. Did you ask him if you could still teach? Have you told him how you feel about children having to go away to get educated?"

"No, I was too shocked when Father told me about the marriage."

But Joseph hadn't objected to the school when she'd talked about it, explained how she hoped that, eventually, children could get a good education and live at home. He'd offered to send men over to clean it up and had, in fact, done so. He'd even agreed not to announce their betrothal until after her school opened and had sent her a gift of oh-so-expensive cocoa.

"I probably am being silly." Meg reached for a cookie but didn't eat it. "I just want to marry a man who makes me look at him like you do Peter, and who looks at me the same way. This just seems like—well, it seems like a business arrangement between my father and Joseph, not a love match."

"I'm sure he must love you though." Sarah gave Meg's arm a squeeze and returned to her coffee and cookies. "You're so pretty and kind and good at so many things."

"But he doesn't look at me like he loves me, and he talks to Father more than he does me. Besides that, I don't love him."

"You'll come to love him."

"But what if—" Meg gazed into her coffee. "What happens if I find someone else to love first?"

"Margaret Jordan, you're one and twenty and haven't yet. What makes you think—" Sarah gasped and set down her cookie. "You have met someone else."

"No. That is—" Meg pushed back her chair and paced to the hearth. She shoved a few sticks onto the already merrily crackling fire. Her face felt as hot as the flames.

"Who? When? Where?" Sarah posed the single words like sharp cracks of a whip. "Tell me."

"It's nothing." Meg pressed her hands to her cheeks. "I only met him once, so I can't have any feelings for him. But there's something about his spirit. His eyes are warm, and he looks right at you like he's not trying to hide anything. He—intrigues me."

"Is this mysterious man handsome?" Sarah sounded like someone placating a child who talked about an imaginary playmate.

"Hmm." Meg closed her eyes and conjured an image of Colin's face. "I think some people would think so. He has very strong bones and beautiful green eyes and red hair."

"Ugh, red hair." Sarah made exaggerated shuddering noises. "That's a vulgar color."

"Yours is auburn." Meg laughed and faced her friend. "He's from Scotland."

Sarah dropped her cookie into her coffee. "The glassblower? Meg, you can't be serious about this!"

"Of course I'm not. A body can't be serious after one meeting and two glances. I said he interests me." Meg squared her shoulders. "And if he interests me more than Joseph does, how can I commit my life to another man?"

"Because you can never commit your life to one of your father's workers." Sarah gave her head a shake violent enough to send a curl tumbling from its pin. "No one would approve."

"Why not?" Meg's jaw hardened. "This is America. Mr. Jefferson himself said that all men are created equal."

"That may be true," Sarah conceded, "but not everyone thinks that, including your father. You know he doesn't like you being friendly with the glassmakers."

"Yes, I know." Meg returned to the table, poured fresh coffee and cream into her cup, and pushed it to Sarah to replace the one now filled with a soggy cookie. "He says he doesn't want to create resentment amongst them by showing favoritism to one and not the other. And I wish I could disagree on that head. But he's a stranger here without any family, unlike all the other men. And I want to be friends with anyone I choose, so long as he's a Christian of course."

Sarah gave her a long, contemplative look. "But what if you end up liking someone as more than a friend? Could you choose between him and your father?"

Meg said nothing. It was a question she hoped never to have to answer.

❧

Colin packed the goblets in a nest of straw and lifted the box onto his shoulder. After two weeks of catching mere glimpses of Margaret Jordan, he must now meet with her face-to-face to get her approval of the goblets for her wedding chest. He would also give her the happy tidings that carpenters were installing the windows in her school that very day, windows he had created with his own craft.

The latter news made him smile. He could imagine her joy, the way her golden brown eyes would light with joy. The former report burdened him in a way that made no sense.

"You do not even ken the lass," he admonished himself. "And you've been warned off."

He had also been given permission to take the first few goblets he'd created to Miss Jordan for her approval. Perhaps he was happier about the opportunity than a brief encounter called for. Nevertheless, his footfalls felt as light as the breeze stirring the bare branches of the trees as he set out for the Jordans' house. Sunshine warmed his shoulders, and the air smelled pungent with fallen leaves and pine.

He made short work of the quarter-mile trek through the woods and arrived at the back door of a fine, big house built of brick and stone, with several sparkling windows on each floor. Beyond the green-painted door, a woman sang a psalm of praise in a high, clear soprano. A hundred feet away, a handful of horses stood in a paddock, munching hay and a few tufts of leftover grass, and outside the adjacent stable, several black-and-white kittens cavorted and tumbled under the supervision of a charcoal-and-silver-striped tabby.

"You wee beasties look happy." He smiled at the felines then knocked on the back door.

The singing stopped. Footfalls tapped on the floor. The door opened, and Miss Margaret Jordan stood framed in the opening.

Colin caught his breath. He'd thought she was a bonnie lass in the gloom of a cloudy day. With sunlight brightening her porcelain-fine features and drawing deep red lights out of her dark curls, she was even prettier than he remembered. That she wore a white apron dusted with flour over a plain blue dress added to her charm.

"Good afternoon, Mr. Grassick." Her smile of greeting seemed as bright as the sunlight. "How good of you to call."

"This isn't a call." He sounded curt and worked to soften his tone. "I've come by way of business."

"I see." Her gaze swept past him. "My father isn't here. I thought he was at the glassworks."

"He is. He sent me over with these." He shifted the box to both his hands, holding it in front of him like a shield. "They're for your approval."

"My approval?" Her eyes danced. "Then please come in. Would you like some coffee?"

"No thank you."

He thought the smell of it brewing fresh in the warm, sunny kitchen was fine, but he'd never cared for the taste.

She laughed. "What am I thinking, offering you coffee? You probably prefer tea. I do have a bit here. Father doesn't like it much. His father forbade them to have it in the house after the tea tax before the Revolution."

"Revolution, you call it?" He stepped over the threshold but went no farther.

No one else seemed to be around, and he thought being alone with her in an empty house was too improper.

"What do you call it?" She busied herself with a canister of tea, her back to him.

"The unpleasantness with America."

She laughed as he hoped she would, the bubbling notes as pure as the song she'd been singing before he knocked.

He set the box on the table. "Tell me if you like these—send word by way of Ilse or your father. I should be going."

He should be running was more like it.

"No need." She spooned tea into a china pot then crossed the kitchen to close the door. "Ilse is around the corner in the housekeeper's room doing some mending. She can hear every word."

Colin relaxed—a bit. "But I should not stay."

"Of course you should. If Father sent you here to show me something for my approval, then he expects you to take the message back to the glassworks."

"Aye, well, probably so." He began to extract a goblet from the straw. "They are of my making."

"What are they?" She left tea scattered about and dashed to his side.

The smell of yeast and apple blossoms rose from her, aromas of new life. A new life like the one he hoped to have here in New Jersey, a life he wouldn't have if he let himself be too friendly with this lady.

Someone else's lady.

He moved to the other side of the table. "They're glasses for you." He lifted a goblet from the straw and set it into her hands.

"Oh my." Cradling the goblet in her fingers as though it were no more substantial than soap bubbles, she turned toward the window and held the glass up to the light.

Sunshine glowed through the bowl of the glass and flashed and sparkled off the twirling stem, turning it into a shimmering amethyst. For several minutes she simply gazed at the piece, turning it, tilting it, holding it to her lips.

Colin had thought the piece still too plain, despite his enhancements to the original design. In Margaret Jordan's hands, it looked fit for a princess.

Yet she stood in silence for so long his mouth went dry and sweat prickled along his upper lip. Any moment now she would turn and thrust the glass at him, tell him to return it, and inform her father it was nothing she wanted on the grand dinner table she would have with her new husband, the man who owned the biggest house in the county.

She faced him all right, but she didn't thrust the goblet at him. She held it out, forcing him to remove it from her fingers, brushing her smooth skin as he did so.

"It's—spectacular." Awe made her voice husky. "I don't think our glasshouse has produced anything so beautiful. Is Father going to sell them in Philadelphia shops?"

"Not these." Colin gave her a quizzical glance. "These are for you."

"For me?" She frowned. "Why would I need purple goblets?"

"For your marriage."

"Oh, that." She waved her hand in a dismissive gesture. "What nonsense. Joseph Pyle has many fine glasses all made in France. Crystal glasses. He doesn't need me to bring more."

"Then you'll be telling Mr. Jordan that, not me."

Colin couldn't stop himself from continuing to stare at her. Never had he met a young lady who was so cavalier about her upcoming nuptials nor one who turned down a fine gift from her father.

"I do the work given to me." He added the last to keep the barrier between them.

"And how many did Father tell you to make?"

"A baker's dozen in the event one breaks in years to come."

"Hmm." She tapped a forefinger on her chin and gazed at the ceiling as though expecting to find some text written there.

She remained in that pose for several moments in which the crackling fire in the stove and the snip of scissors around the corner made the only interruptions.

Then she laughed. "Mr. Grassick, do please tell my father I would like these for my betrothal dinner party, and so I will need two baker's dozen."

"I'm thinking that's not a good idea." Colin repacked the goblet in the straw. "It will take me weeks to make that many with all the other work we have to do."

"Oh, I do hope it does. Many weeks." Her eyes sparkled with mischief. "Maybe the end of January at the earliest?"

"Aye, it could take that long." Colin forced his gaze away from her alluring face.

She was up to some trick, and he wasn't certain he wanted to be involved. Yet Mr. Jordan had said to ask Margaret what she thought of the work before making more.

"If she doesn't like them," her father had said, "we can sell them with ease."

He hadn't given instructions about her reaction if she did like them. Colin would simply tell Mr. Jordan what his daughter said and work from that.

And with every goblet he formed on the end of his pipe, he would wonder why she wanted to postpone even the announcement of her betrothal. He would wish she wanted the work hastened. A lady promised to another man was far easier set from one's dreams than one who remained free.

Not that he was free to be even so much as dreaming about her, but no amount of determination had released his mind from her image. Now it would be even stronger. He had scent and touch to go along with the vision of amber-brown eyes and shining curls; fine, white skin and—

He snatched up the box. "I'd best be going."

"You won't stay for tea?" She gave him a coaxing smile. "It's the least I can do for your effort in bringing the glasses here for me to inspect. And for taking my message back to Father."

"'Tis my work for which I am well paid already." He knew he sounded brusque, but he needed to resist the temptation to stay, and pushing her away seemed like the best way to do so. "I need no extra favors. Good day to you, Miss Jordan." He offered her a bow over the box and exited the house faster than was probably polite.

Standing firm against her attractiveness though he might, he couldn't keep himself from stopping by the stable to admire the kittens. They had grown in the past two weeks. A pan of milk, so yellow it must have come from a goat, stood in the cool shade by the door, and all the cats wandered over to lap from it in the midst of their play.

One kitten perched on the edge of the trough, leaning precariously over the edge to scoop up water with its rough pink tongue. Colin wondered if the one on the trough was the wee beastie who'd scampered up the tree and nearly caused his first would-be rescuer to tumble into the burn.

Smiling, he stroked the silky head with a forefinger. "Good afternoon, you little scamp."

The cat purred and butted its head against his hand.

"Aye, you remember me then?" Colin smiled at another cat trying to grab his sibling's long tail. "Have a care with your perches in the future."

With a pat he turned to be on his way back to the glassworks. From the corner of his eye, he caught the glimpse of Margaret Jordan framed in the kitchen window. She was watching, her face alight with amusement. He touched his cap in acknowledgment of her presence, and she waved in response.

Colin resumed his walk—for about twenty feet. In those few paces he felt something latch onto the back of his boot. He stopped. He hadn't noticed any sort of vine or creeper on the path in which he could have caught his foot.

It was the kitten from the trough, tiny paws wrapped around the back of his ankle as though its few ounces could stop him from going away.

"You daft beast." He stooped and scooped up the kitten.

Purring, it nestled against his neck, warm and soft and smelling of hay. For a moment he considered keeping it. Only for a moment. It wasn't his cat to take, even if it had decided it wanted his company.

"Let's take you back." Resolute he marched back to the stable and deposited the cat among its clan—

The first time. In the next quarter hour he repeated the action three more times. The fourth time, footfalls pattered across the stable yard, and Miss Jordan took the kitten from his hands.

"Let me fetch a basket and some rags so you can take her home with you," she offered.

"Nay, I cannot have one of your cats."

"Why not?" Her gaze swept the horde of felines. "Do you think I'm likely to run out of them?"

"Nay, but—" He laughed. "If 'tis all right, some company would be fine in that great big cottage I have all to myself."

"Then come back inside and have your tea while I prepare the basket." She spun on her heel and marched to the house, apparently expecting him to follow.

Colin hesitated. With her holding the cat, nothing stopped him from going. Nothing stopped him from staying, either.

Nothing except good sense.

Chapter 5

While Ilse served Mr. Grassick a cup of tea at the kitchen table, Meg fairly skipped up the steps to the linen press for clean rags then back down to the pantry for a covered basket. All the while, the kitten rode on her shoulder, purring and kneading its needlelike claws through the fabric of her dress. Meg rubbed her cheek against the kitten's soft fur and smiled into those emerald green eyes, so like the glassblower's.

Not just any glassblower, either. Meg had seen glasses and vases, serving bowls and candlesticks imported from the centuries-old glassworks in Europe, and the craftsmanship was fine. Thus far she had seen little produced in the Salem County works that came close to demonstrating not merely the skill but the artistry Colin Grassick's goblets exhibited. He possessed a gift, and a yearning in her heart told her to find out what made him so humble in accepting her awe and admiration. If she could persuade him to take his time with the tea, perhaps talk to him about a few other pieces Father intended for him to produce, she could learn what lay in his heart.

The idea returned a song to her lips. Before any notes spilled out, however, Sarah's warning cut through her joy. He was one of her father's workers. Father might not—probably wouldn't—approve of her befriending Colin Grassick. And she was supposed to marry another man.

"I don't see the harm in being friendly, kitten." Meg's spirit rebelled. "Father sent him here to get my approval for the goblets."

Her actions thus justified, she tucked the kitten into the basket and returned to the kitchen with her now meowing burden.

"She isn't happy about being confined." Meg set the basket on the floor beside Colin's chair. "Perhaps she's lonely." He lifted the lid and poked a finger inside.

The mews ceased.

"Ach, she's a funny one." Ilse chuckled. "Would you like me to finish with the bread rolls, Miss Meg? They're ready for the oven."

"So they are." Meg glanced at the buns rising near the stove. "I forgot about them. If you stay a few minutes, Mr. Grassick, I'll send a few home with you."

"Nay, I have enough to carry with the wee beastie and the glass." He lifted his teacup. The delicate china looked like a toy in his hand, yet he held it with care. "But I thank you for your thoughtfulness."

"Leave the goblets here." Meg slid the trays of rolls into the baking oven. "Unless you need them for matching the others."

"Nay, I have my drawings. And perhaps these would be safer here."

"Ya, I can tuck them on the top shelf of the pantry." Ilse snatched up the crate of glasses and carried it into the storage room off the kitchen.

Meg drew out a chair and joined Colin at the table. "I didn't notice you at church on Sunday." She tilted her head to one side. "Dare I ask if you go?"

"Aye, I go." He gave her a half smile. "I saw you in the front row. I was in the back."

She was in the family's private box pew with Father and Joseph, perched on cushions to keep them comfortable in the event the sermon lasted a long time. Colin had just reminded her that he had perched on a narrow bench with the other workers, uncomfortable with the shortest of talks.

It wasn't right. The Jordan pew was half empty most of the time.

"Did you enjoy the service anyway?" she ventured.

"He is a fine preacher." Colin set down his cup and pushed it a little away from him. "I missed worshipping at the kirk while aboard ship."

"Have you always gone to church?" Meg grasped the edge of the table. "That's what a kirk is, isn't it, a church?"

"Aye, that it is." He rose. "I went with my family every Sunday until I ran away from home when I was twelve."

Meg stared at him. "You ran away from home?"

"I did." He inclined his head, sending a wave of sunset red hair sliding across his brow.

"Why? I mean—" Meg's face heated. "Never you mind. It's none of my concern."

"I think it is." His voice held a roughness she hadn't noticed before now. "You and your father deserve to know the character of the man you employ. I ran off because I wanted to be a Lowland glassmaker instead of a Highland fisherman like my father. The next time I attended the kirk was two years ago when I went to the funeral of my father."

Raw pain clouded his brilliant eyes.

"I'm so sorry." Despite knowing how useless the words were, Meg didn't know what else to say.

She rose and looked into the oven to see if the rolls were browning too quickly or remaining too doughy. She kept her back to him, waiting for him to compose himself, have a moment to say whatever he chose. She wanted to know how his father died, but she had already probed for more than was appropriate.

"He drowned somewhere near the Hebrides." Colin's voice was soft once again, calm, as though he had spoken these words many times. "The water was rough, and he shouldn't have gone out alone, but his wife and bairns needed to eat, and he didn't have his one son along who was old enough to be of use. If I hadn't been wasting my silver—" He broke off on a sigh. "Thank you for the tea and the wee beastie. I must be on my way."

Before Meg could get the oven door closed, he was halfway outside.

But he hesitated on the threshold. "Your windows should be in your school by now, Miss Jordan. I was forgetting to tell you."

"That's wonderful." She straightened from the stove, allowing the door to shut with a metallic clang. "If you wait another two minutes, the rolls will be ready."

"Thank you, but I must be on my way."

"Yes, Grassick, you should be," Father said from behind them.

≈

Meg counted the kittens lounging about in the feeble rays of the late autumn sun. Four. The adult cats rambled elsewhere, hunting or sleeping or keeping the horses company, but the kittens tended to remain near the door except for the one who had taken a fancy to Colin and now one more.

"Where did your brother or sister go?" she asked the felines as though they could answer.

They didn't even look at her.

"Yes, I know you had quite a mole feast this morning, but where is your brother? Or maybe sister?"

A foot scraped on the beaten earth of the stable yard, and a husky laugh rang out. "I think you need to ask in their language," Sarah said. "A specific series of meows."

She proceeded to meow in several different tones.

The kittens rose, stretched, and wandered into the stable.

"Maybe it's your accent," Meg suggested through her giggles.

"I'm afraid I said something rude." Sarah grinned after the departing felines. "Have you lost one?"

"I have. He was around this morning, but now he seems to have gone off somewhere, and I'm worried he's lost."

"Cats are quite resourceful, you know." Sarah linked her arm with Meg's. "But let's go hunt him down. He shouldn't be out after dark. Foxes can be a menace."

"And the owls. The kittens are so tiny still." Meg adjusted her hat brim so she could look up at her slightly taller friend. "But you came to visit for something more than a kitten hunt."

"I did. I want to go see the new windows in the school before this fine weather ends. Have you seen them yet?"

"I have. They're perfect."

After Father sent Colin back to the glassworks with enough ice in his voice to fill Delaware Bay, Meg had retreated to the school to nurse her humiliated spirit. The windows were far better than Meg suggested, nearly perfectly clear panes set into frames of four squares a window. Light spilled across the hard-packed earth floor, now clear of soot, thanks to Joseph's workers.

"Now all we need is a stove or grate so we don't all freeze, and something on which the students can sit."

"If we have a brazier," Sarah mused aloud, "the children can make do with blankets and slates on their laps."

"I'd rather they were comfortable."

Sarah patted her arm. "You want everyone more comfortable. But you know, the Lord didn't promise us that we wouldn't have to suffer a bit from time to time."

"No."

Meg thought about the suffering in Colin's voice, in his eyes when he talked of abandoning his family. If she possessed the power to do so, she would have removed that pain from his spirit. She could only pray for him, even if praying for him made her feel guilty for thinking of him at all. She should be thinking of Joseph and a future with him because her father wanted that life for her. She should be thinking about the children and helping them have better lives.

"I'm afraid they won't come if they're uncomfortable." Meg kicked a stick off the drive and scanned the area for signs of a black-and-white feline. "We don't need tables and chairs or desks. Simple benches would do."

"Maybe the church has some extra benches." Sarah wrinkled her nose as they turned onto the road, and the wind, tunneling through the lining trees, struck them in the face with the odors of the glassworks. "How do you bear it?"

"I don't notice it most of the time."

Or she tried not to notice, to think of what Colin would look like, blowpipe to his lips, the other end of the tube glowing with molten glass. Purple glass. Would he think of her as he created the twenty-six goblets for her betrothal party?

"You should see the wedding gift Father is giving me." This was a way she could talk about Colin and not give away her attraction to a man besides the one she was to marry. "Co—Mr. Grassick brought them by yesterday for my approval. He stayed a bit because one of the kittens took a liking to him, and I fixed up a basket so he could take it home. Then he told me a little bit more about his family, about his father dying and the children—" Her footfalls sped up. "But I was telling you about the goblets. They're magnificent. When I looked at one with the sun shining through it, I would have thought it was made of an amethyst, the color was so pure and clear. And the workmanship—what's wrong?"

Sarah had stopped and turned to face Meg. Concern radiated from Sarah's hazel eyes. "Did you like the glasses because of the artist, or did you like the artist because of the work?"

Meg blinked. "Did I—what do you mean? I'm talking about the fine workmanship. Mr. Grassick is a talented artisan."

"That's what everyone is saying." Sarah nodded, but her face was tight. "And now he's told you about being all alone here in America and having family back in Scotland."

"Yes, it's rather sad. He ran away from home when he was twelve—"

"Shh." Sarah pressed a gloved forefinger to Meg's lips. "I'm sure it is very sad. But, Meg, he's not a lost kitten you can pack up in your pocket and carry home to feed."

"No, but I can be kind to him."

"While betrothed to another man?"

"It's not official yet."

"It's what your father wants for you."

"But not what I want." Meg heaved a sigh. "Let's go look at the school and try to find the kitten."

"Yes, I'm forgetting how short the daylight is now." Sarah resumed walking.

At intervals one or the other of them called to the kitten, though Meg expected it would be in a field or the woods, hunting or trying to, rather than along the road. When they passed the glassworks, she didn't so much as glance in that direction. She wouldn't see him anyway. Father had told her Colin worked longer hours than any of the men. He also helped out the others and never complained.

"If he works out, he'll be worth every penny it cost me to get him here." Father had laughed at that, his annoyance at finding her chatting cozily with the glassblower diminishing. "I wish it was pennies it cost me instead of a whole lot of dollars."

She mustn't interfere with her father's making a profit from his business. She must be a good daughter. She'd promised to be a good daughter before Momma died. Promised in letters. To be a good daughter, she must do what she was told.

"You're frowning," Sarah said.

"I'm worrying about the kitten. He's so small."

They left the cover of trees and entered the broad intersection of road, charcoal burners lane, and creek. Meg's gaze strayed to the lightning-struck tree, and she caught a flash of movement in the branches.

"That little imp." Picking up her skirt, she raced for the tree. She wasn't mistaken. Twenty feet above the rushing waters of the stream perched a black-and-white kitten.

"I thought the one he took home was the one he rescued, but who can tell them apart?" She began to kilt up her skirt.

"Meg!" Sarah gasped. "Your ankles are showing."

Meg stared down at her stockings, visible above the ribbons tying her blue kid slippers around her ankles. "I forgot. I was wearing boots last time."

"Last time?" Sarah poked Meg in the ribs. "What are you forgetting to tell me?"

"I climbed the tree to rescue a kitten. In the end, he got himself down."

"And probably will this time, too. Now tell me what you meant about the last time you climbed the tree."

As they continued their walk to the school, Meg confessed the entire scene to her friend.

"I can't believe you kept that to yourself." Sarah laughed so hard she had tears in her eyes. "It was too bad of you to climb a tree with your skirt pulled up, even with boots on, but to end up hanging there like an apple—oh my, the picture."

"It was more embarrassing to have a stranger see me like that."

They rounded the curve in the road that led straight to the school building. Meg stopped talking to smile, anticipating Sarah's exclamation of delight when she saw the slanting afternoon sunlight glinting off the panes of glass in the new windows.

Both of them exclaimed, but it wasn't in pleasure. Sunlight glinted off glass, lots of glass. What looked like acres of glass strewed around the little building.

Every windowpane had been smashed.

Chapter 6

Meg started to cry. She'd waited for months to get glass in the frames for her school, and now they lay in fragments on the ground. Gazing at the glittering shards, she felt as though her heart lay mixed in the shining horde.

"Who would do this?" Sarah slipped her arms around Meg and hugged her tightly. "It's simply terrible. Who wouldn't want a school?"

"I thought the soot was bad." Meg sniffled against Sarah's cloak. "But that wasn't expensive to clean up. This"—she straightened and waved her arm in the air—"will take forever to replace, if Father will replace it. Do you have a handkerchief?"

"Of course." Sarah produced a square of linen with a tatted edge.

Meg took it and wiped her eyes—and kept wiping. The tears wouldn't stop.

"How will I ever be able to open a school if it doesn't have windows?" She burst out sobbing again. "It's not as though I'm doing this for myself. I want to serve the Lord through helping the children around here learn to read and write and some history and. . . How can this happen?"

"Meg. Meg, calm yourself." Sarah patted Meg's back then wrapped one arm around her shoulders. "We'll work out something. I mean, if your father was willing to put windows in once, surely he will be willing again."

"It took months to get these."

"Yes, but now he has a new glassblower. You got them within two weeks of Mr. Grassick arriving."

"I know. It's just that he's already doing work for me, making these—goblets—" Meg's voice caught in her throat.

Meg felt sick. Without another word, she turned on her heel and began trudging back toward home. She'd found a way to put off her wedding by convincing Father that she needed glasses enough for a betrothal party. He'd agreed, realizing it would be an opportunity to show off Colin's skill to the county and get orders for their own sets of glassware. Although she intended to use the glasses for such a party, and although they would be fine advertisement for Colin's skill, Meg knew they were an excuse to put off the announcement of the marriage. She wasn't being truly deceitful—or didn't think of it as such at the time. Now, however, she worried that her action was wrong and she was being punished for not being honest with her father.

"What should I do?" Meg spoke to the Lord, but said it aloud.

"Ask your father for more windows. Surely he won't blame you for this."

"No, he won't blame me. It's simply that—" Meg paused in the center of the road and stared at the clear blue sky. "We need to stop at the glassworks on our way back."

"You want to walk up to the gate and ring for admission?" Sarah sounded shocked and justifiably so. Although Meg had visited the glassworks many times to take Father dinner, she had never invited Sarah to go inside the stockade around the factory.

"Yes, we must go now." Meg set out at a trot.

Sarah skipped to catch up with Meg. "Can't this wait?"

"No, I have to talk to Father before—before any more work is done on the goblets."

"Why?"

"Because—" Meg looked down.

A tiny creature whizzed past her.

"The kitten." She dove after it, catching it before it disappeared beneath a clump of shrubbery.

"Wanderer." She tucked him—or her—under her chin.

A purr twice the size of the cat rumbled from beneath a coating of thick fur.

"He's lovely." Sarah stroked the small head between the pointed black ears. "And he likes you."

"One of the cats took a liking to Mr. Grassick. Just wouldn't let him leave."

"Maybe Peter will let me have a cat. They're so useful in the kitchen and pantry."

"Father won't let me have one in the house, but they're happy in the stable. Except this one. He seems to like to wander off and get himself into trouble."

"Looking for you?" Sarah smiled. "And he's making you look happier, too."

"He makes me feel better."

But the sight of the glassworks gates brought the nausea clutching at her middle again. No help for it though. If she wanted to make up for her trick in postponing the official announcement of her betrothal, she must face up to what she'd done, sacrifice what she wanted with the delayed wedding plans for the sake of providing windows for her school. Telling Father in front of his workers would be far easier than telling him in private.

"It's rather smelly in there," Meg pointed out. "If you'd rather go home, I understand."

"I'll come with you. I admit I'm curious."

"They may not let us in." Meg tugged on the bell rope.

A clang rang across the yard. Mr. Weber, wearing a leather apron over his clothes, poked his head out of the factory door. Meg waved to him. Even from the distance to the gate, Meg saw his eyes widen. He nodded and vanished back inside the building.

A moment later Father strode into the yard. "Is something wrong, Margaret?"

"No. I mean yes." Meg put the kitten into the pocket of her cloak. "May I come in and talk to you?"

"It can't wait until I return home tonight?"

Meg shook her head.

"This is no place for a young lady." Father frowned. His gaze fell on Sarah, and he smoothed out his brow. "I beg your pardon, Sarah. How are you doing?"

"Well, thank you." Sarah smiled. "But, if you please, Mr. Jordan, will you allow us to come in? I admit I'm fascinated by the idea of glass."

"All right, but only from the doorway." Father unlatched the gate and pushed it open. "It's not safe inside. We have apprentices running around with molten glass and men working on pieces. It's quite—Margaret, you've been crying."

Meg dabbed at her streaked face with the edge of her cloak. "Yes sir."

"What happened?" He took her arm with one hand and held out the other to Sarah.

"Someone broke my windows. The ones for the school." Fresh tears stung her eyes.

Father's hand tightened on her arm for a second. "How—dare—anyone?" He ground the words through his teeth. "You didn't see anyone about? It was all right yesterday."

"It was perfect yesterday." One tear rolled down Meg's cheek. "I was so pleased. At last I could keep my promise to Momma."

"We didn't see anyone or anything." Sarah answered his question. "Maybe those rough boys from the charcoal burners."

"I helped them get rid of their cats," Meg protested. "And they'll benefit from the school. Why would they harm it?"

"Maybe they don't want the school." Sarah spoke her suggestion with hesitancy.

"No one will make them come." Meg found herself scowling at the still-open door, caught movement from beyond the threshold, and smoothed out her face.

Not until they stepped into the heat and smell did she think of what were surely her red-rimmed eyes and tear-streaked cheeks for everyone there to see. For one man in particular to see.

She glanced around, seeking him out. If not for his red hair, she would have missed him on the other side of one of the great furnaces. He was knocking pieces of excess glass off the bottom of a finished work that appeared to be some sort of serving dish like a soup tureen. The glass shone like amber in the firelight.

"Beautiful," Sarah murmured.

Meg started, rather shocked that Sarah would make such a comment about a man. Then, face flushing, she realized her friend meant the glassware—not Colin.

"Shall we go to your desk, Father?" Meg turned her back on him in pursuit of her father's corner of the factory.

"Yes, just have a care. There's cullet all over the floor." Father picked his way over the flagstones strewn with chunks of glass that had been cut or broken from pieces.

Those shards would be reheated with batches of silica to make more glass. They wasted as little as possible.

Father's desk resided below a broad window formed of eight panes of glass. The afternoon sun blazed through the nearly clear windows and across an open ledger. He slammed that shut and indicated that Meg and Sarah should take the two chairs across from him.

"I'm not in the habit of entertaining ladies here." Father glared at someone behind Meg.

She tilted her head to adjust her hat and saw a young apprentice scurrying away.

"Yes." Father's smile was tight. "It's to keep the men's attention on their work, not pretty girls. Distraction can be dangerous when you're handling molten glass."

"It's wonderful to watch though." Sarah was gazing around, wide-eyed and openmouthed. "I had no idea that's how you make windows. No wonder they're so expensive."

"And now that you've mentioned windows," Father said, "you didn't need to come in here to ask me for more."

"I know. That is—" Meg took a deep breath. "I didn't come in here to ask for more windows. I mean, yes, I would like them and would like to make whoever smashed the other ones pay for them. But I have to tell you something else."

Father and Sarah both stared at her, faces puzzled. Father raised one hand to gesture for someone behind Meg to wait. Meg forced herself not to look.

"Go ahead," Father said.

Meg gulped. "Father, you can tell Mr. Grassick he needn't make so many glasses. Not because—because I don't want them." She spoke the last words in a rush. "I do. They're the most beautiful glasses I've ever seen. But I know they take a long time to make and that I planned not to announce the betrothal until they were done. But if he doesn't make so many, maybe he can make new windows instead." Out of breath, she sagged in her chair as though she had just set down a heavy burden.

Behind her, someone cleared his throat. In front of her, Sarah's face had gone blank, and Father frowned, but not as though he were angry. He looked—sad.

When no one spoke, Meg added, "So I had to come here straightaway to prevent any unnecessary work."

"I appreciate your honesty, daughter." Father stepped away from the desk. "Will you excuse me a moment?"

"Of course." Meg gathered her cloak around her, felt something sharp prick her hand, and remembered the kitten in her pocket. "Would you like us to leave now?"

"No no, I'd rather you stay for a few minutes." Father walked around Meg. "Thank you for finishing that bowl, Grassick. I believe Mrs. Beckett will be pleased with it. Let's take it out back for packing."

Their footfalls rang on the stone floor then died amid the hiss of fires and tinkle of glass falling onto hard surfaces.

"You really don't want to marry Joseph badly, do you?" Sarah whispered.

"You know I don't."

Sarah shook her head. "But I didn't know you would go to such lengths to avoid it."

"I went too far, and now I've been punished by maybe not being able to have my school open after all."

"Punished by whom? I mean, who knows what your plan was?"

"No one except the Lord."

"God doesn't work that way." Sarah drew her nearly straight brows together. "At least I don't think He does."

"I'm supposed to marry Joseph because it's what my father wants for me, and I'm trying to avoid it. So why should I get what I want?"

"Because you thought the Lord wanted you to open the school for the sake of other children?" Sarah suggested.

Meg didn't have a chance to respond. Father returned at that moment with Colin and Joseph accompanying him. Colin met Meg's glance for a heartbeat, gave her a half smile, then spun on his heel and paced to the back of the factory. Father and Joseph approached the desk.

"Good day, ladies." Joseph bowed.

Sunlight drew out the gold in his hair, spinning it around his head like a halo. He was indeed handsome, probably better-looking than Colin.

"Isaac"—Joseph nodded to Father—"has asked me if I'll accompany you ladies home."

And he was nice. She should really want to spend her life with such a good man.

"Thank you." Meg rose, cupping the now squirming kitten in her hand. "Father?" She gave him a questioning glance.

He returned it with a gentle smile. "Grassick has offered to work extra hours to make the windows for your school and to finish the goblets."

"He—but—" Meg swallowed a sudden lump in her throat.

"We'll talk this evening." Father shook Joseph's hand. "Thank you and hurry right back. I want to show you the new windows made with the flint glass. So much clearer, if a bit expensive to produce."

"Maybe not if there's less waste and less need for framing." Joseph laughed. "But we won't bore the ladies with this talk of business matters."

Meg wasn't bored. On the contrary, she was intrigued. She didn't think she should be asking to know more at that moment. She'd received a reprieve.

With a bob of a curtsy to Father, she led the way outside. What had been a pleasant autumn day earlier felt chilly after the heat of the glassworks. She gathered her cloak around her. At the movement her pocket meowed.

"Do you always carry cats in your pocket?" Joseph asked.

Sarah laughed. "You know our Meg. She's always rescuing something."

"Indeed. It's one of the lovable things about her." Joseph held out an arm for each lady. "I'm so pleased she's going to rescue me from a lonely life. And rescue my house from neglect."

"Does Peter feel like you're rescuing him?" Meg asked, blushing over the praise while, she had to admit to herself, pleased by it.

"More like he's rescuing me." Sarah's husky chuckle mingled with the rising wind in the trees. "I won't have to share the kitchen with my mother when I've a mind to bake."

"Meg won't ever have to set foot in the kitchen." To Meg, Joseph's shoulders seemed to straighten and his chin rose a notch as he made this declaration.

She frowned over his pride.

"I have a cook, as well as a housekeeper," he announced.

"But I like to bake," she protested. "My sugar buns are even better than Ilse's, and she taught me to make them."

The instant the words were out of her mouth, she wished she'd bitten her tongue instead of speaking them. She was criticizing Joseph for being boastful—then boasting herself.

"At least she says they are," Meg murmured.

"They are." Sarah toed a pinecone out of her path. "You'll be denying yourself a treat if you don't let her bake now and again, Joseph."

"Well, of course if she wants to." Joseph pressed Meg's hand against his side for a moment too long. "I know how Margaret likes to have her own way."

"I want to be obedient," Meg said then added, "to God."

Sarah gave out an unladylike snort she hastily covered with a cough.

Fortunately, they reached the lane to the Jordan farm at that moment, and Meg looked to the west, where the sun was beginning to drop into the horizon.

"You should take Sarah straight home. If you walk me up to the house, it'll be dark before you get back to the glassworks, and you don't have a lantern."

"Wise you are." Joseph took her hand from his arm and raised it to his lips. "Good evening, my dear."

From beyond his bent head, Meg met Sarah's eyes and read a surprise she hoped wasn't reflected on her own face. She'd never had her hand kissed before. Other than by her parents, she'd never been kissed before.

She didn't think she liked it.

With an effort, she managed not to snatch her fingers free and said something pleasant to Sarah about seeing her at church. Necessary pleasantries over, Meg spun on the flat heel of her slipper and strode up the lane with more haste than dignity or grace.

"I should like him," she made herself say aloud. "He cares for me. I should like him. He cares for me. I should. . ."

No amount of repetition made the words come true. She should or should not do a lot of things she did or did not do. Even Saint Paul had suffered from this affliction. Yet he had been obedient to God even when He made him do things that would send him to prison.

"I will marry him." As she entered the front door of the house, she changed it to a declaration. "I will. I will. I—oops."

She'd forgotten the cat was in her pocket.

She took him out to the stable to join his siblings and friends. They were feasting on some scraps of meat from the supper preparations. His tiny nose twitched, and he scrambled out of Meg's hand and raced across the yard to push his way into the food.

In her bedchamber she washed her face and wrapped a fresh fichu around her neck, one of white linen with a lace edging. Her eyes remained a bit puffy, but her cheeks no longer bore the marks of her tears. Once she had brushed her hair and replaced a few pins, she was ready to help Ilse with the last of the supper preparations. She wasn't sure she would ever be ready to meet her father for the talk he said they would have later.

Yet he hadn't seemed angry. Shocked, distressed, yes, but not angry. Then again, he might have been exhibiting self-control if Joseph and Colin Grassick were within earshot.

When she heard the front door open, her heart began to throb in her chest like galloping hooves. Hastily she picked up the pitcher of lemonade that had been cooling in the springhouse and carried it into the dining room to fill the glasses.

Father entered the room in minutes. Shadows made his eyes appear deep set and dark, and two lines cut grooves on either side of his mouth. But he gave Meg a smile and pulled out her chair.

"You look like your mother tonight," he told her. "She was fond of wearing a white collar with lace."

Meg glowed at his compliment. "Thank you."

"So what do we have for supper tonight?"

"Ragout with noodles."

"Ah, one of my favorite dishes of Ilse's."

They ate in near silence. Despite his claim of the meal being one of his favorites, he ate less than usual, barely managing to finish the plateful Meg served him. Seeing his lack of appetite, Meg lost what was left of hers and sent Ilse back to the kitchen, muttering about wastefulness.

"Take it to the single workers," Meg suggested, following her with the dirty dishes.

"Ach, you know we only have one of those now that Thaddeus has married. It's to that Scot this'll go, and deserving he is, working so hard and eating bachelor fare."

She carried the coffeepot back into the dining room. "Shall I join you, Father?"

"Yes, I have a few things to discuss with you." He folded his hands on the still-pristine tablecloth.

Meg poured coffee for each of them, though she didn't want it, and waited for him to speak.

He cleared his throat. "Why don't you want to marry Joseph?"

"It's too silly." She pressed her hands against her warm cheeks. "It makes sense to me, but when I say it out loud, it sounds—childish."

"To me, Margaret, you are a child."

"I'm not, though. I'm an old maid nearly. You've said so yourself."

"Yes, well, just try to say it."

"I'd like to say it's only because I don't love him, which is true, but I know you and Momma didn't love one another either and grew to over time."

"Marriages were arranged more often in those days than they are now."

Then why had he arranged hers?

Meg tamped down the spirit of rebellion.

"Go on." Father's face showed no expression. "If it's not only that you don't love him, what else is it?"

"He's not my choice." Meg blurted out the words before she lost her courage.

Father said nothing for several minutes, long minutes in which a log fell in the fireplace, sending a shower of sparks spiraling up the chimney and making her jump. Tedious minutes in which she had to clasp her hands together tightly enough to make her knuckles white to prevent herself from drumming her nails on the table.

"And what sort of man would you choose?" Father asked abruptly.

"I don't know." An image of emerald green eyes flashed through her mind, and she amended, "Joseph seems unfriendly."

Except for that kiss on her hand. That was too friendly.

Although she had spoken little to Colin Grassick, Meg felt closer to him after those conversations than she did to Joseph, whom she'd known all her life. Colin spoke of things in his heart. Joseph spoke of—things. Things like his big house. Things like having a cook and a housekeeper.

"He cares too much about his possessions." She spoke on a wave of inspiration.

"Ah." Father gave her his half smile. "But all those possessions will allow you to carry on your charitable work. You can start a whole farm for wayward cats. And provide every child in the county with chapter books."

"If he lets me," she muttered.

"Hmm. Well, yes." Father drummed his fingers on the table. He gazed toward the curtained windows for another minute; then he turned to Meg and covered one of her hands with his. "I can't go back on my word to Joseph about your marrying him. I made a promise to your mother, too, but I broke it. And now—Joseph has agreed to postpone the announcement of the wedding until after the new year."

Meg's eyes stung. Father had broken a promise to Momma? It seemed unbelievable.

"And the wedding?"

"That's still in the spring. The twenty-eighth day of April." Father's lips flattened. "Don't ask me to postpone that, too. Please, for my sake, this wedding must take place."

Chapter 7

The vacant windows of the schoolhouse seemed to glower at Colin as he passed, accusing him of shirking his promise to replace the glass. Given the opportunity, he would be back at the glasshouse working on the panes. But this Saturday afternoon Mr. Jordan insisted he take time off. The great furnaces needed to cool so the pits beneath the fire grates could be cleaned of ashes. So Colin took Thad's offer of the use of his fishing equipment and headed for a pool in the creek the junior glassblower recommended was a fine place.

"You catch them and my wife will cook them," Thad offered.

The pool lay just beyond the school, and Colin couldn't stop himself from hoping Miss Jordan would find a reason to visit her building or go for a walk with her friend Sarah Thompson or call on any number of people along the road in his direction, including the church. She probably wouldn't see him tucked amid the dense growth of trees along the water, but he would hear her coming. He found himself turning to peer through the branches every time he caught the sound of a foot scraping on the hard-packed earth of the lane. Fortunately, for the sake of his line and pole, few people traversed the stretch of road in the middle of the afternoon, even on a Saturday. Too few, since none proved to be Meg Jordan with her light, quick tread and bouncing curls.

Twice Colin found himself starting to pray she would come along, but he stopped before fully forming the words. He should be praying to forget about her. No one had told him not to speak to her, even after Mr. Jordan had been displeased to find them chatting in his kitchen and ordered Colin back to the glassworks. But Colin knew wanting to be near her was wrong. He must think about his work, about his family, about earning a future for them that would make up for what he had caused them to lose.

Yet every time he saw her, his heart lifted. A glance, a smile, a nod from her made him forget the emptiness he had made of his life. To Meg Jordan, who he was and what he'd done didn't seem to matter. He told her the truth about his father, and she still looked at him as though—

She looked at him as though she liked him, and that was wrong. She was marrying another man. Even if the announcement of the betrothal hadn't been made official yet, Colin reminded himself of the truth with each amethyst goblet he produced.

He also knew another truth: Meg Jordan didn't want to marry Joseph Pyle. Since her father obviously loved her, Colin couldn't work out why the man was so insistent that she wed Mr. Pyle. Pure greed? The Pyle fortune was well known in the county, Colin had learned in his four weeks in America. Yet Jordan was a kind and generous man. Marrying off his daughter to a man she didn't care for simply out of a desire to have her marry wealth didn't seem to fit the situation.

A tug on his line stopped Colin from pursuing that thread of consideration further. With pulling on the fish's part, and persistence on his, and enough splashing to mimic a flailing swimmer, Colin landed a fish with a greenish back and silvery sides. He didn't recognize it and wasn't certain it was edible but decided to keep it. Catch in hand, he turned to place it in the basket he'd brought for the purpose and discovered his bucket of bait had disappeared.

Movement through the trees and a muffled giggle hinted at the cause of the disappearance. Throwing the fish into the creel, he shoved through the foliage in time to see five boys charging toward the road. A bucket banged against the leg of the smallest of them. All held their hands to their mouths.

Chuckling, Colin lunged after them. "Halt right there, lads," he called to them.

To his surprise they stopped and faced him. He kept going. In another two yards he intended to stop and lecture them on stealing. He wanted to be close to them, close enough to look down at even the tallest of them.

One boy moved, scooping something from the bucket. Long, brown objects sailed toward Colin. He ducked to avoid an onslaught of worms, and someone behind him screamed.

Colin straightened and turned in time to see Meg Jordan pluck a worm from the shoulder of her cloak and throw it back at the boys.

"How did you miss something the size of Mr. Grassick, children?" She was laughing. Her eyes sparkled.

Colin thought the sun had come out and the temperature had risen to summertime. Tongue-tied, he glanced from her to the boys, who seemed equally struck mute.

"Whose worms are those?" she asked, tilting her head to one side so a curl bobbed against her cheek.

Colin clenched his fingers against a wish to tuck the errant strand behind her ear.

The boys ducked their heads and scuffed their clogs in the dirt.

"I was doing a wee bit of fishing," Colin managed. "While I was bringing in my catch, these lads decided to have a bit of fun with me."

"First cats, now worms." She clucked her tongue. "I don't think they should get away with it. What shall we make them do, Mr. Grassick?"

"We was just playin'," the youngest one cried. "We would have brought 'em back."

"But you all threw them at him and struck me." She shook her head. A limp worm dangled from the brim of her felt hat like a broken plume. "Mr. Grassick, what do you think?"

"I think they'll need to be in the front row of the school when it opens," Colin said.

Meg looked delighted. Expressions of horror crossed the boys' faces.

"An excellent notion." Meg nodded. "The first Monday in January, boys. Be there, or I'll send Mr. Grassick to collect you. Now run along, and don't go stealing things or harming living creatures."

"And I'll take that bucket back." Colin collected the bucket as the youngest one dropped it and fled.

"They don't have a mother, I learned," Meg said. "And their father is busy all the time with the charcoal burner. If I can make them come to school, it will give them something to do an hour or two a day and maybe keep them out of trouble."

"Aye, they're not bad bairns. They simply need a bit of supervision." Pail in one hand, Colin stepped close enough to her to pluck the worm from her hat. "The color does not suit you."

She made a face, laughed, then lifted her chin and looked directly into his eyes. "Thank you."

"Aye. That is, you're welcome." He swallowed. "You're not squeamish about the creepy crawly things then?"

"No, I grew up fishing with my father in these waters before he decided to reopen the glassworks and got too busy." She smiled. "I don't clean them though. E—ew."

"I only have the one pole, but I'm willing to share." He clasped both hands on the handle of the bucket. "If you think 'twould be all right to join me."

"It's all right. I'm on my way back from the church. I was trying to see if they have any extra benches I can use for the school. They don't, so now I'm not promised to anyone." She sighed and muttered, "Yet."

That word *yet* reminded Colin to merely enjoy her company and think no more of it than a pleasant time with a pretty lass. If he told himself that enough, he might believe it. For the moment, he couldn't stop his heart from leaping like a salmon.

"Then, by all means, join me, madam." He offered her his arm.

She took it, and they returned to the pool.

"Who told you about this place?" she asked. "Or did you find it on your own?"

"Thad told me." He retrieved his pole, untangled the line, and hooked a worm. "You may have the first cast. Do you need any help?"

"I should go all missish and say yes." She took the pole and sent the baited hook arcing into the water with scarcely a ripple. "But I'd be fibbing."

"Apparently so." He stooped to gather wet grasses to keep his catch cool and damp, though the misty day would do much of that. Beside him Meg stood motionless except for occasionally moving the tip of the pole.

"You're very good at this." He straightened and gazed down on the crown of her hat, over which curled a pink feather. "How old were you when you last fished?"

"A clever way of asking my age, since you know the glassworks have been open for five years." She leaned a little forward. "I was sixteen."

"I had no intention of being that calculating. My apologies for being so bold."

"None necessary. Hmm." She gave her line a little tug. "Everyone in the county knows I'm practically on the shelf. Finicky Meg—ah yes, I have a bite."

With calm and skill, she reeled in the fish, took one look at the whiskered orange beast, and made a noise of disgust.

"Catfish." She shuddered. "Not something to my liking, but go ahead and keep it. Some people love them."

"Aye, I'll take them all to Martha Dalbow. She can feed them to her pig if she doesn't want them."

"And save the inner bits for your cat." She handed him the pole, allowing him to remove the fish from the hook and rebait it. "How is the wee beastie?"

The sound of the Scots expression on her lips sent his insides quivering. "Fat and spoiled." He cast. "How is your wanderer?"

"Still up to his tricks. I expect I'll be teaching my class one day, and he'll be yowling in the tree outside the windows."

"Some creatures don't have enough sense to stay home where they're loved and safe." He fixed his gaze on the pond.

It lay as still as a mirror, reflecting trees, the gray sky, and their figures side by side on the bank, quiet, comfortable, companionable. It was a vision he would happily keep in his head. In his heart.

"How did the son of a Highland fisherman become a Lowland glassblower?"

Her question yanked him back to the way things really were—him in no position to think about her as anything more than his master's daughter.

"I found a piece of glass on the shore one day." He focused on the past, his father's face as he told him he didn't want to go to sea day after day. "Somehow it managed not to break on the rocks. Probably washed up from a ship. I do not ken. It was only a bowl, but the color was a clear amber like your eyes." He kept his gaze away from her face so he could not see her reaction to his offhand compliment. "The curve of the bowl was so fine I wanted to ken how 'twas done. I asked the minister, he being a learned man from Edinburgh. He told me about the glassblowers, and I had to see for myself. So I sold the bowl to a *sassenach*—an Englishman—visiting the Highlands for the grouse hunting, and I left."

"Did you know you were an artist before then?" Her voice was soft, as though she didn't want the birds in the treetops to hear her.

He snorted. "I am nay artist, Miss Jordan. I am a craftsman."

"You're an artist." Her reflection told him she'd tilted her face toward him. "I know the difference between the two."

"Ah well. Perhaps I have a bit of a gift." He ducked his head, warm with pleasure at her compliment. "I did a bit of drawing with sticks in the dirt, but we didn't have the silver for paper and pencils."

"Do you think your father truly begrudged your seeking a profession that better suited your skills and God-given gifts?"

"Nay, he was not that sort. But I could have sent the money home to help with the bairns. I was a selfish youth who cost them all too much."

"Oh Colin." She laid her hand on his arm.

In the same instant, the tip of his pole swooped toward the water. His foot slid on the grassy bank. With a weight on the hook and thrown off balance, Colin toppled toward the pond.

"Let go," Meg cried.

Contrary to her words, she caught hold—of him. Her arms encircled his waist, and slight as it was, her weight helped him regain his balance and find solid footing.

Colin landed another fish he didn't recognize, something bluish and full of fight, but far enough up on the bank he risked setting down the pole without worrying the catch would flop back into the water and pull Thad's equipment after it.

"I couldn't let go of Thad's fishing pole," Colin said in an even tone. "He may not have another."

"No—no, you couldn't." Meg released him and moved away, out of his sight, away from a reflection in the pool.

Colin faced her. She held her hand to her lips, and she squeezed her eyes shut.

"Lass, what's the trouble?" He raised one hand but stopped short of touching her.

She shook her head, and an odd choking noise came from her throat.

"Lass, are you—" He narrowed his eyes. "Are you laughing at me?"

She nodded, and the mirth burst from her. "I am so sorry." She took a shuddering breath. "But you admit we looked a bit silly."

"Aye, well, I never was verra good at the dancing."

They laughed. They fished together; they talked of growing up in places far different from each other yet sharing a common thread of learning of a faith in God.

"I abandoned mine in the city," Colin admitted. "But I turned my heart back to the Lord after my father died."

"Then good came of it." Meg frowned at the darkening sky. "I fail in my willfulness. I just want things the way I want them."

Colin smiled into her eyes, knowing they must go soon, knowing this was an interlude they would likely never share again. "Aye, I ken what you mean. I wish things were different."

"They will be." Meg clasped her hands in front of her. "If ever I wanted things to be the way I want them, it's more afternoons like this—for us."

Chapter 8

If only she knew why her father insisted she marry Joseph, Meg thought she could persuade him not to go through with the wedding plans. Father said he wanted her to marry because she needed to be settled with a home of her own. Yet now he told her she mustn't call off the inevitable announcement of the betrothal for his sake. For her sake, she must learn what was wrong.

If she could hold off the wedding announcement that long.

Briefly she considered telling Joseph outright that she found her interests lay elsewhere. The risk to Colin stopped her. So she prayed for things to change and worked harder to get her school ready to start the first Monday of the New Year.

Seating was still a problem she hadn't solved. The minister promised to give her some slates and chalk someone had donated to the church, but other than that, he couldn't help her with furnishings. And the windows were still missing glass.

"It seems like it won't open after all," she told Sarah one afternoon.

Sarah's mother was pinning up the hem of a merino traveling dress in which Sarah would accompany her new husband for a week in New York, meeting his family. The deep green complemented Sarah's rich red-brown hair and drew out the color in her cheeks.

"You're so beautiful." Meg poured enthusiasm into her friend's new wardrobe and set worries about her own marriage and school aside. "Peter will fall even more in love with you than he already is."

Sarah laughed and blushed. Her hazel eyes grew dreamy.

With the wedding less than three weeks away, she thought of little else than her husband-to-be and her home. Meg rejoiced for her friend, while feeling a twinge of loneliness cutting inside her. Sarah would never have the same freedom to run about with Meg as she enjoyed now. Yet Sarah wanted the change because she'd met the man she loved and wanted to spend her life with.

Later, when Peter arrived for dinner, Meg watched him and Sarah exchange glances and knew she had spoken the complete truth when she told Sarah she couldn't wed a man until she found one who looked at her that way. Joseph didn't gaze at her with love. She hadn't yet put a name to the emotion in his glances, but it wasn't devotion.

Quiet, she accepted Peter's offer to walk her home rather than Sarah's invitation to spend the night. Father was leaving for Philadelphia the following day, and she wanted to ensure his bags were packed to his satisfaction.

"I'll return tomorrow." Meg kissed Sarah's cheek and headed out for the short walk down the road to home.

Once out of earshot of the house, Peter brought up the subject of glass. "It's a little late, I know, but I thought I could order some fine pieces for our new house. I was thinking candlesticks or glass globes for the wall sconces. Maybe for Christmas?"

"I don't know, but come by the glassworks early in the morning if you can and discuss it with Father before he leaves for the city." She smiled as a thought struck her. "I could go with you to help pick out some ideas."

"I'd like that." Peter heaved a sigh of relief. "I want everything perfect for Sarah."

"She doesn't need perfection, Peter." Meg smiled up at the young man she'd known for many years. He was tall and slim, and his dark hair and eyes were an attractive contrast to Sarah's vivid coloring.

"She would like a kitten, too," Meg added.

Peter laughed. "I'd rather give her glass baubles, but if she wants a cat, she can have one."

"Good. She can pick one out when you return from New York. I found three more abandoned near my school, so that makes nine I've rescued in the past month."

They reached the Jordans' house. Peter bade her good night with the promise to see her in the morning, then strode off down the drive, whistling.

Meg fairly skipped to the door.

<hr>

With the prospect of even catching a glimpse of Colin the next day, she was too excited to sleep well or eat much breakfast.

"You're not sickening, are you?" Ilse asked.

"No, just excited."

"Ah, the friend's wedding." Ilse nodded and carried the oatmeal porridge away.

"I'm going over to the glassworks to help Mr. Strawn pick out a gift for Sarah."

"And that's put you off your food?" Ilse gave her a narrow-eyed look.

"I'd better finish packing." Meg bolted up the steps to her bedchamber.

For the week Father would be in Philadelphia to conduct business, something to do with the glassworks, Meg would stay with Sarah's family. They were happy to have her help with the wedding so close. Too close. Signaling the nearness of Christmas and then the first of the year and the end of her own freedom.

It also meant the opening of her school. She must think about that. Her school and a room full of children needing to learn.

She concentrated on packing until Peter, as he promised, arrived to walk over to the glassworks. The air was clear but cold, and frost still clung to the grass. It kept their steps brisk, and they reached the factory before they had time to exchange more than pleasantries.

Father stood just outside the door, speaking with Joseph. Meg's heart plummeted, her excitement over the possibility of seeing Colin for a moment or two evaporating like the frost beneath the sun's feeble rays. Nonetheless, she managed a polite greeting and explained the purpose of the visit.

"I really need to be on my way." Father looked regretful. "We can't keep the horses waiting in this cold, and they'll be harnessed up by now."

Even as he spoke, the rumble of carriage wheels and hooves resounded from the road.

"They're here now," Father added.

"But it's a fine sale." Joseph laughed. "Sales are money, Jordan. And we all need to make money."

The corners of Father's mouth tightened, but he softened them to smile at Meg. "The designs are on a shelf behind my desk, Margaret. Why don't you take Peter in and show him. Call Grassick or Dalbow for assistance if you need any." He hesitated then added, "And fetch Mrs. Dalbow, so there's another female with you."

"I'll do that." Meg kissed his cheek. "Have a good journey, Father."

She walked off with an even, dignified stride until she was out of sight; then she dashed through the yard, past the outbuildings, and along the walkway to the Dalbow cottage.

Martha Dalbow was a petite, pretty young woman Meg had known all her life. Her father had been a laborer on the Pyle farm, and Meg and Martha played together as children until Meg went to school in Burgen County in the northern part of the state. Now they exchanged smiles and waves at church, but Martha married a glassblower and wasn't invited to the same houses as Meg.

Greeting her childhood friend, Meg experienced a spurt of rebellion and decided to be friendlier with Martha in the future, especially now that Sarah would live farther away.

"So you're going to get married, too." Martha trotted alongside Meg on their way back to the glassworks, her golden curls bobbing with every bouncy step. "I always thought you'd be first."

"It's not certain." Meg figured if she said it enough it would be so. "I haven't said yes."

"Then I'll save my congratulations."

They reached the group of men standing near the door. Father had gone, and Peter and Joseph were engaged in a discussion about the price of shipping goods out of the country. Peter broke off as soon as Meg and Martha arrived, but Joseph took several minutes to finish expounding on tariffs before acknowledging Meg's arrival. He said nothing to Martha. He offered Meg his arm, leaving Martha to follow.

Meg declined the offer and preceded him inside, her hand on Martha's elbow to bring her along.

The heat enveloped her like an extra cloak. Although the desk lay to her left, her gaze shot to the right almost of its own volition, seeking, finding, resting on Colin in his corner. He was working with a piece of glass the consistency of thickened caramel, applying tongs and a cutter to stretch and twist the hot, shimmering mass. Meg's heart suddenly felt the same as that hot glass—malleable, twisted, compressed. She heard voices around her but couldn't comprehend what they said.

"Margaret." Joseph's tone sharpened, and he grasped her arm.

She started. "I–I'm sorry." She swung toward Father's desk. "I'm fascinated by the process of making glass."

And the man making it.

Martha nodded and smiled but said nothing until they all tried to make sense of the diagrams drawn on wide sheets of paper.

"I'll fetch one of the men," she whispered; then she darted off.

Meg watched Martha's progress through the factory, around the furnaces, and past the benches of the blowers. She paused by her husband, who shook his head; then she walked around him and out of sight. Meg tensed, waiting for Martha to reappear, waiting for Colin to appear. Waiting, anticipating, hoping—

"Margaret." Joseph's sharp tone returned Meg to the men beside her.

She blinked up at him. "Did you say something to me?"

Joseph and Peter gave her questioning glances.

"I was woolgathering." Meg turned her back on the workroom. "Peter, I think this design is a glass globe for a wall sconce. See the crimped edges at the top?" She traced a wavy line along the upper edge of a design. "Of course, it's a little too round, so—maybe. . ." Her voice trailed off.

She hadn't heard his footfalls above the clang and clatter of equipment and roar of the furnaces, but she sensed him, caught the scent of smoke and the tang of the silica.

"'Tis a vase." Colin's hand joined hers on the sketch. "See how the bottom is rounded? A sconce would be straight to fit into the holder."

"How silly of me." She felt breathless, too warm in her heavy cloak and wool dress. "I don't think Peter—Mr. Strawn—wants vases, do you, Peter? You mentioned sconces or maybe glasses. Glasses would take longer, since you'd need several, so maybe—" She snapped her teeth together.

She was talking too much.

"Let Grassick help Peter." Joseph's voice was as cold and brittle and sharp as an icicle. "I will walk you home."

"No." Meg stepped away from the desk, away from Colin, and away from Joseph. "I'll go to Martha's house until Peter is ready to help carry my things to Sarah's."

"If you like." Joseph's eyes gleamed pale blue. "I'll see you at church on Sunday." He stalked to the front door of the glassworks.

Meg caught sight of Martha talking to her husband again and waved her over.

They exited out the back door. As Meg turned to pull the heavy panel closed behind her, she caught Colin's eyes upon her and smiled, and her stomach fluttered.

She closed her eyes for a moment to gain her composure, and when she opened them again, Colin stood with his back to her. Her belly settled, and she trotted off behind Martha, an apology on her lips.

"I don't need to stay, since you probably have work to do, Martha. I can walk home on my own."

"But I'd like you to stay." Martha lowered her eyes. "I'm learning how to knit and would love to show someone what I'm making Thad."

"And I'd love to see it."

More time than Meg anticipated passed with Martha. She found herself settling into the cozy kitchen with its herbs hanging from the ceiling and heavy pot simmering over the fire, sending the wonderful aroma of venison throughout the cottage. The entire home seemed to embrace Meg with its plain but comfortable furnishings and embroidered samplers of Bible verses decorating the whitewashed walls. Martha showed Meg everything, her face glowing.

"Will you teach me to knit?" Meg asked. "It's so useful."

"But it's not very ladylike, is it?"

"Neither is fishing, but I do that, too."

Martha laughed. "I heard." She tilted her head and glanced at Meg from the corner of one blue eye. "Colin is a wonderful man."

"Yes." Meg fingered the scarf Martha was knitting, admiring the smoothness of the stitches. "And talented."

"And works for your father."

"It doesn't matter."

But Meg knew it did. It mattered to her father. It mattered to Colin. It should matter to her.

"I'd better be on my way." She stood abruptly. "I want to visit you again. You can teach me to knit, and if I get any girls in my school, I can teach them. Where do I find the needles and yarn?"

Information in hand, Meg returned to the glassworks. Peter seemed to be occupying his time watching the work at hand. Meg wanted to stay but knew she shouldn't. If she were wise, she would leave the glassworks and not return.

She didn't think she was wise—only prudent enough not to mention Colin's name to Peter, to Sarah, to God in her prayers. She tried not to think about him. Like not thinking about her upcoming betrothal, she hoped a lack of thought would make it go away, whatever it was, the tightening inside her whenever she saw him. It was a feeling like she would burst into tears if she couldn't see him and song when she did.

Except she didn't see him. With Father gone, she couldn't even contrive an excuse for visiting the glassworks. Staying with the Thompsons, she couldn't get over to the Dalbow cottage and perhaps encounter him there unless she came up with a good excuse.

The idea came to her while she and Sarah unpacked linens in Sarah's new home. The stacks of sheets, pillowcases, and towels had been stored in wooden crates lined with muslin and sprinkled with lavender, as Sarah had finished embroidering her and Peter's initials on them. Fatigued from a restless night, Meg sat on an unopened crate and suddenly knew how to solve her problem of seating for the students she hoped to have at her school.

"Packing crates!" She leaped to her feet. "We'll use packing crates for benches."

"That's a good idea." Sarah tucked an armful of sheets in the linen press. "You're welcome to take these, but it won't be enough."

"I hope it won't be enough. But Father has acres of them at the glassworks. I'm sure he won't care if I take a few for seats. Shall we go see?"

"Now?" Sarah shook her head. "Your father isn't home or there."

"No one will be there. It's Saturday afternoon, and they stop work early to let the furnaces cool for cleaning."

Not waiting for Sarah to agree, Meg ran down the steps to the entryway and snatched her cloak off a stand by the door. "I'll just run up and look at what's available and see if they're the right size."

"No, don't go alone. The walk will be good." Sarah started down the steps. "If I breathe any more lavender, I'll get a headache."

Cloaks tucked around them against the bite of the early December wind, they strolled along the road. Wood smoke from cooking fires scented the air, and a handful of snowflakes danced around them.

"If it snows," Meg grumbled, "everything in the school will get wet without the windows."

"It won't snow yet. There's sunshine over there." Sarah gestured to the west.

Sunlight glowed around the edges of the clouds like a promise. Meg hugged herself and increased her pace. Sometimes Colin worked extra hours. Maybe today. . .

Although a curl of smoke drifted lazily into the brightening sky from one of the two chimneys at the glassworks, the building was empty, the fires banked in the furnaces.

"They must have just left." Meg closed the door then paused, frowning at it. "But I can't believe they left without locking it."

"Maybe they'll be right back." Sarah tugged on Meg's arm. "We shouldn't be inside without anyone here."

"No, but it's awfully messy. They usually clean up at the end of the day." Though not liking the glassworks left open and unkempt, Meg allowed Sarah to lead her around the building to the shed where packing crates rose in stacks higher than their heads.

"I think these will work." Sarah used her hands to measure one crate.

"They're high enough for children."

"And they're sturdy, since they have to hold glass. Oh, here's someone." Meg glanced over her shoulder, hoping, then suppressing a sigh of disappointment.

Thaddeus Dalbow, not Colin, strode into the yard. "Miss Meg, Miss Sarah, may I be of assistance?"

"I want to look at packing crates." Meg glanced toward the factory building. "Are you the one working late today?" She tried to sound casual. "I thought it was only Mr. Grassick who worked extra hours."

Sarah's breath hissed through her teeth, and Meg realized she'd given herself away just saying his name.

"It is." Thad shoved a lock of unruly hair away from his face. "But there was an accident."

Chapter 9

Colin knew he should be at church and not working, however charitable the work. He heard his mother's admonitions about the need for worship and teaching ringing with nearly every breath he took. But at church he saw Meg, and seeing Meg had begun to hurt as much as did his left hand.

"You understand, do You not, Lord?" As he often did, he prayed while he worked alone.

Today's project took him to Meg's school, a building that appeared to have been an old cottage no one used any longer. Instead of Mr. Jordan having to hire a carpenter to fit the new glass panes into the wooden frames, Colin had offered to do the work. With the glass finished, he decided to risk someone disapproving of him working on a Sunday and set the windows back into the school for Meg's next visit.

"When else would I be having the daylight?" Colin thought something must be wrong if he was trying to justify his actions to the Lord. If he needed to justify them, they couldn't be right.

That knowledge didn't stop him from lifting the first pane of glass from its nest of straw and sliding it into the frame. Around him a few birds chirped and the air smelled clean. He caught a hint of water with the wind blowing from the direction of the nearby bay, and his heart ached with the wish to see his family. He had abandoned them fifteen years ago with scarcely a backward glance, yet now that his father's death had brought them together again, he didn't want to be apart from them.

"So you should stop thinking of the master's daughter, my lad."

Think of Meg he did—too often. He'd ruined a perfectly good candlestick when she walked into the glassworks on Wednesday morning, as bright and effervescent as the morning itself. The excuse to go near her came as a gift, a blessing, and he exerted every bit of willpower he possessed not to run through the factory to her side.

And Joseph Pyle, that man to whom she would be wed too soon, stood near her, too, glaring at Colin as though he intended to shrivel him like last year's apples.

"She can never be yours, lad," Colin cautioned himself over the first pane of glass.

He had no business even considering more than a polite exchange of words with her for however long he remained in Salem County. She was his master's daughter, and he had a family who needed him more than Meg Jordan needed anything.

"Keep your mind on your work and the Lord," he admonished himself.

As though to prove he wasn't doing enough of the latter, church bells began to ring across the countryside, pure and melodic. Soon worshippers would travel along the road, returning to their homes or visiting with friends and neighbors. She would pass by, too. He wanted her to see him and stop. He knew she shouldn't.

His hand throbbed, and he paused to soak it in a bucket of cold water, as Ilse Weber had told him he should. She was right. It wasn't the first time he'd burned himself while learning to manipulate hot glass. But this was the first time the burn hadn't been his fault. Not that he could prove that or do more than speculate how the accident occurred.

The water diminishing the ache in his hand, he resumed his work with the window, fitting a pane into the frame and holding it with the uninjured half of his left hand so he could apply the caulking with his right. The position proved awkward, and when he heard her voice, the glass slipped out of his hold.

He caught it an instant before it struck the ground and broke. The sharp edge nicked his palm. He frowned, figuring it was what he deserved for not resting and worshipping on a Sunday.

And for thinking of Meg Jordan instead of the Lord.

"Mother would be ashamed of you, lad," he muttered.

"I should think she would be indeed." Meg's voice brimmed with laughter. "You should have been in church or home resting that hand."

"Ah, you sound like a schoolmistress." He laughed, too, and turned to face her, his left hand outstretched. "I could not tie a proper cravat for attending the kirk, and I'm hoping the Lord will forgive my work if 'tis for a good cause and not personal gain."

"Oh Colin." She cradled his hand in both of hers, the silk of her gloves snagging on his rough skin. "I was distressed when Thad told us about your accident." She touched the blisters on his palm and pinkie finger so gently she gave him no pain. "How did it happen?"

"'Tis what I'd like to ken myself." He frowned at his hand.

Her gaze flashed to his face. "What do you mean?"

"I mean my grate—you ken where the pipe rests?—'twas hot enough to burn when it should have been as cool as this glass."

"Colin." She curled her fingers around the uninjured part of his hand. "How? I mean, were you in the glassworks alone?"

"I thought I was, but someone could have sneaked in while I was mixing the silica."

"Why? Why would anyone want to hurt you?"

"'Tis not unheard of in the glasshouses. Envy. Fear for their positions. Malice." He set down the pane of glass he still held and smoothed the crease between her brows with the tip of his finger. "Do not fash yourself, lass. I'll be more careful in the future."

"I'll tell my father—"

"Nay, do not. 'Twill cause unnecessary trouble. I'll heal."

"But Colin—"

"Go now." He extracted his grip from hers. "You shouldn't be here, you ken. You're an engaged lady, and he's likely wondering where you are."

"We're not engaged yet." She grimaced. "Father still wants me to marry Mr. Pyle, but nothing is official until after the first of the year. And I'm hopeful— never you mind about that. I'm concerned about your not coming to church."

"You needn't concern yourself with me." He injected as much coolness into his tone as he could manage with her close enough for him to catch her scent of apple blossoms. "The Lord knows the state of my soul."

"Would He be happy with it?"

"Now that is a verra difficult question to answer. But I am thinking the Lord isn't happy with me at all." He turned his back on her and began to fit the glass into the window frame again.

She puffed out a breath. "Colin, you didn't cause your father's death."

"Aye, but there you're wrong. If I'd been with him—"

"You likely would have died, too."

"I might have kept him from going out in a storm."

"So you got your stubbornness from your mother?"

"Ah Meg—Miss Jordan, you make me laugh, you do." He did laugh, and his soul lightened. "Nay, I got my stubbornness from my father. But if I'd been working with him all along, he wouldn't have felt the need to work too hard and be careless with his life."

"I'm sorry. That's a difficult burden to bear." She moved up beside him, tugged off her gloves, and placed one hand on the glass to steady it in its frame while he applied the caulking. "But you've been forgiven if you've asked for it."

"I ken that's what the Bible tells me, but I don't feel it in my heart." He shifted his position for a better angle, and his hand brushed hers.

Like brushing fine porcelain, creamy and as smooth as her silk glove had been.

He took a deep breath to stop his heart from skipping any more beats than it already had. "I need to bring my family here and keep my work to be truly obedient to the Lord. Just like you're needing to marry that fine gentleman your father wishes you to wed."

"I'm not convinced my father really does wish me to marry Joseph."

Colin dropped his knife. "I beg your pardon?"

"I haven't told anyone, even Sarah, and I probably shouldn't say anything to you." She peeked at him from beneath those extraordinary lashes. "I like talking to you. You listen to me and don't treat me like I'm a child who should run along and play."

"You should, you ken. Perhaps not play but run along."

"That's common sense, but my heart says otherwise. I mean—" She pressed her free hand to her cheek. "By my heart, I mean the feeling I get inside when I see others in need, not my heart in how a lady feels for a—should I stop up my mouth?"

"Aye, probably so." Chuckling, Colin made the mistake of looking at her mouth, those pretty lips that always seemed to curve in a smile. His mouth went dry.

She laughed, too. "I talk too much. You do understand what I'm saying, do you not?"

"I understand." Realizing that he held the caulking knife and was doing nothing with it, he set back to work.

He couldn't avoid looking at her though. The windowpane reflected her lovely face.

"You want to make me a charity," he made himself say. "Take me in and pamper me like one of your kittens, or teach me American history like the charcoal burners' children."

His words hurt her. He read it in the way her face stilled and her body tensed.

"Your father's already doing plenty for me, Miss Jordan." He gentled his tone. "I have no need of your help."

"What if I could get your family here faster? Would that help you to—to feel worthy of the Lord's love and forgiveness?"

"You're a kind lady, Margaret Jordan."

So kind, so pretty, so giving, he feared he was more than half in love with her.

"But I have to do this myself. 'Tis the only way I can make up for letting them down."

"You can never make up for letting them down, Colin." She placed a bit of emphasis on his Christian name, an emphasis of her defiance of convention, like talking to him at all was. "We can't make up for any of our mistakes, no matter what we do. That's what God's forgiveness is all about."

"I have to try." He finished with the pane but couldn't place the next one with her standing between him and the frame. "I've been given so much. A runaway lad of twelve years should not have found a place in the Edinburgh glassworks, but I did. They needed assistants to carry the molten glass to the glassblowers, and I was quick. I fell in love with the craft and persuaded the master glassblower to teach me." He faced her instead of her reflection. "I have the gift for it. I have to use it to make up for what learning of that gift stole from my family. You ken? I have to do it."

"I don't agree with you, but I understand. I was away at school when my mother died. I didn't want to be there, but Father wouldn't let me come home. That's partly why this school is so important to me. If it works out, children won't have to leave home to get an education. And children from families without the means to pay for boarding school will have an equal opportunity."

"You're a fine lass." Colin stooped to retrieve another pane of glass. "Thaddeus Dalbow warned me to stay away from you if I wish to keep my employment."

"Thaddeus Dalbow tried to kiss me when he was eighteen and I sixteen." She laughed. "We were friends before that, and he got some notions. Father sent him packing with a flea in his ear."

"But your father doesn't like you being too friendly with the workers," Colin said, still selecting glass from the box on the ground.

"No, but—" She sighed. "He doesn't think it good to possibly play favorites. On the other hand, he is already showing you favoritism, and besides that, Ilse Weber is our housekeeper. She raised me after Momma died. I never talk to her husband because I never see him, but I have few secrets from her, and I'm sure she tells him."

"It makes no difference." He rose, holding the glass between them like a shield, while a wild notion formed in his brain, a spark of hope ignited in his heart. "Will you be asking your father if he cares if you talk to me when we meet up?"

"I—could." She looked dubious.

"If you're thinking he'd say no, then get yourself home now. But if 'tis otherwise, I—" He met her eyes, hoping his look conveyed what he dared not say.

Her heightened color suggested she knew exactly what he was saying—she brought sunshine and warmth into his life, and he cared for her more than he should.

"I'm staying to help you finish." She took the glass from his hands. "It's my school. Now show me how to fit this into the frame."

He showed her. With her assistance, the work sped by. With time together, their conversation grew lighter. As he had the day she stopped to fish with him, he talked to her more in the next hour than he had talked to anyone in the past week. Talking felt like a gift. Listening to her lively way of speaking, gathering the words in his memory felt like treasures he could take out and appreciate in the long hours after work ended for the day and he returned to his empty cottage.

When the work was finished, however, no excuses remained for either of them to stay. Besides, clouds were blowing in from the east, bringing the scent of rain on a chilling breeze.

"We'd best be on our way." He picked up the box the glass had been in and turned to the road without taking a step in that direction.

"I know. I don't want to get my dress soaked in the rain." A stronger gust of wind caught the frill at the bottom of her skirt, and she flattened her hands against the fabric to hold it in place. "Do you have enough provisions to make yourself a fine Sunday dinner?"

"Martha Dalbow sees to my meals. She's a fair good cook."

"That's good then. I worried you weren't eating well."

"You cannot be worrying about me, Miss—Meg."

She wrinkled her nose. "You can't stop me."

"Nay, I have no doubt few people can make you do anything you do not wish to do."

"I expect I'm spoiled."

A blast of wind bearing moisture slammed into their faces.

"We'd better run." Instead of heading to the road, though, she darted around the end of the building. "Leave that box in here." She produced a key from her reticule and unlocked the door. "You can go faster."

"Aye, and the straw won't get wet." He dropped the container inside the building, waited for her to lock the door, then left for the road, being careful to measure his longer strides to her shorter ones.

"I knew the fine weather this morning lasted longer than we deserved in December." She sounded breathless but refused to slow down.

They rounded the curve to the intersection. Already the burn roared louder than when he'd passed it earlier, testimony of rain upstream. Above them the tree branches creaked and groaned, and the lightning-struck tree where he'd first seen her leaned more precariously over the water.

And a bundle of black-and-white fur clung to one of the whipping branches.

"The foolish beastie!" Colin shouted above the wind. "He'll be blown down."

"I don't know how something so small can travel so far. It must be like us walking twenty miles and climbing a mountain." She stopped, and her hat blew off her head. Wind caught her hair and sent her curls flying out like banners. She shoved her hair behind her ears. "We can't just leave him there."

"We should, but, nay, we cannot." Not liking the idea of climbing the unstable tree, Colin began to remove his coat.

"Wait, let's call him first." She laid her hand on his arm then did not remove it when she began to call, "Here, kitty-kitty."

The cat didn't move.

"He's too frightened." Colin removed his arm from her restraining grasp, feeling coldness where her hand had rested. "I'll fetch him. You run along home."

"But what if you fall?"

"I hear a horse. Perhaps 'tis someone who will take you up in a carriage."

"I should go up. I'm lighter."

"Do not dare." He caught the edge of her cloak and found himself holding nothing more than wool.

Meg had slipped out of the garment and darted forward.

"Stubborn braw female," Colin grumbled and sprinted after her.

As Meg set foot on the lowest branch, the kitten leaped from its perch and onto Meg's shoulder. From there it soared to the ground. Colin dove to grab the creature. It slipped past his hands and into the road—right under the hooves of the trotting horse.

Chapter 10

Meg screamed and darted for the road. Her flying skirt tangled in her legs, sending her tumbling to the ground. Gravel stung her hands and knees, and the horse's flailing hooves filled her vision.

"I got you." Colin lifted her aside, as though she weighed no more than the kitten; then he lunged past her and bumped his shoulder against the horse's massive flank.

The animal whinnied and leaped aside. The rider shouted a protest.

Dodging another thrashing hoof, Colin snatched up the kitten; then he turned to offer Meg a hand. "Are you all right then, lass?" His fingers were warm, hard, and strong around hers. A firm, reassuring hand with strength enough in the arm to lift her with a gentle tug.

Meg clung to him, swaying a bit and gazing into his face with awe. "You saved my silly kitten."

"And probably crippled my horse." Joseph Pyle stalked toward them, his face red, his blue eyes flashing. "What nonsense were you about, man?"

"Saving the wee beastie for the lady." Colin gave Joseph a gentle smile, though a muscle in his jaw flexed. "Your horse nigh trampled the silly creature."

"And there are ten more where those came from, but there are few finer horses between here and Charleston."

"I would not ken about the horses," Colin said. "But I do ken that Miss Jordan has a fondness for this mite."

"And I have a fondness for—why are you touching her?" If possible, Joseph's face darkened further, making his eyes appear to lose all color in contrast.

Meg met those pale eyes without flinching and gripped Colin's hand more tightly. "I tripped on my skirt and fell, and now he's making sure I'm steady."

And she loved the excuse to hold his hand again.

"Release him." Joseph's words sounded like the bark of an angry dog. "You demean yourself, Margaret."

"I will in a moment." She still felt off balance, light-headed—more from Joseph's words than the fall and close call with the kitten. "A strong hand for support is welcome."

She glanced at Joseph's long, elegant hand clad in a buttery leather glove.

"You may take my arm." He held out the appendage. "I'll walk you home. Grassick, take my horse to my farm."

Meg didn't move. Every fiber in her being rebelled at taking orders from Joseph and against him for giving Colin directives like he was a groom.

Colin didn't stir either, other than to shift his gaze from Joseph to her.

"Have you two lost your hearing?" Joseph demanded.

"I heard you perfectly well, Joseph." Meg worked to keep her tone even.

"Then stop making a fool of yourself and come home before this storm breaks."

"You'd best go, lass." Colin squeezed her fingers and released her hand. "And perhaps take this kitten into the house so he can't wander so far afield." He placed the trembling feline in her hands.

"Thank you. That will have to wait until I'm home again." She cradled the cat against her throat and gave Colin one more glance. She wanted to speak to him, tell him things about herself and God and hopes and anything that came to mind. Nothing seemed possible, even appropriate, in front of Joseph.

"I'm ready to go," she said to Joseph.

"Finally." He held out the reins. "Grassick, I said to take my horse."

Colin still didn't move.

"What's wrong with you?" Joseph's voice went up half an octave.

"Naught is wrong with me, Mr. Pyle." Colin looked at the gelding, whose back was nearly the height of Colin's chin. "'Tis just that I have no knowledge about how to handle a horse."

"You don't know how to handle a horse?" Joseph's surprise seemed genuine. "What sort of man doesn't know how to handle a horse?"

"Joseph," Meg breathed out in protest.

Colin shrugged. "The kind who's never owned one, perhaps. The kind who goes from fishing to glassmaking and has no need of one."

"Huh." Joseph shook his head. "Then just go about your business. Margaret, come with me."

Because she knew it was what her father would want her to do, Meg nodded to Colin with a silent "thank you," took Joseph's arm, and let him lead her on the one side and his mount on the other.

"What were you doing with him?" Joseph demanded before they were quite out of Colin's earshot.

"He was working on replacing the windows in the school. I stopped to talk to him."

Rain began to fall in big, heavy drops. Joseph increased their pace. "He shouldn't be working on a Sunday."

"He volunteered to replace the windows. He isn't getting paid. I think the Lord will accept charitable work on a Sunday."

"Charitable work that gets him in the good graces of the owner's daughter."

Meg slanted a look at Joseph, wondering if he was jealous, then chastised herself for such a vain thought. "He is trying to please the people who sponsored his coming here to find a better life, Joseph. His dedication to his work is commendable, and Father and I are both happy with him."

"A little too happy," Joseph grumbled. "You were holding his hand."

"I told you—"

"It isn't proper," Joseph interrupted. "You're going to marry me."

Not if she could find a way to avoid it.

"You shouldn't encourage his kind."

"His—kind?" Meg released her grip on Joseph's arm. "What do you mean by that?"

"A man without property or prospects."

"I think his prospects are rather good. He has skill and talent and—"

"Not a roof to call his own, let alone hundreds of acres, as I have." The rain grew heavier, and Joseph walked faster still. "But enough of him. I am assured you won't spend any more time with him."

She had given him no such reassurance and didn't intend to.

"I'm pleased I saw you today, even though we didn't have our dinner as usual."

Meg pulled up her hood for protection but said nothing.

"I know I agreed to hold off making our betrothal official until after the first of the year," Joseph said.

The abrupt change of subject threw Meg off balance, and she stammered out a response. "Ye–es, I have a number of things I need to think about between now and then."

"Frivolous things, from all I can see." Joseph's tone grew indulgent. "Your friend's wedding and Christmas."

"And my school."

"Oh, that." He dismissed her hard work with a wave of one hand. "You'll lose interest in that once you start thinking about a wedding and all the things we'll need to furnish our home properly. I want it fine enough to entertain the governor."

Why not the president?

Meg refrained from asking such a flippant question.

"I can afford the best, you know," Joseph continued. "And you have exhibited fine taste in these matters."

"Thank you." Meg caught sight of the lane to her house and nearly broke into a run.

"But I've decided that the delay to our betrothal is unacceptable," Joseph said.

Meg tripped on the smooth road.

"When your father returns from Philadelphia on Tuesday, I intend to tell him that we will announce our betrothal at Sarah and Peter's wedding."

"You will do no such thing." Despite the rain, Meg stopped in the middle of the road, placed her free hand on her hip, and glared at him. "Sarah and Peter's wedding is their special day. You will not try to steal attention by making such an announcement."

"When else will we have so many people assembled?" Joseph raised one brow, more bemused than angry. "It's when I want it done."

"It's not when I want it announced." Meg took a deep breath. "If you say anything at the wedding celebration, I will—will—I'll denounce you."

"You wouldn't dare," Joseph said through his teeth. "If I say it's so, you will go along with me."

"I won't." Meg took a step backward. Her heart raced, and breathing seemed difficult. "You can't make me."

She didn't care if she sounded childish. She felt like a child—a child frightened of the dark, when she was a woman afraid of the man not a yard away from her.

"In truth I don't ever want our betrothal announced." Turning on her heel, she gathered up her skirt and broke into a trot.

"Margaret, stop this nonsense." Joseph's feet pounded in the forming mud, the horse's hooves clomping along with him.

She kept going.

He grabbed her arm, spun her toward him. "Don't you ever run away from me again. I have paid for your father's permission to court you."

"But not to treat me roughly." She tried to pull free.

Paid for? She would think about the meaning of his remark later.

"I want to go home. I'm cold and wet."

"You should have thought of that before you started flirting with that glassblower."

"I wasn't—" No, she would not defend herself or her friendship with Colin. "Let go of me, Joseph."

"I will when I deliver you to the Thompsons' front door." He gripped her arm, not quite hard enough to hurt but harder than she liked, too hard for her to get free without a struggle.

She couldn't struggle against him, but she needed to get away. She made herself go still. Around her, the rain drummed so hard it sounded like footfalls racing toward them.

It was footfalls. They pounded harder than the rain. Meg twisted around and saw Colin dash up to them, grasp Joseph's wrist, and break his hold.

"The lass said to let go of her." His green eyes glowed like sea fire.

A shiver that had nothing to do with the cold rain raced through Meg. The gelding tossed his head and sidled away from the two men, and Joseph stood, his hair and face shining in the downpour, as though turned into a glass sculpture.

"Verra good." Colin smiled and released Joseph's arm. "If you like, Miss Jordan, I'll escort you the rest of the way to Miss Thompson's house."

"Th–thank you." Meg clenched her teeth to keep them from chattering. "I w–would like that."

"I wouldn't go anywhere with him if I were you." Joseph's voice was as cold as the rain. "You won't like the consequences to your father."

Meg stared at him. "Is that a threat?"

Joseph merely smiled.

Colin curled his fingers around Meg's elbow. "We must get you out of this weather."

Without so much as a nod in Joseph's direction, Colin urged Meg back to the road and toward the Thompson farm. Rain splashed and pounded around them. The road turned to a river of mud. But no thud of hooves resounded behind them. Once Meg glanced back. She spotted no sign of Joseph.

"On horseback he can ride across the fields to his house faster than taking the road," she observed.

"I expect he has." Colin's mouth was set in a grim line. "'Twould be against his pride to follow us after you set your preference for my escort."

"That was probably unwise of me, wasn't it?"

"Aye, probably so." Light pressure on her elbow took the sting from his agreement.

Meg's throat closed. "Do you think he can harm you? I mean, can he make Father dismiss you?"

"Can he harm me? Aye. Can he persuade your father to dismiss me?" Colin said nothing more until they reached Sarah's drive. There he paused beneath the protective canopy of an ancient pine and faced her. "If Joseph Pyle can persuade your father that you should marry him, when 'tis against your wishes, I'm thinking he can persuade your father to make an unwise business decision like dismissing me."

"Colin." Meg pressed her hand to her lips. "You think Joseph has some sort of—control over my father?"

"I'm thinking a father who provides his daughter with a school with fine glass in the windows, a man who lets his daughter bring home stray cats and lets her go fishing with a glassblower is not verra likely to insist she wed a man she does not like."

"Are you saying"—she clutched at his arm—"that Joseph is somehow forcing Father to go along with his wishes?"

"I cannot say anything so bold as all that." He covered her hand with his. "But I'm saying I think some things aren't right, you ken?"

"I know." Meg blinked back tears. "What should I do?"

"Mr. Pyle has a fancy for you and will treat you well when not having his pride pricked, so I'm saying you should go along with your father's wishes and accept his proposal." He turned over his injured left hand. "And when I can work again, I'll make you a fine gift to display in your new home."

She felt as though Joseph's gelding had kicked in her chest, crushing her heart. "You're telling me to marry another man?"

"Aye, that I am." Colin's face was stiff. "I am not worth you having to choose between obeying your father and even being friends with me."

"You are." She could only speak in a whisper.

He gave her a smile though his eyes were sad. "And I cannot put my own wishes before my family another time. I do not feel I have the forgiveness once, let alone twice."

More protests crowded into her throat, but she held them back. She would do everything she could to stop her impending betrothal to Joseph, but she could not compromise Colin's position at the glassworks and his family's better future.

"We'd better get into the house before we both catch a chill." She turned toward the lane. "Come into the kitchen. There'll be something hot to drink and a warm fire where you can dry yourself."

They didn't speak until they reached the walk of flagstones leading to the front door. Colin tried to wish her good-bye there, but she insisted on accompanying him all the way around the house to the kitchen door. The Thompsons' housekeeper greeted them with exclamations over their bedraggled state and sent her daughter running to fetch Sarah.

"We've been worried about you," the housekeeper said. "Sarah thought you would be here long before now."

"I'm sorry." Meg drew Colin to stand beside her at the fire. "One of my kittens—oh." She stuck her hand into her pocket, where the kitten lay curled up and soaked. "Poor thing. I forgot about him. Colin, will you be so kind as to take it to the stable on your way home?"

"Of course." He smiled at Meg, their eyes meeting and holding, as their hands touched in the exchange. "Perhaps this experience will teach him to stop wandering quite so much."

"I think so." She kept her fingers touching his hand. "Feel his little heart. It's beating like a parade drum."

"Aye, I ken how he feels." Colin smiled and drew his hand away. "Now run along with your friend and get yourself dry. This fine lady is making cups of tea, and Miss Thompson is waiting for you."

Meg nodded and turned her back on him, her own heart sinking to her toes.

Sarah stood in the doorway, silent, staring. As soon as Meg faced her, she spun on her heel and marched out of the kitchen. Meg followed. Neither of them spoke until they reached Sarah's bedchamber on the second floor.

"Margaret Jordan, whatever are you thinking?" Sarah sounded out of breath.

Meg removed her sodden cloak and shoes before answering. "I'm thinking that I don't want to marry Joseph even though I know it's for the best that I do."

"That's what I was afraid you'd say when I witnessed that touching scene down there." Sarah pressed her hands to her cheeks. "You're in love with him, aren't you? The glassblower, I mean."

Without needing even a moment to think of her response, Meg nodded. "Yes, I'm in love with him. But if I don't marry Joseph, it could ruin Colin's life and possibly my father's, too."

Chapter 11

Colin spent the evening writing letters to his family. He needed to see each name, conjure every face in his head to remind him of his purpose for being in America, in sending Meg on her way. All for the sake of his family. He could risk nothing that would prevent him from bringing his family to America, where a home to live, a place for them to get an education, the opportunity to have better lives spread out before them.

"This land is vast," he wrote. "People speak of New Jersey being too crowded, but if this is crowded, I cannot imagine the emptiness of the lands beyond the mountains."

Nor the abundance of the fish in the lochs he'd heard of to the west and north, lochs big enough to be seas. He wrote of all of it to his family then set the missive aside for when Mr. Jordan returned. His employer had already promised he would help transfer money to Colin's family, using his agent in England.

Writing to his family, knowing the money would ease their lot a bit, lessened Colin's distress. He had a fine home, warmth, and plenty to eat. He was even making friends, thanks to the Dalbows' warmth and hospitality. Yet his heart ached with every thought of Meg that crept into his head, and in the dark quiet of night, he wished he'd stayed in Edinburgh, though the opportunities to help his family had been too few to count in the crowded, expensive city.

"Haven't I suffered enough, Lord?" he cried out in his empty house. "What else will I have to do to prove I've reformed my ways and am now devoted to my family?"

With his hand injured, he was losing wages. A body couldn't be a master glassblower with the use of only one hand. He needed both to balance the pipe and manipulate the glass. He could manage some drawings, so he stood at a table beneath the windows and began to think of objects he could make for Meg as a wedding present from the glassworks' employees. He considered a vase, but that was too easy, too common, and her friend's fiancé had commissioned a pair of them for his new bride. The same went for candlesticks. She would get plenty of those for wedding gifts. This had to be special, perhaps useless. . .or perhaps simply frivolous.

He chewed on his pencil and gazed out the window, thinking of things he could make, thinking of things Meg could use. Thinking of Meg—her smooth hands, her bright smile, her scent of apple blossoms even in the winter.

Scent—of course. She must wear some sort of scent. He could make her a scent bottle, something delicate yet sturdy, bright and effervescent like Meg herself.

"How's your hand?" Thad joined Colin at the window.

"It's all right." Colin frowned at the blisters. They were healing well. "But I have too much work to be woolgathering here by the windows."

"You can't work with that hand though." Thad leaned toward the windows. "I see the finches have brought some friends. They like the warmth, and Martha sprinkles a bit of grain for them."

"They're not verra attractive birds." Colin eyed the cluster of tiny finches gathered in the yard.

They were a dull brown, but lively and talkative among one another.

"The males turn a bright yellow in the spring," Thad explained. "Martha is convinced they have the same spouses year after year, too. I don't care much for birds unless they're in the cooking pot, but Martha likes them."

Colin studied the finches picking at the ground with their pointed, pink beaks. They were small, not more than four inches long, but their vivacity whirled around them.

"They'll be a fine sight when they're in their courting feathers." Colin grasped his pencil and began to draw.

Thad stood and watched. "That's how you advanced so fast in Edinburgh. You can design, too."

"Aye, I had a good teacher." Colin hesitated, then he changed the bird's position so that it was launching into flight, its beak pointing skyward. "Do you think 'twill do for a perfume bottle? The beak can be the stopper."

"A perfume bottle, eh?" Thad studied the design. "We've made medicine bottles aplenty here—they're easy—but nothing as fancy as this. Do you think ladies would buy it?"

"'Tis not for sale. 'Tis intended as a gift."

"I see." Thad glanced toward the desk, where a box of the purple goblets rested, and Colin understood that Thad saw a great deal.

Neither Colin nor Meg had tried to hide their growing feelings for each other. Inspecting the blisters on his left hand, Colin wondered—not for the first time—if someone had noticed, disapproved, and thought of a way to be rid of Colin without doing him in—just preventing him from working, perhaps long enough to get him dismissed.

"You did not succeed," Colin muttered.

"What was that?" Thad asked.

"I was talking to myself. Is there aught I can do?"

"Carry those glasses to the Jordans' house." Thad started back to his bench. "Miss Jordan has taken it into her head to learn to knit. She's over there having Martha teach her right now."

The message was clear—Meg wouldn't be at home, so going to the Jordans' was safe.

She wasn't home; she was walking around the end of the glassworks as Colin left with the glasses. He couldn't avoid her without being rude, and his heart cried out to God, protesting the encounter at the same time it thrilled at the sight of her.

"Peter and Sarah are coming to fetch me," she told him. "It's not raining or snowing, so I thought I'd walk to the end of the drive. I won't get another chance to walk for another two days at the least, and I do love to—" She broke off and giggled. "I'm talking too much, aren't I?"

"Aye, that you are." Colin grinned at her. "But I like the sound of your voice."

"No no, you're the one with the fine voice. It's"—she tilted her head and smiled up at him—"musical."

"You flatter me." He looked away from her so he could regain his composure. "Shall I escort you to the gate, Miss Jordan?"

She took a step closer to him. "I was Meg yesterday."

"You should not have been." He adjusted his grip on the box. "Perhaps I should be delivering this half of your wedding present to your house, as Thad told me to."

"There will be no wedding." Meg spoke through her teeth. "Tomorrow, when my father returns home, I will tell him absolutely I will not marry Joseph Pyle."

"You do as you think is right, but you will still have to be Miss Jordan to me."

"I don't want—"

The ringing of the gate bell interrupted her.

"Good day." Colin inclined his head and headed toward the side gate that led to the fields of the Jordan farm, a rough shortcut to the house. Behind him, he heard Meg make a noise, something like a sob. He refused to look back. He'd be doomed if he did. A man only had so much strength for resisting even a few minutes with the lady he loved.

~⊰~

While hunting up work to keep himself occupied, from sweeping up the cullet off the floor, to nailing crates together for Meg to use as benches in her school, Colin prayed for no more encounters with Meg. That another errand took him into her presence again the following morning proved to him how little God paid attention to him. He was still doing wrong in the Lord's eyes.

If only the Thompsons had waited another day to ask for someone from the glassworks to measure the globes in their sconces to make some replacements, Meg would have been back home. Instead, she perched on the edge of a sofa, snippets of white yarn sticking to her dress like snowflakes, while she counted stitches on a knitting needle in the room into which Mrs. Thompson led him.

"I don't know how I ended up with thirty-four stitches when I started out with thirty. Martha warned me about dropping stitches, but—" She stopped talking to her friend Sarah, and pink tinged her cheeks.

"I beg your pardon, ladies." He bowed his head and tried to turn his back on Meg so he could concentrate on the business at hand—the measurement of a sconce globe made of glass that was far too dark to be of much use.

"Did you knit two stitches from the same loop?" Sarah asked a little too loudly.

"Did I what?" Meg sounded vague.

Colin smiled and took out his caliper to measure the base and height of the globe.

"Are you going to replace the glass, Mrs. Thompson?" Meg asked.

"I was thinking of it," Mrs. Thompson said. "The glass in these is so gray the candlelight doesn't show through very well."

"Will you use flint glass to make them, um, Mr. Grassick?" Meg's voice emerged breathless.

Colin glanced over his shoulder at her and smiled. The sight of her with her hair in loose curls tumbling down her back, confined only by a blue velvet ribbon, the white wool yarn in her hands, stole his breath, robbed him of anything sensible beyond the ability to nod.

"Maybe Sarah and I can come watch you work one day." Meg smiled. "I've seen them make the windows, but something like these globes is much more interesting."

"If Mr. Jordan says 'tis all right, I'd be honored." He made himself turn to Mrs. Thompson. "Is there anything else, ma'am?"

"No." She drew out the single word, and her hazel eyes flitted between him and Meg. "Send us the estimate on the cost of four globes for this room as soon as you can."

"Aye, er, yes ma'am." As he exited the room, he allowed himself one more look at Meg, met and held her gaze for a moment longer than necessary. A moment longer than was good for his heart.

Outside, a blast of cold, damp air slapped him in the face along with the sight of Joseph Pyle riding up on his fine chestnut horse. Pyle, who had a right to call on Meg.

Colin returned to the glassworks, where he assisted one of the other workers to break some rather well-done bowls out of the new molds. They lacked the artistry of blown glass pieces, but they were also far cheaper.

In the early afternoon, Colin returned to his cottage for his dinner and found Meg placing a basket on his back stoop.

"I do not think you should be here, Miss Jordan." He made his posture and manner as formal as he knew how.

She tossed her head back. "Martha Dalbow is right next door, and I was just leaving this here. Mrs. Weber made dinner for Father, but he didn't come home, so I brought it over to you."

"And I'm an ungrateful beast for not thanking you. But, my dear—I mean, Miss Jordan—"

"I prefer 'my dear.'" She took a step closer to him, one hand outstretched. "Colin—"

Footfalls sounded on the gravel path between the cottages, and Meg's face paled. Colin knew what—or who—he would see even before Meg spoke.

"Father, you're home at last. And, Mr. Pyle, good afternoon."

"Run along home, Margaret," Jordan said. "Joseph will escort you. Grassick, shall we go inside your house and talk?"

"Aye sir." Without so much as a glance in Meg's direction, Colin picked up the basket she had carried with her own soft hands to his doorstep, and he opened the door.

The cottage was cold. Colin made haste to build up the fire from the banked coals and set a kettle of water on for tea. Purring, the cat rubbed around his ankles.

Jordan arrived in a few moments and closed the door. He didn't sit; he stood with his back to the panels, his arms folded across his chest. "How's the hand?"

Colin started at the question, expecting something quite different. "It's healing nicely, sir. I should be back to work shortly. In the meantime, I'm making myself as useful as possible."

"Good. We have a number of new orders from my journey to Philadelphia." Jordan cleared his throat. "The others are learning finer work from you, but they aren't up to your standards and won't be for a long time. You know all this, and I reiterate it to emphasize how much I need you."

Colin said nothing. He sensed Jordan intended to say more—more Colin wouldn't like.

"However," Jordan continued, "Pyle tells me you've been annoying my daughter."

Colin stiffened. "Nay sir, I would not call it annoying."

"Neither would I, which is the difficulty." Jordan sighed, and his arms dropped to his sides. "Margaret enjoys your company. That's all too apparent, and it cannot continue. To secure my daughter's future, I must tell you that if this friendship between you continues, I will have to discharge you."

Chapter 12

You disappoint me, Margaret." Father spoke from the head of the dining room table as Meg poured the after-supper coffee. "I thought you'd be too occupied helping Sarah with her wedding, and now I understand you've spent half your time with a glassblower."

"You exaggerate, Father." Meg softened her words with a smile. "Only a wee bit of my time, all told."

"Any time is too much." Father's frown warned her not to speak with haste. "You know how I feel about your being friendly with the workers, but you've been at the Dalbows' and today were standing outside Grassick's cottage talking to him. The impropriety shames me and should shame you, too."

Meg set down the coffeepot before she dropped it and clutched the back of her chair. "I am ashamed of nothing I've done, sir. Mr. Grassick is a kind, Christian man who has behaved with utmost propriety whenever in my company."

"And Joseph tells me you continue to rebuff his attentions." Father spoke as though she had said nothing. "Why?"

"I've made that clear, Father. I don't wish to marry him."

"But I want you to." His tone gentled. "My dear, I need to see your future secure, for my peace of mind."

"Father?" Meg rushed to his side. "You're not ill, are you? Please, tell me you're not ill. Did you go to Philadelphia to see a physician? Father—"

"Hush." He caressed her cheek. "I'm fit as a fiddle. But I wasn't a young man when I married your mother, and we must all face our mortality one day. I want this farm and the glassworks in the hands of a man who can see them prosper and regain the investment I've made to get the glassworks going again. Your mother said I shouldn't start up until I had saved enough to remain debt free, but I broke that promise in my grief and borrowed too much money. So we need someone who can keep the glassworks building profits. Joseph is that man."

And Colin wasn't. Father didn't need to say so for Meg to understand this. He knew nothing of farming. Colin was a fine artisan, but he had never managed a business, didn't know about sales and accounts and bankers. She knew how to run a household and cook a fine meal, sew a nearly invisible seam and almost knit, but no one had taught her more management skills than being wise with the household accounts. Too many people depended on them for their livelihoods to entrust the land to inexperienced persons.

"Please, Father, not yet." She sank to her knees and laid her cheek against his arm as she had as a child. "Give me time to learn. I did well with my sums. I can learn. Many women run their own farms and businesses, too."

Father patted her on the head. "I'll try to keep him from pushing his suit until after the first of the year as I promised, daughter, but Joseph is a man who goes after what he wants with fervor. Right now, he wants two things—you as his wife and repayment of the money I borrowed from him. Now, let us go into the parlor and read some scripture."

She chose Colossians and stumbled over the third chapter. "If ye then be risen with Christ, seek those things which are above, where Christ sitteth on the right hand of God. Set your affection on things above, not on things on the earth." Then the later verses about obedience to one's parents being pleasing to God.

She wanted to agree to marry Joseph, even let him announce their betrothal at Sarah's wedding, but because her heart rebelled, she could say nothing. If she kept herself occupied, she didn't need to think about it and nearly managed not to think about Colin.

Occupation was easy with the wedding three days off. A local seamstress had made Meg's gown, but she needed to finish the embroidery around the neck and hem. She and Sarah helped make pastries and breads and peel mounds of potatoes for the fifty guests who would enjoy a buffet at the Thompsons' after the ceremony. She spent the night at the Thompson house so she could assist Sarah in washing, curling, and pinning up her heavy auburn tresses.

At last Sarah, quiet but smiling, glowing in her pink velvet gown, stood ready to go to the church. Her female cousins surrounded her in their own velvet dresses, like a pastel flower garden of primrose, lilac, and pale blue.

Meg had chosen a darker blue for her own gown and stitched the neck and hem with tiny white roses. She wore white silk roses in her hair. Everyone told her she looked stunning. She didn't once glance in a mirror to verify the truth of their words. Her looks didn't matter.

As quiet as Sarah, Meg climbed into the carriage Father had sent over to fetch her, and she managed not to sigh with disappointment when she saw Joseph sitting beside her parent.

"Next winter," Joseph said, "I'll buy you a fur-lined cloak."

Meg clenched her hands together inside her muff. "I'm quite warm enough in this one, thank you."

But if he was her husband, she couldn't stop him from buying anything he liked. Nor, since he was the man her father had chosen for her, could she stop him from escorting her into the church for the ceremony. She could, however, ignore him as Sarah and Peter exchanged their vows, their faces glowing brighter than the candles massed along the altar to counteract the gloom of a winter day.

Meg's eyes dimmed and blurred with tears. She wanted that kind of love. She rejoiced for her friend, but her heart ached.

When she stood and turned to go at the end of the service, she caught a glimpse of sunset red hair at the back of the sanctuary. Her heart constricted. With all her will, she stopped herself from pushing through the throng of the congregation to join Colin at the back. But no will in the world stopped the prayer she sent to the Lord, asking, pleading, begging Him to change her circumstances. She then took Joseph's proffered arm to exit the church. When she reached the benches at the rear of the church, Colin was gone.

Outside, snow fell like sugar crystals to ice the ground. Ladies paused to strap on the wooden pattens that added inches to their height and kept their light slippers and long dresses dry. Meg clung to Joseph's arm then to keep her balance and received the warmest smile he'd ever bestowed upon her.

"Peter may be the luckiest man today," Joseph said, "but I'm surely the second luckiest to have you on my arm."

"They look so happy." Meg sighed. "And Sarah is beautiful."

"You're even prettier." Joseph patted her hand. "How did you get such a pretty daughter, Jordan?"

Father laughed. "Her mother."

"Guessed as much." Joseph nodded to the line of carriages and horses heading to the Thompson house. "How will they manage all these vehicles?"

"They hired extra men from around the county," Father explained. "It won't be easy with all the snow."

"That's why I'm willing to wait for a spring wedding." Joseph patted a lock of his hair away from his brow. "One runs the risk of mud, but it's not as bad as snow. And I do like to think of Margaret in silk. Pale blue silk. I'll buy a bolt when I'm in New York the week after Christmas."

"You mustn't," Meg cried. "That's far too much."

"No no, it's not beyond my budget." Joseph chuckled. "Nor is a fine wedding."

"I will pay for my daughter's wedding." Father's voice turned as frosty as the air.

Meg gritted her teeth.

"Will there be dancing tonight?" Joseph asked.

"No, the house isn't big enough." Meg caught a glimpse of the house, ablaze with light and bursting with guests, and smiled. "But there is music."

"Too bad." Joseph prepared to exit the carriage first. "I did want to dance with you, Margaret, and I'll be gone for the Christmas party."

"That's unfortunate for you."

The carriage stopped. Joseph alighted and assisted Meg to the ground then led her inside. Warmth and noise and the aromas of roasting meats and candied fruits greeted them. Meg managed to elude Joseph long enough to take her cloak to an upstairs bedchamber and tuck a few pins more securely into her hair. Once downstairs, she found Sarah and Peter and hugged them both.

"It'll be you next," Sarah said.

Meg merely smiled and turned to greet some neighbors who lived farther away and usually attended a different church.

"When are you getting married?" two matrons asked her in succession.

"When I find a man who loves me like Peter loves Sarah," she responded.

"You young girls read too many novels, to have those kinds of notions." An elderly lady patted Meg's cheek. "You want a man who can provide you with a good home and fine children."

"Yes, ma'am." She smiled and agreed until her face hurt, and all the while she wished Colin stood beside her, his hand tucked into the crook of her arm as Peter held Sarah close to his side. She would smile up at him and let everyone see how much she loved him—

"I've brought you a plate of food." Joseph stood in front of her bearing two laden plates. "Come. There's a table here in the dining room where we can be comfortable. I paid one of the servants to keep it empty for us."

Martha Dalbow, in her Sunday best, guarded the two places. She smiled at Meg then darted away to pick up an empty serving plate.

"Martha isn't a servant." Meg seated herself in the chair Joseph pulled out. "She's my friend."

"If she were your friend," Joseph drawled, "she would be sitting at the table, not waiting on it."

Meg closed her eyes and prayed for a still tongue.

"Aren't you going to eat?" Joseph asked. "The food is good. Plain but good. When we get married—"

"Will you please excuse me?" Feeling so hot she couldn't breathe, Meg pushed back her chair. She rose and exited the room before Joseph managed to stand.

The house wasn't big enough nor the crowd dense enough for her to hide from him. So she kept going through the parlor, into the entryway, and out the front door. The blast of snow-laden air cleared her head instantly. She stood on the porch for a moment, breathing in gulps of clear air; then, hearing the scrape of shovels on the flagstones of the walk, she descended the steps and walked into the darkness of the yard, heedless of snow soaking into her shoes. She wouldn't be there for long, just enough to regain her composure and set her roiling stomach to rights.

She heard no footfalls on the white carpet, but when a hand curved over her shoulder, she neither jumped nor cried out. A scent, a touch, or perhaps pure instinct told her who stood behind her before he spoke.

"Are you all right then, lass?"

"I am now." She rested her head against his shoulder. "But why are you here?"

"I'm helping out with the snow shoveling."

"What about your hand?"

"'Tis all right." For a moment he rested his cheek atop her head. "What drove you into the snow?"

"It was hot and noisy inside, and everyone kept asking me when I'm going to get married. And Joseph keeps talking about how much better our wedding will be than Sarah and Peter's."

"I expect it will be." He lowered his hand from her shoulder but didn't move away from her. "If you marry him, that is."

"If? I don't see that I have a choice."

"I wish it weren't so."

"Me, too. I just wish—I wish I knew why he is so determined to marry me."

"'Tis simple for me to understand." Tenderness infused his tone. "He wants to be an important man. To him, that means having possessions he can show off. And you, lass, are a wife to show off."

"I'm not an ornament." She shuddered.

"Well, having you on one's arm would do a man's pride good." He sounded as though he smiled. "What concerns me about Mr. Pyle is the lengths to which he will go to get what he wants."

Meg gasped. "What are you saying?"

"Naught for which I have the proof." His accent thickened. "But if I did, I would be standing up in the kirk to denounce his right to wed you."

"Colin, you couldn't. You could lose your position at the glassworks. Your family would suffer if you angered him and Father."

"Aye, they might, but what about you suffering if I have the knowledge and do naught about it?"

"Do you know something?" She clenched her fists. "If so, tell me."

"I'm gathering the proof first, lass. Meanwhile, try not to announce your marriage. Unless—" Frost tinged his voice. "Unless you want to marry an important man."

"You know I don't want to be important," Meg cried. "I want to be loved."

Someone opened the door of the house, and fiddle music and laughter danced into the night. Then the door closed. The music ceased.

In the ensuing stillness Colin murmured, "You are, lass. You are most certainly loved."

She straightened, turned, faced him. "Colin, I lo—"

"Nay." He pressed a finger to her lips. "Do not say it until you're certain you will not wed the man."

"You know I must. Father—Colin, I'm afraid Joseph is using Father's debt to him to force this marriage."

"Aye, it seems likely, and 'tis a good reason why you should not wed the man."

"What do you know?"

"I do not ken for certain, but one cannot help but overhear bits of conversation from time to time. It seems Pyle loaned your father money to restart the glassworks," Colin explained, "and now the note is due without the profit to pay it yet."

"And I'm payment for the debt." Despite the crisp, clear air, Meg could scarcely breathe. "I can take care of my own future, but I don't know what Father would do without the glassworks or maybe even the farm."

"Aye, which is why I am hoping I'm wrong in thinking what I am of Joseph Pyle, if you will wed him."

"I can't abandon the needs of my father any more than you can abandon the needs of your family."

"I'll do my best to change things. There must be a way out."

"If there were, I'd take it."

Colin's chest rose and fell in a silent sigh. "You should go back inside before you catch a chill." He brushed snow from her hair then let his fingertips linger against her cheek.

She didn't move. She feared even a breath would dislodge his hand from her face, would send her skittering across the snowy grass in an opposite direction to his. If she remained motionless, the moment would last as long as she wanted it to. There in the night, a gauzy curtain of snow sheltered them from the music and laughter in the house, where half a hundred people celebrated someone else's wedding.

"I can't go in there." Meg clasped his hand against her face. "I can't go back there and pretend I'm happy. I want to stay out here with you, where I don't have to pretend."

"Aye lass, the pretending lies in thinking we don't have to say good-bye." He curved his other hand beneath her chin. "Or that I have a right to this."

He touched his lips to hers. His kiss was warm and gentle and far too brief. Before her heart remembered to beat, before she thought to respond, he drew his hands away from her face, turned his back on her, and vanished behind the swirling mantle of snow.

Chapter 13

Meg decided to set up a Christmas party to introduce her school to the county. She could serve hot cider and coffee and little cakes and give the children some sort of gift, like a bag of sweets. The planning would keep her occupied, would steer her mind away from thoughts of Colin, of the kiss, of his walking away from her because she insisted she must marry Joseph for everyone's sake. Activity must fill up the empty place in her heart.

Christmas lay three weeks off, and Father and she always entertained on Christmas Eve. She must plan for that, too, not to mention help Ilse clean and cook and decorate the house with evergreen boughs and holly berries. But no mistletoe this year. Meg wouldn't risk Joseph coming across her standing beneath it. After Colin's kiss, she never wanted another man to so much as touch her hand.

Colin had kissed her.

Meg paused in the middle of the planning that was supposed to make her forget, and she pressed her fingertips to her lips, as though the gesture could seal in the memory of that all-too-brief contact. He had held her face as tenderly as a blown glass ornament.

"I love you, too," she whispered.

No answer returned from the four walls of her bedchamber. Beyond the windows the world lay in white silence. They would need the sleigh to get to church.

She hurried to dress and descend to make breakfast. Father came in the door as Meg finished toasting slices of bread. Snow clung to his hair in streaks of white, making him look ten years older until the flakes melted from the kitchen's warmth in moments. Those were enough moments to give Meg a pang of apprehension, a reminder that Father, although not old, was certainly no longer young.

"I should have come out to help you," she said.

"No need. We got the sleigh out yesterday when the sky grew so dark. But that coffee won't go amiss." He seated himself at the table.

Meg served him coffee, toast, and eggs then seated herself. "It's early for so much snow."

"A bit." Father spread apple butter on his toast. "Where did you disappear to last night?"

"I needed some air." Meg stared at her plate, the food untouched. "I'm going to miss Sarah."

"She's only a mile farther up the road."

"Yes, but it won't be the same, will it? I mean with her married and me—"

Too late she realized her error.

"You can be married, too." Father wasn't eating either, though he held his toast. "When Joseph asks you again, you will accept."

"Yes Father."

She knew she must, for her father's sake, for Colin's sake. She mustn't let Joseph have the right to take over the glassworks, or then Colin would lose his position and his family would remain in a tiny, damp, and drafty cottage without enough fuel to burn or food to eat.

Father relaxed. "I'm glad to see you've gotten sense about this."

"Yes Father."

Sense enough to pray that Joseph would not ask her. For surely this was not God's will for her life, especially if Colin was right. God didn't want her to spend money on fine furnishings so they could entertain the governor. God wanted her to open her school and knit mufflers for the children, aid the poor with soup and blankets, and make sweets for the church's spring fete. Surely God wouldn't give her a man she loved and one who loved her, only to tear them apart. God would never expect her to sacrifice her happiness for the sake of a man's greed and desire to possess things.

"I just wish," she ventured, "that Joseph weren't so interested in owning things."

"He was raised that way." Father buttered more toast. "His father made a great deal of money as a privateer during the Revolution. But he didn't live very long to enjoy it."

"That's very sad." Meg rose. "I'll go fetch the lap robes from the linen press. We'll need them with this cold." She hesitated in the doorway. "I've decided to open the school early, as a sort of Christmas present to the local children. A week from tomorrow. I'll have a bit of a party. Is that all right with you?"

"Yes daughter, it'll keep your mind off Sarah being away." Father gave her an indulgent smile.

Strength flowing back into her limbs, Meg raced upstairs to collect the heavy rugs they used to keep themselves warm in the sleigh. She could start with her school. She could concentrate on the children and not think about Colin or Joseph.

Not thinking of either of them at church proved impossible. Joseph sat beside her in the Jordan pew rather than alone in his own family section, and Colin sat in the back. She exchanged pleasantries with Joseph, giving him an invitation to dinner, and turned as soon as the service ended in order to catch the merest glimpse of Colin.

With his height and bright hair, he stood out in the crowd, standing beside Martha and Thad Dalbow—and what appeared to be half a dozen young women surrounded him, fluttering their lashes and making their side curls bob against rosy cheeks. In response he smiled and turned a reddish hue that clashed with his hair.

Meg laughed. Seeing him with friends and well made her smile. His dis-comfiture over the female attention amused her.

"I'm pleased your father told him to stop annoying you," Joseph said beside her. "He appears to get enough female attention without demanding yours."

"He never demanded it, Joseph. He has a kind and gentle spirit."

Joseph snorted. "Which is why he's working for someone else."

Meg swung around to stare at Joseph, sharp words burning on her tongue. A group of neighbors wanting to discuss the wedding prevented her from speaking her mind.

And from seeing more of Colin. By the time everyone drifted toward the waiting sleighs, he had departed. She probably wouldn't see him for another week.

Heart lightened from the mere glimpse of him, Meg tucked herself into the sleigh. Father stepped in beside her, and they set out across the snowy landscape. Craning her neck, Meg observed her school. Snow piled on its roof gave it the appearance of an iced cake. Above it, branches of the oak sagged with their fluffy, white burden, and in their midst someone perched, knocking the snow away.

"Why is he doing that?" Meg cried.

Father pulled up the horse. "What?"

Meg gestured to the tree and Colin relieving the branches of their excess weight. "He's going to hurt himself."

"Not if he's careful. It's a sturdy tree." Father nodded. "Thoughtful of him. Those branches could go through that roof if they got too heavy and broke off. He's a nice young man."

"Yes." Meg craned her neck around so she could watch him as Father snapped the reins and got the horse going again.

"I'm sorry I can't allow you to associate with him." Father spoke after a few minutes. "If circumstances were different. . ." He sighed. "But they're not. You need a man of substance and property."

Meg caught her breath. "Are you saying you would approve of him if he had property, even though he's a glassblower?"

"It's beside the point, Margaret. He doesn't and never will. Now, what's for dinner?"

"We're having a roast chicken."

"That's good. Very good."

The chicken would be good. The afternoon would not. She must spend it with Joseph, but she could bear it. Father's words lit a spark of hope in her heart, and she determined to nurture it to a flame.

The spark gave her the strength to muster warmth as she served dinner. She needed to say nothing when the men talked of business, but she brought up her plans for a Christmas party at the school during a lull in the discussion.

"Isn't that a great deal of work for you, my dear?" Joseph asked. "Don't you and your father have a party on Christmas Eve, too?"

"Yes, but with Sarah gone, I need something to do, and why delay starting the school until after the first of the year? It's ready now."

Joseph turned to Father. "And you haven't been able to talk her out of this... notion of teaching the charcoal burners' and farm laborers' children?"

"It's harmless." Father shrugged. "And working on it makes her happy."

"But those children are such ruffians." Joseph's eyes held concern.

"I want to include all local children eventually. Most of them are well-behaved. The five boys from the charcoal burners are a bit high-spirited," Meg admitted. "But I've managed to get them in line the two times I've encountered them."

"You encountered them twice?" Father and Joseph both frowned at her.

"I knew about the kittens," Father said. "When was the second time?"

"The day I went fishing with—" She pressed her serviette to her lips and sprang off her chair. "We have a spiced cake for dessert. I'll go make coffee."

She escaped from the dining room before they could question her further.

Meg stood at the window while the coffee brewed, and she watched some gray-green finches pecking at grain scattered across the snow. Clustered in the stable doorway, five cats stared at the birds but didn't venture into the cold wetness even for a bit of a hunt.

"Five cats." Meg counted the kittens again. "Wanderer is missing."

She wanted to escape out the back door and hunt down the little creature. His size must make traveling in the snow difficult. Surely he merely slept or hunted inside the stable and wasn't so foolish that he thought he could climb white mountains for adventure. She needed to persuade Father to let her have the wee beastie in the house for his own sake.

In her head, she heard Colin calling the kitten a wee beastie, and her heart fluttered. A man who showed such tenderness to a tiny creature deserved to have someone who could love him without reservation. She wanted to. Oh how she wanted to! But her father wouldn't approve, and the man she was supposed to marry waited for her.

Colin and the missing kitten still on her mind, Meg took her tray of coffee and cake into the dining room and discovered her father no longer sat at his place.

"Your father wanted to look over some contracts before he posts them back to Philadelphia tomorrow," Joseph explained. "He thought we would be comfortable here, since the fire is already bright and the room warm."

"Then I'll take coffee in to him." Before Joseph could object, Meg snatched up a plate, fork, and coffee cup.

She intended to ask Father if she and Joseph could look for the kitten. Tramping through the snow, calling for a cat did not give rise to personal conversation. But Father merely nodded in acknowledgment of the refreshment and kept reading. Meg waited a moment, hoping he would understand she wanted his attention. It failed to materialize, so she trudged back to the dining room.

Joseph greeted her with one of his thin-lipped smiles. "Do sit down. We can talk for a while."

"I'd like to go look for my cat." Meg bunched her ruffled white apron between her fingers. "He may be in the stable, but he's not with the other cats, and I don't want him in the snow when night falls."

Joseph stared at her. "You want to tramp about in the snow looking for a useless creature like a cat?"

"Cats are not useless. They keep vermin away from the grain."

"Not if you make pets of them."

"I like animals. They're fun to watch and nice to pet."

"I do not believe in pets." Joseph set the pot down with a thud. "Dogs are for herding and guarding, and cats are for killing mice. Horses are for pulling or riding. One does not pamper them or worry about them. Especially with a cat. If it dies, ten more are available to take its place."

Now Meg stared, her mouth open on a gasp. "Surely you don't mean that. We are to care for all God's creatures. They are precious to Him and should be to us."

"Oh, that." Joseph waved his hand in the air as though erasing a slate. "Animals, like some men, are here to serve the rest of us."

"No." Meg took a step backward. "We are the ones who serve. We serve God and His creatures and our fellow man. The more fortunate we are, the more responsibility we have."

"Of course." Joseph smiled, his eyes flat and cool. "We have a responsibility to be good stewards of what we're given and be generous when possible."

"But what of ourselves?" Feeling a little weak in the knees, Meg dropped onto the nearest chair. "We are supposed to give of our abilities to do the Lord's work. I have some skill with teaching; I learned in school with the younger girls, so I want to teach children close to their homes."

"Not after we're married."

"As long as I'm able."

"You won't be able. You won't have time." He drew his chair closer to her, his knees mere inches from hers. "You'll be too busy setting up our home and entertaining."

"Of course I'll do those things for my husband," Meg said, choosing her words with care, "but I will still teach and knit and take food to the sick."

"Not as my wife. I won't have you associating with those people and risk becoming ill."

"But what about church activities? What about serving the Lord?"

"Arranging fetes and so forth, of course." He leaned forward and patted her hand. "That's completely appropriate. And you may embroider handkerchiefs but not knit. Knitting is common."

"I can embroider handkerchiefs?" Meg nearly choked on the words. "When a child is cold, what good is an embroidered handkerchief? How does that demonstrate God's love?"

Joseph shrugged and reached for the coffee. "You take cream and sugar, don't you?"

"I've worked hard to prepare this school," Meg plunged on. "I'm not going to give the children a taste of education then pull it away while I live in luxury."

"Come, come. You make too much of it." He slid a cup of coffee toward her. "It's not as though these children expect to go to school or even will if it's offered."

Meg held her breath. She counted to ten. When she didn't feel as though she would strangle if she spoke to him, she leaned forward, her hands folded on her knees. "Joseph—"

A knock on the kitchen door interrupted her. She sprang to her feet and sped from Joseph to whoever called at the kitchen on a Sunday afternoon.

"I found the wee beastie outside the glassworks." Colin greeted her with a sodden mass of black-and-white fur limp on his palms. "He'd been chasing the birds that far, I'm thinking."

"Thank you." Her heart soared like a winged creature the cat might chase. "Is he all right?"

"Aye, that he is." Colin smiled. "Now that he's with you."

His eyes held hers, conveying the message he referred to more than the kitten's being all right in her presence. She grinned in return, feeling the same about him, and held out her hands to accept the bedraggled burden.

"I'll make him a box here by the fire. Maybe you would—"

"Good of you to return the cat," Joseph pronounced. "Allow me to recompense you for your time."

A flash shot through Meg's side vision. A silver coin sailed toward Colin's still outstretched hand. An instant before it should have landed in his palm, he shoved his hands into the pockets of his coat, allowing the money to hit the floor with a resounding ping.

"I did not bring the cat home for money," Colin said in a voice icier than the snow behind him. "I did it as a favor to Miss Jordan. Now I'll be on my way. 'Tis her wish, you ken."

For your sake, she wanted to cry out.

"Take care of yourself." She hugged the kitten to her. "I'm going to keep this beastie near me all the time now for his own good."

"Thank you." Smiling, Colin tipped his hat to her then spun on his heel and strode off through the packed snow.

"Revolting." Joseph reached past her and slammed the kitchen door. "You lower yourself, Margaret."

"Because I'm going to care for a kitten?"

"Because you care for a mere glassblower. When we're married, you will never associate with the glassblowers or their families."

Meg turned on him. "I will associate with whomever I please. I want to be with glassblowers or anyone else. I'm sure it's what God wants for me."

"Not possible." Joseph curled his upper lip. "You are gently bred and beautiful. You deserve better associates than that."

"I don't deserve anything. I've been blessed is all." She carried the kitten to the arc of warmth around the stove but kept her gaze on Joseph. "Since you think to associate with only those you consider worthy of notice, what is your notion of serving the Lord?"

"I go to church on Sundays and holidays and give generously." He cut himself a slice of the cake still sitting on the worktable and bit off a generous hunk, chewed, and swallowed while Meg waited for him to say more. "Other than that, I'm far too occupied with my properties to do anything."

"I see." Meg's spine stiffened. "And you're saying that you won't allow your wife to do much more than work on the church fetes?"

"You won't have time."

"Even if I want to use my time for something other than housekeeping and entertaining important people?"

"You won't have a choice."

"I see." Meg took a deep, shaky breath. The kitten's claws dug into her shoulder like a pricking conscience. "Joseph, I need to go to my room. Please excuse me."

Without waiting for him to respond, she strode past him, through the dining room, and up the steps to her bedchamber. Once there she tucked the kitten into a quilt on the floor then fell to her knees.

"Lord, I don't want to marry him. I simply can't do it. Surely You don't want this for me either."

She so disliked the idea of marriage to Joseph that she couldn't believe God wanted the union. Yet she couldn't figure out how to make things change. Her father's future depended on the marriage. Colin's future depended on the marriage. His family's future depended on the marriage. As for her future. . .

"God, I can't do this. I believe You want me to serve You with the school, yet I'm being forced to marry a man who doesn't serve You at all. It's wrong. I can't—I can't—"

She sobbed and didn't care who heard her.

"I thought if I did enough, You would honor that and give me what I want. Is that too much, Lord?" She pounded her fist against her mattress. "I want to teach at the school. I want to bring home kittens or orphans or whoever needs help. I want—"

Her own words began to ring in her ears, and she stopped, choking down the next sob.

She was telling God what she wanted to do for Him. Rocking back on her heels in a puddle of crumpled muslin skirts, she scanned through her mind to think of when she had asked God what He wanted her to do. No time came to mind, not a single prayer, even a brief one. All her prayers regarded what she wanted to happen. She told God; she didn't ask Him.

"But I haven't done anything wrong." The minute she made the statement, she knew it was a poor excuse for going her own way.

Going her own way was doing something wrong. Father denied her little, so she asked for the school, knowing she would get it. And the school cost Father money and resources he couldn't afford. She pursued Colin, knowing he found her attractive. And their relationship put him in Joseph's sights, endangering Colin's future at the glassworks. She had no idea what sort of troubles she had caused others with her willful behavior.

"Lord, I need You to show me what You want for me." She gulped. "Even if that means marrying Joseph."

More peaceful, if not entirely settled in her heart and mind, Meg returned downstairs to clear away the dinner dishes. Joseph was nowhere in sight. Neither was Father. She sliced bread and buttered it; then she set it on a plate with pieces of cheese and ham and some apples and left them on the kitchen table for Father's supper. Back in her bedchamber, she decided to push forward with her party for the potential schoolchildren and listed things she needed to accomplish for both that event and the one for neighbors on Christmas Eve. She worked until the candle guttered and her eyelids drooped. She still hadn't heard Father come home, but she crawled into bed to sleep.

Sometime during the night, she heard the sleigh swoosh into the stable yard, harness jingling, and a few minutes later the back door closed. Father had returned from wherever he had gone. Meg rolled over and fell into a deep sleep that lasted until Ilse arrived and the aroma of coffee drifted up to Meg's room.

She dressed with haste and ran downstairs for breakfast.

"You look pretty today." Ilse set a mug of coffee before Meg at the kitchen table. "The wedding must have pleased you."

Only Colin's kiss had pleased her about the wedding, but she mustn't think about that, let alone admit it to the older woman.

"I'm excited," Meg said. "I'm going over to the school to see if I can make tables out of the crates so I can have a bit of a party for the children there next Monday."

"Ya, that would be kind of you." Ilse smiled. "My children are looking forward to the school."

"That pleases me. No eggs. Just some toasted bread."

Meg wolfed down her breakfast and hastened into pattens, warm cloak, hat, and gloves. She would have to walk slowly, and a brisk wind warned her she would be chilled by the time she reached the school. But she didn't care. She was working for the Lord now, not herself.

Despite the cumbersome iron rings on the bottom of the pattens, she trotted along the road, following the ruts of sleigh runners and heavy wagons. Her heart twisted a bit as she passed the glassworks with its twin curls of smoke spiraling into the gray-white sky. She employed all her willpower not to stop and pull the bell for admission. She couldn't see Colin again unless something changed.

"It can, Lord. I know it can with Your help."

Though she had no idea how.

She reached the crossroad, where chunks of ice flowed in the stream. A glance at the lightning-struck tree assured her no kitten clung to the branches. Only another hundred yards to her school.

She rounded the corner and stopped, her heart freezing in her chest.

Yesterday an aging oak spread its snow-laden branches over the roof of the school. Today that same tree lay with its branches inside the roof of the school.

Half the roof and one wall were completely destroyed.

Chapter 14

The goldfinch perfume bottle lay in fragments atop Colin's workbench. He found it the moment he walked into the glassworks on Monday. Considering he left it in the lehr to cool Saturday evening, the ornament could not have broken on its own.

"Aye, and I suspect I ken who 'twas." He let his gaze travel the length of the glasshouse to where Joseph Pyle stood talking with Isaac Jordan.

The men's faces appeared grim. Gray tinged Jordan's complexion, and he stood with his arms crossed over his chest. Pyle leaned forward, making his height advantage over Jordan appear far greater, rather as though he were a bird of prey.

Another image of the man flashed into Colin's mind—Pyle standing behind Meg, his hands clenched, his eyes colder than the snow blanketing the countryside, while he challenged Colin's presence in the kitchen.

The cat had merely been an excuse. Colin could have warmed the creature in his own house and returned it to the stable without disturbing Meg. The need to see her, to receive one of her smiles, to hear her voice flared inside him, and he allowed his feet to carry him to her door.

The sight of her, the hint of apple blossoms mingling with fresh coffee and spices, the brush of her fingers against his added up like treasures, and he stored them in his heart in case she married Pyle.

But she couldn't marry him. Colin understood, empathized with Pyle's wish to marry Meg and have her near him. Colin didn't approve of how Pyle went about compelling her to wed him. At the same time, Jordan had made the debt, had agreed to the bargain. Surely a father who loved his daughter as Jordan loved Meg would never ally her to an unworthy man. Pyle would take care of Meg, cherish her, give her the kind of life Colin could scarcely imagine living, let alone bestow upon a wife. He had to convince himself she was better off with Joseph Pyle in the end so he could let her go. His conscience demanded it. He couldn't let his family down again. She couldn't see her father suffer.

The broken perfume bottle changed all Colin's careful thinking. A man who deliberately smashed a piece of work lacked kindness. Worse, he possessed a streak of meanness that might not stop with cruelty to a glass ornament.

"What happened?"

Colin startled at Thad's voice close behind him, knocking several shards of the finch bottle onto the floor.

"Somebody smashed it." Colin shoved the other pieces onto the stone to be swept up for cullet later. "I left it in the lehr."

"Who would do something like that?" Thad glanced from the fragments to the head of the room.

"Who can get into the glassworks?" Colin asked.

"Any of us with keys. That's you, me, Weber, and the senior apprentice. And Jordan, of course."

"And who was here first this morning?"

"Jordan and Pyle. But if you're thinking someone snuck in here and broke your piece—" Thad shrugged. "I hate to say it, but anyone could bribe someone to open the glassworks. Weber and I wouldn't do it, but the apprentices might wish a little income."

"Or someone welcome in Jordan's house could take his key," Colin mused aloud.

"Colin?" Thad lowered his voice. "What are you suggesting?"

"I'd say 'tis a warning." Colin picked up his pipe and called over an assistant. "Just the green glass, Louis."

"You're not working on more goblets today?" Louis asked.

"Nay, nor will I be. I'll be making the medicine bottles."

"Yes sir." The lad darted off with Colin's pipe to fetch the molten glass.

Thad fixed Colin with a crease set between his brows. "A warning for what?"

"To stay away from Meg—Miss Jordan." Colin slid onto his bench to wait for his pipe.

"No, Jordan would never do something like that. He'd just dismiss you. I warned you about that."

"Aye, so you did. So Jordan did." Colin returned his gaze to the two men by the desk. "But I did not say 'twas a warning from himself."

"Pyle?" Thad snatched up his own pipe. "Why would he be in a position to threaten you over Miss Jordan?"

"I should not say. 'Tis only speculation." Colin turned to take the pipe from the assistant.

A glowing mass of molten glass clung to the end of the metal tube. With the pipe balanced on the grating before the bench, Colin inhaled deeply through his nose, set the end of the instrument to his lips, and began to blow in a slow, steady stream of air. A bubble formed in the glass. Colin turned his pipe. The glass shifted, began to form. All that mattered was the glass, the object he created, his work.

The glass would free him from the guilt of abandoning his family. It gave him the means to change their lives. He must not dwell on the pain of giving up Meg for the glass. Surely God would honor his sacrifice.

The glass began to cool, began to turn viscous. Colin removed his tongs from the set of tools at his side and commenced manipulating the caramelized silica into the flat, wide shape of a bottle to hold laudanum to ease pain or an elixir to soothe a sore throat.

The glassworks receded into a background hum of voices, hiss of fire, chink of cooled glass, the music of his life. Peace flowed through him like air through his pipe. All that mattered was the glass, the nearly completed bottle. Part of his mind knew he heard the gate bell ring. On the far side of the furnace from the door, he felt no draft if someone opened it. He focused on the forming mass of green before him, the tongs in his hand, the twist of his wrist—

The door flew open. "Father!" Meg charged into the glassworks, hair tumbling down her back, hat askew. "Father, the school is destroyed!"

Colin dropped his pipe and the nearly finished medicine bottle. The metal pipe hit the grate then the floor with a resounding clang and clatter like a bell losing its clapper. The eyes of the three people in the front of the factory swung his way. No one moved. No one spoke. Leaving the pipe and useless lump of green glass, Colin slid off his bench and stalked to the front of the glassworks.

"What happened?" he asked.

Pyle took a step toward him. "This is none of your concern. Get back to work."

"But 'tis my concern, sir." Colin bowed his head. "I was at the school yesterday after church, and all was well."

"I saw you." Meg still breathed too quickly, and color flamed along her cheekbones. "You were removing snow from the tree branches. But it didn't do any good. The tree has fallen into the building."

"Impossible," Jordan snapped. "That's a sturdy tree."

"It's a very old tree." Pyle yawned behind his rather red hand. "Apparently having a hulking brute like you in its branches wore it out." He snorted as though amused by his insulting words.

"'Tis possible." Colin remained calm on the outside, while his innards roiled. "But unlikely."

"I'd say it's unlikely." Jordan rubbed his temples. "The wind was blowing last night, but not that strongly."

"What does it matter how it happened?" Tears spilled down Meg's cheeks.

Colin clasped his hands behind his back to stop himself from pulling her head against his shoulder.

"I don't have my school now," she sobbed.

"Such a shame," Pyle murmured. "After all that work." He took her hand and tucked it into the crook of his arm. "Come along, m'dear. I'll walk you home and let Mrs. Weber spoil you." He started to pull a glove from his coat pocket then tucked it back again.

"I don't want to be spoiled. I want my school." Meg wiped her gloved fingers over her cheeks. "Please, Father, what can be done?"

"I don't know." A muscle twitched at the corner of Jordan's jaw. "I don't know." He cleared his throat. "I'll have to—uh—assess the damage. Joseph, do take her home. Grassick, you have an order to fill."

"Aye sir." Colin waited until Meg and Pyle left the glassworks before returning his attention to Jordan. "Sir, I'll work through the dinnertime if you'll allow me to do that assessing for you."

"Hmm, well, you may need to come back after supper, too."

"Aye sir, I'll get that order fulfilled on time." *And remake the goldfinch bottle, though not for its original purpose, the Lord willing.* "Every night, sir, I'll work late if necessary."

"All right then, go." Jordan swept an arm toward the door then pivoted on his heel and shuffled to the desk like a man twenty years his senior.

Colin pulled his coat and hat from hooks by the door, donned them, then set out across the hard-packed snow in the yard. Ice had formed in the ruts from wagon wheels and sleigh runners, so he kept to the deeper snow. The countryside lay in silence save for his footfalls crunching and an occasional branch cracking beneath its burden of white. When he reached the crossroad, he thought he heard children's laughter. Children who wouldn't have their school now, thanks to—

He stopped himself from drawing a conclusion without proof. Just because he didn't like a man, just because that man used his money and influence to gain the lady Colin loved, didn't grant him license to make unfounded accusations against him.

"If I found the proof, Lord, I could change Meg's mind."

He rounded the corner and saw the school, half crushed like a child's kicked-in sand castle.

Feeling as though the tree had landed on him, Colin made his inspection then returned the way he had come. He didn't stop at the glassworks. He continued down the road to the Jordans' lane. Around the back he encountered Ilse Weber collecting logs.

"I'll get those for you." Colin relieved her of the burden.

Ilse opened the kitchen door to warmth and the smell of baking apples. "*Danke*, Colin, but you should be working."

"Aye, but I need to speak to Miss Jordan first." He set the logs in the wood box by the stove and smiled at her. "Please."

"Ah, you, you flirt with those eyes, and I'm a married woman."

"No such thing. I'm begging like a stray cur. 'Tis verra important I speak with Miss Jordan."

"I sent her to her room with a cup of chamomile tea. She's upset, she is."

"Please fetch her. She's going to be more—" Colin broke off at the sound of light footfalls on the steps.

A moment later, Meg pushed through the kitchen door. "Colin, what are you doing here?"

"I've come to see you, Meg." Ignoring Ilse's gasp, he closed the distance between him and Meg and took both of her hands in his. "You cannot marry Joseph Pyle."

"I beg your pardon?" Her hands writhed in his, but she made no move to pull away. "How can you say something so outrageous? Of course I can marry him. I have no choice but to marry him."

"Aye, that you do. Furthermore, you must make the choice not to marry him."

"And be responsible for you losing your position and your family suffering?" She drew her hands away now and clasped them on her elbows. "The destruction of the school is God's way of telling me I was wrong to think that's what He wanted me to do—teach, that is. I'm supposed to marry Joseph as my father wishes. Now, please leave."

"Please hear me out." Colin kept his hands outstretched in a supplicant's pose. "Meg—"

"She said to leave, Colin." Ilse glided up beside him and laid a gentle hand on his arm. "For your own sake if nothing else, you must get back to the glassworks."

"Aye, I must." Colin met and held Meg's gaze. "But let me have my say, first. Please."

Meg sighed. "All right. Speak, then be gone."

"Thank you." Although for most of his life, he'd spoken nothing but English, except on his brief journeys home, his thoughts suddenly began to form in Gaelic. He struggled to unscramble the languages and spoke with care. "I cannot believe that 'tis God's will for you to marry Joseph Pyle when I have reason to believe the destruction of your school was nay accident and he is responsible."

Chapter 15

Meg felt as though someone pulled the kitchen floor out from beneath her feet. In a moment, she would land in the root cellar or wake from a nightmare. Air refused to reach her lungs, and she swayed.

Colin caught hold of her shoulders and held her steady. "You're all right, lass. I'm here. Nay harm will come to you."

"No." She gave her head a violent shake. "You can't be right. I prayed last night—" She squeezed her eyes shut. "Last night I told Joseph to go away; then I prayed for God to show me what He wanted. I always do what I want, I'm so selfish, and—"

"You're the last person anyone would call selfish." His fingertips brushed across her cheek, and she realized she was crying.

"Ya," Ilse said, "she's kindness itself."

"No no." Meg made herself open her eyes and look into Colin's. "Listen to me. Last night I prayed for God to show me what He wants for me. Joseph said I couldn't keep the school, and I came close to saying I wouldn't marry him because he won't allow me to have my kittens or my school or my knitting." She spoke fast to get all the words out. "I prayed for God to show me what He wants and—and the school is destroyed today. Surely this means God wants me to marry Joseph and save you and Father and everything else and serve the Lord as Joseph's wife."

"Not if the tree was destroyed on purpose." Colin's hold on her shoulders tightened. "Meg, it was cut with an ax. I ken the marks. No snow or wind blew that tree over."

"Then God used some mischief maker." Meg stepped away from him and turned her face toward the windows so she could think clearly. "Joseph wouldn't be so cruel."

"Someone made me burn my hand." Colin's voice grew soft. "Joseph Pyle was near the glassworks at the time. Someone smashed a piece of work I was making for you. Joseph Pyle—"

"No, you mustn't say these things about him. He's going to be your master soon."

"And the tree—"

"You need to leave." Meg stepped around him, heading for the door.

"Ya Colin, you'd best be gone," Ilse added.

"Nay, I will not leave until you hear me out, Margaret Jordan." He followed her to the door and laid his hand against her cheek, gently turning her face toward his. "Please, for your sake. I found a glove in the schoolyard. Did you notice he wasn't wearing gloves today in spite of the cold? His hands were red from it, but only one glove stuck out of his coat pocket."

The scene in the glassworks flashed through her mind, Joseph taking her hand to place on his arm. Then she remembered Joseph bowing over her hand when he left her at the house. No gloves. Red hands. A supple leather mitt protruding from one coat pocket.

"But what—what does this mean?" she whispered. "Colin?"

She held out her hands, needing something solid to cling to, as her world that seemed so certain—unhappy but certain—an hour ago crumbled beneath her. Colin took her hands then released them and wrapped his arms around her. She buried her face in the rough wool of his coat, inhaling his scent of wood smoke and the freshness of the winter day.

He crooned to her, words that weren't English yet comforting in their sibilant melody. "God has a plan for you, lass," he said, switching to English. "I can't accept He will use a deliberately cut tree to reveal it to you."

"But—"

"Miss Meg," Ilse broke in. "Your father—"

The back door sprang open. Meg jumped away from Colin, her face flaming. "Father, I—"

"What are you doing here, Grassick?" Father's dark amber eyes blazed.

Meg pressed her hand to her lips. "Father, please, don't misunderstand—"

"Hush, lass, I can explain." Colin took her hand in his. "I came to warn your daughter of Joseph Pyle's treachery."

"I beg your pardon?" Father enunciated each word with care. "Ilse, what sort of carrying-on are you allowing behind my back and in my own house? I hold you responsible."

"He was comforting me." Meg tugged on Father's sleeve. "Please, listen to what Colin has to say. It's—distressing."

"What I find distressing," Father said, "is finding my daughter being embraced by one of my employees. Now get yourself back to work, Grassick, or you can go pack your things and leave."

"No," Meg protested.

"Nay sir." Colin stood his ground, a full head taller than Father and far broader in the shoulders. Solid. Dependable. Noble.

Meg's heart cried out for a life beside this man.

"You may dismiss me if you wish, sir," Colin said, "but my conscience would never stop pricking me if I left to save my own skin and risked Meg's."

"She is Miss Jordan to you, Grassick." Father planted his hands on his hips. "You've been warned once too often."

"Aye sir." Colin sighed. "And the matter stands. I will not risk her future with a man who destroys property, when it could be people one day."

Meg shivered and wanted the warmth of Colin's arm around her again.

Father scowled. "You make a grave accusation, Grassick. The consequences could be serious."

"Aye, I ken the risk, but the truth speaks for itself." Colin reached past Father and opened the door. "Will you come with me, sir, Miss Jordan? I'll show you the evidence."

Father hesitated, and Meg held her breath. Then Father nodded. "Because I think you're a good man, I'll let you have your say in full. Margaret—"

Meg was already racing to find her cloak and pattens. She joined the men in the stable yard, where Father was harnessing the horses to the sleigh. With three passengers, they sat close together like a family. If only. . .

Surely God didn't want her married to a man who could be dangerous at the worst and destroyed things important to others in order to get his own way at the least.

The sleigh runners hissed over the snow, and the horses' hooves crunched through the icy crust. The air lay so still, smoke from the glassworks and charcoal burners soared straight into the sky, white columns against the pale blue. Meg clasped her arms across her middle and willed the sleigh to go faster while her stomach churned with the anticipation of seeing her school in ruins.

"All those beautiful windows you made," she murmured.

"The building can be repaired, lass." Colin smiled down at her.

Meg knew she should say she didn't want to restore the building, that she must marry Joseph and be done with the school. It had brought nothing but trouble and expense. She should have known from the day she found the smashed windows she wasn't supposed to carry on her work. Yet her heart ached at the prospect of giving up her school or the cats or her newfound pleasure in knitting. Her insides quaked at the notion of marrying a man who treated others with such disregard and things with disrespect.

Her lower lip began to hurt, and she realized she held it clamped between her teeth. She made herself stop, but her jaw felt as rigid as the trunk of the oak beside her school. The trunk of the oak that used to stand beside her school.

The sleigh swept around the curve in the road, and the sight of the school sprang into view. Meg covered her eyes, unable to see the caved-in roof, the sagging wall.

"Did you see anything unusual here, Margaret?" Father asked.

"No sir." Meg gulped. "I saw the tree down and ran back to the glassworks. It's—horrible."

"Aye, hinnie, 'tis a pathetic sight." Colin touched her cheek.

Father glared at him. "You haven't proven anything to us yet."

"I will." Colin sprang from the sleigh and held out a hand to Meg.

She took it and stepped to the snowy ground. They stood, hands still clasped, while Father secured the horses. She avoided Colin's eyes but welcomed the strength of his hand.

"Let's see this proof." Father tramped through the snow, his footfalls sounding like an ax cutting through wood.

As an ax had cut through the tree trunk. Meg stood between Father and Colin and stared at the slashes in the trunk, not all the way through, just enough to weaken the oak.

"I could not clear the higher branches of their snow." Colin spoke in a low voice as though afraid someone would overhear. "They were too thin to hold my weight. But I thought what I did would be enough to protect the building."

"It would have been without this." Father gestured to the split trunk. "Maybe a branch or two would have taken off a couple of shingles but not this destruction."

His face appeared gray in the brilliant light of sun on snow.

"But this is no proof that Joseph did this," Father added. "Anyone wanting to make mischief could have. Think of those broken windows."

"Aye, but who would have wanted to smash windows?" Colin asked. "Have you or your daughter the enemies?"

"No, but Joseph hasn't any cause either."

"He does." Meg felt ill. "I made it clear to him that I thought the school more important than he is. I didn't like him telling me I could only arrange fetes for the church and things like that when I'm his wife. I was willful about it." She swallowed. "Like I'm willful about everything."

"You've been indulged." Father squeezed her shoulder. "But don't blame yourself for this. We don't have proof one way or another."

"Except for that." Colin pointed to something nearly the color of the bark snagged on a knot protruding from the side of the trunk.

Meg leaned forward to get a better look. So soft and supple it molded itself to the tree, the glove hung torn and dirty, a mute testimony to its owner. A match to the glove in Joseph's pocket.

"I'm thinking he doesn't know where he lost it," Colin said. "But he'll come here to look eventually."

"He should have come here first," Meg whispered. "We'd never have known."

"He might have intended to." Father stepped away from the tree. "He wouldn't expect you to come here and find the disaster so early if at all until the snow melts."

"Nor I." Colin faced Father. "Do you believe me, sir? And shall I tell you about the accidents in the glassworks? Nay proof there, you ken, and who else would wish to harm or discredit me?"

"Why would Joseph?" Father returned.

"Because of me." Meg curled her fingers and squeezed for something to hold on to. "Because I insisted on being friendly with Colin and showed my preference for him over Joseph. If I didn't insist on having everything my own way, he might not be pressuring Father over the loan money and—and—"

"Even if that were true, 'tis no excuse for a man's behavior," Colin said.

"And little proof to lay against a man of Joseph's prominence," Father pointed out. "I won't make accusations against him."

Meg stared at Father. "But shouldn't we ask him? That is, are you going to let him get away with this?"

"We don't know he's getting away with anything." Father removed the glove from the tree. "Maybe he was here inspecting the damage, as we are."

"With all due respect, sir," Colin said, "this was here before Mr. Pyle could have gotten here."

"Oh, uh, true."

Now that he held the glove, Meg saw it was sodden, as though melting snow had soaked through the leather. No snow remained on the tree to drip as the sun melted it. None had remained on the tree when they arrived.

"We should at least ask him," she pointed out.

Father turned on his heel and tramped back to the sleigh. Meg gazed after him for a moment then turned to Colin.

He gripped her hand. "We need to persuade your father to talk to Pyle, you ken."

"Yes." Head down, Meg followed her father, drawing Colin with her.

Father stood at the horses' heads, stroking their gray noses and staring at the sky. "If we're wrong," he said as though talking to himself, "he will forget he's given me a two-week grace period and call in the loan now. I can't let him have the glassworks. I've worked too hard for it." He faced Colin. "And you know as soon as he is the owner, he'll dismiss you to get you away from Meg."

"Aye, I ken." Colin's face paled against the vivid red of his hair. "My faith has been lacking in a number of areas in my life, mostly that I haven't trusted the Lord to take care of my family, insisting I do it all myself. But how can I see my family in comfort here in America, giving them the grand futures, when Meg's future as that man's wife looks to be one of misery? I'll risk losing my position here and return to Scotland before I see Meg married to that man."

"Colin, no." Meg clasped his hand between both of hers. "No, you can't do that. I want your family here and you to keep your position."

"Aye, you want." Colin smiled at her. "But is that what the Lord wants? Or are we to trust Him to show us a different plan, one that is different from what we're thinking?"

Meg started to speak; then she clamped her lips together. Colin was right. If Joseph continued to go around causing damage to property when people thwarted his will, he might end up harming a person.

She took a deep breath. "I'll do what you wish, Father."

"And I also, sir."

"It's a risk that could hurt all of us," Father said. "But it's one we have to take."

Chapter 16

"Is it faith or foolishness?" Father asked the question as he entered the house.

They were the first words he'd spoken since leaving the school. They paused at the glassworks long enough for Colin to return to work; then they swept up the lane to the house. While Father took the horses to the stable, Meg ran inside to warm herself by the fire and prepare hot tea. She told Ilse to go home, that she would see to their meals.

Now Father stood wiping snow from his boots, rubbing his hands together, and gazing past Meg as though posing the question to someone other than her.

She chose to answer. "I'm trying to work that out, but I think it's faith. I've been going my own way and not asking which way to go."

"You had a good teacher in me, daughter." Father came forward and hugged her. "I did the same in not asking the Lord if I should open the glassworks. I wanted to do this in memory of my father. I should have kept my promise to your mother. But Joseph offered to lend the money, so I went ahead. We'll be profitable soon. The orders are coming in. But it's not soon enough. Joseph will break his word to extend the contract past Christmas because you won't agree to marry him."

"And there's nothing you can do about it?" Meg clung to him as she had when a small child, seeking comfort from a nightmare or skinned knee. "There's no one else you can borrow from?"

"There is." Father moved to the stove and held his hands to the warmth. "I approached some bankers on my last journey to Philadelphia. They didn't want to take the risk, but I have orders I can show them. Joseph would be a fool to get rid of Grassick, but he will out of spite."

"Because I pursued him."

"I didn't see him running away, daughter." Father gave her a sad smile. "The two of you. . ."

Meg waited. Father remained silent.

She licked her dry lips. "When will we talk to Joseph?"

"Call it the weakness of my belief that the Lord will work this out according to His will," Father said, "but I'd rather wait until I hear from the bankers."

"And if they say no?"

Father squared his shoulders. "We will still talk to Joseph about the incidents. In the meantime, my dear, don't let him press his suit."

Meg squirmed. "He'll suspect something. I can't do this to you or Colin. I'd rather marry Joseph than see the two of you suffer."

"It's not your decision, Margaret."

"But—" She bowed her head. "Yes sir."

She didn't know how she would obey her father, knowing it risked his future and Colin's.

"Go pack your things," Father said. "I'll go ask the Webers if you can stay with them."

Her proximity to Colin alone would anger Joseph. Nonetheless, Meg ran upstairs and began to pack a small trunk with clothing for several days. In the kitchen again, she filled a basket with some delicacies for the Webers—a loaf of sugar, a tin of chocolate, butter, jam, and a packet of raisins. She thought for a moment then hefted in flour and spices and more dried fruits. They would bake for the Christmas Eve party, and the children could help, stealing as much dough as they liked. It was the least she could do for destroying their chance at an education.

When Father returned to collect her, she was hauling a sack of flour from the pantry. He raised his eyebrows but said nothing. He took the bag from her and carried it to the waiting sleigh. He returned for her trunk, and she followed him, swinging the basket. In moments Father drew the horses up before the Webers' cottage.

The Webers ran out to greet Meg and her father, Ilse and Hans along with their three children, who ranged in age from six to fourteen. Neat and clean and smiling, the children seized the food and insisted they carry it into the house for Meg.

"Do you enjoy baking, Gretta?" she asked the eldest.

She nodded, her blond braids flopping against her shoulders. "Yes, I always help Momma."

"I don't bake." Hans, the youngest and only boy, wrinkled his nose. "I only eat because I'm going to be a glassblower."

If the glassworks still existed.

Meg determined to make things work out for the sake of these children, too.

"You can eat as much as your momma says you can." Meg resisted the urge to hug him, and she returned to the yard to bid her father farewell. "God be with you and the bankers," she whispered.

He kissed the top of her head and climbed aboard the sleigh. "I'll leave the horses at the inn and take the next stage."

He clucked his tongue and snapped the reins. The horses trotted forward. The sleigh swept around the corner and disappeared.

Meg pressed her folded arms to her belly to minimize the emptiness inside. "Lord, what is the right answer? I want to know now."

No answer came to her, so she returned to the house and plunged into baking preparations. Martha Dalbow joined them later in the day, and the time flew by. As occupied as she was, Meg kept glancing out the windows, hoping for a glimpse of Colin, fearing a sight of Joseph. She saw neither of them. Hans

Weber said Colin was working late at the glassworks.

"He will be all the week." Mr. Weber shook his head. "That young man works too hard. He needs a pretty wife to come home to like I do."

Ilse laughed and blushed, and the emptiness inside Meg grew. This kind of love was what she wanted. She saw it in them, in Martha and Thad, in Sarah and Peter. She doubted she would find it with Joseph. His actions, even if he were not guilty of cutting the tree and destroying Colin's work, assured her that her first impression stood solid. What she would say to him upon their next meeting, she didn't know.

Late the following afternoon she needed to find out. He rode up to the Webers' front door shortly after dinner. Meg saw him through the parlor window and grabbed her cloak off a hook in the kitchen before running to answer his knock.

"Don't go anywhere with him," Ilse insisted.

"I won't." Meg opened the door and stepped onto the stoop, shutting herself outside. "How are you, Joseph?"

"I'm well." He eyed her up and down. "You have flour on your hem."

"I wasn't expecting a guest." She shook out her skirt, sending some of the flour onto his shining boots. "May I assist you with something?"

"Why are you here, and where is your father?" He delivered the questions like a volley of gunfire.

"Father is away, so I'm staying here."

"I should have been told."

"Why?"

"I'm your affianced husband."

Meg wrapped her cloak more tightly around her shoulders against the brisk wind. "No, you're not." She made herself look into his eyes. "Nor will you be until we have made the impending marriage official."

"Which is right now. If your father is so irresponsible he runs off and leaves you in the protection of these people"—he sneered at the simple, white-washed cottage—"then you need to be allied with my name for the sake of your reputation."

"My reputation?" Meg drew herself up to her full height. "No one in this county is more respectable than Ilse and Hans Weber. My reputation is likely safer with them than with you."

"Indeed." Joseph smiled, and his eyes glowed with such a cold blue light that Meg felt as though he shoved an icicle through her chest. "You don't understand, Margaret. I can destroy your father and that Scot you fancy. If I can't have you as my wife, I will have the glassworks as my business, and all these good people you think so highly of for no good reason will be out of work. They'll be on the roads and so will you."

"No." Meg flattened her hands against the door behind her for support. "I won't let that happen."

"You'll have no choice unless it's to marry me."

"Why?" She cried out in desperation. "Why do you want to marry me so much that you'd destroy others' lives?"

Joseph shrugged. "Because I want what I want. You're the prettiest and most loved girl in the county. The best. I must have the best."

Meg stared at him, wide-eyed. "I'm not the best, Joseph. I'm selfish and self-centered and want—"

She caught her breath. With her words seeming to ring around the yard like the gate bell, she heard them again and again and realized how close to Joseph's words they sounded. *I want. . . I want. . .*

"We can talk again after Father returns." She turned the door handle.

Joseph caught her wrist. "You will not walk away from me until I say you can."

"You have no right to tell me to stay here." She struggled to free herself.

His grip tightened. "When you're my wife or I own the glassworks—"

"Stop it." Meg wrenched her hand free and pounded her fist on the door. "I will never be your wife, and you will never own the glassworks, once Father hears of this."

"You'd prefer your father lose everything for the sake of your delicate sensibilities?" Joseph laughed. "That won't get you very far when you're homeless."

"We won't be homeless once the bank—" Meg slapped her hand across her lips—too late. She'd let the cat out of the bag.

❧

Colin nodded to Louis, the senior apprentice who usually helped him. "This is the last of the purple bowls we'll making for this order if you'd like to go to your supper."

"Not if you're going to stay and work, sir." Louis, young, fair, and eager to please, hovered near Colin's bench. "We still have the purple silica if you'd like to finish that set of goblets. I was counting them, and with the twelve at the Jordan house, you only have three to go."

Colin had made several of Meg's goblets on Monday out of pique that she insisted she was responsible for fixing everything. Other than carrying her off to one of the states he'd heard about, where couples could marry without any sort of notice—rather like Scotland's own Gretna Green—he didn't know how else to stop her, except to pray for the truth to come forth and the situation to resolve. Even if that meant he was wrong and Joseph Pyle was a decent, if somewhat greedy, man, Colin wanted the best for Meg.

Finishing the goblets felt like defeat, as though he had given in—or up. Yet his practical side told him not to let the already-heated purple glass go to waste and have to be reheated at another time.

"All right," he agreed, "we'll finish the goblets."

"Right." Louis took Colin's pipe and dashed off for the vat of molten glass.

Colin pulled the crate of finished goblets off the shelf and set several on top to study their lines. His tongs, pincers, and calipers lay spread out on his workbench. Other than the crackle of the fire in one furnace and the grate of the door as Louis reached in to draw out the hot glass, the factory lay quiet. Lamps lit the interior. Darkness spread across the outside save for the luminescence of the snow.

A shadow moved against the whiteness. Footfalls crunched past the windows. Then the door opened and Joseph Pyle stood in the opening, frigid air swirling around him and through the building.

"You're dismissed, Grassick," he announced.

Colin met Louis's gaze and indicated he should proceed with the glass, before turning back to Pyle. "By whose orders?"

"Mine." Pyle smiled, his eyes cold. "I own this glassworks now."

"Is that so?" Colin reached out one hand for his pipe, molten glass glowing on the end. "I'll be hearing that from Mr. Jordan before I take an order from you."

He set the pipe to his lips and began to blow in a slow, steady stream that belied the turmoil inside him. Pyle couldn't possibly own the glassworks yet. Jordan said he had until Christmas.

"Put that pipe down, and get out of here." Pyle marched forward.

"The door, sir." Louis ran to close it. "The cold air will ruin the glass."

"Quitting will ruin the glass, too." Pyle's smile widened. "Quite unfortunate for Isaac Jordan's former customer."

If he didn't need to maintain an even exhalation, Colin would have laughed.

Pyle turned to Louis. "Get out, boy. I wish to say a few things to Grassick in private."

"But—but—" Louis stammered.

Never taking his eyes from his work, Colin pointed a pinkie toward the door.

"If you think it's all right." Louis snatched up his coat and cap and fled.

Colin continued to work, turning the pipe, watching the bubble form, the glass shape.

"If you weren't here, Grassick," Joseph growled, "Margaret would be grateful to me for offering her marriage."

Colin picked up his tongs.

"You've turned her head." Pyle advanced, stepping sideways to avoid the hot glass at the end of the pipe. "You, a mere workman."

Colin applied the tongs to pinch the glass for the stem.

Pyle slid behind him, raising the hairs on the back of Colin's neck. "I could make her a governor's wife, and she wants a glassblower."

Contempt dripped from Pyle's tone.

The tone, the words rang like sweet music in Colin's ears. Meg must have said something to Pyle.

"You'll give her nothing but grief," Pyle continued.

Not so. Colin would give her love.

"That is, if you're still here. Which you won't—" Pyle lunged, snatching the pipe from Colin's hand.

The glass flew off the end. Colin ducked, twisted, rolled away from the pipe's hot tip.

"Think she'll like you with your face scarred?" Pyle plunged the pipe toward Colin.

He snatched up one of the finished goblets and threw it. Pyle deflected it with the pipe like a cricket ball and bat, sending the heavy glass soaring toward Colin. He sprang to his feet. The goblet missed and smashed against a workbench.

Colin vaulted the bench and snatched up the crate. Glasses flew, shattering like discordant music.

Another note sounded, high-pitched and shrill. Meg's scream. Colin looked. A mistake. Pyle leaped at him, the pipe swooping toward Colin's face.

"No!" Meg cried.

Colin dove for Pyle's legs. Meg sprang at his back. They struck at the same time. Pyle dropped with a shout, a thud and tinkle of glass, and a clang of metal on stone. He lay in a shower of shattered amethyst glass, the hot end of the blowpipe against his cheek.

Chapter 17

For several seconds, nothing, no one in the glasshouse moved. Even the fire merely hissed as it began to die on its grate. Then Colin shot to his feet, kicked aside shards of glass, its tinkling breaking the stillness, and crouched beside Joseph to pull the pipe free.

"Is he—gone?" Meg whispered.

It sounded like a shout to her ears.

"Stunned is all." Colin touched the blowpipe. "And he'll have a frightful scar."

"He intended you to have one." Meg staggered to her feet and closed the distance between her and Colin. She wanted to touch him, hold on to his solidity and strength, but she kept her hands pressed to her sides. "He was swinging it at your face."

"Aye, he thought you would not care for me if I had the scar on my face." Colin set the pipe on his workbench then slipped his arms around Joseph and rose, all without looking at Meg. "If you'll be kind enough to get the door for me, I'll carry him to my cottage. Perhaps Hans could be fetching the apothecary."

"Of course."

Before Meg or Colin reached the door, it flew open and Louis, Thad, and Hans rushed in. They halted at the sight of Colin's burden.

"What happened?" Mr. Weber asked.

"He had a wee bit of an accident." Colin shifted Joseph to drape him over his shoulder. "Louis, be a good lad and fetch an apothecary or whatever you have here."

"Yes sir." Louis bolted out the door.

"He said Pyle was talking ugly," Thad explained, "so he came to fetch us. We're sorry we didn't get here sooner. Are you or Miss Margaret injured?"

"I'm all right," Meg said.

Except for her spirit, which ached like a wound.

"I am, too." Colin headed out the door, paused on the threshold long enough to face Meg. "I'll be calling on you later, if I may."

"Of course." Her response was automatic not warm.

A light flared in Colin's eyes then dimmed. Without another word, he spun on his heel and vanished into the night.

Thad slipped his arm around Meg. "Let's get you back to the Webers'. Ilse and Martha will likely have gallons of coffee brewing and piles of sandwiches waiting."

"I'm sure Colin will be hungry." Meg felt too numb to be hungry, though a hot drink sounded good.

Thad led her away. Hans stayed in the glassworks to close up the furnace and extinguish the lamps. The broken glass would be swept up and melted down to make something else. What, Meg neither knew nor cared. It wouldn't be goblets for her new home. The notion should elate her. Joseph had shown his true nature, and no one would expect her to marry him.

Not that anyone would want to marry her, she realized, now that she knew her own true nature.

They reached the Webers' cottage. Thad took her cloak. Ilse nudged her into a kitchen chair and curled Meg's hands around a mug of hot coffee with instructions to drink. Meg felt like a marionette with several people pulling her strings.

"We all want to know what happened," Ilse said. "Thad, go see what's afoot. Where did they all go?"

"Colin's." Thad opened the door. "I'll send Martha over and head to Colin's."

"I should go do something to help." Meg started to rise.

Ilse held her in place with a hand on her shoulder. "You stay there and warm yourself."

"I'm not cold." Yet as she took a sip of coffee, Meg realized she was.

Ilse draped a quilt over Meg's shoulders. "There now, you've had a terrible shock. We all thought Mr. Pyle was such a good man."

"He always wanted his own way." Meg's hands shook, and she set her cup down. "He picked out things he wanted and did anything necessary to get them. I was one of those things—like fine windows and furnishings for his house. And Colin—" She put her head on her folded arms atop the table. "I nearly killed Colin."

"*Nein. Nein.*" Ilse knelt and wrapped her arms around Meg. "You did no such thing. Now then, would you like to go to your bed?"

"I'd rather wait."

Colin arrived within the hour, along with Hans and Thad.

"The sheriff took Pyle to Salem City," Thad announced.

Meg dropped the knife with which she was cutting slices of cake. "The sheriff took him?"

"Aye, Louis is a quick-thinking lad." Colin retrieved the knife from the table and slid it into her hand. "He sent the apothecary here then went on to collect the sheriff."

"And Pyle was arrested?" Ilse shook her head. "I never thought I'd see it."

"Is he well enough to go to jail?" Meg gazed up at Colin, so close to her yet too far away.

"He'll do." He tucked a curl behind her ear. "He's got a headache and a nasty burn, but he's awake and blaming—well, he's a frightened man."

"You can say it, Colin." Meg gripped the edge of the table. "He's blaming me. It's all my fault, and I'm no better than he is."

A chorus of protests rose.

Colin tilted her chin up with a forefinger and looked into her eyes. "What makes you say something like that, hinnie?"

"He would stop at nothing to get his own way. I insist on mine, too." Meg licked her dry lips. "I claimed I was doing the Lord's work, but I was doing mine. Is that so different than Joseph wanting the best of everything to glorify himself?"

"You were not trying to bring glory to yourself. How could you ever think so?"

A murmur of agreement ran around the kitchen.

"Isn't going my own way, saying that I want to do this and I want to do that, bringing glory to myself?" Meg hugged her middle. "I never once asked God if I was doing what He wanted. I asked my earthly father, who always gives me what I want, except for freedom from Joseph, and I've brought harm through my willfulness. I was so determined I wouldn't marry Joseph that I told him too much and he went straight to the glassworks to attack you."

Colin gave her a gentle smile. "Nay harm's been done. We're all right."

"Are we?" Meg flung out her arms and stalked across the kitchen so she could face everyone. "Joseph may be in jail, but my father still owes him money. He will still own the glassworks, and Colin can still lose his position if Father can't get the loan he needs. You could all lose your positions. You've witnessed Joseph at his worst, and he apparently harms those who thwart him."

"Which is why you cannot wed him," Colin said.

"No, I cannot, and although I want to marry you so much, I can't ever hope to do so."

⁓

Colin set down his pipe and rubbed his eyes. He felt as though the sand that went into making the silica had been poured into his sockets. He needed rest. Yet sleep eluded him and had in the three nights since Joseph Pyle tried to attack him with a hot blowpipe.

Pyle was out of the jail, though facing charges of assault. He claimed he was defending himself, but even if people doubted the word of a mere glassblower, no one questioned Meg's integrity in her account of the incident.

The other incidents, the hot grate on the workbench, the broken bottle, and the hacked tree, Pyle denied and no one could prove. Since he lay at home, suffering a septic wound from his assault on Colin, he would likely have to pay a fine and nothing more. That left him free to do as he pleased with the glassworks if Jordan didn't obtain the loan money by other means, since Pyle no longer wished to marry Meg for payment. Despite her freedom from that burden, Meg refused to let Colin court her.

"My wanting to be with you has caused nothing but trouble," she insisted.

"But surely You don't want us apart now, Lord," Colin cried aloud to the empty factory.

And why not?

That question sent him pacing the aisles of the glassworks between work-benches and molds, furnaces and lehrs, until he came to rest at one of the windows, his brow against the cold glass.

He'd come to America to help his family. Or so he had told himself. Now he began to wonder if he acted no differently than Meg—going his own way because it was something he wanted, yet excusing the behavior with the claim it was what God wanted.

"But I'm here now, Lord, and my family is thousands of miles away. Meg may as well be. I don't know what to do."

Which might be the best place in the world to be—so uncertain he had no choice but to let the Lord take over.

"But my family—" He stopped, recalling a verse his mother often quoted.

"Wherefore, if God so clothe the grass of the field, which to day is, and to morrow is cast into the oven, shall he not much more clothe you, O ye of little faith? . . . Take therefore no thought for the morrow: for the morrow shall take thought for the things of itself."

She was a great one for having the faith through difficult times. If she, a widow with five children to care for, believed the Lord would show them a way to get through life, then Colin could do the same. Or at the least, he could try. He would trust that the Lord would see to the future and keep working as long as he was allowed to do so. He knew exactly where to start.

Fatigue slipping from his shoulders, Colin returned to his workbench and picked up the drawing he'd made of the goldfinch.

⁓

Candles blazed in every room of the Jordan house, and fires blazed on the hearths, staving off the cold sweeping through the rooms each time the front door opened to admit another group of people. Thus far on this Christmas Eve, friends and neighbors braved another snowstorm to partake of the Jordans' Christmas Eve party. People Meg loved to see were laughing and chattering and consuming mounds of food and bowls of hot, spiced cider. She especially enjoyed watching Peter and Sarah together. They glowed whenever they caught each other's gaze. Meg's heart leaped with joy for her dearest friend's happiness.

She jumped with anticipation and apprehension every time the door swung in; Gretta rushed up to take hats and cloaks, and Ilse collected contributions of sweets and savories. She anticipated Father's arrival, hoping, praying for good news, fearing the answer because she wanted it so much.

She wanted Colin to walk through the door, too. But she'd given him up, and only the Lord could give him back if He wished.

Knowing this didn't stop her from jumping and staring toward the kitchen every time she moved near enough to hear the back door open.

"Mar–ga–ret." Sarah drew the name out close to Meg's ear. "I've been talking to you for five minutes, and you keep staring at that door."

"I'm sorry." Meg rubbed her hot cheeks. "I thought I heard someone arrive through the back door."

"How can you hear anything above this din?" Sarah slipped her arm through the crook of Meg's elbow. "Let's steal five minutes in your room. No one will miss us, and I simply must know what happened with Joseph. How could we have all been so wrong?"

"We were deceived by his good looks and wealth."

"You weren't deceived." Sarah hugged Meg. "I owe you an apology."

"You had my future security in your heart, as Father did. So no apology—oh!"

"Isaac, you're home!" someone cried from the parlor.

"Father." Meg whirled on her heel, sending the lace flounces on her gown swirling around her like snow. "You got home in time." She dashed through the crowd of guests and flung herself into his outstretched arms.

Snow covered his coat, and he smelled of leather, wet wool, and pipe smoke. Dark circles rimmed his eyes, but the dark amber irises glowed as though candles burned behind them.

"You look lovely, daughter." He held her at arm's length.

Around them guests stood back and grinned at the reunion.

"I didn't think you'd get here and feared I'd be spending Christmas alone."

"I wouldn't make you do that if I had to swim across the bay to get here." He hugged her again then released her. "If my study isn't full of people, may we have a few minutes there?"

"Shed that wet coat first," Meg said, "and I'll shoo anyone out."

By the time she'd displaced a handful of gentlemen complaining about how President Madison's policies would ruin them all then collected a hot drink and plate of food, Father had changed his clothes and joined her in his study. Not until the door closed, blocking out the gaiety of the guests and clatter of crockery, did Meg realize what news he might bring. Her stomach began to ache, and she sank onto the edge of a chair.

"What—happened in Philadelphia?"

"First things first." Father began to munch on a slice of ham rolled around a hunk of cheese and spread with mustard. "Tell me what happened here. I've heard some of it, but I want to know everything."

Meg told him. "It was all my fault. I slipped and told Joseph what you were doing in Philadelphia."

"He was bound to find out anyway." Father selected a dried cherry tart and took a healthy bite. "They don't have food like this in the city."

"But, Father." Meg slid farther forward in her chair. "I told him, and he attacked Colin. Or tried to."

"He failed."

"But he won't next time. Next time he'll dismiss him, and that could be worse than a scar. I can't marry Joseph now, even if he still wanted to marry me— which he doesn't—but I've decided I can't associate with Colin either."

"The poor lad. Why would you break his heart like this? Don't you care for him after all?"

"I do." Meg gulped. "More than anything. But I caused so much trouble setting my cap for him it can't be right."

"Seems to me Joseph caused the trouble, not you, my dear."

"Well yes, but if I hadn't been so willful, wanting everything my own way—"

"We don't know what would have happened instead." Father gave her a gentle smile. "One thing I did while waiting about in the city was talk to an old friend from Princeton. He's a man of deep faith, but I've never asked him about it until now." He leaned forward. "I see now that we've been going our own way and not trusting the Lord to either guide us or help us. We are doing good, we say, so we think it's right."

Meg nodded.

"And that makes us worry when things don't go our own way."

She nodded harder.

"But good doesn't mean right." Father rose and rounded the desk. "I got a no the first time I tried a city banker, so I took Joseph's terms, thinking I was doing good for you. But after the incident with the tree, I knew I had to try again, humble myself if necessary. But first I prayed and left it in the Lord's hands. It may be the first time in my life I've done that."

"I prayed, and the next day the school caved in."

"Destroyed by someone's hand. Don't you understand?" Father moved to crouch before her and took her hands in his. "God allowed this so I would see Joseph for the greedy, selfish, and dangerous man he is, not so you would think you should marry him."

Tension inside Meg eased just a bit. She still had to ask, "What about the glassworks? Everyone's positions there?"

"Safe." Father broke into the biggest grin she'd ever seen on his face. "When I asked for a loan before, I didn't have the orders I do now. With these new contracts for glass, we'll make a profit in no time and pay off my debt to Joseph. In fact, I paid him before I came home. He can't threaten any of us any longer."

She covered up the stab of disappointment that she couldn't celebrate this moment with Colin and grinned back. "Then let us join our friends and give thanks to God for the birth of His Son."

"Let's. I believe I just heard some people arrive." Father rose, a little stiffly, and drew Meg with him.

They exited the study. Indeed, several more people were crowding through the front door: Sarah's parents and brothers, and behind them, a parcel in his hands, his bright hair dusted with snow, was Colin.

Meg pressed her hand to her lips to stop herself from calling his name. She didn't know why he'd come. Father began to introduce him to everyone, his voice ringing out with pride.

"This is my master glassblower, Colin Grassick, come all the way from

Edinburgh, Scotland, to bless us with his presence."

Colin smiled to the ladies, who preened before his charm, and shook hands with the men, who appeared a bit surprised. No one snubbed him. They wouldn't. He had been presented as Father's guest.

Across the entry hall, Meg caught Sarah's questioning glance and shrugged. She didn't know what was afoot. She ached for Colin to speak to her, wish her a blessed Christmas if nothing else. Hearing his voice, seeing his smile, even past the heads of two dozen people, smoothed balm on her bruised spirit.

Then only a dozen people stood between them. Half a dozen melted away. Three. Two. . .

He stood in front of her, holding out his parcel. "A wee gift for you, hinnie."

"Th–thank you." Aware that the crowd watched her, Meg took the package and looked at him. "Should I open it?"

"Of course," people chorused.

"Aye, open it." Colin smiled. "'Twas to be a wedding gift and perhaps still is."

"No no. I don't have to marry Joseph now. That is—" Her hands shook.

"Aye, I ken. Your father stopped to talk to me on his way home." He took back the parcel. "I'll be holding it."

"Thank you." Fingers clumsy, Meg untied the string and allowed the brown paper wrapping to fall back. Meg thought she gasped, but she couldn't be sure amid the collective inhalation.

Before her, nestled in a bed of tissue paper, rested a goldfinch as delicate and detailed as the ones who populated the countryside, brownish in the winter but golden in summer.

"'Tis a perfume bottle in which to store your apple blossom scent."

"Colin, I—" Tears blurred the work of art before her, and her throat closed.

"Martha Dalbow says the goldfinch takes a partner for all his life," Colin said, his rich voice flowing around her like music.

"If he sings as well as he talks," the pastor said from the parlor doorway, "we have to get him into the choir."

Meg choked on a giggle.

"So what better gift for a bride than a goldfinch?" Colin continued as though no one had spoken.

"But I'm not going to be a bride," Meg murmured. "You know that."

"I ken nay such thing." He tucked one hand beneath her chin and tilted her face up. "I cannot offer you many fine servants and a grand house, hinnie, but I can give you my heart, my devotion, my enduring love, if you'll consent to becoming my wife."

All too aware of a score of people witnessing this proposal, Meg struggled for an appropriate response.

"Yes," someone hissed. "Just say yes."

"F–Father," Meg stammered.

"I have his blessing, if you can bear to be wed to a mere glassblower."

"Colin Grassick, I've never thought of you as a mere anything." Meg's tongue released with a spate of words. "How dare you think I would turn down the man I love because he works with his hands instead of ordering people about. Never has it been my choice to separate myself from people because—"

He raised his thumb from her chin to her lips, stilling the flow of speech. "Then I understand you are saying yes?"

"Yes!" Meg cried.

And as the Christmas party guests laughed and cheered, Colin lowered his head and kissed her in front of what sounded like half the residents of Salem County, New Jersey.

Epilogue

Carriage wheels rumbled on the hard-packed lane leading to the Jordan house, and Colin grasped the railing around the porch to keep himself from jumping up and down like a small boy. Beside him Meg danced in place, sending her curls and hat ribbons bouncing.

"It's them, Colin, I know it is."

"Aye, lass, I believe so. But perhaps a wee bit of decorum before you meet my mother?" Grinning, he tucked a pin back into her hair.

"Oh no, is she strict? You never told me she's strict."

"Nay, she's as gentle as a—well, she's more like a ewe than a lamb, but smarter."

"She won't like me." Meg began fussing with her curls, her ribbons, the puffed sleeves of her muslin gown. "She'll take one look at me and say I'm not good enough for you. And she's right. You're so thoughtful and good, and I'm still willful and—oh, that cat!"

Wanderer rambled onto the porch, leaped atop the railing, and proceeded to bat at Meg's hat ribbons fluttering in the summer breeze.

"Leave her be, you beastie." Colin scooped the cat to the ground.

"Did he mess them up? Please make certain I look all right. I don't have time to go find a mirror."

"You look as bonnie as ever." Colin cupped her face in his hands and smiled into her eyes.

Behind her extraordinarily long lashes, the amber irises shimmered like gemstones. Her lips parted in a half smile, and he kissed them.

"Now they've come, we can wed, aye?"

"Aye, I mean, yes. Tomorrow. No, tomorrow is the Fourth of July. The day after. There they are."

"And none too soon."

Meg had refused to marry him until his family arrived. Sending messages to Scotland and making the arrangements for six Grassicks to pack up their home and sail across an ocean made hazardous by the war between England and France and uncomfortable relations with England and America, proved time-consuming and sometimes seemed impossible. But a messenger arrived on horse-back the previous day announcing they would reach Salem County the next day.

That came, and there they were, five brothers and sisters tumbling from a coach, pushing and shoving, shrieking and crying, and looking as if they'd grown a foot apiece.

Colin landed on the ground without use of the steps and raced forward to greet them. All of them at once. He gathered as many into his arms as he could reach and didn't mind that his eyes misted so badly he could scarcely see their faces.

"This country is huge."

"Are we going to live here?"

"Where can we go fishing?"

The questions poured over him, bombarded him, felt like a shower of gifts.

"And have you forgotten your mother, hinnie?" a soft voice asked from close beside him.

"I could never forget you." Colin drew her into the circle of his arms, too. "'Tis glad I am to have you here."

"And you." She stepped back and scanned him from head to toe. "America agrees with you."

"My bride-to-be takes good care of me." Colin glanced over his shoulder and saw Meg poised at the top of the steps, her fingers fluttering like her ribbons. "Will you come to meet them, Meg?"

She headed down the steps and glided over the gravel with the grace of a princess. The children fell silent. The eldest of his brothers, a mere lad of eleven, stared with open admiration. The eldest girl, a woman of five and twenty, tilted her head to one side and pursed her lips then glanced down at her own muslin gown. She didn't need to speak for Colin to guess the comparisons she was making. If he knew his Meg, she would be giving Fiona and the other lasses half her gowns within the hour.

His Meg. The mere thought of that sent joy surging through him, and he stepped forward to take her hand in his. "Meg, let me present you to my mother and the rest of the clan; Fiona, Annabel, Jean, Jock, and Douglas."

"How do you do?" Her voice came out breathy, and her hand shook.

"Do not fash yourself over remembering all of them," Mother said, taking Meg's hand in both of hers. "Sometimes I forget them myself."

"How could you forget such beautiful children?" Meg glanced at Colin. "And you look too young to have a son as ancient as Colin."

Mother laughed. "I see you found yourself a flatterer."

"Oh no, I'm not like that. I'm simply on my best behavior today. I'm so afraid you'll meet me and not want me marrying your son and—"

"Hush, hinnie." Colin touched his finger to her lips. "They'll love you as much as I do soon enough."

"Indeed we will." Mother glanced from one of them to the other. "As long as you love my son and the Lord, you have my blessing."

"Well yes, I do, very much. And—oh, here's Father." She waved to Isaac as he exited the house. "Father, come meet Colin's family. Aren't they beautiful?"

"They are a fine sight to see in my yard." Meg's father descended the steps and held out his hand to Mother.

And as their hands and eyes met, Colin caught the flash of a bird taking flight, the bright yellow plumage of a goldfinch in full summer glory.

THE HEIRESS

Dedication

To Louise, Marylu, Paige, and Ramona, whose input makes my writing and my life so much richer.

Chapter 1

D aire Grassick paced back and forth on the sidewalk in front of the pawnshop. He possessed only one valuable object, and the dealer didn't want to buy it.

"I've got to get home, Lord. Please." The murmured prayer sounded strange to his ears. Weeks, perhaps months, had passed since he last spoke to the Lord. He relied on his own wit and strength—and failed.

Head bowed in shame, he plodded on one more circuit of the pavement, hoping, trying to pray further, that the pawnbroker would change his mind and step outside to hail Daire back into the shop. Doors along the street opened at regular intervals, disgorging or admitting men, women, and children. They talked and laughed and skirted Daire, as though they didn't want to touch him. He supposed he did look a bit odd, a young man in fine, if somewhat rumpled clothes, striding to and fro in front of a door that remained closed, its toys and trinkets obscured behind dusty glass. His own bauble shimmered in his hands, golden glass as delicate as mist, as detailed as a snowflake, too fragile for him to carry about unprotected.

With one last hope that the secondhand shop dealer would see the ornament and step out of his store, Daire leaned against the front window and pulled the cotton wool wrapping from a bag flung over his shoulder. The scent of lilacs rose from the batting, a hint of the perfume his mother kept in the blown glass bottle shaped like a goldfinch, until she gave it to him, as his father's mother had given it to him.

"For your future wife."

The wife he'd been so certain he could win if only he left the farm in Salem County and headed for the city.

Another shudder of shame washed through him, and he shoved a strip of fabric around the bird.

"Don't break it." Two small hands in gray kid gloves curved around the sides of the goldfinch bottle. "It's beautiful."

Daire glanced up at the soft-voiced speaker and caught his breath. The bottle wasn't the only beautiful creation on the sidewalk. Eyes, the purplish blue of the flowers growing by Grandmother's summerhouse, gazed back at him from an oval face with skin so fine it resembled rare porcelain.

"May I look at it?" Without waiting for his reply, she lifted the goldfinch bottle from his hold and held it up to the sunlight. "Oh. The detail is perfect, but you can't see through it."

"Light ruins perfume. That's why it's opaque."

"I didn't know that." She turned and tilted the bottle, drawing out the beak that formed the stopper. Her nostrils flared at the strength of lilac scent rising above the odor of pavement dust and horses. "Is it empty?"

"Momma stopped using this for a perfume bottle a few years ago." Daire shifted. People were staring at them, and he thought their interaction looked unseemly. Yet if he had any chance that this young lady wished to purchase the goldfinch, he mustn't send her away.

"Is it cracked?" Her questions and gazing at the object persisted.

"No. I wouldn't try to sell a cracked perfume bottle." His tone turned indignant, and he took a deep breath to calm himself. "Momma simply chose to use the bottle for an ornament on the mantel in the parlor until she gave it to me for—" He stopped. The young lady didn't need to know about his disastrous betrothal.

"It would surely brighten up our parlor," the young lady murmured. She smiled up at him. "Where did it come from?"

"My grandfather made it." Daire couldn't keep the pride from his voice. "It's nearly fifty years old and the only one like it. It was part of the Great Exhibition at the Crystal Palace in London in '51."

"That's truly amazing." She sounded awed. "You shouldn't sell it, or be standing about with it in the middle of all these people." She held the bauble out to him. "It might get broken."

"I was hoping it would get purchased." Daire glanced at the shop. "But the broker said it's useless. I'm afraid he's right."

"Nothing that beautiful is useless, especially not if your grandfather made it." Wistfulness added smoke to the purple blue of her eyes. "If I owned something so precious, I'd keep it safe."

"Do you want to own it?" If he didn't need the money so desperately, Daire would have given the young lady the ornament right then and there, without knowing her name, without her being his future bride. Stomach knotted like a sail line, he held the goldfinch up to the sunshine as she had. "You can have it for twenty dollars."

"Twenty—" She laughed. "No wonder the broker wouldn't buy it if that's what you expected."

The trill of her mirth made Daire chuckle. "You can't blame a man for trying."

"No, but I can blame a man for dishonesty." She took a step backward. "Good day."

"Wait." Daire shot out one hand and touched the sleeve of her dress. "Why are you saying I'm dishonest?"

She tossed her head, sending maple syrup–colored curls bobbing against her cheeks. "You ask twenty dollars for a piece of glass? However pretty it is, it's not worth that much, so you really have no intention of selling."

"But I do." Daire's cheeks heated despite the coolness of the spring day. "I—need the money to get home. This is all I have other than the clothes on my back."

"I'm sorry." She gazed up at him in silence while a score of people passed them, some staring, others scurrying along and looking straight ahead.

A breeze off the harbor caught at the girl's wide skirt, lifting the ruffled blue fabric to reveal a mended bit of lace edging. Considering they stood outside a pawnshop and no maid accompanied her, Daire figured she must be heading inside to sell something of her own concealed inside her basket.

"But my troubles aren't your concern." With more care than before, Daire began to wrap the goldfinch in its protective cloth. "Maybe another broker or shopkeeper will be interested."

Except he'd tried every place in town since receiving the telegram telling him to get home as quickly as possible.

"I'm interested." She glanced at her mended ruffle. "I've never owned anything so pretty."

Words burned on the tip of Daire's tongue, the notion of telling her she owned something more than pretty and would see it if she only glanced into a mirror. But his days of wooing compliments like that ended with his last failed attempt at love and business.

"I only need enough money to get home," he said instead.

"How much?"

He told her. He expected her to laugh at him again.

Instead, she drew a threadbare silk purse from a pocket in her voluminous skirt and extracted several coins. "My aunt told me to purchase something pretty. This will fit the request."

She held out the money. Silver and one gold piece glimmered against the dull gray of her glove. With great restraint, Daire managed not to snatch the wealth from her and run to the train station.

"If you're certain." He cradled the goldfinch bottle as though it were alive and injured.

"I'm certain." She tilted her head and peered up at him from beneath gold-tipped lashes. "Are you?"

"I—um. . ." He swallowed.

Sun warmed the glass. For a heartbeat, he pictured the ornament forming at the end of his grandfather's blowpipe, the silica still hot from the furnace. The coins glittered before his eyes. The bird clung to his hands.

"I have no choice." He thrust the ornament toward her. "Take it, please. The train leaves in half an hour."

They made the exchange with care, while several passersby gawked at them and the wind, smelling of the Hudson River and smoke from the steamboats, billowed the girl's skirts against his legs. Once the goldfinch left his fingers, he felt as though he'd just sold his soul for thirty pieces of silver.

But it was only a piece of glass. A cunningly designed piece of glass, formed at the hands of a master, and only a bauble for a lady's vanity. Its purpose of gifting a beloved lady had only been for two generations, so ending with him wasn't all that serious.

He slipped the coins into the pocket of his trousers and turned away.

"Thank you." Her tone held awe. "I'll take good care of it."

"Do that." He took several paces then swung back to face her. She stood where he'd left her, her head bowed over the goldfinch, the brim of her hat obscuring her delicate features. "Give it to someone you love."

She glanced up at him and smiled. "I will."

A whistle from the harbor reminded him he needed to hurry to buy his ticket and board a train. He nodded at the girl and ran for the station. In his pocket, the coins jangled like discordant notes on a pianoforte. His bag flopped against his side, as empty as his heart.

"It's only a bauble," he told himself again and again.

In a few hours, he would be home. Reaching his father's bedside on time was worth losing the goldfinch. If Father forgave him for his failures in business and love, for selling the goldfinch instead of giving it to the love of his life, Daire could maybe forgive himself, maybe start again.

~∽~

Susan Morris resisted the urge to stop on her way home and take out the bird to gaze at it one more time. Never in her life, as the fourth daughter, had she owned anything quite so pretty, so unique, so entirely hers. The young man who had sold it to her must have suffered a serious catastrophe to part with something so old and cherished.

His face had been troubled, his emerald green eyes holding a grief she'd only seen at funerals.

No young man with his looks and manners should appear that devastated. Susan wanted to give him every coin in her purse, if a lack of money was all that troubled him. She regretted not presenting him with a higher amount for the goldfinch bottle. But a lifetime of frugality insisted she negotiate for every purchase, even one as frivolous as the glass ornament tucked into her basket along with thread for her to alter one more of her elder sisters' gowns.

Maybe she should have purchased fine fabric instead of the bird. With three older sisters, she had never owned a new gown, and perhaps Aunt Susan Morris had meant her namesake great-niece should use her inheritance to buy pretty clothes made to fit her.

That she could afford to buy fabric and frivolities hadn't sunk into Susan's mind. She knew how much her great-aunt had left her, but she couldn't bring herself to visit the banker, her trustee, and find out if she could spend more than she would normally pay out of her allowance. She remained frugal with her funds the banker had given her—until she saw the stunning ornament glimmering in the hands of an equally striking young man. She couldn't wait to tell her family of her purchase. Surely they would be in as much awe as she was and notice her instead of everything else that distracted them.

"Momma, I bought something pretty today," she rehearsed beneath her breath. "As Aunt Susan Morris told me to in her will. . . ."

Momma would be more interested in the man from whom she'd bought it, since Susan, at twenty-two, hadn't yet found herself a husband. Not quite as bad as Deborah at twenty-four, but she, at least, had a steady beau. Susan didn't have one, and she certainly wouldn't mention her attraction to the young man. He'd been catching a train out of town. Even if he hadn't, he would never find her interesting with her toast-colored hair and funny-colored eyes, too-pale skin even for fashion, and figure so thin she only wore a corset because not doing so was indecent. A man who looked like the one she'd bought the ornament from sought out ladies like her older sisters, who had china blue eyes and golden curls, fine figures and flirtatious demeanors. Susan would be left at home, playing governess to the younger two of her three brothers and whatever nieces and nephews happened to be in the house on any given day.

Thoughts of showing off her prize quickened her footfalls. Her house came into view, where it perched on the corner, a two-story brick building in need of paint on the trim, inside a wooden fence in need of whitewashing. Now that spring had come, the lawn and garden appeared more ragged than her mended ruffle.

Susan shuddered and ducked her head in a vain hope that none of the neighbors would see her enter the gate and recognize her as a member of the Morris family. The rest of the houses on their block sported fresh paint and gleaming fences, trimmed lawns and spruce gardens. One would think the Morrises were poor. Probably people thought they were with their seven children.

Three of those children, boys ranging from nine to sixteen, tossed a ball around the yard, accompanied by shouts of glee for a good catch and jeers when one of them let it drop. Paul, the youngest, called Susan's name. The ball flew in her direction. Remembering her precious burden, she spun around instead of reaching for the ball, and it smacked her on the shoulder.

"You little scamp." Tears of pain stung her eyes. "What did you do that for?"

"You were supposed to catch it." Paul looked stricken.

The other two boys slunk around the corner of the house.

Susan glanced from their retreating forms to Paul then to the sun. "Why aren't you boys in school?"

"No one made us go." Paul retrieved the ball. "You and everyone else left, except for Gran, so we just stayed home to play."

"You wait until Daddy hears of this." Susan frowned at him. "He'll make you regret playing hooky here at home."

"Aw Sue, he won't do nothing." Paul grinned, his bright eyes dancing. "He's too busy writing another poem."

"Is that why he didn't say good morning to me?" Susan sighed. "I won't waste time telling him then. But you'll go to school tomorrow."

"Tomorrow is Saturday." Laughing, Paul scooped up his ball and ran after his older brothers.

"If you don't get an education—" Susan stopped in midcall.

No sense in drawing attention to her brothers' delinquency. From the corner of her eye, she saw two neighbor ladies in their gardens and making no pretense of working on weeding or planting. They were watching the antics of the Morrises yet again.

Wishing she owned a poke bonnet that would hide her features, Susan entered the house through a front door left half open. A few leaves from last autumn had blown in through the gap, and she used the toe of her shoe to shove them over the threshold. They had a maid. Laundry and cooking for the eight Morrises still living in the house kept Bridget too busy for mundane tasks like sweeping. Susan would get the broom later. Right now she wanted to show off her new purchase.

Gran was the only family member home. She sat in her corner of the parlor, sketch pad on her knees, an array of colored chalks in a box beside her. She didn't look up when Susan entered.

"Gran, I bought something pretty today." Susan set the basket on the floor and began to unwrap the goldfinch bottle. "This young man was selling it outside a pawnshop. I was going into the haberdashery to get thread. . . ." She sighed.

The only part of Gran that moved was her hand holding a pencil. It flew across the paper in quick, decisive strokes.

"It's the prettiest thing I've ever owned," Susan murmured. "The young man said it was part of the Great Exhibition in London."

She held the bottle to the light, marveling at the rich golden color of the glass, the detail of wings and feathers. Were it not so delicate and shiny, she could imagine it taking off from her palm. And to think it was nearly fifty years old, had survived all this time for her to see and buy, a bauble good for nothing but the pleasure of its beauty.

Unless she poured perfume into it, of course. The bottle smelled of lilac. Susan thought she would prefer something crisp and clean like lemon.

"If I put this on the windowsill in my room," Susan continued, "the morning sun will make it glow."

"Hmm." Gran tore a sheet off the pad and dropped it onto the floor.

Susan set the goldfinch into its nest of cotton wool and reached for the sketch. It showed her in caricature form, her eyes double normal size, gazing at a giant bug captured between her fingers.

"Ugh." Susan dropped the picture back onto the floor. "Why a bug?"

"It's useless and destined to be smashed." Gran kept sketching. "You'd best tuck it away before the others get home."

"But I want Momma to see it."

"No, child, you don't. She'll never approve. Now run along and get us some lunch. Bridget is busy with the laundry."

"Yes ma'am." Susan tucked the basket behind a chair and headed for the kitchen.

Bridget, as plump as Susan was thin and as dark as the Morrises were fair, stood over the stove, stirring a pot of soup. "It'll be ready soon, Miss Susan. I made the boys hang out the sheets as punishment for not going to school."

"You should have made them go to school." Susan snatched a handful of raisins out of a bowl on the table. "They're going to end up working on the docks if they don't get an education."

"And what's wrong with working on the docks?" Bridget cast Susan a glare. "Me entire family works on the docks, and we're all respectable. Seems to me that eldest brother of yours would prefer that to his sums."

"I'm sorry. I only meant. . ." Susan turned to the table and began slicing bread. "They're supposed to be bankers like Daddy."

"And not one of them likes sitting behind a desk." Bridget banged the spoon against the side of the pot. "But speaking of supposed to dos, missy, you're supposed to be married by now."

"Tell me where I can meet young men, and I'll do so."

She knew the answer before Bridget opened her mouth. "You can go to church."

And hear about a God who noticed her as little as her own father? Susan shook her head but didn't argue. She went to church; she simply took care of the children instead of joining the adults for the service.

"I'll get started on the mending if you don't need my help here." She started to exit the kitchen.

"You can set the table for six in the dining room. Your mother and sisters said to expect them for lunch. I'll feed the children in here."

Susan carried plates and bowls into the dining room. If Momma and the sisters were coming together, they must have been off on one of their charitable projects and planned to do something else that afternoon. She tried to remember what drew their interest this month. India? Yes, that was it. They were sewing clothes for the orphans in India. Susan's sewing had been deemed not good enough. A glance at her badly mended ruffle reminded her they were right.

Bad at sewing and worse at being a Christian, Susan took comfort in knowing she'd done well with her purchase. She recognized beauty when she saw it.

The sound of female voices in the hall drew her out of the dining room, the table half laid, to join her mother and older sisters. As though she were a hat stand, they piled their straw bonnets into her arms and continued their conversation about packing boxes for India.

"We must line them with oilcloth," said Daisy, the eldest. "That will protect them from sea damp."

"That much oilcloth will be expensive," Momma said. "But if we—"

"I bought something special today," Susan broke in. "It was part of the Great Exhibition in London. You know, the Crystal Palace."

Her four relations glanced at her. "For the orphans?" asked Opal, her next to the eldest sister.

"No, for me, as Aunt Morris told me to." Before they could say more, Susan darted into the parlor and retrieved the basket.

Gran held up another sketch. This one showed Momma and Susan's older sisters upside down in a packing crate.

Susan laughed. "Gran, you should make cartoons for a newspaper. People would pay money to have these."

"That would take all the fun out of it." Gran chuckled. "Is lunch ready?"

"Yes. Do you need my help rising?"

The basket with the goldfinch in it slung over one arm, Susan held out her hands to assist Gran to her feet. Arthritis crippled her knees so badly she could scarcely walk, but she refused to use a cane or bath chair, preferring that her youngest granddaughter supported her from room to room. They crept toward the dining room, where the others still chattered about packing crates and shipping costs.

"We need another bazaar to raise money to pay for the shipping costs." Momma pulled out her chair. "Daisy, you ask the blessing."

Daisy prayed over the food that hadn't come from the kitchen yet. They all sat. Clattering of crockery from the kitchen suggested that Bridget would serve soon, so Susan pulled the goldfinch bottle from the basket before Momma and the others resumed their dialogue.

"Look what I bought today." She held the ornament to the light, wishing sunshine came through these windows to show the bird to its best advantage.

Everyone stared at it in silence.

"A young man was holding it up outside the pawnshop, and I just had to have it." Susan's voice squeaked into the stillness. "Aunt Morris said to buy something pretty."

"Aunt Morris never should have entrusted you with her fortune." Opal shook her head. "We all said you'd waste it, and look what you've done."

"Sell it," Momma directed. "It'll help pay for the shipping cost to India."

"I can donate money for that—"

"Sell it," everyone chorused.

"That'll help us get materials to make things for a bazaar to raise more money," piped up Deborah.

"But I've never owned anything. . . ." Susan slumped beneath their china blue stares, joy in her purchase draining from her. "All right. I'll see if I can find someone to buy it."

Her heart a leaden weight in her chest, Susan rose, carried the goldfinch bottle to the mantel, and stuck it behind Daisy's wedding photograph. Out of sight, out of mind—something to forget like the young man from whom she'd made the purchase.

Chapter 2

Halfway up the drive to the Grassick farmhouse, Daire reined in the mount he'd hired in town and sat staring at the array of vehicles crowding the gravel lane. Broughams, landaulets, and buggies lay cheek by jowl from the trees on one side to sweeping pastureland on the other. Horses filled the pasture, a few familiar to Daire as the teams of neighbors. Beyond the vehicles, smoke poured from the kitchen chimney, and the aroma of roasting meat permeated the evening air.

The Grassicks were entertaining what appeared to be most of the county.

"No. No." He slid to the ground then stood with one arm draped over the gelding's withers for support. "No Father, no."

He didn't know if he prayed to Father God, who couldn't be much interested in the grief Daire had brought upon himself, or if he called out to his earthly parent now gone beyond hearing him.

Either way, he feared the answer was, "Yes son, yes."

According to the telegram Daire received, his father lay near death, the victim of a bad-tempered bull, who had gored him and tossed him a dozen feet. Two days later, Daire knew of only one event that accounted for so many vehicles cluttering the drive—a funeral. He was too late to obtain his father's forgiveness.

"If only I had the money. . . ." He leaned his head against the horse's neck, a shudder racing through him.

How he'd finally obtained the means to get home would make the rest of them dislike him.

If the coins he'd received from the pretty young lady wanting to buy something frivolous hadn't all gone to purchasing his way home, he would have climbed astride the hired hack again and ridden away, kept riding until he or the horse collapsed from exhaustion. He didn't know how he could face any of his family, but face them he must.

Feeling as though his boots had turned to millstones around his feet, he trudged around the house to the stable and left the gelding with a youth he didn't recognize. "Treat him well. He may have to travel again soon."

He turned away and scanned the house. A brush against his ankles drew his attention downward. Two black-and-white cats rubbed around his legs, meowing and purring their recognition. He stooped and gave them each a pat and a scratch behind the ears. "Good beasties. You never forget a free bit of fish, do you?"

He glanced toward the kitchen door, where he, too, had obtained many a treat over the years. If he slipped in that way, he might be able to avoid the bulk of the guests and find a member of his family to break the news that he had come home at last.

Too late. Too late. Too late.

The words pounding through him with each heartbeat, he left the cats to their own devices and headed for the kitchen door. Beyond the panels, women talked and laughed and called orders to one another. Mixed with the aroma of roasting meat, cinnamon, cloves, and nutmeg swirled around the door frame like a wreath. Daire's mouth watered. His stomach growled.

A cat meowed at his feet and slipped inside ahead of him.

"Get that animal out of here," a woman shrieked. "I nearly dropped the ham. Who let the—" She glanced at Daire from beneath a ruffled white cap. "No guests in the kitchen. You'll get fed when everyone else does. Go around to the front door."

Daire stared at the strange lady, a cook or housekeeper, judging by her black gown and white apron. He hadn't expected a fatted calf to be killed to welcome him home, not under these circumstances. Neither had he expected to be shooed away.

"Take that cat out of here and go around to the front," the woman directed again. "Please."

Daire glanced around the room for a face he recognized. No one among the three maids and one scullion engaged in various stages of food preparation appeared familiar. They gave him blank stares in return.

"I'm just passing through." He shooed the cat outside then wended his way through the kitchen staff, finally reaching the door leading to the entry hall.

What sounded like a hundred people talked and laughed behind it. The talk didn't surprise him. Grassicks were sociable people. But the laughter seemed odd for such an occasion. Yet maybe not. Father had been full of joy. The only time Daire remembered seeing him sad was when he said good-bye to his eldest son.

Burdened by this last memory of his father, Daire pushed through the swinging door and stepped into the hall. Men in frock coats and bright waistcoats and women in bell-shaped skirts swept past him. Not one looked in his direction, not even his sister. She stood five feet from him chattering and gesturing to one of the apprentices from the glassworks.

Daire leaned against the wall like a fallen portrait. Even if he didn't expect the homecoming welcome of the prodigal son, he also didn't expect no one to notice him in their midst. If he slipped up the steps to his bedchamber, perhaps he could make himself presentable, wash away the travel dust, before he needed to face them, face the truth.

He couldn't find the energy to move. Every drop of blood seemed drained from his limbs.

The kitchen door flew open and smacked him on the shoulder. He jumped and knocked the platter of sliced meat from the maid's hands. Food and crockery smashed against the floorboards. The girl shrieked. Conversations ceased, and footfalls rushed along the hall.

Face hot, Daire dropped to his knees to help gather up the mess. He had everyone's attention now.

Above him, someone gasped. "Daire. Grandma, it's Daire." His sister, Maggie, dropped onto the floor beside him, heedless of meat juice staining her gown, and flung her arms around his neck. "Oh Daire, I thought we'd never see you again when you didn't come to see Daddy. We were so worried. He was so worried." Crying, she buried her face against his shoulder, her high-piled red curls tickling his nose.

"I got here as fast as I could." He stroked Maggie's vibrant hair. "I'm sorry it took me so long." He swallowed against the tightness in his throat. "Too long."

"But not long enough to keep away from my party." The jovial tones of Jock, his youngest brother, rang through the hall. "I can't have everything my way."

Confused, Daire glanced up. "Party? But I thought—" Warmth spreading through him, he glanced at the gathering guests and family.

None wore the somber hues of mourning. Maggie wore green the color of her eyes, the color of all the Grassicks' eyes. Jock's waistcoat sported green and gold stripes, and the stunning young lady beside him glowed in a gown of crimson and gold.

"Are you saying this isn't a—a—" Daire shot to his feet, broken china and ruined meat forgotten. "Father?"

"He's in his room resting as comfortably as possible," Maggie said. "We thought we were going to lose him, but he's on the mend, so we went ahead with Jock's engagement party. But you haven't met Violet yet, have you?"

"No, but please. . ." Daire offered the pretty young lady a smile. "I'm not fit for a celebration. Traveling. . ." He glanced about for a way to extricate himself from the staring family, neighbors, and strangers. "May I see Father?"

Would Father want to see him?

He pressed his hands against his legs to stop himself from dashing up the steps to his father's room. "I came back to see him."

"Aye, and see him you will." Grandpa's voice, still holding its Scots burr after nearly fifty years in America, pushed through the crowd and grasped Daire's hand in both of his. "Now we've three grand things to celebrate."

"Four, if you count the—" Maggie gasped as Jock elbowed her in the ribs.

"Thank you, sir." Daire coughed. "I don't deserve to be celebrated."

"Aye, but you do." Grandpa slipped his still burly arm around Daire's shoulders. "The lost lamb has returned. But he looks tired, so if you'll be excusing us, I'll take him up to his father."

Murmuring and smiling, the crowd made a path clear to the steps. Daire preceded Grandpa up the treads. His leg muscles spasmed as though he were the old man of seventy-eight and not a young one of twenty-five. At the top of the steps, Daire stopped, his gaze fixed on Father's closed door. "Maybe I should change my clothes first."

"Nay, he'll want to see you now." Grandpa laid his hand on Daire's shoulder. "You ken he'll forgive you, lad. Whatever kept you from us, 'tis not too much to forgive."

"Easy to say when failure has never been a part of this family." Daire squared his shoulders and marched toward the door.

Voices murmured on the other side of the panel: Father's distinct, if somewhat weak, and Momma's gentle, loving.

Daire's hand shook on the faceted glass knob. "This is new."

"Aye, 'tis Jock's design."

"It's a handsome piece, as fine as anything I saw in the city."

"It turns well, too." Grandpa nudged Daire. "Try it."

Daire obeyed. The knob twisted with a light touch. The door swung inward to reveal Momma lighting a lamp beside the bed. The flame emphasized her still golden hair and smooth complexion. Propped on pillows against the headboard, Father didn't fare so well. His skin shown pale beneath his normally ruddy complexion, and new threads of silver streaked his dark hair. But the Grassick green eyes still shone brightly.

They widened and blurred at Daire's entrance. "My son, you've returned."

"If you'll have me." Daire managed a smile.

For response, Father held out one hand. The other lay limp and bandaged atop the coverlet.

One arm was enough for Daire. He crossed the carpet in a handful of strides and clasped Father's hand. "I got here as soon as I could."

"You should have come home sooner." Father blinked hard, and his eyes cleared. "I didn't like having to get myself gored just to get you back."

"I'm glad my telegram found you." Momma hugged Daire. "I was afraid you'd moved on, it had been so long since we heard from you. And when you didn't come right away. . ."

"I'm sorry for the delay." Daire released Father's hand and clasped his fingers behind his back. His face heated. "I had difficulty coming up with the money to get here."

There, the truth was out, admission of his failure to succeed on his own. And he'd made the confession in front of more than his parents and grandfather. Voices in the corridor outside the bedroom warned him that his brothers, grandmother, and sister had come to join the family reunion.

Daire wondered if he could simply crawl under the bed and hide. But he'd been running and hiding for six months. He needed to face the consequences of his bad decisions and work out a way to win his way back into worthiness to be a part of this godly and gifted family.

"You should have let us know," Momma said. "We could have arranged for you to get money up there."

Daire swallowed and avoided her eyes. "I didn't have the funds for a telegram."

In the ensuing silence, someone gasped. No one asked him what had happened to the money Father had given him for investments in the city. No one asked him what had happened to his relationship with the young lady whose family had lured him north. They didn't need to. His lack of money and a fiancée told their own tale.

"Then how did you get here?" Maggie asked.

It was the question Daire didn't want to answer.

He kept his gaze on Father. "I had to sell something."

"Like what?" Maggie pressed.

"Let the lad alone." Grandma's voice entered the crowd behind Daire. "He looks tired and hungry. When did you last eat, Daire?"

"Awhile ago." His stomach, empty since he left the city, growled.

"Take him down for a good meal," Momma suggested. "We can talk more later."

"Maybe he'd prefer to change his clothes." Jock chuckled. "He looks a little dusty."

"No, I'm not fit for a party." Daire touched Father's hand again. "And you look tired, sir. If I may come back later?"

"You may return at any time, son." Father smiled. "Whatever you tell me, it doesn't matter now that you're here."

"I wish that were true." Daire compressed his lips. "But thank you."

Heart lighter despite the shame of his past behavior, he turned to leave the bedroom. For the first time, he noticed that Jordan, his quiet second brother, had also joined the family group. He caught Daire's hand and shook it without saying a word but showing support and kindness with that single gesture.

"Daire." Maggie grasped his other arm. "It's terrible you were so badly off. How did it happen? I mean, where's Lucinda and—"

"Later, Maggie," Jordan murmured.

"But—" She sighed and released her hold on Daire. "That's right. You're home, and that's what matters most. Well, bringing the goldfinch home, too, of course."

"I didn't bring it home." Daire spoke quickly to get the moment over with as quickly as possible. "I had to sell it to pay for my fare home."

Silence filled the room, a silence profound enough to make conversation and the clink of silver on glassware below stairs audible through the closed bedroom door. But the glances exchanged between family members spoke volumes—shock, dismay, even anger.

Daire backed against a bedpost as though each look were a blow. "I knew you all would be disappointed. I mean, I know this is an important piece to the family, but its value isn't that high on the market, I learned, and any one of you can make another one."

"Aye lad, we can make another one," Grandfather confirmed. " 'Tis naught more than a bauble after all, whatever the sentiment attached to it. But 'tis what's inside the bottle that matters."

"What's inside?" Daire blinked, trying to push fatigue away. Surely his confusion lay in weariness, not in the fact that what Grandfather said made no sense to him. "The bottle was empty."

"Not precisely." Jock scowled, but at Maggie, not Daire. "Our little sister put something in there the moment it was entrusted to her."

"I didn't know Daire would run off like he did and take the goldfinch with him. I thought it would be the best place for it, like in that story by Mr. Poe—hidden in plain sight."

"You entrusted a family treasure to a tale by a dissolute poet." Jock's voice rose. "Fiction, Mag—"

"Well, Momma entrusted the goldfinch to Daire," Maggie shot back, "and look what he—" She slapped her hand across her mouth. Her eyes filled with tears.

"You can apologize to your mother and your brother later." Father's voice drifted from the bed, weak but in command. "Right now, I suggest you keep your mouth shut before it gets you into more trouble."

"Her lips have more talent for glassblowing than for speaking," Jordan said.

"If you please"—Daire spoke between stiff lips to hold back anger swelling in his chest—"will someone tell me what this is all about, or am I to be indicted by my family without knowing the charges?"

"Nay lad, no one is indicting you." Grandfather slung a burly arm across Daire's shoulders. "You did not ken what wee Maggie had slipped into the bottle, since you do not work at the glasshouse."

Daire stiffened. That comment in itself felt like an indictment. His younger sister worked as a glassblower, though few females did, alongside his grandfather, brothers, and several uncles. He was the only one in his generation who showed no talent for the art. His father hadn't been a glassblower either. He preferred to work the land. And because Daire showed no aptitude for farming, he'd tried his hand at business—and had been swindled.

"And we didn't dare write you about the problem with the goldfinch once you'd gone with it," Momma added.

"In other words, I'm the only member of the family who doesn't know what the difficulty here is." Daire feared a hint of bitterness had crept into his tone, and he swallowed to clear it away. "May I know now?"

"You have to," Jordan said, "so you can retrieve it from the goldfinch."

"Retrieve what?" Daire persisted.

"A formula," Jordan explained.

"For the special crystal we displayed at the Great Exhibition in London seven years ago," Jock added.

"You ken how Queen Victoria was so taken with it?" Grandfather began.

"Taken with you is more like it." Despite her seventy years, Grandmomma's eyes still shimmered amber gold when she was trying not to laugh.

"Aye, well. . ." Grandfather cleared his throat. "She has a liking for the Scots and wanted that crystal for her wee castle at Balmoral."

"But she's broken a piece," Maggie burst out, as though too many words had piled up for her to hold them back. "And I got to help make the parison for the new pieces. But the formula has been such a secret, I wanted to hide it. And we had company arrive unexpectedly one day when I had forgotten to put the formula back in the safe at the glassworks, so I rolled up the paper—it is just a little slip—into a little tube and stuffed it down the neck of the goldfinch."

"And how do you think we'll get it out without breaking the—"

"Tweezers," Maggie interrupted Jock again. "I wouldn't have done it if I thought we'd have to break—"

"And not destroy—"

"Not another word out of either of you until I say so." Once more, Father's voice rose from the bed. "Father, please finish."

"We got word last week that we need to make even more pieces," Grandfather complied. "And we do not wish to depend on anyone's memory for the exact formula, as we all recall it just a wee bit differently."

"And without the formula?" Daire asked, his stomach clenching. "What will happen?"

"We'll be in breach of contract to the Queen of England," Grandfather said, "as we got that order under the condition we would always be able to make replacement pieces for Balmoral."

Daire didn't need to ask what breach of contract with Queen Victoria meant—ruin for the company. And, worse, with the way Jock and Maggie had been speaking to, and now glared at, one another, the loss of the formula because of Maggie's carelessness first and now Daire's further irresponsibility, meant strife within the family, possibly an irreparable rift.

"But you can get the formula back," Jordan said.

"I don't know." Daire felt sick at how his gullibility and pride could so easily ruin his family. "I don't know the name or address of the lady who bought it."

Chapter 3

Susan stared across the mahogany desk at the bank manager. "What do you mean you can't give me more money? Isn't it mine?"

"Yes, Miss Morris, but under the terms of your aunt's will, you can only spend this money on yourself." The banker, at a different financial institution than the one at which Daddy worked, gave her an indulgent smile. "Per her instructions, I've set up accounts for you at dressmakers and hatters and cobblers. You can buy all the pretty clothes you like, and even some jewelry, but you can't spend your money on shipping crates."

"I don't like this." Susan twisted her gloves between her fingers, noticing one finger was about to split at the seam. "I don't want pretty clothes. That is—" She glanced down at her dress, another hand-me-down from Deborah, a blue that matched her sister's eyes but made hers look like sickly lilacs. "One or two would be nice, but the children in India need things more than I do."

"And 10 percent of your quarterly interest payments went to the church." The bank manager took a sheet of paper from a desk drawer. "If you want to specify that the church use the money for mission projects, we can arrange for that for the next payment."

"Which is nearly two months off." Susan sighed. "But let's see to that. The children will just have to wait."

The children would wait even longer for assistance, while she indulged herself with pretty clothes and useless baubles. Momma and her sisters would never approve. They would continue to criticize her for buying the goldfinch bottle. She'd tried to sell it, but no one wanted it or insisted on paying no more than a few pennies for it. So she shoved it behind the wedding picture again and approached the bank manager about giving her enough of her inheritance to pay for packing crates and shipping costs.

"Why was my aunt so insistent I fritter away this money?" Susan demanded.

The banker's smile turned gentle. "She wanted you to be happy, Miss Morris."

"What do you mean? Am I expected to buy happiness?" Tears blurred her eyes. "Was she happy with all her wealth?"

"She was, but she was happy before she obtained her wealth." The manager stood. "I'll draw up that agreement and have you come back to sign it in a day or two. I'm sorry I can't do more for you now in the way of cash, other than your allowance, but do make some purchases of things you want. Tell the store clerks to send the accounts to me."

Susan nodded, rose, and allowed him to escort her through the quiet lobby of the bank. The tellers and customers—all men—gazed at her, a young female alone in a financial institution, being treated like royalty by the manager yet wearing a shabby dress. Her cheeks heated at the attention. It wasn't the sort she wanted.

She wanted Momma's and her sisters' approval. She wanted them to ask her to join in their charity work. Even if she couldn't sew, she could do something useful like play the pianoforte while they worked. Her musical ability wasn't terrible. She could make them cups of tea and serve them Bridget's cookies. But they didn't eat while working for fear of soiling the fabric, and they said the pianoforte music interfered with conversation.

Reluctant to go home to a house empty of everyone except for Gran and Bridget, since she'd gotten the boys off to school that morning, she stopped and made one purchase—new gloves. A hat with frothy pink netting and ribbons caught her eye. The color suited her better than the endless blue from her sisters, so she bought that, too. Then she noticed the darn on her right stocking was giving her a blister on her heel, so she indulged in two pairs of fine lisle hose and delicate lace garters.

Though light, the purchases felt as heavy as the burden Christian carried in *Pilgrim's Progress*. Maybe if she bought gifts for the family, she wouldn't feel so guilty about spending money on herself.

A stationer's shop drew her inside to obtain paper and pastels for Gran and a new notebook for Daddy to write down his poems. Candy for the boys completed her spending. She couldn't work out what Momma or her sisters would like. They preferred doing good works, except for buying the pretty clothes their husbands or Momma insisted they wear. They claimed one could raise more money if one didn't look like it was for oneself.

All the way home, she racked her brain to work out what she could do. By the time they arrived for lunch, she knew what it was.

"I'll watch the children on your nannies' days off," she announced. "That way, Deborah can help you, too."

Four pairs of bright blue eyes stared at her.

"You want to look after all six of our children?" Daisy asked.

"I'm good with the children at church," Susan pointed out. "They scarcely ever cry."

"It would be rather nice," Opal admitted. "Tomorrow?"

Basking in her second sister's approval, Susan nodded with enthusiasm.

Enthusiasm that died as her sisters arrived with their broods. Daisy had presented her husband with three boys, and Opal had three girls. They deposited the horde in the middle of the parlor and swept off to decorate the church hall for someone's wedding. The next one, they all believed, would be Deborah's, though her beau hadn't proposed to her in three years of courtship.

"What have I done?" Susan groaned.

She gazed at the mob of children from ages one to ten and wondered what she'd been thinking. Maybe that a school day would be the nannies' days off and half of the children would be under someone else's care.

"Paul, Roger, Samuel?" she called to her brothers, wherever they were. "Come help."

Paul and Roger, the two younger boys, thundered down the steps. Paul was the same age as his eldest nephew, but Roger, at fourteen, balked at playing nursemaid.

"Sam isn't here," Roger said, referring to their eldest brother.

"Where is he?"

Susan hadn't noticed him leaving the house that morning.

"Off to the harbor to watch the ships." Roger's lavender gaze tracked to the street. "He wouldn't let me come with him, but I want to go. There's a ship in from the Far East, and I want to see what kinds of things it brought back."

"You're too young to go to the docks alone."

So was Sam. Someone should have stopped him, but evidently no one had even noticed him leaving.

Sighing, she began to bribe Roger to help corral their nieces and nephews into the back garden and form up games. If running about in the May sunshine for an hour wouldn't fatigue them enough for naps, Susan knew it would make her drop where she stood. After a quarter hour, her hair had come loose from its chignon and hung down her back like a schoolgirl's. Grass stains marred her blue muslin skirt from several little ones tackling her to the ground, and a tumble into a rosebush had left a long, red scratch on her hand. But she was laughing.

Until she noticed she wasn't alone in the yard with the children.

Poised on the balls of his feet, as though he intended to race off at a moment's notice, a man stood between a lilac bush and a rose trellis. The former shot fragrant blossoms in haphazard profusion halfway across the walk, and the latter threatened to topple over and bury the unwary in a profusion of thorns. They shaded the man's features, but something about the lift of his strong chin and set of his broad shoulders struck a chord of familiarity in Susan.

Extricating herself from the clutches of her youngest nephew, she took a step forward. The man removed his hat, and a bubble of joy warmed her heart as much as the sun warmed her skin. He was familiar. Not even in the shadow of overgrown flowers could she mistake those brilliant green eyes and the perfect wave of the thick black hair, his high-bridged nose, and broad cheekbones.

The handsome young man with the goldfinch bottle had found her.

⁓

Daire Grassick stared at the scene before him. When no one had answered his knock, the cacophony of children at play had drawn him around the house to the back garden. There, amid a jumble of children, he caught sight of one female who appeared older than the rest, though her stained gown and disordered hair were more appropriate for a schoolgirl half the young woman's age. Yet the rich golden brown of the waist-length tresses and glowing countenance assured him she was indeed the young woman who had been so happy to purchase his family treasure, more of a bona fide treasure than its sentimental value. When she drew nearer, her footsteps hesitant, her hands held before her as though warding off danger, he saw her eyes. Wisteria, Grandma had told him the flowers were called when he asked her about the purplish blue blossoms. Wisteria.

Behind her, the children ceased their play and stood or sprawled in a tableau of curious faces, except for a toddler, who stared at a laden lilac bush. Only the young lady moved. Miss Susan Morris, according to the shop girl who'd put a name to his description. She glided across the overly long grass, a torn flounce trailing behind like a train, and that shining expression of joy he'd noticed upon their previous meeting lit her delicate features even in the shade.

"Miss Morris?" Daire stepped forward to greet her.

His arm brushed the lilac bush, sending a cascade of blossoms into the air. They clung to his coat, his trousers, his hair.

"I'm Susan Morris, yes." She swept her hand over his sleeve, removing the petals and sending a jolt like a lightning streak through him.

He swallowed against a sudden dryness in his mouth. "I'm Daire Grassick."

"I'm pleased to meet you." She held out her hand. She wore no gloves as she had in town, and he noticed the long, red scratches and a hint of roughness around the short nails, as though she was not a lady of leisure. "That is, we have already met, in a way, have we not?"

"Yes." Daire shook her hand and experienced that tingle again, an awareness of being near a pretty girl and something more he couldn't put a name to. "I've had a time of it finding you."

"I expect you did." She gestured to the children, who resumed their game with a ball and much yelling. "I don't look like the rest of my family, except for my father. But that's neither here nor there. You found me." Her voice turned breathy, like someone who'd been running, and her eyes glowed. "How may I— *Oomph.*"

The ball sailed past the toddler and struck Miss Morris between the shoulder blades. She staggered forward, caught her toe in the hem of her bedraggled skirt, and fell against him.

Daire caught her in his arms and held her a little too tightly to ensure she regained her balance. She pushed her hands to his chest so hard he swayed back against the rose trellis. Thorns caught in his coat and held him captive. The children shrieked with laughter. Miss Morris groaned and flung her hands over her face. Behind her, one of the older boys raced up, grabbed the ball, and streaked back to his companions, still laughing, apparently unconcerned whether the young lady had been injured or was in danger from this stranger who embraced her so improperly, whatever his good intentions.

"Are you hurt?" Daire asked for lack of anything better to say.

She shook her head, sending maple-syrup hair cascading around her shoulders.

"Then perhaps you could assist me."

"You?" She peeked at him from over her fingertips. "Oh no." Her eyes widened and she dropped her hands. Her cheeks had turned the color of a sunset. "I am so sorry. Here, don't move."

"I won't," Daire drawled.

"No no, you don't want to ruin your beautiful coat." She scurried around to his side and rested one hand on his shoulder. "This will take awhile."

"Perhaps one of the boys should do this."

He didn't like her standing so close to him. He'd made enough mistakes in the past six months. He didn't need to add to his bad behavior with attraction to a female about whom he knew almost nothing. He did know, however, that the shabby appearance of the girl and her house didn't make sense when he considered how much she'd paid for the goldfinch bottle. Surely this family couldn't be as poor as they looked.

"They're young," Daire remarked on the children, "but—"

"Don't move." She increased the pressure on his shoulder. "This trellis is about to fall."

"If one of those boys could hold it up, it might be safer."

"No, it wouldn't." She glanced toward the throng of youngsters.

They showed no interest in him or Miss Morris. All but the littlest one seemed engaged in a game of tag. The baby had curled up in a patch of sunlight near the lilac bush and fallen asleep like a kitten.

"They're all too young to be responsible." She made a hissing sound through her lips, and the wooden latticework frame for the climbing roses rattled. "I could get my eldest brother—he's sixteen. But Roger, one of my other brothers, said Sam's gone down to the docks. I don't know that for sure. We haven't seen him today."

"You haven't seen one of your brothers?" He couldn't keep the astonishment from his voice. "How is that possible?"

She laughed. "The rest of them are here. But it's all right. I can manage—ah, it's not as bad as I feared. Just one—ouch."

"Miss Morris?" He tried to twist his head around so he could see what she was doing.

"No, don't move. It's just a scratch, I think. There." She released her hold on him and glanced at him through a curtain of hair. "You're free now."

He wasn't free with those pretty wisteria blue eyes gazing at him through a waterfall of burnished gold. He felt bound to her by an invisible thread.

He stiffened and cleared his throat. He must get his mission accomplished and return home before temptation took over his life again. Six months was more than enough to abandon his family and his Christian faith. It brought nothing but disaster, and this girl was the culmination of that time. He must put it behind him, and that meant putting her behind him, however pretty she was. However sweet and soft her voice. However fragrant her hair and—

He stepped away from her. "I apologize for barging in on your day, Miss

Morris. With your permission, I'll conclude my business quickly and be on my way."

"Business?" A shadow darkened her eyes, and she turned her head so she looked past his shoulder to the boisterous crowd of children. "Of course. I assume this has something to do with the goldfinch bottle? I mean, it's the only business transaction we have shared."

"Yes." Daire tried not to cringe at the sudden coolness of her tone. "I wish to buy it back."

With money his father had given him. More money than he'd received to go out on his own, making him worse than the prodigal; this wasn't even part of his inheritance. Of course, what that bottle held *was* part of his inheritance.

"You do?" She spun toward the house on her heel, sending the ends of her hair flying out like fringe on a shawl. "Come inside, and I'll wrap it up for you."

Daire hastened to catch up with her. "You don't want to negotiate a price for it?"

"Why would I do that?" She rounded the front of the house and trotted up a set of porch steps in need of a good sweeping. "We both know how much I paid you for it. So I expect that's what you'll give me in—"

The grate of ripping fabric interrupted her.

Daire glanced down to see he'd stepped on her torn ruffle. His face flamed. If he didn't want the goldfinch bottle back so badly, he would have raced for the front gate and fled back to the train station to ride as far away from this slapdash female as he could before he committed some other faux pas beyond holding her in his arms, even if it was just to catch her from falling, making her scratch herself extricating him from rose thorns, and now ripping the bottom of her dress far enough to reveal a grass-stained underskirt.

"Perhaps I'd better wait out here," he murmured. "Since there's no one at home inside the house."

"There isn't?" She glanced back at him, her cheeks the color of June roses. "Gran surely is. But she wouldn't come to the door. Walking is too difficult for her." She glanced down. "If you remove your foot, we can go into the parlor while I get the goldfinch."

"Uh, yes, my apologies." Sure his entire body was blushing, Daire backed up.

He expected her to secure the ruffle somehow. Instead, she grasped it in both hands and yanked until it tore off the rest of the way.

"I never liked this dress anyway," she said, head down. "Blue makes my eyes a funny color."

Her eyes a funny color? If she meant not boring plain blue, then she was right. But surely she didn't believe something was wrong with the color of her eyes.

Daire shook his head. "Miss Morris..." He stopped. He mustn't give a female compliments. She belonged to this city, where he'd met nothing but trouble. He wouldn't encourage friendliness. He just wanted away, back to the safety of home, formula in hand to stop the bickering between Jock and Maggie and the rest of the family silently siding with Jock.

"Come inside." The bundle of fabric in her hand, she opened the front door.

The cool interior of the house displayed as much neglect as the outside. Dust gathered on picture frames. The molding needed paint. And the room most people would save for their guest parlor looked more like a nursery than a chamber for receiving visitors. Lead soldiers lay scattered about the floor like casualties of a battle, a half-full glass of milk stood spoiling on the mantel, and an old lady perched on a straight-backed chair with sheets of paper scattered around her like molting feathers.

No wonder she was eager to have him buy back the goldfinch. No doubt she had spent money on it she shouldn't have and was eager to get it back so they could hire a maid or maybe buy a new dress.

"Gran," she called to the elderly woman, "we have company."

"How lovely." The woman never looked up from her sketch. "He might find a clear seat. And if you bring him some lemonade, will you get me some, too?"

Daire nearly gasped in shock that she didn't want to know his name, what he was doing there, what connection brought him to their house. That the children seemed uninterested in his arrival wasn't surprising, but a grandmother should show more curiosity or concern for the company her granddaughter kept.

"Would you like some?" Miss Morris asked him.

Afraid if he said no the grandmother wouldn't get hers, Daire nodded. "Thank you. It is a warm day."

He hoped the glass was clean.

"I'll fetch that then get your bottle." She darted from the room, pausing in the doorway long enough to say, "Do sit down."

Not certain which chair to clear of baby paraphernalia, books, or dolls, Daire remained standing. "Would you like me to pick up your drawings for you, ma'am?"

"That would be kind of you, young man." Gran dropped another sketch onto the pile.

Daire stooped to gather them up. He didn't know what he expected to see, a still life, perhaps, or nice landscapes, the sort of thing females usually drew. But this lady was a caricature artist. When he saw that the most recent one to land on the floor showed him cringing away from an oversized glass of liquid, he laughed aloud.

She might look indifferent hunched over her tablet, but she was an observant old lady.

"Nice." She gave him an approving glance from beneath bushy eyebrows. "Susan is the only one in my family who ever laughs at my drawings."

"I come from a family of artists." Daire stacked the drawings into a neat heap. "I know talent when I see it."

144

"Wish one of my grandchildren got it. The older girls don't care for drawing, and Susan couldn't draw flies."

Daire flinched at the unkindness. He sought for something complimentary to say about her to counteract the bluntness. "She's very pretty."

"Not compared to her sisters. Susan is our ugly duckling who isn't going to turn into a swan."

Daire was glad to hear footfalls heading toward the parlor so he didn't have to respond. Contradicting his elders wasn't proper, but he wanted to. Susan might not be likely to turn into a graceful swan, but ugly she was not.

She strode into the room bearing two glasses of lemonade. The glasses looked clean, and their fine quality surprised him considering the shabbiness of the house.

He rose and went to greet her. "Thank you." The beverage was cool, and his mouth watered for the refreshment of sweetened lemon. "But none for you?"

"I'll serve some to the children after you go." She swept past him, her face so stony he wondered if she'd overheard her grandmother's remark. "Here you go, Gran. Where's Bridget?"

Gran shrugged. "Haven't seen her all day. But take care of this fine young man and just ignore me."

"We could never ignore you, Gran." The smile she gave her grandmother lit her face to loveliness an artist like the old lady should notice. "I think Mr. Grassick will only be here for a few more minutes." She glanced around then darted over to a chair and gathered up the pile of magazines sliding across the cushion. "Do sit down, sir. I'll fetch the goldfinch."

Before Daire could respond with something polite, she dashed off through the doorway again. Her footfalls rang on the floorboards then died abruptly, likely reaching a rug. Silence stretched for several moments, broken only by the distant yelling of the children and the nearby scratch of the grandmother's pencil.

A sudden crash sent Daire charging from the parlor, lemonade splashing out of his glass and over his hand. "Miss Morris?"

"In here." Her voice sounded odd, thick.

Daire's heart stopped. He envisioned her standing amid shards of broken yellow glass. Instead, he found her standing in the dining room amid broken glass, but it was clear, having covered the faces of several photographs that now lay with the glass at her feet.

"It's gone," she wailed, flinging her hands up to her face. "I am so sorry, Mr. Grassick, but your goldfinch bottle is missing."

145

Chapter 4

Anger flashed in Daire Grassick's green eyes—anger and something more Susan couldn't name. Disgust perhaps, or disdain. And no wonder. She'd lost a valuable piece of artwork and hadn't noticed it was gone. With the chaos of the house, no wonder she hadn't missed the object.

Looking away from the aversion tightening his face, Susan became aware of her bedraggled dress, her loose hair, and the bread crumbs on the dining room carpet. No one took care of the house as well as they should, including her. Their only maid came and went as she pleased, her two eldest sisters—Daisy and Opal—were off to their own homes, and Momma and Deborah simply didn't care about housework. That left the household management to Susan, and she wasn't any better with it than she was with sewing or drawing.

Maybe the bank manager would let her use her inheritance to hire a maid. Not that that would help now with the pictures on the floor where she'd knocked them in her frantic search for the goldfinch bottle. She heard the children coming toward the back door and realized she needed to clean up the glass immediately before the younger ones crawled into it and hurt themselves.

"I'm so sorry." She dropped to her knees and began to gather up the shards of broken glass.

At least she could pay to replace the damaged frames.

"I set it on the mantel here the day I got it from you," she babbled on. "No one liked it. They thought I spent my money foolishly. So I stuck it behind the frame. Then I tried to sell it on Monday, but no one wanted to buy it. And I put it back here. I know I put it back here."

"Are you certain you didn't put it on a different mantel?" Mr. Grassick's voice, though quiet, resonated through the room like a bell tolling her doom. "Like the parlor or a sitting room or even the kitchen?"

"No, not the kitchen. I'm as bad at cooking as I am—" She realized she was talking too much and concentrated for a few moments on clearing the carpet of glass and a number of other things that shouldn't have been there, such as the silver button from a child's coat and a teaspoon, and dumping them into her lap.

"Perhaps I should go look in the parlor," Mr. Grassick suggested. "The mantel looked. . .crowded."

"All right. Do so." Susan popped her finger in her mouth to remove a fleck of blood obtained from a sliver of glass. "Gran won't care. But be careful of the toys on the floor."

"Don't you all have a nursery?" His tone held more curiosity than censure—she hoped.

She glanced up at him through the curtain of her hair. "We do, but it's at the top of the house and is only large enough for two children. So when all of them are here like today, we keep them downstairs."

"And the weather is too fine to confine them to an upstairs room." Daire started to smile.

A shriek from the backyard wiped the smile from his face and sent her surging to her feet. Glass sprinkled from her skirt in a ringing cascade. "I should never have left them alone." She charged for the door.

The kitchen door stood open, allowing a swarm of flies to swoop around the room, but giving her clear access to the garden and children. All of them huddled near the lilac bushes, some talking, some standing still, their thumbs in their mouths, others crying.

One bellowed the loudest, a toddler from the sound of it. Unable to see who it was for certain, through the phalanx of children, Susan began picking them up and moving them aside.

"Let me by." She reached Paul and dropped a hand onto his shoulder. "Who is it?"

"Jerald." Paul stepped aside.

The youngest of the nephews huddled on the ground, a bunch of lilacs crushed in one hand, his face as red as beet juice. Wails loud enough to awaken a sleeping Australian in Sydney pierced the afternoon.

Resisting the urge to cover her ears, Susan dropped to her knees beside the baby and tried to pick him up. If possible, he bellowed louder.

"What happened?" she shouted to the others.

"We don't know," Paul yelled back. "We were playing tag, and he started crying."

"I suppose no one was watching him?" The flash of anger sharpening her voice lent more to distress with herself than with the children's neglect.

She'd been so thrilled to have Daire Grassick find her, she hadn't thought for a moment about leaving the children unattended. They were in the yard after all, and Roger was old enough to be responsible.

Except Roger wasn't there.

"Where's your brother?" she asked Paul.

He shrugged, his thin shoulder feeling like a bag of bones beneath her hand. "He said he was going to get some water and never came back."

"He didn't come into the house."

So she'd lost track of Sam and Roger, all for Daire Grassick, who had only gone to the trouble of tracking her down so he could get his silly bottle back. And she couldn't return it to him, let alone sell it back to him. It was missing, and now she had a mess in the dining room, a ruined dress, and most definitely nothing that would make the handsome stranger want to stay a moment longer than it took to find his artwork.

With a bit of regret that she couldn't curl up on the grass and wail like her nephew, Susan tried to pick him up again. When she touched his chubby little arm, his scream sounded as though she had just taken a hacksaw to the limb. She recoiled and did start to cry, though silently.

"Let me." A shadow fell across the scene; then Daire Grassick crouched beside her.

He reached for Jerald, too, but made no attempt to pick him up. Instead, he cradled the boy's hand in his own long, strong fingers and touched the exposed skin just above the baby's wrist. With a flick of his fingers, he seemed to stop the yowling. At least Jerald stopped crying more than a few hiccuping sobs, and he gazed up at Mr. Grassick with huge blue eyes full of wonder.

Susan gazed at him with wonder, too. "What did you do?"

Behind them, the children murmured in tones of awe.

Mr. Grassick shrugged. "I removed a stinger from a bee." He gestured to the flowering bushes. "They're all over, and he was clutching some of the flowers."

"And you found the stinger." Susan reached for her nephew.

This time Jerald flung himself into her arms and clung to her neck.

"Come into the house, baby." She tried to stand, but her feet caught in the ragged hem of her skirt, and she swayed to one side, bumping into a nearby child.

A scene of her and the children tumbling onto the grass like pieces in a game of dominoes flashed through her mind. But she couldn't catch herself without dropping Jerald.

Daire Grassick snatched the baby from her. With her hands free, she caught her balance and scrambled to her feet. She didn't want to look at the gentleman, afraid of what his expression would be this time.

A snort drew her attention anyway. Instead of the disgust she expected, his eyes danced and his lips twitched. He coughed, but one of the children giggled, then another and another, and Daire Grassick joined in the hilarity.

Wordlessly, Susan took Jerald from his arms and headed for the house. Now that Mr. Grassick had removed the stinger, she saw the spot on the baby's wrist, a small red welt.

"We'll take care of that in a minute, sweetie." She held her nephew close. "Then I'll give you a cracker."

"We're hungry, too," the other children chorused.

"I expect you are." Susan gave Daire Grassick a helpless glance. "I'm sorry, but I should feed the children."

"I'll help. It might get done faster." His dry tone matched the resigned expression on his face.

Susan winced. "I'm sorry. Why don't you let me know where you're staying? I'll look for the goldfinch after I get the little ones down for a nap. When I find it, I'll get word to you."

148

"I'll help," he repeated. To Susan's astonishment, he hefted the other two toddlers into his arms and headed for the kitchen door.

"Come along, everyone." Susan addressed the rest of the throng. "There's bread and cheese and lemonade."

And Mr. Grassick was going to regret the day she'd caught sight of the goldfinch bottle from the corner of her eye and stopped to admire it. But he'd seemed desperate to sell it then. Now he looked anything but desperate. His clothes were impeccable, his hair was trimmed with a perfect crest above the brow, and he smelled of sandalwood. If he'd been poor a week ago, his fortunes had changed drastically.

Maybe he was a gambler. The notion made Susan shudder with revulsion. Then annoyance tightened her lips. If so, his disdain of their chaotic house was unfounded.

If he wasn't, the shabbiness of the house was embarrassing, not to mention her appearance. She must look like a ragamuffin from the street instead of a young lady who had inherited a small fortune from her great-aunt. Probably most of his dislike of his surroundings focused on her.

Susan wanted to crawl under the kitchen table or maybe even descend to the cellar until Mr. Grassick left. She knew after they located the goldfinch bottle she would never see him again, so her appearance didn't matter. But if this was an example of how matters would lie if she managed to have another gentleman call on her, whatever the reason, she would end up an old maid. She couldn't think how her brothers-in-law had wanted to marry into such a haphazard family. But then, her sisters were intelligent and beautiful, talented and friendly—everything Susan was not. At least she wasn't in comparison to them.

Unable to hide away with all the children to feed and half of them to put down for a rest, Susan entered the kitchen and set about slicing bread from an array of loaves someone had either baked or purchased. Daire Grassick joined her at the worktable and commenced slicing off hunks of cheese to lay atop the bread. Paul, bless him, distributed the food to the rest of the group then poured lemonade. At last, the noise settled down as everyone ate. Susan's stomach growled, but she wasn't about to take a bite in front of Mr. Grassick. She feared she would end up with bread crumbs down her front and cheese smeared on her upper lip.

"Would you like something to eat?" she asked him.

"No, thank you. I'd rather get on with things." He glanced at the mantel. It jutted out over the stove, since they had installed that instead of using the fireplace for cooking many years earlier. Pots and pans rested atop the mantel, along with a spoon that belonged with the dirty dishes.

Susan snatched it up and dumped it into the sink with the plates from someone else's meal. "It's not there, either."

"No." Mr. Grassick looked at the table and children devouring their food. "Should we take something to your grandmother?"

"Oh, goodness, yes." Susan closed her eyes.

How could she have forgotten Gran?

"She'll just want some butter on her bread, no cheese."

"I want butter and no cheese," one of the children cried.

"You eat your cheese." Susan gave the girl a stern glance. "You need to grow big and strong. Paul, will you take this to Gran?"

"I'll take it." Daire took the plate from her hands. "And I'll look for the goldfinch in there."

"Thank you. That's very kind of you." Susan picked a piece of soggy bread off the floor from beneath Jerald's chair. "No, baby, you have to eat this. See, I gave you only the soft part."

When she straightened, Daire had vanished. She wanted to pray that he would find his family treasure. But prayers were for people like her mother and sisters, those who did good work and God noticed. Still, she found her heart yearning for a good outcome. Otherwise—

"It's not here." Daire returned bearing a glass of milk that reeked from all the way across the room.

"Ugh." Susan wrinkled her nose and wished she could hide her face. "Who left that there?"

"It hardly matters." Daire carried the glass outside then returned in a moment to set the empty glass with the other dishes. "I didn't see the goldfinch anywhere."

"I am so sorry."

More than he could know. She was used to her chaotic home, and although she didn't like it, it was familiar. Seen through the eyes of this well-dressed and handsome stranger, the flaws of her surroundings glared like sunlight on tin. The sooner he left, the sooner she could stop being ashamed of her house and family—and herself.

"Let me get the babies down for a nap, and I'll look elsewhere." She glanced around at the older children who would never agree to resting. "Will you play outside again or take a book and read? I need you all to be a bit quieter so the babies will sleep. Mr. Grassick, maybe you should come back later or—or meet us at church tomorrow."

Daire said nothing but looked pensive. The older children filed around him like a stream dividing around a rock. They slipped outside, as she knew they would do, rather than read with Gran in the parlor.

"Mr. Grassick?" Susan arched one brow at him.

He shook his head. "Perhaps that would be best. Which church?"

She told him.

"I'll be there. No need to see me out." Unsmiling, he left the kitchen. His footfalls echoed on the hall floor; then the front door clicked shut.

Although the children had begun another boisterous game outside and the two youngest toddlers were beginning to whimper from fatigue, the house felt empty, barren of light.

Heart heavy, Susan picked up Jerald and called to the others to follow her into her mother's sitting room across from the big parlor. It was cool and dark with its curtains drawn. She laid them in a row atop a blanket on the rug and covered them with another blanket.

"Sleep well, little ones." She gave them each a kiss. "I'll stay here until you fall asleep."

She spent the next moments searching for the goldfinch. She couldn't imagine any way in which the object could have found its way into the sitting room, but she didn't know how it would have gotten out of the dining room either.

Thinking of the dining room, she recalled her need to clear away the broken glass. Once the babies slept, she left for the other room. But the glass had been cleared away and the frames set back on the mantel. The sound of clattering dishes in the kitchen drew her into that chamber. Bridget stood at the sink, scrubbing plates.

"Where were you?" Susan asked.

"Shopping." Bridget pointed her sharp chin toward the table.

Several baskets of foodstuffs sat there.

"We were out of nearly everything," she continued. "I don't know when anyone did the shopping last, and with all these little ones here, there wasn't a thing left."

"No, I suppose I should have gone. Momma's so busy." Susan began to unpack the baskets. "Bridget, have you seen that goldfinch bottle I brought home last Friday?"

"Not today." Bridget dipped water from the reservoir behind the stove and poured it over the dishes to rinse them. "Weren't it on the mantel in the dining room?"

"Yes, behind Daisy's wedding picture." Susan stood gazing at a wrapped sugar loaf as though she could read an answer on the plain white paper. "But it's not there now."

"I've got to get supper started, or I'd be helping you." Bridget took the loaf from Susan and carried it to the pantry. "I'll watch the children so you can look."

"Thank you."

Susan looked. She hunted behind cushions and under chairs, atop mantels and inside cupboards. The only room she didn't inspect was the one belonging to her parents. She wouldn't invade their privacy. Besides that, she couldn't believe they would have it there. Momma had been so opposed to the bottle, she wouldn't want it around as a reminder of her daughter's foolishness, and Daddy had never known of its existence.

At last Susan admitted defeat. She stood in the middle of the parlor, watching Gran draw something more detailed than usual, and wondered how she would face Mr. Daire Grassick in the morning. The temptation to remain with the little ones and send a message through one of her brothers ran high. But she'd agreed to meet him there; thus, for the first time in at least a year, perhaps longer if she thought about the exact date, she was going to attend an actual church service—because of Daire Grassick.

Chapter 5

Daire heaved a sigh of relief as the front gate banged shut behind him. Although children played in other gardens and a chorus of birds serenaded the neighborhood from the tops of tall oaks and maples lining the street, compared to the Morris household, the rest of the world lay in stillness and neat array.

As Daire traversed the brick walkway back to the harbor and his hotel, he thanked God for his own home. Nothing ever went missing in his family until the secret formula for the Balmoral crystal. Grandma and Momma kept the household running as smoothly as Grandpa and his brother ran the glassworks, and Father, the farm. He'd mislaid himself for a while, but no more. His family wanted him back, and as soon as he returned the goldfinch and formula to the household from which he'd taken it, he would rejoin them and start to make himself useful.

But he would never achieve his goal if he depended on Susan Morris.

At the end of the block, he glanced back at her home. He doubted they were poor. The house was large amid other fine homes that signaled prosperity. Yet everything appeared neglected, including Susan herself.

Thought of the bedraggled young woman, apparently overwhelmed by too many children to look after and his arrival, sent his heart twisting with pity, frustration, or attraction, or perhaps all three. Her care for her grandmother and children, whatever their relationship to her—brothers and sisters or nieces and nephews—struck a chord of approval inside Daire, to whom his family had once again become all important. Her prettiness beneath the bedraggled hair and gown added to her appeal for him. And that jolt when she'd brushed the lilac petals from his sleeve—

"No, not again." He spoke aloud to make the words more important, more definite.

A passerby glanced in his direction then ducked his head and hastened past.

Daire grinned. Living in the country most of his life, where he often saw no one on his long walks or afternoons fishing, he'd gotten used to giving himself an audible talking-to without worrying what others thought. There in Hudson City, he'd broken himself of the habit, but a few days back in Salem County had changed all that. He'd spent hours walking through the fields and woods, absorbing the peace and serenity of his surroundings and the joy of knowing he had a fine home and loving family to return to.

Until he went back into the parlor and saw the empty place on the mantel beneath Grandma's portrait, where Momma had set the goldfinch bottle when he was a child, declaring it was too special to the family to reside on her dressing table and hold perfume for her alone to enjoy.

"It's yours to give to your bride, Daire," she had told him. "Until then, it will sit here."

He'd taken it, believing he had found that bride—though his parents didn't approve—believing his future lay in the city, away from glass and farmland, neither of which had been his vocation. Her father was a customer of the glassworks. She came with him on a buying visit. One glance at her raven-haired beauty, and he'd believed every word she said about falling for him at first sight, about wanting a future together, about her faith in God.

"Stop thinking of that time." Daire paused to rest his hand on a streetlamp, welcoming its solidity, its steadiness. He let the cool metal anchor him in place like thoughts of his family.

He must go straight, not turn right toward Lucinda's house. His feet had taken him there so often, doing so now seemed natural, welcome. He wouldn't face an evening alone in the city. She would greet him with her warmth and smiles.

"I knew you'd come back," she would say as she had the first time he returned. "Daddy will be overjoyed to see you."

Daddy, with his questionable business practices; Daddy, who used his daughter to reel Daire into joining the Grassick name to the enterprise of luring young men into jobs out west, promising them riches in no time and good conditions in the meantime. He'd succeeded at first. Daire so wanted to make a fortune on his own, he invested all the money his father had given him for a stake in his future. Then, when Daire realized the business was dishonest, that the young men ended up working backbreaking labor for little food and low wages, he couldn't get the money back.

"Only if you stay," Lucinda told him. "That's what Daddy says."

He hadn't stayed, but when hunger took over because of his lack of income, he had returned to the temptation of Lucinda's adoration and beauty and constant searching after another form of revelry. With Lucinda came another future stake in the form of her dowry. He could have her, start his life anew, pay Father back—if he didn't think about the source of the money.

He'd thought about the source and grew weary of her flirtations. He'd thought of what his family had instilled in him as right and wrong and chose hunger once more until his pride in refusing to go home penniless compelled him to sell the goldfinch and the precious formula inside.

He hadn't chosen Susan as the person to whom he should sell it. She had approached him. Yet he couldn't help feeling as though he should have been wiser, started walking home, found a ride on a farm cart, even if it took him days to reach home—anything but sell the goldfinch to a lady who was careless with the possessions of others.

No, that wasn't fair to Susan. The goldfinch belonged to her. She had paid him well for the bauble. But she hadn't cared for it as a Grassick would.

Lucinda had been the same the one time he showed it to her. She made a careless remark about it being pretty then handed it back to him with such inattention she nearly dropped it on the maple floorboards, where it would have smashed to bits if Daire hadn't caught it.

Lucinda—careless with possessions, careless with hearts.

With evening falling on the city, others like her began to surround Daire. They spilled onto the sidewalks in their finery, girls too young to be out on their own and young men with faces already hardened by the world. Daire wanted to escape from the temptation of the city. He'd fallen back into it easily the first time and wasn't convinced his new resolve to remain worthy of his family's forgiveness would prove strong enough for him not to wish to mask his shame with noise and flirtations and. . .

He started walking again, his footfalls firm and determined to take him to his hotel. He would dine in his room and compose a letter for his family. Tomorrow he would meet Susan at her church, which was good. He didn't want to set foot inside the house again. The tumult reminded him too much of his life for the past six months. And he didn't like the guilt that had squeezed his insides at every turn. He needed order and answers, a sense that everything lay in its place, from his purpose in the world to his relationship with God.

Tomorrow all would be well and he could return home. Without doubt, Miss Susan Morris would have found the goldfinch by then. The house was chaotic, but surely no object the size of the perfume bottle would vanish completely, even in that mess.

~

Susan could never face Daire Grassick at church or anywhere else without the goldfinch bottle. She couldn't imagine why it was so important to him now, when a week ago he'd been anxious to get rid of it. But maybe his family had been upset with him over selling the family piece. He certainly looked distressed that the bottle was missing.

Its absence from the places she expected it to be distressed Susan. It emphasized the chaos of her home. How embarrassing to have him see such disarray. Finding his trinket would make up for him seeing her and her family at their worst.

As the children trickled inside, weary from play and seeking more food, she began to question them. "Have any of you seen a pretty yellow bird statue?" She glanced from the three eldest to the younger ones. "It's really a perfume bottle but stands about six inches high—"

"That silly thing you bought off some stranger?" Paul asked.

"Yes, have you seen it?" Susan leaned toward him, eager to have an answer.

"I saw it when Momma was showing it to Father and saying how silly you are," Paul said. "She wants you to support her missions not spend your money on toys."

"And she's right." Susan bit her lower lip and glanced at the other children.

No, none of them would know anything. They weren't tall enough to reach the mantel, though Opal's daughters were old enough to move a chair, stand on it, and reach anything on the shelf.

"I'll have to ask Momma when she gets home."

She paced to the parlor, where Gran sat reading instead of drawing. A pile of sketches lay on the floor beside her. Susan stooped to gather them up and glance through them. Several depicted children playing in a garden. Since Gran couldn't see the back lawn from her chair, Susan presumed Gran had drawn from imagination what she thought her grandchildren and great-grandchildren looked like playing outside.

"They're not nearly that gentle." Susan smiled at Gran. "Show the boys knocking one another down, and you have it."

"I like to think of them being kind to one another." Paper crackled as Gran turned the page of her book. "None of my great-grandchildren are mean."

"No, there's no meanness in them." Susan turned over another sheet. "This is precious."

Since Gran could see through the doorway to the sitting room, this must have come from observation. It showed three little heads poking from a blanket like puppets in a Punch and Judy show popping their heads up above a curtain.

Gran shrugged. "They're best when they're sleeping."

"That's—oh my." Susan caught her breath.

The next sketch in the pile showed Daire Grassick gazing at her. Rather than the contempt Susan believed he felt toward her, his dreamy eyes and half smile depicted wonder, as though. . . As though. . .

"As though he likes me." Susan felt warm all over, like when she drank a cup of hot chocolate.

"He's noticed you." Gran turned another page. "He didn't like me saying you're not pretty—that's for certain." She chuckled.

Susan winced in reaction to Gran saying she wasn't pretty. Yet if Daire Grassick didn't like it, he must think she was. And one of Gran's observant sketches said he'd noticed her, noticed her as a lady, not a flibbertigibbet.

Buoyed into further action on his behalf, Susan made another search of the house for the goldfinch. Not until she came up empty-handed did she think that, when she found it, he would be off to his family again. If they couldn't find it, he would likely be off to his family anyway, and he would think less of her.

Susan was under no legal obligation to give or sell the goldfinch back to Daire Grassick, but she wanted to. She needed to have the purchase off her conscience. If the bottle was so important to him, he should have it at all costs. Once it was gone, if Daire Grassick vanished from her life, too, she would still be free to pursue a purpose for her life other than spending the inheritance her great-aunt had given her to catch herself a husband. She needed something special to take to a husband besides money so she knew he loved her first.

Daire Grassick would never love a female for money. He would prefer beauty and grace and poise and talent.

Could one buy poise and talent?

Susan pondered this notion as she rejoined the children. She was glad her sisters' children had spent the day with her. Opal and Daisy would have to come home with Momma and Deborah to collect the young ones, and Susan could ask them about the bottle then.

Father returned home first. Susan broke off in the middle of helping one of the girls put a new dress on her doll and ran up the steps after Father before he disappeared into his room.

"Have you seen that goldfinch bottle I bought last week?" she asked between gasps for air.

"Goldfinch bottle?" He gave her a befuddled look from his lavender blue eyes so like her own. "What is a goldfinch bottle?"

"It's a glass ornament, a perfume bottle, in the shape of a goldfinch taking off in flight. I bought it from Daire Grassick last week."

"Grassick." Father's face grew pensive. "Why do I know that name?"

"I don't know. I've never heard it before." She turned away. "But I really want to find that bottle again so I can get my money back."

"A goldfinch, you say?"

"Yes, a bottle shaped like one." Susan managed to keep the impatience from her tone, as the familiar gleam brightened her father's eyes.

He was starting to compose a new poem.

"Fascinating." Father closed his eyes. "Sounds like a work of art."

"It is. Please. Have you seen it?"

"No, I haven't, but I'm sure I know the name Grassick. Tell me more about the bottle. It sounds interesting. Goldfinches are beautiful in the summer when their plumage changes color. Was this bottle yellow?"

"Yes, though more amber and made opaque to protect the perfume, except it was empty when I bought it. But surely you saw it." She grasped his arm. "It was on the mantel in the dining room."

"Nothing but wedding pictures on that mantel. Used to be a painting there before the girls insisted they needed photographs." He grimaced. "No poetry in those stiff poses." He patted her hand. "And that reminds me. Thank you for the notebooks. That's the sort of thing to be buying, not some bottle shaped like a bird."

"I know it was foolish of me." Susan removed her hand from his arm and clutched her fingers together behind her back. "I saw it and had the money and. . ."

The man holding it had caught her attention as much as the ornament had.

"Never you mind, Father. I want to sell it back to the young man I bought it from, but I can't find it."

157

"Not surprising you've misplaced something. I lost a book of my poems last night."

"Oh no, do you need me to help you find it?"

"No, child, thank you." He smiled, making his eyes go dreamy. "I found it inside my Bible. Just shows reading your Bible every day is good for you." Chuckling as though he'd made a great joke, he patted her cheek and slipped into the suite of rooms he shared with Momma.

Stabbed with guilt that her Bible lay collecting dust on her bedside table, Susan returned to the children playing in the parlor. Silence on the other side of the door sent the hairs on the back of her neck rising as though brushed by a frosty hand. No way should a room holding Gran and more than half a dozen children be that quiet.

Heart thumping like a fleeing rabbit, she pushed open the door and shrieked. A red substance like blood covered the face of nearly every child and the hands of most. Red also appeared on cushions and the carpet beside an overturned jar of raspberry preserves that hadn't been set down properly.

"Where did you get that?" Relief sharpened her tone.

"The look on your face." Gran's rusty laugh scraped through the room. "Did you think someone was stabbed?"

"Several of them." Heart still running away inside her chest, Susan skewered Paul. "Did Bridget get that down for you?"

"We wanted something sweet, and Bridget and you weren't around." He looked sullen. "I tried to spread it on bread, but it was too watery, so we just got spoons."

"Then I suggest you go get a bucket of water and several rags." Susan glanced at the rug. "And Bridget with some soda."

Paul jumped to his feet and raced for the door. The instant the clatter of his footfalls diminished, Susan understood the reason for his haste to obey her.

Momma and the sisters were coming up the front walk.

Susan groaned. "I shouldn't have left them alone for even a minute."

The first time that day she'd left the children unattended, Jerald had gotten stung by a bee. This second time, clothes, cushions, and carpet had likely gotten ruined. And all for the same reason.

Susan wished she could run away for the day like the two eldest of her brothers had. But she stood to face the women in her family. She had forgotten about her own bedraggled appearance until they swept into the parlor on a wave of floral scents and rustling skirts and all four of them stopped to goggle at her.

"What happened to your hair?" Deborah asked.

"And your dress?" Opal added. "I liked that dress. What did you do to ruin it?"

"It's a long story." Susan took a deep breath. "We have a bit of a mess with the children—"

Opal spotted her offspring and exclaimed in horror at the same time Momma cried out over the carpet.

"How did this happen?" Momma demanded of Susan.

"I was talking to Father. . . ." She shook her head. "It has to do with that goldfinch bottle I bought. Have any of you seen it?"

They stared at her.

"The children, you, and this room are a mess," Momma said, her lips tight, "and you're asking about that bit of frivolity you wasted your money on?"

"None of this would have happened if the goldfinch was where I left it." Afraid her response sounded disrespectful, she bowed her head. "The young man I bought it from found me and wanted to buy it back, but I can't find it anywhere. Mr. Grassick and I were looking for it when Jerald got stung—"

With a wail of horror, Daisy swooped down on her baby and scooped him up, raspberry jam and all. Momma tapped her fan against her chin, murmuring, "Grassick," as though she, too, thought she should know the name. Then Paul and Bridget returned with buckets of water, soap, rags, and soda, and the cleanup process began.

An hour later, with the parlor damp but fairly clean, perhaps cleaner than it had been before, and the children bundled off to their homes, Susan found time to mend her own appearance. She finished changing her gown and pinning up her hair in time to join Momma, Deborah, and Daddy for dinner. From the cacophony in the kitchen, the older boys had returned home and decided to eat in there, as usual.

Once she sat across from Momma at one end of the long dining table, Susan wished she could dine with Bridget supervising the meal instead of Momma. She and Daddy cast disapproving glances in Susan's direction but said little directly to her. Susan picked at her food and said nothing. The conversation revolved around Deborah and her plans to go with her longtime beau, Gerrit Vandervoort, to a hymn-singing at church that night.

"It'll be the last time I let him court me if he doesn't propose on the way home." Deborah pouted. "He's been courting me for three years, so no other man at church will court me, but he won't ask me to marry him either."

"He hasn't asked my permission to make you an offer," Father admitted.

"Then you're right not to court him." Momma nodded. "Don't even let him sit near us in church tomorrow. Let everyone know you've jilted him instead of the other way around."

"Oh, indeed I shall." Deborah's blue eyes gleamed.

Susan pitied Gerrit. He didn't have a chance, and maybe he shouldn't. He wasn't being fair to Deborah, staking a claim on her but never offering marriage. And maybe if Deborah were safely wed and out of the house, Momma would notice Susan was unmarried and without so much as a beau.

Thoughts of courting and beaux led Susan back to Daire Grassick and the goldfinch bottle. She racked her brain to figure out where the goldfinch could have gone. She determined to find it. Until she did, she couldn't justify the disasters of the day or redeem her poor decision in purchasing the object in the first place. Once she had her money back, she would find something to spend it on that would give her a purpose in her life, a way to make her family happy with, if not proud of, her.

When Deborah came home later, still without an engagement, she gained everyone's attention by bursting into tears the instant the front door closed behind her. "He brought his stepmother's younger sister along with his little sister." Her wails were loud enough for Gerrit to hear them from his house three blocks away. "She's only eighteen and so very pretty."

"No one's prettier than you," Susan said with all sincerity.

"Nell is." Deborah yanked the hat from her head and tossed it onto the table. "Her hat was brand-new, and I've worn this at least three times."

"You're frugal with your allowance." Momma hugged Deborah so she had a shoulder to cry on. "You care more for those less fortunate than frivolities." Momma shot Susan a glare.

"You can wear my new hat tomorrow," Susan offered.

It wasn't generous of her; she could buy a new one in a minute.

Deborah stopped crying long enough to smile at Susan. "That's very sweet of you, Sue, but that shade of pink is too dark for my coloring."

"Then I'll get you a new hat on Monday." Susan knew just the one.

"Silly of Aunt Susan to give you her money." Father shook his head. "If Deborah had a fortune like that, Gerrit would marry her."

"Then I wouldn't want him." Deborah straightened and wiped her eyes. "If he can't take me in an old hat and without a fortune, then I'll let everyone know I'm not spoken for."

Back straight, she marched upstairs.

Neither parent looked happy.

They weren't any happier the next morning than the night before. Deborah's eyes were red rimmed and Susan spent so much time locating, then needing to iron a gown that matched her new hat, that she ended up running downstairs and out the front door as the others were leaving the gate.

"You should have been there already to help with the children," Momma said.

"I'm not helping with the children this morning." Susan twisted her gloved hands in the cords of her reticule. "Mr. Grassick is meeting me at the church to learn if I found his goldfinch bottle."

"Mr. Grassick?" Momma and Daddy both gave Susan their full attention.

"Is he related to the Grassick Glassworks?" Daddy asked. "I remembered where I heard the name."

"I—I don't know." Susan stumbled over a bit of rough pavement. "I've never heard of the glassworks."

"You drink out of tumblers they make nearly every meal," Momma said. "They—Paul, Roger, don't run ahead of us."

The boys slowed but remained a dozen yards ahead.

Momma drew her brows together for a moment then continued. "They've been making glass down in Salem County for over fifty years. Very successful."

"They had a display at the Great Exhibition in London seven years ago," Deborah added. "Now they make glass for the queen."

"Then I wonder why he would have had to sell a piece of glass to get enough money to get home," Susan mused aloud.

"The city has many ways to steal money from the unwary." Daddy gave Susan a pointed glance.

She winced. "Yes, I know. I shouldn't have bought it. But I'm puzzled. Why would one little piece of glass be so important to him if his family makes glass?"

"Whatever the reason," Momma said, "we need to get it back to him as soon as possible. You said he was meeting us here?" Her gaze traveled across the lawn of the church, where several people gathered beneath the spreading branches of an oak to shade themselves from the late spring sunshine.

One man stood on the church steps engaged in conversation with the pastor. At the sight of his tall, broad frame, Susan felt as though her insides had turned the consistency of the badly set jelly on the parlor rug. She had nothing to tell him. She'd questioned every member of her family, and none had known a bit of the goldfinch's whereabouts. Perhaps she should ask them again, take the children aside one by one to see if maybe one of them had taken the trinket and now feared the consequences of their action.

She glanced around, letting her gaze gather the scattered members of her family. They were all there—her two eldest sisters, their husbands, and their children. Momma and Daddy and Deborah with her, as well as—

She stopped so abruptly her hoops swayed as though a high wind blew across the lawn. "Momma, Daddy, where's Sam?"

Momma halted. "What do you mean where's Sam? He's—" The crease between her brows appeared again, and she turned to Daddy. "Have you seen Sam this morning?"

"I haven't seen him since yesterday morning," Father admitted. "Ask the boys."

As discreetly as possible in a crowd, Momma called Roger and Paul to her side and asked about Sam. They shrugged in response.

"He was around yesterday morning," Paul said. "I know, because he was talking about playing some game where you hit the ball with sticks like cricket but more fun."

"I saw him on Market Street yesterday afternoon," Roger said. "We'd been down to the docks to see a clipper from China; then we had an ice cream and I came home. He said he'd be along later."

"Maybe he went to Opal's or Daisy's." Noting that Daire had spotted her and was headed her way, Susan hastened to catch up with her sisters and ask about their eldest brother, sixteen-year-old Sam. By the time she reached Opal, Daire had caught up with her.

"Did you lose something else?" he asked, one dark brow arched, the corners of his mouth twitching.

Susan wanted to snap that this was no joke. But she merely nodded and gave a brief explanation. "No one has seen our brother Samuel since yesterday afternoon. We all thought he was with someone else. But no one's seen him."

"I see." His lips stopped twitching. His eyes narrowed, intensifying the brilliant green. "The goldfinch bottle and your brother have both gone missing from your household without anyone noticing for at least a day. Very peculiar."

"Yes, it's—" Susan stopped as his words sunk in. Understanding of the meaning behind his words knotted her stomach, and she grew aware of the staring faces, the lull in the conversations around them. Nonetheless, she had to ask him what he suggested, just to make certain. "Are you hinting that my brother stole the goldfinch?"

Chapter 6

Daire thought he should shrivel under Susan's glare. Although their looks were vastly different, Daire recognized his sister Maggie in Susan's fierce expression, her challenging demand to know if he was maligning a member of her family. Maggie was like that—defending every one of them whether they deserved it or not. And gazing into Susan's lovely wisteria-colored eyes, he felt something inside him give way, a thrilling twist in the middle like swooping over rapids on a raft.

"I'm sorry." He took her hand in both of his and applied just a bit of pressure. "I guess that didn't come out well."

Falling for another city female wouldn't come out well either, and for that he was sorrier than making an accusation against one of the Morris clan.

"Of course Mr. Grassick wouldn't mean anything so rude as to accuse Samuel of theft." A middle-aged beauty smiled up at him. "You are Daire Grassick, are you not?"

"Yes ma'am." Daire released Susan's hand.

"This is my mother, Mrs. Morris," Susan said. Her face was flushed, her eyes veiled behind their gold-tipped lashes. "And this is the rest of them." She gestured to the growing crowd, all the sisters looking like their mother, the two brothers and Susan taking after the father. "Except for the eldest boy, Samuel. He's. . .missing, like your goldfinch."

"It's your goldfinch, Miss Morris." Daire still cringed at having so much as hinted at an accusation against a young man he didn't even know. "You purchased it from me quite honestly."

"And a foolish waste of her money it was." Mrs. Morris shook her head and bestowed an indulgent glance on her youngest daughter. "But I suppose we should send some people out to hunt for Samuel. He's probably sound asleep in his bed. William, Marcus?" She directed her attention to her two sons-in-law. "Will you go see if you can find Samuel? If he's not in bed, he'll be playing ball in the park."

"How old is your brother?" Daire asked Susan in an undertone.

"Sixteen." She drew her brows together over her tip-tilted nose. "He's usually more responsible about his disappearances."

"He's done this before?" Daire couldn't keep the astonishment from his voice. "And no one sees that he is with the family?"

"Someone always thinks he's with someone else." Susan looked from her sisters' husbands to her parents, to her younger brothers, and finally to Deborah, who couldn't take her eyes off Daire, before giving him a sidelong glance. "You've seen my house. You can understand how one of us could go missing. One time I—" She snapped her teeth together, biting off her words, as her cheeks turned a darker pink than the ribbons on her bonnet. "Samuel can take care of himself."

"In the city at sixteen?" Daire clamped his own teeth against saying more.

He knew better. The world offered too many temptations for young men on their own, and the city magnified them by having all the lures so close together.

"I'll be happy to go looking for him," Daire finished instead.

"That's so kind of you to offer." Mrs. Morris turned back to him and touched his arm. "My sons-in-law will find him. They always have in the past. And we'll find your trinket, too. Right now, it's time for the service. Susan, take your father's arm."

"Maybe I should help look for Sam, too," Susan murmured.

"Nonsense." Mrs. Morris laughed. "Why ever would you skip services for something the men can do better, when we have a guest? You will be our guest, will you not, Mr. Grassick? We all have dinner together after church, and you're more than welcome."

"Thank you." He glanced at Susan for a clue as to why her family was so friendly to him.

Another sister, Deborah, caught his eye instead and smiled. He nodded then turned toward Susan.

She kept her face averted just enough that the brim of her rather fetching hat hid her expression, and she drew back into the throng of her family, edging to the outskirts with the married siblings and their offspring.

"I'd like to hear more about this goldfinch object." Miss Deborah Morris fell into step beside Daire as the lot of them headed for the church doors. "I've seen other *objets d'art* of the Grassick Glassworks, but never a goldfinch."

Understanding dawned. He wasn't really a stranger. At least his family name was familiar to Susan's parents and at least one sibling. They knew the Grassick Glassworks and thus probably something of the family, which included him, an excellent catch for their unmarried daughters.

"The goldfinch is special," Daire answered Miss Deborah. "I should never have sold it."

If he'd known what lay inside, he'd never have taken it. No, Maggie shouldn't have left the formula inside the goldfinch, but his need to impress Lucinda had done the damage.

Lucinda's face flashed across his mind's eye. He shouldn't have been without money. Until he'd refused to work further with her father, he'd been a good catch for her, too. Her father had brought her to Salem County deliberately to meet him. Lucinda's family had appeared just as qualified for an alliance—prosperous and warm. Daire ignored his father's warnings about their lack of adherence to their spiritual lives. Church, to Lucinda, was for socializing and for business connections for her father.

In his brief talk with the pastor before the Morrises arrived, Daire discovered a man of deep convictions who expected his congregation came to grow in their relationship with the Lord, not show off their newest gowns or walking sticks. That lay in the Morrises' favor. Coupled with a family so careless with their possessions that a missing son didn't raise alarm, however, Daire didn't think they were a family with whom he would like to ally himself.

"Is there a story behind this goldfinch?" Mrs. Morris asked. "It seems an odd object to be so valuable to the family."

"Yes, I agree that it's odd." Daire smiled over memory of the story often told in the family. "It was my grandfather's betrothal gift to my grandmother in 1809. Grandfather won't allow any more of them to be made in our glasshouse."

"A betrothal gift." Miss Deborah fairly cooed. "So sweet and romantic." She gave him a melting glance from beneath the brim of her flower-bedecked hat.

Across the porch, a man of about his own age glared at him with a sharpness that should have sliced the buttons off Daire's coat then gave Deborah the same look. The message was clear—the other man didn't like Deborah with Daire.

Deborah stepped a bit closer to him, her hand curving around his forearm. "How did you manage to find our little house to buy back your trinket?"

"I asked around the shops with Miss Susan's description until I found someone who knew where she lived."

Daire couldn't even see where Susan was at that moment between Morrises, hats, and the scowling man.

"I never imagined she wouldn't still have it," he added.

If they hadn't reached the door of the church at that moment, he would have made a hasty exit. But exiting meant giving up hope of finding the goldfinch, and that meant returning home empty-handed. Going home empty-handed once had been bad enough. Now that he knew the consequences of doing so, he wouldn't do so again. He couldn't watch his family ruined.

He endured the second youngest Morris daughter's attention, the glowers from the stranger, and numerous curious glances until they reached the sanctuary. The Morrises took up three pews because of the large number of children and the ladies' voluminous skirts. Daire found himself wedged between two pairs of hoops—Deborah's and Susan's. All through the service, which was truly excellent, he found himself watching Susan instead of paying as much attention to the sermon as he should have been. She kept her gaze either toward the pastor or choir or down at her hymnal or Bible. He didn't catch so much as a sidelong glance from her. She seemed intent on the service, singing softly but in a voice as pure and sweet as he would expect an angel's to sound. Around them, the other Morrises sang in a less tuneful manner. Music, apparently, was not a talent the Morrises shared with Susan.

Once the sermon began, she sat twisting her hands in her lap so hard he expected the seams of her gloves to split open. Once he caught the toe of her shoe tapping against the floor. Several times she glanced to the pastor then toward the window.

Daire wondered if she disliked the message. It was good, solid teaching but not convicting to a person whose heart was right with the Lord. Of course, hers might not be.

Or perhaps she was simply distressed about her brother. He would be. He wouldn't sit still in a service not knowing where a member of his family had gone. He knew his family had been praying for him over the last six months and hadn't come after him because he'd insisted on being on his own, and they understood dragging him back would accomplish nothing for the stubborn and wayward heart. But he was a man of five and twenty. Samuel was a boy of sixteen, far too young to be on his own for a day.

Daire wanted to take Susan's hand and leave the church so they could begin the hunt. Foolishness. The family knew their own. The boy was merely playing or sleeping. They should have noticed he was gone, and maybe this was a lesson to them to take more care in the future.

"What man of you," the pastor read from the fifteenth chapter of Luke, "having an hundred sheep, if he lose one of them, doth not leave the ninety and nine in the wilderness, and go after that which is lost, until he find it? And when he hath found it, he layeth it on his shoulders, rejoicing. And when he cometh home, he calleth together his friends and neighbours, saying unto them, Rejoice with me; for I have found my sheep which was lost. I say unto you, that likewise joy shall be in heaven over one sinner that repenteth, more than over ninety and nine just persons, which need no repentance."

Daire smiled, taking comfort in the words. He was the lost sheep who had gotten home. His family had rejoiced. They would rejoice again when he got back to Salem County. But he couldn't feel redeemed yet. He'd let them down and must make sure he deserved to go back with his soul spotless once more. Finding the precious formula would accomplish that.

Beside him, Susan shifted and twisted her hands and glanced toward the stained-glass window. She, at least, seemed concerned about her brother, another lost sheep.

Daire's smile faded, and he prayed for the young man. He prayed that Sam hadn't taken the heirloom. Daire didn't care about the legal implications of the figurine; he simply wanted it back. Needed it back. And her brother having stolen something would hurt Susan.

The idea of Susan being hurt by anyone twisted his heart, and he cut off that thought and focused on the sermon. He needed to hear all he could about redemption.

At last they stood and sang the last hymn. Susan's voice rose pure and sweet, and a glowing peace settled over her face as she sang, "Jesus, lover of my soul, let me to Thy bosom fly, While the nearer waters roll. . ."

Listening to her instead of singing himself, Daire glanced at her and experienced that wild-ride-through-the-rapids feeling in his middle. He hated to be rude, since he had accepted an invitation to dinner with the Morrises, but he needed to get away from Susan. Yet how could he expect to get the formula back if he did? People so careless with a living being wouldn't care much about an inanimate object they didn't even like.

The hymn ended. The pastor blessed the congregation and sent them on their way. Though he knew how the action would look to the assembly, he turned to Susan and offered her his arm out of the building. Behind him, he thought he heard Miss Deborah huff out a sigh of displeasure.

"I expect you're a bit worried about your brother," he said.

"I am." She nodded, sending a curl bobbing against her cheek and the flower petals on her hat fluttering. "He's never been gone this long. I'm terribly afraid—" She tilted up her head and looked directly into his eyes, hers nearly violet with emotion. "I'm terribly afraid you're right and he did take the goldfinch."

"But why would he do that?" Aware of everyone headed for the front door, Daire paused in the vestibule and edged into the aisle. "I spoke in haste, but with some thought, I can't imagine what a young man would want with such a trinket."

"To sell." Susan's fingers lay as light as thistledown on his arm, and she held herself farther away from him than even hoops necessitated.

"But neither of us did well trying to sell it. Why would he think he could?" He resisted the urge to cover her hand with his and draw her nearer—so they could talk more freely in the crowd, of course, nothing more.

Already they drew curious glances and a few knowing smiles or raised eyebrows. Miss Deborah started toward them. Mrs. Morris headed her off. Daire couldn't hear their conversation, but the looks cast in Susan's and his direction told him what the subject was.

"Sam might not know he can't sell it," Susan said. "He only knows I paid a lot of money for it, not that I couldn't sell it to anyone. And you sold it to me. Maybe if people around here knew about the Grassick Glassworks like Daddy does, they would find your goldfinch more valuable."

"Let's hope not." Daire led Susan out of the church in the wake of her substantial family.

At the door, the two brothers-in-law who'd gone hunting for Samuel waited without the youth. Their faces were grim.

"We didn't find him," one of the men announced. "He wasn't at home and he wasn't in the park."

"The lads in the park say they haven't seen him in a week," the other spouse added.

Susan's fingers tightened on Daire's arm, and a low moan emerged from her throat.

His heart twisted, and he touched her hand with his. "He can't have gotten very far since yesterday."

Yet even as he spoke, Daire reminded himself about just how much trouble a young man could get into in the city. Certain establishments flashed through his head, the bittersweet aroma, the raucous noise, the illusion of pleasure.

"Is he prone to disappearing?" he asked.

"Not like this." A stricken look contorted Susan's features. "I mean, he hates school and wants to go off on an adventure instead of to the university, but surely he wouldn't just pick up and run off."

"He might."

Daire pictured himself at sixteen, restless, no good at glassmaking, not interested in farming. . . .

"Shall we go back to your house and organize the search?" Daire suggested.

Now gathered around him, the Morrises looked at him as though he were some sort of miracle worker.

"That would be such a blessing," Mr. Morris said. "We're not good at organization. But if you are, we welcome your aid."

He led the way down the church steps. The rest of the Morris family and others followed. Susan still held Daire's arm, and as they reached the main sidewalk, Deborah fell into step on his other side.

"You're very kind to help us, Mr. Grassick." Deborah spoke in a sweetly modulated tone. "I mean, we're really strangers to you, nothing more."

"He wants his goldfinch back." Susan's voice was sweeter than Deborah's, but her words sounded a little cynical, and he could do nothing to counter her claim.

"But that's what I mean." Deborah touched his arm. "If you hadn't bought it, he wouldn't have to bother with our ramshackle ways."

"If Miss Susan hadn't bought it, I might not have been able to find out who else had." Daire spoke the words to be polite, but once said, he realized they were true. "This way, I have a better idea where it could be."

"When we find Sam?" Susan's fingers flexed on his arm; then she released him.

Daire glanced at her, took in her set face, and wished he could assure her that her brother hadn't taken the object. Any number of people could have walked through their house without anyone knowing. But Sam Morris likely knew how much his sister had paid for the goldfinch, a lot of money to some, not enough to get a young man far unless. . .

But Sam wouldn't be in the sorts of places where Heath, Lucinda's father, lured the unwary and eager, Daire hoped. Those places, that scene, preyed on the young men who didn't have homes or families.

Minutes later, the entire Morris clan, minus one son, as well as several men and women from the church, gathered in the Morrises' back garden. Daire counted the men. Eighteen.

In moments, the eighteen men set out to various areas of the city. The ladies entered the house to prepare food and simply be near the Morris females as a comfort. Daire set out for the front gate alone. His destination was the harbor, a place much like the one he had sought as a young man, a youth like Samuel Morris, to find adventure. The one brother, Roger, had mentioned something about a clipper returned from China.

The front gate swung shut behind him with a clatter. Footfalls followed, the gate clanged again, and more heels clicked along the pavement. Daire paused, glanced back, and sighed.

"Mr. Grassick?" A gentle voice sounded behind him. A gentler hand touched his arm.

"Miss Morris?" He glanced down at Susan. "What is it?"

She tucked her hand into the crook of his elbow. "I'm coming with you."

"You can't." His response shot out with finality. "I'm—"

"Susan." Miss Deborah called from the front steps as she surged toward them on a froth of sky blue ruffles and lace. "You should be in the backyard helping with the children."

Susan's hand tightened on Daire's arm, but her face remained serene. "Opal and Daisy are here, along with a half dozen other ladies. They don't need me, but Mr. Grassick does." She cast him a pleading glance from beneath her gold-tipped lashes. "You don't know the city well."

"You didn't hear him giving everyone directions, did you?" Deborah reached the gate, laughing. "It sounded to me as though he knows it better than you." She tilted her head and gave him a coquettish smile. "But not better than I do. I do charitable work in some of the. . .less desirable areas, and we may need to look for Sam there if he's decided to get himself lost. I think I should go with you."

"I don't think either of you ladies should go with me." Daire touched Susan's hand on his arm. He intended to remove her fingers from his sleeve but found himself clasping her hand instead. "I'm going places that are inappropriate for a lady."

"I don't care." Susan tightened her hold on his arm. "I need to be useful. I won't be anything if I stay here." Her purplish blue eyes met and held his. Her chin set with determination. "No one will even miss me."

"Nor me." Deborah blinked rapidly several times as though clearing a speck from her eye, although a brightness to the blue suggested perhaps she was trying not to cry. "Gerrit didn't even come to help us look for Sam."

He wished he could disagree with the ladies on the notion that no one would miss them, but he feared both spoke the truth. The grandmother might. He spied her through the front window, nodding to something a befeathered matron was saying. She glanced out the window and nodded, as though she approved of her granddaughters vying for his attention.

"Miss Deborah, Miss Susan, please don't be foolish." Looking at their resolute faces, he felt his resolve become as wobbly as Deborah's chin. "These places I'm going if your brother isn't at the harbor could be dangerous."

"Then you shouldn't go alone, either." Deborah pushed through the gate and joined Daire and Susan on the sidewalk.

"But if you want to. . ." Susan released his arm and stepped back a foot. "If you don't let us go with you, I'll simply follow."

"I don't think your parents would like that." He made one last attempt to stop them.

Susan grimaced. "I wouldn't be so certain about that."

Remembering how Mrs. Morris had fawned over him—Mr. Morris, too, for that matter—Daire understood what she meant. Still, he glanced back toward the house in hopes of seeing someone he could employ to hold the ladies back. No one came into view, no one imploring them to return. In fact, the grandmother grinned and turned her back on the window.

He heaved a sigh and gave them a brisk nod. "All right, but stick close to my side and do exactly what I say."

Chapter 7

Susan frowned at her sister. Flirting a bit with Daire to make Gerrit jealous, Susan understood. It seemed to have worked, too, judging from the way he'd glowered at Daire in church. But Gerrit wasn't even there to see Deborah take Daire's other arm, nor hear her thank him profusely for allowing her to accompany him.

"I doubt you'll be thanking me in an hour or two." Daire's mouth set in a grim line. "Nor will your parents be pleased you two are with me."

"They'll thank both of us if we find our brother."

"All three of us," Deborah said. Then she launched into a line of prattle Susan doubted Daire would find interesting. "I think I've been in every part of this city. Momma and my sisters and I do a great deal of sewing for the less fortunate. My elder sisters, that is. Susan isn't good at sewing, so she stays home to see to things there."

Nicely put in her place.

Susan turned her face away from Daire and her sister and tried not to listen to Deborah go on and on about all her good works for orphans at home and now in India. Daire interspersed an occasional question, enough to keep Deborah chattering, and Susan said nothing. She trotted along at Daire's side, her heels clicking in rhythm with his and Deborah's, her skirt rustling. Few people moved about in the middle of a Sunday afternoon. Those who did smiled at the trio, the gentlemen lifting their hats.

Then the pavement grew less evenly distributed. Sidewalks turned into missing patches of brick, as though someone had hauled them away for building. The houses grew closer together until no more than a narrow passageway ran between buildings, and front doors opened directly onto the walkway. Men and women sat on the stoops, and dusty children played around them. Then the homes and people grew scarcer. Structures grew larger and taller. The aromas of spices and coffee, rope, and tar permeated the air, and the whistle of boat horns sounded through the towering building canyons.

"This isn't the harbor, is it?" Susan spoke up for the first time since leaving home.

Daire and Deborah paused to stare at her.

Her cheeks grew warmer than the mild spring day warranted. "I hear the boats and can smell the river, but it's never looked like this when we've gone anywhere by water."

"This is the warehouse area," Daire explained. "You probably took pleasure

171

boats and left from the passenger side."

"Yes, of course." Susan ducked her head and wished she'd kept her mouth shut.

"As much as I've enjoyed the walk," Deborah said, sounding a bit winded, "I don't know why you'd think Sam would be down here."

"Miss Susan said he wants adventure." Daire smiled down at her. "I tried to go aboard a merchantman when I was about his age. But if you need a rest, I'm certain we can find someplace to let you ladies sit while I ask around."

"You can't leave us alone here." Deborah glanced at a towering warehouse. "Some of the people who loiter here are unsavory at best."

"No, this is no place for a lady." Daire's jaw hardened. "But you two insisted you come with me or follow me, and coming with me seemed the safest course for the two of you."

"I was hoping—" Susan looked at her sister and snapped her teeth together.

In no way would she admit in front of Deborah that she hoped their parents would be proud of her if she helped to find Sam and bring him home. And she couldn't admit to Daire she preferred to find Sam if he was guilty of stealing the goldfinch bottle.

"Sam's always been a good boy." Deborah filled in the silence left by Susan's refusal to talk further. "I think once he sees the two of us, if we do find him, he'll realize running off is foolish. But—oh dear."

Susan followed Deborah's gaze to where an old woman slept in the doorway of one of the storage facilities.

"Doesn't she have a home?" Susan whispered.

"Probably not." Daire sighed. "There are too many people living like that since the financial panic last year."

"That's so sad." Susan glanced at the grimy buildings and litter in the gutters, and her throat tightened. "I never go anywhere to see things like this."

"Your family protects you." Daire touched the back of her hand. "Should I take you home? Things might get uglier than this in another block."

"Not like that poor old lady," Deborah said. "The harbor area is just full of sailors, but they might make some vulgar remarks. If you ignore them, though, they'll go away."

"How do you know this?" Susan stared at her elder sister.

Deborah shrugged. "I come down here once a week."

"You—" Susan thought her eyes would bug from her head.

Daire looked bemused, too. "Why does a gently bred lady come down here once a week?" he asked.

"I help make food for men and women who don't have work." Deborah ducked her head so the brim of her hat hid her face. "Mostly I serve food, since I'm not a very good cook."

"You—" It was all Susan could get out for a moment. After a long breath, she managed, "But I thought you were at the church sewing or trying to get donations for the orphans."

"Not on Mondays." Deborah kept her face averted.

Susan's eyes stung with tears. "And you never asked me to join you? You know—"

The clatter of boot heels on pavement and raucous voices interrupted her.

"Perhaps we should have this discussion elsewhere." Daire started forward, away from the noisy men. "I'd rather not be here with two lovely ladies when that lot comes around the corner."

Susan fell into step with him again, and Deborah did the same. The rowdy men emerged from an alleyway a hundred yards behind them. Even from that distance, their ribald remarks swept toward Susan's ears. Those ears grew hot, and the heat spread to her cheeks.

"Just ignore them," Deborah advised. "They'll lose interest. They won't do anything in daylight. It's nighttime that is dangerous."

"How do you know all this, and who do you come here with?" Susan blurted out the questions. "Momma and the others wouldn't come down here."

"No, but Gerrit does." Deborah's voice fell so quiet, Susan nearly missed the words beneath the blast of a steamboat whistle. When they sank in, she understood Deborah's reluctance to talk about her excursions to this sad part of town—her heart hurt over Gerrit's reluctance to propose, or lack of interest in proposing. That he hadn't come along to help search for Sam was troubling. Sam looked up to Gerrit.

"We'll just have to be the ones to find Sam," Susan declared aloud. "Regardless of what these sailors shout to us."

"It can be pretty rude," Daire cautioned. "Your parents aren't going to like me bringing you here." He glanced at Deborah. "I admit I'm surprised they let you come every week."

"They'll let me go anywhere with Gerrit Vandervoort." Deborah grimaced. "They never ask where we're going, they trust him so much."

Susan blinked. She thought her parents ignored only her whereabouts, but they seemed to pay little attention to Deborah, too, and, obviously, Sam.

She wanted to stop and ask Deborah if she thought they didn't care or if they trusted their children to behave themselves. But the unruly men gained ground behind them, and she sensed Daire wished to enter the greater crowd near the harbor, so she picked up her pace and said nothing, her heart partly more burdened and partly lighter. She liked knowing that her sister sometimes felt neglected, too, but felt burdened that frivolity filled her days, especially since she'd inherited Great-aunt Susan Morris's fortune.

Pensive, she scarcely noticed her surroundings until the sweet notes of a hymn drifted through the shouts of boatmen and cacophony of the steam engines.

"It's a church." She stopped and gazed at the whitewashed building perched amid the warehouses and wharves like a pearl amid boulders. "Why is there a church down here?"

"It's a mission to the sailors," Deborah said.

"You know a great deal about the work going on down here." Daire gazed at Deborah with admiration.

Susan felt sick. All she could tell him about was the best place to buy hats or how to get raspberry jam out of a carpet.

"I didn't want to be a useless spinster," Deborah said, returning Daire's look of approbation, "so I started asking around about how I could serve. Gerrit Vandervoort brought me down here with some other people from the church a few years ago, and I've come ever since."

"I thought he was courting you with the intent to marry you," Susan said. "At least you've led the rest of the family to believe it."

Such an expression of pain crossed Deborah's face, Susan immediately regretted her words.

"I'm sorry." She wished Daire weren't between them so she could take her sister's hand. "That was mean of me, but we really did think. . ."

"So did I." Deborah coughed. "Let's go into the mission. I'd like to rest while Mr. Grassick looks for Sam."

"But he doesn't know what he looks like."

"He has a sketch." Deborah released Daire's arm and crossed to Susan's side. "Come along. They'll enjoy hearing you sing."

Susan remained where she stood, though she saw two sailors ogling her and Deborah. The mouths of the men moved, but the noise around them blocked their words from her hearing, for which she was grateful. "But I need to find him. If I do—"

No, she couldn't admit to Deborah that she wanted to be the one to bring Sam home so her family would notice her, would admire her for something. In light of the new revelations about Deborah's work in the poor part of town, it made her look selfish and mean.

"Miss Deborah is right," Daire said. "I may need to go inside places a lady can't go into if I don't find him along the wharves."

"We'll be inside." Deborah tugged on Susan's arm.

Still reluctant, Susan paused outside the church that was no larger than the first floor of their house and perhaps smaller. A box had been nailed to the side of the structure and filled with soil and flowers. She reached out one hand and stroked a scarlet tulip petal. "I wonder if this came from Holland."

"Possibly." Daire averted his gaze from her, as though he didn't like the sight of her.

No wonder. Old people slept in doorways, and her sister served food to the needy once a week, while she bought fripperies from an inheritance given to her to catch a husband. All she'd caught so far was a glass bauble important to no one but the man beside her, who seemed interested in her sister, if he didn't simply want to find his family heirloom and get away from all the Morrises.

"Let's go inside," Deborah urged.

Susan nodded and followed her sister through the doorway so narrow they each had to turn sideways to accommodate the breadth of their hoops. A few people glanced at them, men and women alike, and smiled. Susan returned the friendly greetings and slipped between two backless benches at the rear of the room. The singing continued. After a moment, Susan joined in the familiar words, letting her voice soar with the others.

She didn't realize she sang alone until the chorus ended and a ragged older lady, who smelled like boiled cabbage, turned and clasped Susan's hands.

❧

From inside his coat, Daire removed a sketch Gran Morris had given him. Sam apparently resembled his father, as did Susan. How to find one youth among the throng of men and boys Daire didn't know, but he began to show the sketch around and ask if anyone had seen such a young man. The answers varied in politeness. The result was the same—no one had seen him. Finding a stack of unattended boxes, Daire climbed atop them and scanned the crowd from his height advantage. He caught no glimpse of maple syrup–colored hair, though a hat would obscure that if the lad wore one.

What Daire did see made his gut tighten. Besides the dozens of mostly men, who seemed not to care that today was a Sunday, he noted two establishments with which he had grown too familiar over the past months, businesses owned and operated by Lucinda's father. Establishments set up to lure in and swindle the unwary young man seeking adventure or easy profit.

Samuel Morris wanted adventure, according to his sister, and might wish to turn an easy profit to fund that adventure. If he had taken the goldfinch and discovered, as Daire had, that it wasn't worth a great deal of money, he might find his way—or be lured into—one of Leonard Heath's establishments.

Knowing he had to look, Daire darted across the thoroughfare and into a building he'd sworn he would never enter again. Even on a Sunday, men of all ages sat playing their games of chance while discussing business that was as much a game of chance as the dice and cards. Those vices hadn't lured him, but the prospect of making lots of money quickly had. He'd thought he would go home rich, making up for his lack of talent in farming or glassmaking with his independence.

He shuddered, took too deep a breath of the smoky air, and scanned the room for a familiar face.

"Grassick," someone called. "You're looking prosperous. Ready for another venture?"

The room erupted in laughter. Daire had been a great dupe for these men, who took from the unsuspecting to invest in land in the West or railroad stock that might be worth something if the tracks went across the plains someday. Daire had fallen for the scheme. The only game that hadn't taken him in was the prospect of work in the West. He didn't want to be that far from home.

Seeing these men, knowing they operated inside the law just enough to keep them from getting prosecuted while taking people's hard-earned money or inheritances, he wished he weren't as far from home as he was. He wanted the strength of his family's love.

You need the strength of the Lord, he heard his father saying.

In his head, Daire knew Father was right, but at that moment, he thought of how disappointed his family would be if he fell back into his old ways. How ruined they'd be if he failed to find the goldfinch and the formula.

"I'm looking for someone," he said as though the man hadn't spoken. "A young man with eyes the color of wisteria—"

Laughter burst out in a roar.

"Turned poet now that you're penniless?" another man taunted.

"Only until the railroad moves west," someone else pointed out. "Then he'll be rich."

Daire glanced at the cards in front of the man and expected his investments had gone into a game of chance and not any railroad stock.

Daire smiled. "Perhaps. But it's the most distinguished feature about him."

"He wouldn't come in here without money." Heath strolled from a back room, a gold watch chain gleaming across his vest. "How are you, lad? Lucinda misses you."

Daire tried not to picture her beautiful face, hear her sweet voice. He should think of Susan or, perhaps better yet, Deborah. She possessed a giving spirit along with her beautiful face.

"Give Miss Heath my regards." Daire injected polite coolness into his tone. "I'm looking for the brother of some acquaintances. He may have been carrying my goldfinch bottle, trying to sell it."

"Haven't seen him or it." Heath's dark eyes gleamed. "I'd have bought it off him if he had. Discovered it's more valuable than I realized."

"Indeed?" Hairs rose across the back of Daire's neck and along his arms beneath the sleeves of his white linen shirt. "How's that?"

Heath shrugged. "One of a kind from the glassworks Queen Victoria uses."

"You already knew that."

Had he somehow discovered the formula had been hidden inside the goldfinch? No, not possible.

"I didn't realize that made it valuable." Heath laughed, while the other men fell silent. "Lucinda said I never should have let it get away. Or you, for that matter. You know you're welcome back at any time. I think she pines for you."

Temptation flashed through him. Lucinda was always orderly, purposeful, determined. He had felt secure in her presence.

He shook off the image of her in his head. He didn't need to feel secure in a person. Security came from the Lord, his family had reminded him. He wanted to be with them for more of that reminding.

He gave Heath a polite smile. "Give her my regards, but I've had enough of life up here. I prefer to be with my family."

"Doing what?" Heath started to laugh.

Others joined him.

"If this young man comes here"—Daire held up the sketch—"please send word to the Main Street Hotel."

A few people nodded as though they'd heard him. Doubting them, knowing too much of their lack of generosity and kindness, Daire spun on his heel and exited.

Despite the sourness of garbage from a nearby alley, the air outside smelled as fresh as the Morrises' garden compared to the reek of cigar smoke, macassar oil, and fear inside the building he'd just left. He considered calling on another establishment where Heath lured young men in with false promises, but a glance down the street told Daire the windows were dark, the curtains drawn.

He heaved a sigh of relief and headed to the church. As he approached the doorway, one voice stood out against the background of steam whistles and rough talk. A clear soprano sang with a warmth and sincerity that brought a lump into his throat. After his visit to Heath's business and thoughts of calling on Lucinda, however fleeting, he felt unclean, not worthy to step into the presence of such beauty of spirit. Yet feeling as though the singer had attached a length of Mr. Goodyear's vulcanized rubber to his belt to draw him in, Daire charged to the church.

He paused in the doorway. The church's coolness and peacefulness closed around him like loving arms. With a glance about, he realized that the singer was Susan. She caught his eye, faltered, and stopped.

Everyone faced Daire.

"I apologize for interrupting." He twisted his hat in his hands. "I came to collect the ladies."

"We've enjoyed having them for our hymn singing." A burly man with a peg leg thumped down the aisle toward Daire. "The young lady has been a blessing to us all."

"Oh no, I—I just like to sing." Susan's face turned as pink as her hat.

Deborah gave her younger sister a bemused look. "And I never knew you could sing like *that*. How have we missed that...? Well, never you mind. Maybe we can come back someday."

"Please do." The man, who seemed to be the spokesman for the congregation, though he didn't wear the typical suit of a pastor, held out his hand to Daire. "Jeb Macy. I lead this mission now that my sailing days are over. We have a singin' every Sunday and Wednesday. Come back and bring as many as you like."

"I'll do that if I'm still around." Daire shook the man's calloused hand.

He hoped he wasn't around that long. By Wednesday he would be in the arms of his family again with the formula in the glassworks safe. Yet part of him felt a twinge of regret that he wouldn't hear Susan singing again, nor the rest of these people, whose faces glowed with a joy he had never understood, even with all his worldly goods.

As he led Susan and Deborah out of the mission, a chorus of thank-yous and invitations to return followed them. He wished he'd found this church in the city instead of Heath's comrades. If he had, he would have returned home and all would be well.

"Why don't you sing like that around us?" Deborah demanded of Susan once they reached the sidewalk. "You know the rest of us can scarcely tell one note from another."

"Momma told me not to sing loudly whenever I go to church," Susan admitted. "She said I am showing off and—" She turned abruptly toward Daire. "Any news?"

"Not from the men I asked." He took her hand and tucked it into the crook of his elbow. Deborah took his other arm without invitation. "So we should look for him at the harbor."

"Why?" Susan's fingers flexed on his arm. "Surely he isn't trying to run away, is he?"

"I don't think he would consider it running away," Daire said.

"He is always fascinated with boats," Deborah added. "Gerrit and I caught him down here one day. But that was about a year ago, and we scared him off, we thought."

"Young men can get adventurous." Daire gazed at the smokestacks protruding into the blue sky, many puffing out clouds of steam and soot like the glassworks' chimneys. "We can only hope he hasn't gone aboard somewhere."

They headed toward Elizabeth Street and the harbor. Daire gave a brief account of his inquiries.

"So he hasn't tried to sell the goldfinch to men who deal in stolen goods," he concluded.

"I see." Susan started to remove her hand from his arm.

"Please don't be angry." He stopped, pulled free of Deborah's grasp, and caught hold of Susan's fingers. He held them. "You need to understand the possibility."

"I know." She blinked rapidly and hard. "I just can't bear the idea of my brother taking something that isn't his and running off. I mean, it's obviously not valuable or you would have been able to sell it to these men."

"I could have, but I wouldn't." He resumed walking. "They're not nice people."

"How do you know?" Deborah and Susan asked together.

"To my shame, I did some business with them."

Deborah gasped. "You dealt in stolen goods?" Horror filled her voice, rising above the blast of a steam whistle.

"No." He wouldn't tell them the rest.

"Then how—" Susan stopped. "I suppose it's none of my concern if you help me find my brother."

"Someone will find him." Daire cast a quick smile in her direction. "Tell me about the church. Did you enjoy waiting there?"

"I did." Her tone turned reverent. "Those people looked. . . Well, they're not prosperous. But their joy glowed from them. It's almost as though. . ." She paused in the middle of the sidewalk and gazed up at him. "It's almost as though they believe every word they sing and pray, as though they really believe God is with them."

"You don't?" Daire's stomach clenched with the sorrow that coursed through him.

She shook her head. "God doesn't have time for me. I'm too unimportant."

"Susan—I mean, Miss Morris, God has as much time for you as He does everyone else who wants it."

"Then why. . . ?" She started walking again. "Let's look this last place for my brother."

"All right, but we should talk more—"

Daire stopped himself. No, they should not talk more. He needed a young lady certain in her faith. Never again would he care about a female who went through the motion of worship without feeling it in her heart.

Silence stretched between them. Deborah made no more move to take his arm, though she kept pace with him and her sister. Beneath Deborah's bonnet, her face looked still, pensive. A furrow creased Susan's smooth brow.

As they drew closer to the harbor, the noise of the steam engines and whistles made speech difficult anyway. With relief, Daire noticed several ladies amid the crowd around the docks, embarking or disembarking passengers from pleasure cruises on the river. Susan and Deborah didn't stand out, and although a few men cast admiring glances Susan's way, no one said anything inappropriate. Like him, she turned her head and looked at everyone. He could only guess at Samuel Morris's appearance. Most of the men were older, though, weathered sailors and stevedores, or middle-aged sightseers, so Daire hoped Samuel's youth would make him stand out. He saw no one he could even guess was the young man.

Beside him, Susan gripped his arm and tipped up the brim of her hat. "I wish I were taller. Maybe if I stood on—" Before he knew what she was about, she released his arm, darted forward, and clambered onto a crate.

"Susan, that doesn't look very stur—"A crack like gunfire penetrated the noise around them as the lid of the crate split.

Daire lunged forward to catch her, but she leaped to safety and kept going, plunging into the crowd, her hoops pushing people aside more effectively than strong elbow thrusts. Daire followed and caught her cry.

"Sam. Samuel Morris, stop right there." She then flung herself onto a gangly youth with rumpled clothes and maple-colored hair.

"Aw Sue, what are you doing here?" The boy held her off at arm's length. "This isn't a place for a lady alone."

"I'm not alone." Susan grasped Sam's shoulders and shook him. "I'm with you, and I'm with Daire Grassick and Deborah. Now what are you doing scaring us all, taking off like this? If I were Daddy, I'd—oh, you make me so angry. Did you take the goldfinch?"

Chapter 8

Sam stared at Susan as though she'd lost her reason. "Why would I take that piece of yellow glass?"

"Because it's valuable." Susan glanced at Daire, realizing she'd just admitted her brother could be a thief. "It's a unique piece of glass made by the Grassick Glassworks."

"But you couldn't get anything for it." Sam's upper lip dusted with a pale line of fuzz, curled in the slightest of sneers. "And he had to sell it to you to get any money for it."

"Mr. Morris," Daire said in his rich timbre, "you should show your sister more respect."

"Respect Susan?" Sam laughed.

Susan flinched as though he'd struck her. "Really, Mr. Grassick, I'm just his sister."

"You're a lady and deserve to be spoken to with courtesy." Daire frowned at Sam. "Now if you please, answer your sister with a civil tongue."

"Susan's not a lady." Sam kicked at a crumpled piece of paper lying on the wharf. "She doesn't do anything that—"

"She's spent the afternoon in the heat helping me look for you." Daire's voice, still low, cut through Sam's protest.

Susan looked at Daire, feeling as though she had been set aglow like a lantern in a dark room. No one ever championed her, except for Paul upon occasion. But Daire had done so with Gran yesterday and now Sam today.

If she wasn't careful, she could fall in love with this man. Deborah's arched eyebrows told Susan her older sister saw the danger signs, too.

Sam ducked his head and ground the toe of his boot into the wharf. "She didn't need to. I should've been gone by now, but the paddle wheel broke on the *Mary Sue*."

"You really were running away?" Susan forgot Daire slipping into her heart and his goldfinch and Sam's disrespect of her. "Sam, why?"

"I don't want to be a banker." Sam gestured to the line of vessels from the tiny pleasure crafts to the enormous seafaring ships, and to the river leading to New York City on the other side, then the sea beyond Long Island. "I want to see the world. India. China." His voice took on an awed tone. "Rio de Janeiro. I want to do something. . .important, not be just another one of the Morrises no one can keep track of."

181

"Oh Sam." Susan blinked back tears. "I wish I didn't understand how you feel."

"But running away isn't the answer." Daire rested a hand on Sam's shoulder, making him look like the boy he still was. "I know. I did it more than once. No good ever came from it."

"Did you go to sea?" Sam's face lit.

"Just a riverboat the first time." Daire turned Sam toward the street. "I'll tell you about it while we walk back to your house."

Sam balked. "I don't want to go home. The captain of the *Mary Sue* hired me on. My gear's already aboard."

"You're too young," Deborah protested.

"When is she due to leave?" Daire asked.

Susan shot him a disapproving glance. Surely he didn't intend to give in to her brother's insistence that he remain at the docks.

"Tomorrow now." Sam made a face. "Can't get the wheel fixed on a Sunday, so we missed the tide last night and this morning and tonight. Probably won't be until tomorrow night now."

"Then you've got time to go home and persuade your father to give you his permission." Still gripping Sam's shoulder with one hand, and with Susan and Deborah falling into step behind him, Daire headed away from the harbor. "Wouldn't you rather go with your father's blessing?" His voice drifted back to Susan's ears.

"I won't get it." Sam sounded like a sullen ten-year-old rather than the grown and independent man he wanted to be. "He'll go write a poem about sailing out to sea."

"You shouldn't talk about Daddy like that." Susan bristled. "His poems are beautiful."

"They're useless, just like Momma's and Deborah's sewing and—"

"That's enough, laddy." Daire's tone turned steely. "Families are to be honored and cherished, not scorned."

"But mine—"

"Was terribly worried when they discovered you were missing," Daire said, cutting off Sam's protest.

"Yeah, and how long was I missing before they figured it out?" Sam gave a stone in the road a vicious kick.

"It was too long, Sam." Susan felt as though her bodice and hoop skirt had grown too big for her. She hastened her steps so she could walk beside her brother. "Will you please forgive me? I've been so concerned about myself, I didn't give you a thought."

"What do you have to be concerned about?" Sam demanded. "You got all that money from Great-aunt Susan. You can pay your way to anywhere you want to go."

"I can't pay for—" Susan stopped and glanced sideways at Daire.

He'd already learned too much about her family yesterday and today. She wasn't ready to share her heart, her disappointments and frustrations, any more than she had already revealed to him.

Not to think of Deborah overhearing revelations of her younger sister's heart. Deborah was oddly quiet, her face set, but not like someone who was angry—more like someone deep in difficult thought.

"I was sixteen the first time I ran off." Daire spoke into the silence broken only by the crunch of their footfalls on the walk and the voices of passersby. "I hopped aboard a boat going up the Delaware River. My father was in the middle of harvest and didn't miss me either. He thought I was working where I was supposed to be because he trusted me to do my work. So my grandfather came after me. He left an important customer to find me and bring me home." He fell silent.

When he said no more for an entire block, Sam asked, "What kind of trouble did you get for that?"

Susan was glad he'd asked and she didn't have to.

"None." Daire's face grew sad. "We got home to find my father had fallen asleep over his supper he was so weary from doing his work and mine, too. And the next month, Grandfather showed me the books to the glassworks and how much money the company lost because of my escapade."

"That must have stung," Susan murmured.

"Not enough," Daire said. "I left them again."

"No one loses sleep or money by me leaving." Sam snapped a low-hanging branch off a tree and began to whip it through the air with a hoarse whistle as they walked. "They won't have to feed me, so it'll save money."

"They'll lose your school fees," Deborah spoke at last. "You'll never get into university."

"I don't want to go to university." Sam smacked the branch against a fence, snapping the limb in two. He tossed the pieces onto the sidewalk.

Daire stopped. He said nothing, just stood motionless staring at the litter.

Susan opened her mouth to tell Sam to pick up the broken branch. Before she formed the words, her brother glanced at Daire then retrieved the sticks with a muttered apology.

"Leaving your family will hurt them," Daire said. "At least ask for permission."

"I'll never get it." Sam sounded more sad than sullen.

Susan wanted to cheer him. "You know Momma and Daddy don't say no to you, Sam."

"But if they do—"

Two men stepped from a side street, and Sam halted his speech and body.

"Daddy," Susan called. "We have him."

Their father spun on his heel and strode toward them. A smile lit his face. "You're all right, son."

"Yes sir." Sam took the hand his father stretched out to him and shook it.

"I signed on to the *Mary Sue*. She's a merchantman headed for Madagascar. I don't want to give up my berth on her."

"Well, now, we'll have to talk about that." Father and son strolled toward home.

The other man, a member of the church, nodded at Susan and Deborah, shook Daire's hand, and followed.

A lump swelled into Susan's throat. She grasped the picket of a neighbor's fence, heedless of how the rough wood could snag her glove, and blinked hard against the moisture in her eyes.

"Miss Morris?" Daire moved to stand in front of her. "Are you all right?"

"Yes, I'm just. . .embarrassed." A shudder ran through her. "You've spent your afternoon hunting down my brother, and no one even thanks you. And we aren't any closer to finding your goldfinch."

"Your father was happy to have his son home safe." Daire touched a fingertip to her cheek, and she realized a tear had rolled there.

"He's here at last," Deborah murmured, her gaze fixed on the house and a handful of men milling about the front garden.

Gerrit leaned against a pillar of the front porch, one hand shielding his eyes, as though he gazed into the distance for an incoming ship.

Or maybe just his lady.

"It's far more important to bring home a lost lamb than a piece of glass."

"Well yes, but—" Susan snapped her teeth together to keep from bursting out that her father hadn't noticed her back home, either, or that she'd even been gone; it sounded selfish, as though she should be more important than her brother. She didn't want that. She just wanted to be *as* important. For once, she wanted them to notice her above all the others.

"Let's go home," Daire said. "You must be tired and hungry."

"I am." Susan took a handkerchief from her reticule and dabbed at her eyes. "And let me thank you if no one else does."

"Seeing him safe is thanks enough." Daire offered her his arm then held out his other arm for Deborah.

She declined it and ducked behind Susan and Daire. Thus, the three of them completed the last two blocks to home. Most of the people remained from earlier. Children ran about the yard, playing a game of tag. Inside the house, women had set out food on the dining room table. Sam sat with several other men, explaining about the *Mary Sue* in between and around bites of ham and salad.

Gerrit was nowhere to be seen, and Deborah had also vanished.

Good. Perhaps they would mend their fences and Gerrit would speak up at last.

The notion that Deborah would be engaged at last saddened Susan. She'd wanted it so she would be the last daughter at home, but she'd glimpsed a different side of Deborah today and wondered if perhaps she was ignoring her sisters as much as she believed they ignored her.

Hoping to find Momma, Daisy, and Opal in the kitchen, Susan turned to Daire. "Go join the men. I'll bring you a plate."

"Why don't you sit down and let me bring you a plate." Daire smiled at her. "You look tired."

She instantly wished for a mirror to see how bad she must appear for him to say her fatigue showed.

"Thank you," she began instead of rushing off to find a looking glass. "I think—"

"Mr. Grassick."

Momma and Daisy descended upon them—or more accurately, Daire. Their faces beamed. Plates of food filled their hands.

"Thank you for bringing Sam back to us." Daisy shot her brother an indulgent glance. "He's such a wanderer, I think they should just let him go off somewhere."

"But he's too young," Momma protested. "Don't you think, Mr. Grassick?"

"It depends on the captain," Daire said. "If he's a good, Christian man, the experience could be good."

"Just what I said to my husband not two minutes ago." Daisy gestured across the room. "I told him to save you a chair. Do sit down."

"I think Susan needs the seat more," Daire said.

Susan gazed up at him. Her middle felt like melted caramel. Her heart. . . She feared she'd just lost that.

Momma and Daisy glanced at Susan as though they'd just noticed her, which they probably had.

"You look tired," Momma said. "What have you been doing?"

"I was looking for Sam with Deborah and Mr. Grassick."

"You were?" Momma and Daisy said together.

They narrowed their eyes in twin speculative gazes and glanced at Daire then back to Susan.

"Clear a space at the table for Susan, too," Momma said.

"I was going to get Mr. Grassick some food." Susan gestured toward the buffet. "He gave up his day for us."

"Nonsense." Daisy's smile glowed with all its beauty. "You were out, too. I'll bring you a plate, as well."

Before Susan knew how to respond, Momma and Daisy ushered her to the table and made her sit beside Daire. Within moments, plates of food and glasses of lemonade rested on the cloth before them. Momma and Daisy fawned over Daire all the while they served, as they had earlier at church. Some of their effusiveness spilled over onto Susan, mainly because Daire sat turned in his chair to look at her and included her in every remark. In those minutes, Susan received more attention from female members of her family than she had since bringing home the goldfinch.

Because of Daire.

She cast him a sidelong glance. He was a remarkably attractive man and so very kind. Best of all, her family liked him. If she managed to attract him, her family would notice her because she'd be with him.

As soon as the notion struck her, she dismissed it. It seemed far too mercenary to set her cap for a man because her family liked him. On the other hand, she remembered the way his touch, the sound of his voice, simply being near him made her feel warm and pretty and. . .needed.

Only until they found the goldfinch. Or until he gave up seeking the bauble.

She fixed her attention on her plate. She mustn't even let herself for a moment consider a match with Daire Grassick. A man like him would want a far prettier girl and one with a family that didn't lose one of its children for a whole day. Daire came from the sort of family that married heiresses.

And she was an heiress.

She squirmed on her chair, her appetite gone. She couldn't let herself be interested in Daire for more than a passing acquaintance. She thought she was starting to have strong feelings for him, but maybe they came from the attention she received when she was in his company and not from the man himself. Only time would show her the truth, and she didn't have time with him.

Daire seemed to have his attention fixed on the dialogue between the other men and Sam. They discussed the good and bad aspects of allowing her brother to head off to Madagascar—wherever that was—with an unknown sea captain.

"You could get to know him," Daire suggested during a lull, while Deborah circled the table with a pitcher of lemonade. "If the *Mary Sue* isn't leaving port until tomorrow night's tide, you could invite him here for a talk or go down there to the docks, Mr. Morris."

"Well, um, yes, I suppose I could." Daddy's face turned ruddy. "Not, um, much good with strangers, but for my son. . ." He cast a frantic glance to Sam.

Poor Daddy. He was shy. Susan wondered why she'd never noticed that before. She thought he didn't talk to any of them because he didn't care. But she couldn't think that with the way he had panicked over Sam's absence earlier and now looked at the eldest son as though he were truly a precious gift.

If he just looked at her like that once, she would never feel unimportant.

"I'll take you to him." Sam's face lit as though he had a lamp inside his head. "He has a good reputation. I asked around before I approached him."

"That shows maturity," Daire murmured to Susan.

"All right." Daddy took out a kerchief and mopped his brow. "Tomorrow. No, no, it'll have to be tonight. Tomorrow is a workday. Hmm. It'll be difficult to find the man after dark, and it's getting on to that. I don't know, Sam."

"Father." The glow on Sam's face died. "I'll show you where the boat is."

"I'll go with you, Mr. Morris." Daire set down his fork. "If you've finished eating, we can leave right now and be at the docks before the sun sets."

"Why would you do that?" Susan couldn't stop herself from asking. "We're strangers to you."

"We'll go, too," William and Marcus said.

Susan kept looking at Daire, waiting for an answer.

He glanced from Sam to Susan. "I understand what he wants. If the captain is a good man, it could be the best thing for your brother. He'll either find what he wants and have a career started, or he'll keep running off until he finds what he wants and too likely end up in bad company."

"Have you found what you want from running off?" Susan thought her tone was a bit sharp but didn't understand why.

"I have found one thing"—Daire spoke with an even cadence, though the corners of his eyes and mouth tightened—"that nothing is more important to me than my family. I just wish—" He pushed back his chair and rose. "Mr. Morris?"

All the men rose. Susan followed. She knew she would never be allowed to go to the harbor with the men, but she walked with them to the entryway, clinging to the fringe of the group in the hope someone would notice her. Someone like Daire Grassick. She wanted to say good-bye to him. All too likely, he wouldn't return. They'd lost his goldfinch bottle. She'd lost his goldfinch bottle. He had no need to return. And now Sam was likely to leave her. She never paid much attention to her brother, but she didn't like seeing him leave, heading off for the other side of the world for months or years.

As though he felt her gazing at him, or perhaps he was simply polite, Daire made his way to her side. "May I call on you tomorrow?"

"Ye—yes." Susan's heart began to gallop so hard she thought her lace fichu should start fluttering as though in a high wind. "I didn't think—there's no need. . ."

"Perhaps the two of us can think up another place to look for the goldfinch," Daire said.

"I don't know—yes, maybe we can." Susan felt breathless. "Tomorrow. The goldfinch has to be somewhere around here. Maybe Gran has seen it after all, or—"

"I did see your goldfinch yesterday." Sam turned around, blocking the doorway and everyone's exit. "I'm sorry I didn't tell you earlier." He looked down and ground his toe into the floorboards, scuffing them. "I didn't like being dragged home like a recalcitrant schoolboy, so I didn't say anything."

"What are you talking about, son?" Daddy asked.

"That glass goldfinch." Sam looked up at Daire. "I honestly don't know where it is, sir, but I saw a man with it. He was heading toward those tenements on the other side of Market Street."

Chapter 9

Daire didn't think Samuel Morris should exchange his family for the discomfort of shipboard life and a voyage to the other side of the world. He was too young to be on his own. Yet he wasn't impulsive as Daire had been. Samuel thought out his plan and executed it. If not for a broken paddle wheel, the lad would be well into the Atlantic and beyond his family's reach to draw him back. If he didn't go with their blessing, he would succeed in making his escape the next time.

Why he was aiding these people, who were near strangers, in managing their recalcitrant son, Daire didn't know. But there he was, striding along beside the other men in the family and discussing the merits of travel, something none of them had done much of beyond crossing the Hudson River to go into New York City or traveling south to Philadelphia. All the while, Daire waited for the opportunity to talk to Sam alone and ask him more details about seeing someone with the goldfinch bottle. From the sound of it, finding the bauble again sounded hopeless unless Sam knew the identity of the man or could describe a unique characteristic that would help in identifying him. Daire suspected that was a vain hope and the goldfinch was forever lost.

Its precious secret gone forever or, worse, waiting to be found by strangers.

He cringed at the notion of unknown hands retrieving the formula and either throwing it away as useless or recognizing its value and selling it to— whom?

Heath had said he would buy the goldfinch now, that he hadn't known its value when Daire might have, in desperation, sold it to him. Was it possible that Heath knew the formula lay inside the goldfinch? No, not possible. He couldn't have learned that in just a few days.

Except that Leonard Heath could have learned something. He knew far too much about far too many people for Daire to doubt the man's ability to gather information on the Grassicks. He had done business with them, after all. He'd infiltrated the family, using his daughter as a lure.

Which meant Daire would have to rejoin the Heath social circle to learn if his notion held any merit.

His gut tensed at the idea. He would try to get information from Sam.

He maneuvered himself so that he fell into step beside the youth. "Why do you want to run away from people who love you?"

The others grew quiet, including Sam. He ducked his head as though the brick sidewalk at his feet required all his focus.

"I suppose if your father gives you permission to leave, it's not running away," Daire amended.

His father had given him permission to leave the last time. He'd spoken his disapproval of Lucinda and her crowd, but he had given Daire part of his inheritance to invest, to make a go of life on his own.

"But the world can be cruel to a young man without proper guidance," Daire continued. "It's none of my concern, but I speak from experience."

"We won't let him go if the captain isn't a good man," Mr. Morris said. "I'd rather Sam finishes school and goes to university."

"I don't like school." Sam raised his head and brushed his hair out of his eyes. "I'm no good at mathematics or reading."

"Your work was fine this past term." Mr. Morris set a hand on his son's shoulder as they neared the harbor. "I was pleased."

"Then tell Susan." Sam's face grew flushed. "She helped me through."

"Susan?" The chorus of male voices rang out against the walls of warehouses and shipping offices, as though no one recognized the name.

Daire glanced around, reading astonishment in faces lit by the setting sun. Not one of them believed Susan had aided in the attainment of Sam's school-work to a degree that he had earned good reports.

"She's excellent at arithmetic," Sam said. "I always put the numbers backwards and end up with the wrong answer if I try it on my own. And she helped me figure out my sums and get my reading straight."

And Susan thought she didn't pay enough attention to her family or think they noticed her? Sam did. No wonder she wanted to find him.

"Once I started to read better," the youth said, his face lighting, "I looked through the books in Father's study and found some about faraway places. I wrote a report for school on India, and the teacher read it to the whole class. And, well—" He shrugged. "I want to see more than words about a place. If I could write things after I see the place, it might make people here think about the people there and maybe that would help Momma and the girls with this mission and. . ." His voice trailed off, his cheeks turning more scarlet than the sunset.

"I never knew, son." Mr. Morris stopped and brushed a hand across his brow. "I just read about those faraway lands and dream in verse, but I never thought to go see them."

"Then let me, please, sir." Sam fairly bounced from foot to foot as the group recommenced their trek to the harbor.

"We'll see what the captain's like," Mr. Morris said.

"Or perhaps find a better one?" Daire suggested.

Unlike him, Sam held a purpose in his desire to wander, and Daire wanted to see the youth attain his goal, if his soul and body would be safe.

If Daire had known a reason for his wanderings other than the vague notion of proving himself as good at something as were his brothers and sister, he would not have sought after easy wealth and gotten himself mixed up with the wrong sort of people and damaged his relationship with his family and God.

If only he possessed a purpose for his life now, then—what?

No no, he must find the goldfinch, take it home, and do what his family wanted of him, whether that was acting as a mere clerk in the glassworks or plowing fields alongside his father, regardless of how both activities made him restless and longing for something more for his life, some sort of... purpose.

His lips twisted in an ironic smile. He would have no work with the Grassick glasshouses, and possibly the farm, if he didn't find the formula inside the goldfinch before someone else did.

Someone like Leonard Heath.

Regardless of whether the gesture appeared rude and intrusive, Daire clasped Sam's shoulder and drew him away from the other men. "Tell me more about the man you saw with the goldfinch. How do you know it was my—the piece your sister purchased from me?"

"Couldn't mistake it." Sam frowned. "I thought maybe she managed to sell it after all, though the man didn't look like he had enough money to buy something like that."

"What did he look like?" Daire pressed.

"Well, he was kind of tall." Sam frowned and rubbed the bridge of his nose. "Kind of your height. And his hair was about your color. Dark. And he wasn't quite so broad in the shoulders." He shrugged. "Can't think of anything else."

"Can you tell me where he went?" Daire kept his tone even, trying not to sound too eager and encourage Sam to forget details out of nervousness or make something up to get Daire to stop asking questions. "You said something about a tenement."

"Yeah. They're like a rabbit warren there near the harbor. Lots of sailors' families live in them. Lots of Irish who came here from the famine."

A rabbit warren. Lots of families living in tight quarters.

Daire knew the place, knew of its cramped, dark apartments with rooms like railroad cars shared by a dozen family members and facilities in the yard the entire building used. Finding one man who was roughly his height and coloring amid that crowd was impossible even if he didn't get assaulted and robbed the minute he stepped into the throng of immigrants trying to survive on too little money and even less hope.

Those were the young men Heath tried to lure into his schemes, promising them jobs out west. Hope sprang into the faces of those men—hope that they could support their families and find a better life for them away from the city. They disappeared west, but no one ever heard from them again. Daire had found out why. Heath gave them jobs mining, digging wells on land Heath owned so he could sell it for more money—backbreaking labor for which they never saw a cent because... Heath had provided Daire with a dozen excuses, none of which Daire accepted. The men needed clothes, so Heath provided them—for a fee. They needed transportation and food and shelter. Heath provided them—for a fee.

No one heard from the men, because most took off on their own or died or simply could not afford the cost of postage back to family members who too often couldn't read.

Daire's hands balled into fists at the memories of how his involvement with Heath had helped fund such adventures. Except Heath and his cronies were the only ones getting rich from land deals and mines.

Heath again, a man who could easily pay one of those men in the tenements to steal the goldfinch.

Jaw tight, Daire addressed Sam again. "Can you think of anything else?"

"No. Sorry, sir." Sam looked sincere, though his gaze quickly traveled from Daire to the harbor and a stocky steamboat, whose name blazed across her bow in silver gilt lettering: *Mary Sue*. Closer inspection showed a clean deck and smokestack. The sailors working around the deck spoke to the visitors with respect, and no foul language passed between them. If the captain proved to be responsible for this behavior, which was likely, Daire decided he would take advantage of his seeming influence with Mr. Morris and encourage him to let Sam go to sea. A lad with a purpose should be encouraged.

~

Catching sight of Deborah at last, Susan balanced a stack of dirty plates on her hip and charged out the back door. She didn't care that her sister and Gerrit Vandervoort stood in what appeared to be serious conversation, judging from their set faces and tight lips. Susan couldn't wait any longer to talk to Deborah about her work with the mission and possibly the people in the tenements, where someone carrying Daire's goldfinch bottle had disappeared.

"Are you going to wash those in the well?" Deborah asked.

"What? Oh." Susan set the plates on the grass. "Deborah, do you know people in the tenements?"

"I wouldn't say I know them—"

"Miss Susan," Gerrit said, breaking into Deborah's hesitation, "will you ask about that later? Your sister and I were having a talk about—"

"We all know Bridget," Deborah interrupted in turn. "She lives there with her sister and her sons. I believe they all work—or try to work—on the docks, when there's work, that is."

"Bridget." Susan felt a little ill. "Deb, you don't think Bridget would take the goldfinch, do you?"

"It's useless," Gerrit said. "Why would she take it?"

"Because it's pretty," Deborah snapped, "and she probably doesn't have many pretty things."

"But she's never taken anything from us before," Susan protested.

"We don't have frivolous ornaments lying about, either." Deborah half turned her back on Gerrit and faced Susan fully. "And it was tucked behind the pictures because none of us wanted it. She might not have considered it stealing any more than it's stealing if she takes leftover food home with her."

"But it's wrong to take things anyway." Susan twisted her fingers together. "We told her she could take the food. Taking the goldfinch is. . .different."

"Then ask her in the morning," Gerrit suggested, sounding bored.

"I will." Susan picked up the plates and marched back to the house.

But in the morning, Bridget didn't arrive for work. Everyone scurried about so much trying to get Sam off to his ship and the younger boys off to school, despite their protests that they wanted to watch Sam sail, Susan didn't take time to wonder about the maid's whereabouts until Daire arrived at the front door.

"There's your young man." Gran chuckled and dropped a sketch onto the floor.

Susan picked it up while Deborah answered Daire's knock. The drawing showed a young man with wild dark hair puzzling over a young lady and an adult human–sized goldfinch, as though trying to choose between the two.

"You are so droll, Gran." Susan kissed her grandmother's cheek. "But please hide this one away." She tucked it at the bottom of the stack. "He's not in the least interested in me. He just wants his glass ornament."

"And he doesn't need you to find it, now that he knows you don't have it."

"But I have information for him."

It wasn't much, but it was a gossamer thread of hope.

"He doesn't know that." Gran grinned and bent over her sketch again.

Susan turned toward the front hall, where Deborah laughed with a flirtatious note, and Daire's deep voice rumbled in return. "He could be here for Deborah."

"Deborah will marry Gerrit when she's done making him suffer."

Susan glanced back at Gran. She'd started outlining a drawing with a man holding up his hands in supplication.

"Is that Gerrit?" she asked.

Gran laughed. "I give him another week."

"Or less." Susan smiled and headed into the hall.

"Good afternoon, Miss Susan." Daire bowed. "Miss Morris tells me that your brother got off to his ship safely."

"Yes, thank you. I've never seen him so happy."

"Knowing one's purpose in life can make a body happy." Daire gazed past Susan, as though something important hung on the wall behind her. "I've seen it in my family."

"But not you?" Susan dared to ask the question.

"Not as much as I'd like." Daire shimmied his shoulders as though shaking off rain and turned his brilliant smile on Deborah. "You will help me search today, won't you? You know something of the tenements, you said."

"I do, but Susan has more information than I do right now." Deborah gave Susan a little nudge on the arm. "Go ahead without me. Today is my day for the soup kitchen with Gerrit."

"But—" Susan didn't want to go without her elder sister. "I don't know where Bridget lives."

"If you can't find her," Deborah said, "I'll come with you tomorrow."

"Deb—"

"Time's wasting." With another trill of laughter and a wave of her hand, Deborah swept out of the entry hall and up the stairs.

"I don't know if it's proper for me to go with you alone," Susan murmured, her cheeks growing warm.

"We'll always be in the daylight." Daire held out his hand. "And your family approves of me." His lips twisted into a mocking smile at this last.

Susan squirmed. "They approve of you being a Grassick."

"It's approval nonetheless." His smile turned genuine. "And I'd like to hear about what this Bridget has to do with our search."

"She's our maid," Susan began.

By the time she finished her tale, she wore her bonnet and a light shawl and was strolling down the pavement with her hand tucked into the crook of Daire's elbow.

"But I don't know where she lives," she concluded.

"You have a full name," Daire said. "That will help."

"But I—" Susan halted, her face burning with shame. "I don't know her last name. That is, I'm not certain of it. O'Malley? Mulligan. I—I never asked her."

She wished the maid stood before her so she could ask her forgiveness, ask her last name, ask about her family and native country and hopes.

Daire started walking again. "We'll find her. I found you, after all, and with little trouble, and I didn't even have so much as your Christian name."

"My Christian name." Susan mused over the familiar reference to a first name. "I wonder why it's called that, when so many of us don't deserve it."

"Don't you consider yourself a Christian?" A muscle bunched at the corner of Daire's strong jaw.

Susan gnawed her lower lip. "Well, I mostly help with the children at church, but I don't attend services much. And my Bible is dusty from disuse. And now—" She stopped.

Just because she was gaining a great deal of attention from Daire Grassick didn't mean she should unburden herself to him. A man who was little more than a stranger didn't want to hear about how she felt neglected and yet, apparently, did little herself to pay attention to others.

"I don't think God has much interest in me," she finished.

"He does, Susan." Daire covered her hand with his, sending a thrill all the way through her. "I thought He didn't care about me, either, but I realized how wrong I was when I went home and my family welcomed me with unconditional love and acceptance. God used their kindness to remind me that He always loves us, regardless of how we behave, and I have behaved far more badly than you ever could have."

"I'm completely self-centered." She made herself look up at him. He was gazing down at her, so she met his gaze full on. The intensity of his green eyes made her stomach clench and her mouth go dry. She wanted to blink, break the connection, but she felt rooted to the pavement. A passerby bumped her hoop, sending it swaying, and still she couldn't move.

"Who are you?" She asked possibly the stupidest question in the world and tried to cover up for her silliness. "I mean, I know your name is Daire Grassick and your family makes glass, but I don't know anything about you, and yet—" No, she would not say she felt as though she knew as much as she needed to, to know to experience a yearning in her heart far stronger than any wish she felt to have her family proud of her for something.

"I come from Salem County, where my grandmother's family has lived for over a hundred years." Daire started walking again as he talked, his words emerging slowly, as though he chose each one with care. "My grandfather came from Scotland nearly fifty years ago to work in the glassworks. We also have a large farm. But I'm not much good at farming or glassmaking, and I didn't want to just take orders while the others worked. So I came up here to make my fortune."

"But you didn't?" She posed the query but knew the answer. He hadn't. He'd sold her the goldfinch.

"Why Hudson City and not New York?" she asked in addition.

He remained silent for so long she thought he wasn't going to answer. Amid the crowd of Monday morning shoppers and clerks running errands, she wasn't certain she would have heard him. They walked through the heart of the city, past her great-aunt's bank, past her father's bank, past the pawnshop where she'd seen Daire for the first time.

And started dreaming of him as more than a person in a chance meeting like a shopkeeper?

Oh yes, she dared admit that now. The man, as much as the goldfinch bottle, had caught her attention, with his good looks and air of bewilderment. She wanted to help him, make him smile, encourage him to smile at her. And when he had, she yearned for attention from him, as she had never wanted it from her family. And all he wanted from her was help finding his goldfinch, a silly, frivolous piece of glass.

"Leonard Heath encouraged me to come here." Daire spoke so abruptly Susan jumped. "He did business with my family, and his daughter. . . But that's all behind me now unless Heath wants the goldfinch."

"Why would he want it?" Susan asked. "Surely, he knows it's not valuable."

"It's more valuable than I realized." He guided her around a bit of broken pavement.

They had entered the less prosperous part of the city, where the shops grew dingier and the houses narrower and more crowded.

"How could it increase in value?"

Had she not made a foolish acquisition after all?

"I'd rather not say any more than—" Daire paused and stared down the street toward the tenements. "My family will be ruined financially if I don't find it."

"Goodness me." Susan blinked up at him. "Surely you exaggerate."

"Perhaps a little." Daire shrugged. "We'll still have the farm, but we could lose the glassworks."

"Oh no." Susan wished to run down the street calling Bridget's name aloud.

Instead, she paced along beside Daire until they stood across the narrow thoroughfare from the first row of tenements. Courtyards nestled in the shadows of the three-story buildings, courtyards mostly full of women, children, and old men. Some washed clothes at the single pump each building offered. Others cooked over open fires, sending the greasy tang of cheap sausages and smoke into the humid air. Others simply lazed about, their faces devoid of joy or—

"They look so hopeless," Susan murmured, her eyes stinging with tears.

"They are, mostly. That's why men like Heath can take advantage of them. He promises hope, where he delivers none."

"Does God care about them, too?"

"Most definitely."

"Then why are they so unhappy?"

"Unless we seek Him, we all are without the Lord in our lives, regardless of how much money we have."

The words struck home. Susan opened her mouth to ask him more questions, but a swarm of children surged toward them, hands outstretched. "Sweets?" they demanded.

"No, but I have—"

When she reached for her purse, Daire stayed her hand. "Not coin. Too often bigger children or even adults take it from them for gaming or drink."

"But they look hungry," Susan whispered.

"They probably are." Daire smiled at the youngsters. "I'll buy you some meat pies if you can tell me where to find Bridget."

"Bridget who?" the children demanded. "Bridget O'Malley? Bridget O'Halleran? Bridget McConnell?"

Susan felt her own hope slipping away with each name the children mentioned. The muscle tightening in the corner of Daire's jaw warned her he felt the same.

"All of them," Daire finally said.

They got directions. With a gaggle of youngsters following them, they sought out and found ten Bridgets. None were the Morrises' maid. None claimed to know who she was. The morning slipped into afternoon with no progress. Susan's feet felt as though her shoes were made for one of the little girls trailing in her wake, and her stomach growled loud enough to mimic a steam engine. Daire proved relentless, though, climbing steep, narrow steps that smelled of cabbage and other things Susan didn't want to consider, or ducking down alleyways that sent fear crawling up her spine for fear they would meet more than another Bridget at the end.

At last he paused to buy a dozen meat pies from a street vendor, handed them out to the children, who stuffed the pastries into their mouths, and divided the last one between Susan and himself.

"You look tired." He traced a fingertip along her cheekbone. "I should take you home. Perhaps your Bridget has come to work by now."

"Maybe." Susan thought her face must reflect the hopelessness of the people in the courtyard. "But even if she hasn't come to work—especially if she hasn't come to work—I should go home and make dinner and see if the boys need help with their schoolwork. And Gran is all alone unless Momma came home for lunch. I must stop neglecting my family. Maybe then—" She turned her face away.

"Yes, let's stop for today. It's getting too late to remain here." Holding her hand instead of letting her take his arm, Daire led her out of the tenements and back to the more prosperous part of the city.

Once she trod on pavement with shops and houses she recognized, Susan expected she would feel less downcast, less. . . hopeless. But the feeling remained, a deep sorrow eating away at her heart like rot on a piece of fruit. There she was, with more money than she knew how to spend, unable to spend it on anyone beyond herself in any meaningful quantities, and she was so very unhappy. She had a fine home, if somewhat neglected, and a family, also neglected, and her heart ached. The most attractive man she'd ever met held her hand, and she wanted to crawl into a private place and weep.

To her relief, Daire didn't try to talk either, though he kept a firm, warm grip on her hand, as though he needed the contact. As though he welcomed the contact.

As though he liked the contact.

But no, not her. He wouldn't be attracted to her that way. He came from an old family, a famous family. He would want a girl who came from the same sort of people, not an heiress with selfish intent.

Nor one who couldn't say specifically that she was a Christian.

They arrived home to find Gran munching bread and jam in the kitchen.

"I've never seen you without your sketching, ma'am," Daire greeted her. "I'm pleased to see you up and about."

"Need to be if you're going to drag my granddaughter all over who knows where." Despite the sharpness of her words, Gran grinned, showing her still good teeth. "Of course, if you enjoy her company, I won't complain."

"I do enjoy her company, ma'am." Daire drew a chair out from the table. "Do sit down, Miss Susan. I see the icebox. Will it have something cold to drink inside?"

"I made lemonade this morning." Susan didn't sit. "But you sit. I'll serve."

"Sit down, girl," Gran ordered. "You look like you're about to fall down."

"I'm all right," Susan declared.

Then she burst into tears.

Chapter 10

Daire swung away from the icebox and stared from Susan to Gran then back to Susan. His sister, Maggie, never cried. He had no idea what to do with a weeping female.

"She needs comfort," Gran said in an exaggerated whisper. "Or maybe just a nap."

"Then I'll leave." As much as he wished to, Daire couldn't bolt with Susan so distraught.

"I'm all right," she insisted again, drawing a handkerchief from a pocket in her gown. "Those poor people just made me so sad, and I can't help them. I'm rich, but I don't have control of my money and can't help them."

"Where did you take her today?" Gran asked.

"To look for your maid." Daire's heart felt like lead in his chest—guilt, regret, and understanding of Susan's feelings. "We saw many people who aren't doing well in life."

"And I'm so selfish, I just want attention from everyone." Susan buried her face in her hands. "But the bankers won't give me control of my money."

"Then you'll have to get married," Gran pronounced. "Your aunt wanted you to use that money to catch a husband." She glanced at Daire from the corner of one still sharp eye. "A nice Christian man."

"I don't deserve a nice Christian man." From between her fingers, Susan's face shone as red as strawberries, but not unattractively so.

She cried rather prettily. Rather appealingly. Daire's arm twitched with the impulse to wrap it around her shoulders, draw her close so she could weep on his shoulder.

Before he realized what he was doing, he did just that. She felt so tiny against him, except for the ridiculously wide skirt women found necessary to parade about in to fulfill fashion's demands. He imagined protecting her always, offering her the shelter of his name, the abundant gift of his family's love. Together they could—what?

His lack of a purpose in life kept him from doing something truly foolish like kissing her in front of her grandmother, which would have been tantamount to a proposal. He didn't know Susan well enough for that.

Yet he'd run off to the city, away from his family, after a far more brief acquaintance with Lucinda.

And that was all the more reason to take himself off, as far away from Susan Morris as he could. But not while she grasped his shoulders like one of his own grandmother's kittens clinging to a limb by only their front paws. As the kittens trusted him to lift them to safety, Susan seemed to expect him to lift her spirits from despair.

"If you can't give them money," he suggested tentatively, "perhaps you can work alongside your sister, serve them food, take care of their children so they can get some rest or even do a little work."

"Do you think I could?" Her voice sounded as tiny as one of those kittens, too.

"You could," Gran broke in, "if we didn't need you at home."

A shudder ran through Susan, and she drew away from Daire. "I'm not needed here. I do so little for any of you. I even left you alone all day."

"You spoil me, child." Gran reached out a hand with fingertips bearing testimony to the many colors of her pastels. "As you see, I'm not as helpless as you let me behave. And the boys—"

The cries of children outside echoed Gran's words about brothers.

"They're home, and I look a fright." Without so much as another glance at Daire, Susan fled from the kitchen, her bonnet dangling down her back.

"If you're only interested in having her help you find that piece of bric-a-brac," Gran said, her jowls quivering beneath a set chin, "then I suggest you stay away. We take advantage of her desire to please us so much, she's going to fall in love with the first man who pays her attention—as you are."

"Yes ma'am." Daire smoothed his damp neck cloth. "I'm in no position to consider courting a lady right now. Though if I were. . ."

He couldn't finish that sentence. He didn't know if he could court Susan even if he did know what he was supposed to be doing with his life.

The kitchen door burst open, saving him from having to speak of Susan any further. Two youths charged into the house, faces shining, books tucked under one arm. Immediately they dropped the books onto the floor.

"Where's Susan?" the younger one cried. "I'm starving."

"Mind your manners," Gran ordered. "We have company."

The boys halted and nodded to Daire. "Good afternoon, Mr. Grassick. Are you here calling on Susan?"

"No, I'm just leaving." Daire shook the boys' hands and bowed to Gran. "Thank you for your words of wisdom, ma'am. I have taken them to heart."

And, for no logical reason, his heart hurt at the notion of not seeing Susan again.

And with the realization that, with no success at finding the Morrises' maid, he had no choice but to visit Leonard Heath—and Lucinda.

~⊷~

If she could crawl under her bed and hide, Susan would do so. But the raucous entry of the boys reminded her she was going to pay more attention to her family, and that meant feeding Paul and Roger, helping Gran back to the parlor, perhaps even making dinner, such as it would be with her poor cooking skills. She could only hope that Daire had gone home to his real home, far from Hudson City, so she wouldn't even accidentally encounter him. After her mortifying display in the kitchen, she doubted she could face him without dissolving into a puddle of humiliation.

She was of no use to him now that she couldn't find Bridget or any other clue to the whereabouts of his goldfinch. He wouldn't be back. She needed to stop dreaming about him caring for her and find a way to make her life valuable to others so God would want her. Somewhere in her mind, she was sure that if God and she shared a relationship, she didn't need anyone else. But He wouldn't have any more use for her than anyone else unless she did something special like her mother and sisters did.

Momma and the eldest girls didn't want her to work with them, but maybe Daire was right and Deborah would let her hand out food on Mondays. Surely one had an easier time finding hope in life if one had a full stomach.

The notion of full stomachs reminded her again of her brothers. She splashed cold water on her face from the basin in her room then tidied her hair and descended to the kitchen in time to stop Paul and Roger from devouring all the bread in the house.

"Go to the bakery and buy more," she told them. "We won't have anything for supper if you don't, since Bridget didn't come to work today."

"Did she steal that glass thing?" Paul asked. "I mean, it disappears, and she stops coming to work."

"It's possible." Susan thought of all the tired women in the tenements. "Or maybe someone needed her more than we do. Now, run along. I'll help you with your schoolwork when you get back."

"We want to play ball," Roger protested.

"You'll have enough light to play ball after you do your schoolwork. Where's Gran?"

"She got herself back to the parlor." Paul scooped up a crumb with his moistened fingertip and popped it into his mouth. "Can we buy sugar buns?"

"One apiece if they have any left, but you can't eat them on the way home. Not until after supper." Susan shooed the boys out of the house then set about cleaning up dishes and trying to work out what the family would eat for supper.

All the while she worked, she thought of how to ask Deborah if she could go with her. Maybe they could even go more often. In the end, for all her practiced speech, she simply asked outright.

"I'd love for you to join us," Deborah responded without hesitation. "I didn't think you'd like it, or I would have asked you to come along."

"Why did you think I wouldn't like it?" Susan asked.

"Because you seem to like to stay here at home. Even after you inherited Great-aunt Morris's money, you didn't even try to spend any of it for months."

"And look what silliness I created when I did spend it." Susan picked up the hem of her skirt to examine a tear in the bottom flounce. "If I hadn't bought that goldfinch—"

"You wouldn't have met Daire Grassick." Deborah's eyes glinted with gentle teasing.

Susan feared her eyes sparkled with tears. "There's nothing in that. I can't help him find his bauble, and he's gone off to hunt for it on his own. Or perhaps reacquaint himself with the lady who had lured him to Hudson City instead of New York or Philadelphia."

Deborah clasped Susan's hands in hers. "I'm so sorry if that's true. But he'll come back if he cares."

"He's only interested in his goldfinch. And I need to be interested in some sort of good works like what you're doing."

"It's little enough." Deborah sighed. "We fill their bellies and hope we show some of God's love through this small act."

"Can we do more?" Susan wanted to stamp her foot like a child. "If only I could spend Great-aunt's money, I could—oh, I don't know. But it's wasted on me. I don't need a husband to do good for you all and for those poor people and to show God I want to be a Christian."

"Being a Christian takes more than just doing good, Susie, or even going to church. You need to give your heart to Him and trust in Him and serve Him as He directs you."

Susan crossed her arms over her middle. "Does God lead us in a direction even if I don't—I mean, haven't—given my heart to Him?"

"Yes, it's possible." Deborah looked thoughtful. "Everything that happens in life has a purpose God uses."

A tingle of excitement raced through Susan at the notion that maybe God did notice her, had been leading her in a direction after all.

"If I hadn't bought that goldfinch from Daire and lost it, I wouldn't have realized that we have so many needy people right here on our doorstep," she added. "Momma and Opal and Daisy, and you, too, are always worrying about children in India, which is important, but what about the children in the tenements? They're so sad, so lost, so. . .hopeless."

She gazed up at her elder sister. "Is feeding them enough to give them hope?"

"No, not for long enough. They need to know that they have a future to look forward to."

"How can we give them that future?" Susan began to pace about the kitchen, where Deborah and she had been cobbling together a supper of bread, cold meats, and salad. "Isn't there land out West? I heard about how a man promises people land but never delivers on it. But what if they had real land, learned how to farm—or maybe they already know how—and were given a way to get out there and make claims in, where would that be?"

"Iowa, Illinois, Kansas. . ." Deborah sounded thoughtful. "But that would take a great deal of money, Susie."

"Which I have and can't use for anything but catching a husband." Susan banged the teakettle onto the stove. "And what husband would want to spend my money like that? He'll want to spend it on himself."

"Not the right husband." Deborah chuckled. "You need a man with his own means and a sense of responsibility. A man like Daire Grassick."

"Daire Grassick will never be back. I'm not good enough for a man like him."

"What are you talking about?" Deborah slipped up behind Susan and rested her hands on her sister's shoulders. "Why do you think you're not good enough for Daire Grassick?"

"I want attention for myself, and I'm not good at much but singing."

"I would have said that a day ago, but now I realize that you have a kind and generous heart, and we've all been so good at saving the world around us that we've forgotten our little sister needs some guidance, too."

"Guidance toward what?" Susan faced her sister. "I've tried to join Momma and you and Opal and Daisy with the mission work, but only so you'd notice me, not because I cared about poor children in India."

"And you feel differently about working with the kitchen at the tenements?" Deborah's eyes turned deep blue with her seriousness. "Or do you want to glorify Susan?"

"I want to help. I know now there's so much suffering there. I want to give them hope."

"We can fill their bellies for a day, Susie," Deborah said, her voice a little rough. "But true hope comes only from God. Do you understand that?"

"I. . .don't know."

Daire had said something similar. Maybe if she hadn't given the wrong response to him, he would be coming back.

"I hear the boys coming." Deborah cocked her head to one side. "And Father will be home soon. But after supper, I'll read some scripture with you. The Bible says things so much better than I can."

The boys flung themselves through the back door right then, bearing bread loaves, sugar buns, and telltale dustings of the latter confections around their mouths. Susan didn't scold them, though she knew she should. She was too preoccupied with thoughts of hope beyond the material, not to mention the practical matters of helping the boys with their sums and reading, then finishing preparations for the meager supper.

⁓

"We must find out what has happened to Bridget," Momma said as she dissected a slice of tomato. "Your father needs a hot meal after a day at the bank. If Sam were here, I'd send him to her flat, but maybe you can go, Susan, if Roger and Paul accompany you."

Susan stared at her mother. "You know where Bridget lives?"

"Of course I do." Momma looked indignant that Susan even needed to ask.

"And do you know her last name?" Susan pressed.

"Yes." Momma arched one perfect golden brow. "It's McCorkle."

201

Susan jabbed her fork into a sliver of hard-boiled egg. "Then I'm happy to go."

⤃

"I wondered how long you would stay away." Lucinda swept into the parlor in a red silk gown over wide hoops, her raven hair scooped atop her head like a crown, her dark eyes brilliant with triumph. "Papa said he saw you wandering about looking prosperous again. Did your daddy fill the coffers with more money to invest in our little schemes?"

"Good evening to you, too, Miss Heath." Daire gave Lucinda a formal bow, ignoring her taunting query. "You are as lovely as ever. Are you going out tonight? I don't wish to keep you from your friends."

"Oh, la, they're not important compared to you." Her voice purred. She tossed her head, sending curls dancing over her bare shoulders and wafting the scent of attar of roses into the crowded parlor.

Not so long ago, that voice, the gesture with the bouncing ringlets, and the aroma of roses stirred Daire. Now he thought of Susan's lilting voice, speaking truth as she saw it, light and pure, of her maple-syrup curls tumbling over a modest fichu with artless grace, and her light fragrance more reminiscent of sun-warmed grass than bottle perfumes. Her mere smile or the brush of her fingers thrilled him more than all of Lucinda's flirtatious gestures.

Tamping down images of a young lady he mustn't care about for far different reasons than he had applied to stifle feelings for Lucinda, Daire injected a chill into his voice. "I doubt your father feels that way, depending on the company."

"But no, dearest Daire." Lucinda laid her hand on his arm and squeezed. "Papa would love for me to renew our engagement."

"Yes, the Grassick fortunes would make a nice addition to the Heaths'." Daire removed her hand from his arm and stepped out of range of her reach. "When will he be home?"

"You mean to tell me you came to call on him?" Lucinda's full red lips pouted. "And here I thought I was the lure. I'm crushed."

"For your father, not for any interest you have in me."

"Daire, you're so cruel." A tightening around her eyes made Daire wonder if she spoke a fraction of truth in her latter words.

"You were. . .at first." Daire softened his tone. "But I need a Christian wife willing to live in the country near my family, and if you're honest with both your-self and me, you'll admit that isn't what you want."

"Well no." Lucinda sighed. "I often wished it were." She fingered one of her pomaded curls. "I think I was a little in love with you. But church and the country are so boring compared to parties here in the city."

"Then why did you set your cap for me?" Daire hadn't meant to bring up this much of the past, yet the words sprang to his lips, and he couldn't help but let them emerge.

"Papa promised me a wedding trip to Europe if I could get you to the altar."

Lucinda laughed. "So you see, your value is high."

Daire felt a little ill.

"What about when the honeymoon was over?" he asked.

"No one in my set spends much time with her spouse." Lucinda settled herself onto a chair, her skirts billowing around her like a pile of discarded petals. "But since you don't like Papa's promises of how he can make you rich one day, and you don't want to marry me, why did you come back?"

"To find something that belongs to me." Daire didn't sit. He remained on the far side of the room. "My goldfinch bottle is missing, and I want to know if you or your father have anything to do with that."

"Your goldfinch bottle? Daire, Daire, Daire, you are so unnaturally attached to that hunk of glass. Forget about it and find a nice girl to marry instead."

Jaw set, Daire remained silent, meeting and holding Lucinda's gaze. Her words told him she knew something about the goldfinch. Otherwise, she wouldn't be telling him to forget about it.

She broke the eye contact first and let out a titter. "Why would you think we would know anything about it? Last I knew, you were trying to pawn—" She covered her mouth with her hand. Above the white fingers, her eyes clouded.

"How do you know I wanted to pawn it?" Daire questioned in a low, intense voice.

Lucinda shook her head.

"Your father was looking for it, wasn't he?" Daire pressed.

Lucinda blinked. She didn't confirm his claim. Nor did she deny it.

"Why?" Daire persisted. "I know he isn't trying to get it for you. You were so careless when I showed it to you that you nearly dropped it on the floor."

"No, I have no interest in a silly little glass bird," Lucinda burst out. "But if I'd dropped it, getting the formula would have been so much easier."

Chapter 11

Susan wore an old gown without hoops for her foray into the tenements with her brothers. She'd spent the day cleaning the house and studying a cookery book to come up with a meal that was more substantial than bread and cold meat and salad. The stew she left simmering on the stove smelled savory, though she didn't like the looks of the layer of grease on the top. Bridget's stews never bore the slimy stuff when she served it. Maybe she could find a way to scoop the nasty substance away before they ate it.

Or maybe she could persuade Bridget to come back to work. If the maid did return, Susan vowed to learn how to cook. Even if being a true Christian and real hope came from God, as the Bible said, she thought He might appreciate a lady who possessed useful skills, too, even if that lady would always have enough money to live on, while paying someone to cook for her.

And if all You want is my heart, God, she prayed silently as she marched along between the two boys, *then show me what that means.*

Deborah explained how all Susan needed to do was ask, but Susan had given up asking for things when her mother and sisters said no to her coming along to help them.

Yet Deborah hadn't said no the day before, had she? On the contrary, they had acted like close sisters ever since.

"Can it be that simple?" she murmured.

Paul and Roger glanced at her.

"What did you say?" Paul asked.

"I was talking to God," she told them.

"I do that, too," Paul said. "I ask Him to take care of Sam and keep him safe."

"I asked God to find me boys who can hit a ball as well as I can, but He hasn't answered it," Roger piped up.

Susan laughed. "Roger, do you think God is some kind of rich uncle who hands out toys at Christmas?"

"It was worth a try." Roger grinned. "Paul plays all right, but he's still too short."

"You miss when I pitch to you." Paul swung his arm for demonstration.

"Only sometimes."

"Only most of the time."

"Not once yesterday."

"Boys." Susan headed off an argument. "I want you to stay with me until we get back home, just like Daddy said you must. If we get separated, we might never find one another again."

"We'll all just go home then." Paul flipped onto his hands and began to walk.

Passersby stopped to stare.

"Paul," Susan tried to snap between chuckles, "you're not in the circus."

"But I don't have any schoolwork tonight." He righted himself. "How much farther do we have to go?"

"Another two blocks, I think—where's Roger?"

Sometime during Paul's antics with a handstand, Roger had rounded a corner ahead of them and encountered a throng of boys his age and older batting a dilapidated ball and racing from point to point in the interminable game Roger loved to play.

"He caught it!" Paul cried. "Did you see that, Susan? Roger caught their ball from a block away."

"I saw it." Susan raised her voice. "Roger, get back here."

He either did not hear her or chose to ignore her. Cheered on by the group of youths, her middle brother threw the ball. For whatever reason he did that, it must have been good, for half of the boys cheered and the other half booed.

"Go get him back, Paul," Susan directed.

"All right." Paul plunged into the melee—and disappeared.

Susan cried out in protest but could do nothing to retrieve either brother unless she, too, ran into the crowd surrounding and participating in the game.

Daire wouldn't have abandoned her on the pavement.

Yet Daire had abandoned her, not sent a single word of regret or appreciation for her help. Not that she blamed him. She had lost his precious family piece. Even if it was hers, she should have taken better care of something that bore more sentimental than monetary value.

Without his chivalrous attentions, she must extricate Paul and Roger by herself.

Clutching her shawl across her front like a shield, she edged her way into the first circle of youths. They elbowed her back with rude remarks, the kindest of which was, "No girls here."

"But my brothers—"

A cheer and chorus of whistles drowned her out.

"Paul, Roger," she tried to shout above the tumult.

The shoving boys grew more insistent.

"Go bake bread or something," a young man a foot taller than her suggested. "Leave them to their fun."

"But I need them to help me find—" She stopped.

The youth had turned his back on her, blocking her view of the playing field—the street.

Extracting her brothers looked impossible, and she still needed to find

Bridget. Maybe if she did, the maid would help get the boys away from the game. She always could manage them better than anyone else.

Glad she had left the hoops off today, Susan slipped away from the rowdy boys, glanced about for someone she could ask for directions, and headed toward a slip of a girl with a baby in her arms. "Will you tell me how to get to Mulberry Street?"

"Thataway." The young woman pointed with her chin to a narrow alley appearing dim in the shadow of the tall, narrow flats. "Why you want to know?"

"I'm looking for Bridget McCorkle." Despite the warmth of the day, Susan shivered at the notion of going into that tangle of passages alone.

But she would go, for Daire's sake. For Bridget's sake. Maybe even for her own sake—she didn't know.

"Please." She licked her dry lips. "I need to find Bridget. Not to cause her any trouble," she added with haste.

The girl shrugged. "Turn left, then right, then right again—" She thrust out her hand. "I'll take you."

For a fee. Susan understood the gesture and dug in her purse for a nickel.

The coin disappeared down the girl's bodice, and without a word, she turned and stalked toward the first street. Susan followed, ignoring some catcalls from a group of lounging men. In the girl's footsteps, around refuse and cooking fires, corners and crooked passages too narrow to be called streets, Susan trod with care. She feared the girl led her astray, they turned so many corners, but kept up the walk with dogged pursuit until, at last, the young woman pointed to a whitewashed door.

"There she lives."

Before Susan could thank her or pay her another nickel, the girl and her too-silent infant disappeared back into the warren.

"Wait," Susan called.

What would she do if Bridget wasn't there? She could never find her way out again. "Please, come back. I'll give you another—"

The whitewashed door opened. For a heartbeat, Bridget, solid and white-faced, stood in the frame. Then she spun on her heel and vanished into the flat.

"Bridget, stop." Susan raced in after her.

One dark room led to another. All lay empty, silent save for the patter of fleeing footsteps, sparse of furnishings and spotlessly clean.

"Bridget." Susan slammed into a door painted the same whitewash as the flat's walls.

She staggered back, holding her bruised nose. Her head spun. Stars danced before her eyes. And the silence grew intense inside, not much louder beyond the walls.

Still holding the bridge of her nose with one hand, Susan opened the door. A courtyard lay beyond. Many women worked there washing clothes, tending to children, cooking on braziers. None of them was Bridget.

Daire experienced a lightness of spirit he hadn't known since leaving home in pursuit of wealth and Lucinda Heath. At last he'd shed his heart and soul of any lingering interest in her. Yes, she was beautiful. Yes, she could be charming. No, she was nothing like what he wanted in a wife.

He wasn't certain what that was and refused to contemplate it at present. Each time he did, while walking back to his hotel from the Heaths', while eating his breakfast, while planning his next step in finding the goldfinch, he saw Susan's pretty face.

Susan Morris was most definitely not right for him either. Yes, she was pretty. Yes, she was sweet-natured and open and honest in a refreshing manner after the Heaths' set of friends. But her family needed her. She didn't think they did, but that they depended on her presence at home appeared obvious to Daire. He couldn't dream of dragging her away to Salem County.

Yet hadn't her aunt left her a fortune in order for her to provide herself with a husband? The aunt must have realized that her family would forever keep Susan with them, fetching and carrying, helping with the children and replacing the unreliable maid, until she was a spinster beyond a marriageable age. And her parents, if not her siblings, seemed interested in him as a prospect.

But she did not have a heart for the Lord. Not that his heart felt completely at peace. He was still a wastrel, which was surely not God's will for his life. He needed a purpose, something to make him worthy of his family's love and respect.

He needed to find the goldfinch before he took time to think about his future.

With that in mind, he made his way back to Heath's office near the harbor.

The older man met Daire with a broad grin and outstretched hands. "Come in, lad. So good to see you. May I fetch you something to drink?"

"No thank you." Daire stood in front of the chair a lackey set behind him. "I won't be here long."

"I'm sorry to hear that." With a gesture, Heath sent his assistants from the room. "Lucinda said you two had a rather unpleasant conversation last evening. I'm sorry I missed it." He chuckled deep in his thick chest. "Not the unpleasantness. I'm sure I could have smoothed things over if I'd been there."

"How did you find out about the formula?" Daire demanded.

"Ah, the formula." Heath raised a glass of amber liquid to his lips, though noon had just arrived, later than Daire wanted, the earliest Heath would see him, too early for the man's sort of drink. "Everyone knows the Balmoral crystal is special. I've been trying to get the formula for years."

"But you only export glass sometimes." Daire hooked his hands together behind his back. "You don't make it."

"No, but many a glasshouse here and in Europe would pay for that formula and the queen's favor instead of that paltry business of your family's."

"But how did you know it is in the goldfinch?" Daire asked.

Heath grinned. "Not all of your apprentices are as loyal as you would like to think they are. A little pocket money, and they are happy to write me of any upheavals at Grassicks'."

"Indeed."

Daire would have to telegraph his family and warn them of a spy in their midst.

"By the time I knew you were trying to sell it," Heath continued, "you'd pawned it off on some stranger and left town."

"So you don't know where it is?" Daire hoped he didn't sound too eager.

"I've offered some true land deals to half a dozen men in the tenements if they can get their hands on it, but none have come through." Heath snorted. "Too lazy to really work the land, I expect. They want gold for little work."

"Most of their families were farmers before the famine forced them to come here." Daire jumped to the ready defense of the city's poorest people. "And most of them are honest despite being poor and wouldn't steal."

He shot Heath a glare from beneath half-lowered lids.

Heath let out a booming laugh. "I caught that arrow straight to the heart. But it won't stop me from trying. I will have that formula if it's the last possession I gain."

"And I will stop you from ruining my family if it's the last thing I do."

Daire walked out on Heath, the man's laughter echoing in his ears.

This was Heath's city. He knew too many men in all walks of life, from the poorest to the wealthiest, the least important to the most influential. His chances of tracking down the goldfinch ran higher than Daire's. Heath had sent out the word that he would give land to any man who obtained the formula. That gave him the advantage of many potential leads.

Daire had but one.

Heart pounding as though he ran all the way, Daire approached Susan's house. No one answered his knock. He caught no glimpse of even Gran in the front window. No boys played in the back garden. The dwelling was the quietest he'd ever seen it. Quiet and too neat.

Uneasiness sent him knocking on the kitchen door and circling the premises more than once. It wasn't right for this home of boisterous, untidy, yet friendly and giving people to be silent. The large lot needed to be full of children playing. Gran should be sitting in her window drawing her insights into the family. Susan should be rushing about, her hair and a frill on her gown trailing behind her.

The image sent Daire's heart plummeting into his middle. If he didn't need Susan's help once again, he would have fled right then and there. He couldn't have such strong feelings for her. He'd made many mistakes over the years, but falling for Susan Morris would not be one of them.

Jaw set, he returned to downtown and strolled around a park, where nursemaids watched over babies and old men dozed over newspapers. When numbers boys began to fill up the open green, Daire returned to the Morris house. Surely the two boys would be long since home and someone would be there to meet them.

Once again, the house lay in unnatural silence. Daire paced around and around and around until a neighbor stepped onto her front porch and demanded to know what he was about.

"None of them are home," he said. "Do you know where they've gone?"

"You can look at the church." The woman's smooth face creased into a frown. "It has been quiet there today. I hope nothing's wrong."

"So do I." Daire started to let himself out of the gate.

"Don't you want to know which church?" the woman called after him.

"I already know." Daire waved to her and quickened his pace.

The church lay only a few blocks away. He hoped that someone there would know the whereabouts of at least one of the Morrises, and they all hadn't been mislaid, as Sam had been.

Daire smiled at the notion, where he would have been disgusted just the other day. The Morrises weren't uncaring. He'd seen how they worried. They simply kept their minds focused on others so much they tended to forget what was under their noses.

At the church entrance, he heard the sound of female voices and started in that direction. But he passed the sanctuary on the way, and its quiet dimness drew him in, called to him to stop and do more than hope. He'd told Susan that true hope came from God, yet he hadn't asked for it himself. He'd been trusting in his own devices to find the goldfinch in order to save his family, in order to make himself acceptable to them again. But what of putting his hope, his future, in God and being acceptable to Him?

He talked and thought a great deal about faith in God, even repented of his months with the Heaths. He had not, however, since leaving home, focused on anything beyond finding the goldfinch, trying not to be attracted to Susan Morris, and being able to return triumphant to his family. The safety of his family, where being a Christian, or at least living like one, was easy.

"And I criticize her for not being a Christian." He dropped onto one of the pews and closed his eyes. "Lord, I am failing on my own once again, yet if I do not find the goldfinch, I can't go home. I can't face them. Please let me find it."

He believed God could help him find the ornament with its precious contents, yet peace eluded him. The swell of female voices grew louder, as though they approached, and he scrambled to his feet, afraid they would leave before he finished his devotion or worked out why finally asking for God's help in finding the goldfinch didn't make him feel better.

Neither did seeing Mrs. Morris leading the pack of ladies toward the church entrance, her three eldest daughters following in her wake like ducklings.

"Mr. Grassick." She stopped and gave him her brilliant smile. "What a pleasure to see you here. But if you've come to meet Deborah, I'm afraid she's spoken for." She laughed.

Daire felt warm under his collar. "I, um, am actually looking for Miss Susan."

"Susan?" Mrs. Morris looked blank. "She never comes to help us here. We need her at home."

"She isn't there," Daire said.

"She's gone with the boys to find our maid, Bridget McCorkle," Deborah informed him. "Remember, Momma? We didn't want another cold supper."

"Oh yes. I was so occupied with the bazaar I completely forgot. Didn't my mother tell you where to find Susan?"

Her mother? Oh, that must be Gran.

"She wasn't there either," Daire said.

The four Morris ladies' faces registered shock.

"Where could she be?" Mrs. Morris wailed. "Mother never goes anywhere."

"She probably just didn't come to the door," Daisy murmured, patting her mother's arm. "We'll all go to the house and find everyone safely there."

"Allow me to escort you." Daire offered his arm to Mrs. Morris.

She took it, and her hand shook a little. "Susan should be home by now, too."

"I'm sure they all will be, ma'am."

At least he hoped they were.

But no one was, except for Gran. Moving with the slowness of a giant turtle, Gran tottered around the kitchen, leaning against the worktable or gripping the handle of the oven door, as she appeared to prepare supper—and to do well with it, judging from the delicious aroma of stew wafting through the house.

"Mother, you're cooking." Mrs. Morris's eyes widened. "You haven't cooked for twenty years."

"That's twenty years too long." Gran chuckled. "At least in the summer, when the arthritis isn't so bad. But someone had to do it. Susan tried. She left stew simmering earlier—"

"Susan!" the ladies cried.

"She doesn't know how to cook," Opal said.

"She was trying," Gran explained. "But when she didn't come home soon enough, it started to burn, so I got Mr. Lamb to take me to the market in his buggy for fresh provisions and started over."

"Why?" was all anyone could seem to ask.

"I was afraid once Susan knew how to cook, none of you would ever let her go get herself a husband." Gran stirred the kettle on the stove. "She wants to make you all so happy she would give up her own happiness to ensure yours. And I couldn't let that happen, even if—" She cast a pleading glance at Daire. "Will you help an old lady to that chair?"

He saw the lines of pain then, etching deep grooves on either side of her mouth.

If Susan saw what her grandmother suffered for her sake, she would never doubt that at least one member of her family loved her and cherished her.

"I can carry you into the parlor if you prefer, ma'am," he offered.

"No, the kitchen chair will do." She clasped his arm. "Someone needs to supervise."

"I can cook." Opal rushed to the stove. "William gives the maid two days a week off, and I do for us on those days."

"Where is Susan?" Deborah asked. "She should be home by now."

"And the boys." Mrs. Morris fluttered her long, narrow hands in front of her. "The boys should have come home by now, too. They just had to go find Bridget."

Hairs along the back of Daire's neck rose. "How long ago would they have gone?"

"Two hours and more," Gran said. "They left as soon as the boys returned from school."

"Left for where?" He kept his tone even with effort.

"To find our maid." Mrs. Morris's eyes had reddened, as though she were trying not to cry. "I know where she lives and her surname, so I sent Susan and the boys to find her. I was so sure they'd be all right in the daylight. But two hours is far too long."

"Where would they have gone?" Daire headed for the door. "I'll go."

"I'll go with you." Deborah followed him.

"But Gerrit is coming over shortly," Daisy said.

"He can wait if he has a mind to." Deborah tossed her head. "My little sister needs me."

"Do you know where to go?" Daire asked.

"I know the name of the street." Deborah made a face. "Maybe we can find that."

"I expect we can."

"If we know where to start."

Back at the tenements, Daire stared where a group of boys played a boisterous game with balls and sticks. He was about to lead Deborah around them when he caught sight of the youngest Morris boy jumping up and down on the sidelines.

"Paul," Deborah cried.

He turned, caught sight of her, and tried to duck in front of two bigger boys.

Daire lunged forward and caught him by the shirt collar. "Stop right there, young man." He drew Paul from the crowd. "You are supposed to be with Susan. Where is she?"

"She's not here?" Paul glanced around.

"Paul." Deborah loomed over him, her face tight. "You were supposed to accompany Susan here to Bridget's, not play ball. Where is she? And where is Roger?"

"Roger's there." Paul pointed his thumb to the center of the circled spectators.

Roger swung a stick at a flying ball. *Thwack*. The connection of ball and stick sounded over cheers.

"He's so good," Paul said on a sigh. "If I were taller—"

"Susan," Daire interrupted.

Paul stuck out his lower lip. "I don't know. We got invited to play and—er—sort of forgot about her."

"Don't we all." Deborah shook her head. "Do you think she's gone off to find Bridget on her own?"

Daire glanced around the street. "Since she's not here and not at home, we can only hope that's where she is. I should say *pray* where she is," he added.

"All right." Paul squirmed in Daire's hold. "Can I return to the game?"

"No, you cannot." Daire glanced at Deborah. "Will you hold him while I retrieve the other one? Roger, is it?"

"Yes and yes." Deborah clamped her hand onto Paul's collar in Daire's place. "Don't move, little brother. If you so much as blink, I'll. . ."

Daire didn't hear the rest of the threat as he shouldered his way through the youths, enduring a number of unpleasant names directed at him, and found Roger as his comrades shouted him back to where he'd hit the ball.

"Take your bow and leave," Daire commanded.

"Who are—oh, Mr. Grassick." Roger mopped his sweaty face with a shirt-sleeve. "What're you doing here?"

"Looking for the sister you seem to have mislaid."

"Susan? She's not here?" Roger glanced around as Paul had.

"No, she's not." Daire resisted the urge to shake the lad.

It wouldn't have been right or fair. He knew the lure of a ball game and friends. Roger should have obeyed his parents and stayed with Susan, and that was his parents' place to correct him for his actions. He should have called on Susan earlier instead of abandoning her because he didn't have the strength to resist a lady's attractions.

"We'll go find her now," he said in a calmer tone.

"All right." Roger called a farewell to his companions, receiving many protests in return, and followed Daire back to where Deborah still gripped Paul.

"We need to find someone to direct us to this Mulberry Street," Daire said.

"There's a hundred people around," Paul pointed out. "Ask any of them."

Daire chose a young woman with two small children clinging to her skirt and a baby in her arms. In response, she held out her hand. Daire gave her a quarter, and she gave them directions.

"Left, then right, then right again. . ."

All of them lost the directions after the fourth turn. They stopped an old man, who demanded four bits for his trouble. Daire gave him a quarter instead of fifty cents then gave another quarter to an urchin in a clean shirt and short pants with a dirty face.

A dollar later, they reached the whitewashed door a neighbor assured them belonged to the flat of Bridget McCorkle. The portal stood open onto dimly lit rooms.

"Should we go in?" Paul whispered.

"We won't find anyone standing in the street," Roger retorted.

"We'll knock first," Deborah suggested.

Knocking produced nothing more than a few curious glances from people in other doorways and one old lady's information that Bridget might be in the courtyard.

"How do we get to the courtyard?" Daire asked.

"Go on through," the woman told them. "She won't mind, least I didn't hear her complaining about the young lady earlier."

"Susan," the three Morrises and Daire said together.

Daire held out an arm to bar the boys from charging through the flat, though he wished to do the same himself. At a sedate pace, Deborah's skirts swishing over the bare floorboards, they tramped through the narrow, dark rooms of the flat until reaching the rear door. It, too, stood open. Beyond it, the courtyard teemed with life, everyone in constant motion except for a young lady in a crumpled blue dress, who sat on the pavement with one of her maple syrup–colored curls clutched in the hand of a laughing baby.

Gazing at the image of Susan holding a child in her arms, Daire couldn't remember why he'd wanted to stay away from her.

"I never knew she was so beautiful," Deborah murmured.

"She's that and more," Daire responded in an awed voice. "I think—"

"There's Bridget!" Paul shouted.

Daire jumped and swung toward where the boy pointed. Half a dozen middle-aged matrons gathered around a cooking pot.

"Which one?" he asked.

"That one." Paul raced forward. "Bridget, we've been looking for you."

"Aye, and you found me." One woman detached herself from the others and trudged forward. "But you shouldn't have been sending Miss Susan here on her own. She's been here for hours, caring for the little ones while we got some washing up done."

"We've come for her now," Daire said. "But you could have gotten her home."

"Aye, I could have, but she wouldn't leave." Bridget glared at him from brilliant dark eyes. "Not that you'll be believing me. You'll be saying I've kept her here against her will."

Daire glanced at Susan, who was gazing at them but not moving.

"Why would you think that I'd have such uncharitable thoughts about you?" he asked.

"Because I took your goldfinch bottle," Bridget confessed.

Chapter 12

Susan couldn't move. The child in her arms had finally stopped crying after she'd sent an older boy running for some milky mush to feed the little one. His mother had died the day before, and the distraught father didn't know what to do, so he left the boy in charge of the other children. They couldn't spare much food from the mouths of their own children for the baby, so he wailed with hunger until mere pennies from Susan gave him enough sustenance to quiet him down.

As long as she continued to hold him.

When Bridget returned to the courtyard, Susan couldn't approach her. With the child in her arms, she couldn't get to her feet, and she feared setting him down might get him trampled. Moreover, after the way he had displayed the power of his lungs the other two times she'd tried to relinquish her hold on him, she feared he would throw another fit.

Bridget didn't come to Susan, though their eyes met across the courtyard. Suspicion turned to certainty over the maid's part in the goldfinch's disappearance. Otherwise, she would have spoken, demanding what Susan was doing there, if nothing else.

Susan wished she could see Daire's face as he talked to Bridget. Hers was stony, cold. His stance was rigid.

He'd been taut since he stepped out of Bridget's flat and caught sight of Susan. She hadn't looked at him directly, but she caught the flash of tenderness in his face, a softening that made her heart feel like mush, before he turned his back on her and marched toward Bridget with shoulders as rigid as a building wall.

Such nice shoulders.

"I love him," Susan murmured to the baby.

He cooed in response and took two fistfuls of her hair.

"But he'll never love me. He'll get his goldfinch back and leave."

The baby giggled.

Smiling, Susan cuddled him close. "I can live without him if I can make babies like you laugh."

If she could bring hope to the little ones and their parents.

"How can I do this, Lord? I don't know You enough to talk to people like Deborah talked to me, but I must do. . . something."

Her gaze strayed to Daire. Her heart had reformed itself from the ball of mush and now bounced off the wall of her chest like a ball. It hurt to have him ignore her. Physically hurt.

"There, Lord, I have no hope."

As though he felt the intensity of her gaze, Daire turned his head and looked at her. Saying something to Bridget that Susan couldn't hear, he crossed the courtyard and stooped before Susan. "We were worried about you."

"I was worried about me, too, for a while." Susan stared at him with her feelings bursting forth. "Then I helped with this little one, and I forgot about being lost and Bridget and your goldfinch." She glanced down. "Did she take it?"

"Yes." Daire held out his hands. "I'll help you up and you can hear what she has to say for herself."

"You aren't going to have her arrested?"

"I should." Daire's mouth went grim. "But I doubt I will. Now, how do we manage this if you won't let go of that baby?"

"Maybe Deborah can hold him for a minute."

They called for Deborah to join them. The boys trailing behind her, she crossed the courtyard to where Susan sat. She took the child, who immediately started to wail. Daire assisted Susan to her feet. He didn't let go of her hands as soon as she stood but remained holding them in a firm, warm grip, while he smiled down at her, an odd expression on his face, as though he didn't recognize her and thought he should.

"Bridget," Susan said in a breathless voice.

"This baby is making a scene," Deborah piped up.

Daire dropped Susan's hands as though they'd turned into hot pokers, and she took the child from Deborah.

"I don't know what to do with him," she admitted. "His father has gone off to find work, and he doesn't have a mamma now, poor thing. The baby, not the father."

"I doubt anyone will notice if you take him home." Deborah laughed to show she wasn't serious.

"Since he's quiet now," Daire said, "can we think of his future after we talk some sense into Bridget?"

"You won't get sense out of her," Deborah predicted. "She's adamant."

"About what?" Susan asked.

"Not telling us where the goldfinch is," Daire grumbled. "She took it, but I can't even persuade her to sell it back to me."

"Why not?" Susan glowered at the woman who had been their maid for nearly a year. "Bridget, why won't you sell the goldfinch back to Mr. Grassick?"

"It isn't his to buy back," Bridget answered. "Nor mine to sell," she added.

Behind her, the other women drew away, turning their backs on Bridget. Space encircled the Morrises, Daire, and Bridget. Beyond the gap, the courtyard fell silent. Those who remained watched and listened in silence.

Feeling as though she performed on a stage, Susan moved closer to Bridget. "No, the goldfinch isn't Mr. Grassick's. It's mine, and I will give it back to him. This piece is important to his family."

"So important he sold it on the street?" Bridget curled her upper lip. "And you shoved it into a corner to do nothing but collect dust? Well, now it's important to my son."

"You have a son?" Susan blurted out the words before she realized the possible consequences.

Bridget slapped her hands onto her hips. "You see me nearly every day for a year, and you don't ask my surname. You don't know where I live. You don't know I have a son, who wants to be married if he can prove to his girl's family he's good enough for them. But he won't be doing that without the work, will he?"

"How can he do it with the goldfinch?" Daire asked in an exaggeratedly calm manner.

"He'll sell it to Leonard Heath," Bridget said. "Then he'll have land and money to get a new start."

"And you'd let him do that at the expense of Mr. Grassick's family?" Susan demanded so harshly the baby whimpered.

"They have land already," Bridget reasoned. "A man can have hope if he has land to work and a future."

"Will his conscience let him enjoy his prosperity?" Deborah spoke in gentle tones. "Mr. Grassick and Susan may have discarded the goldfinch because they thought it held little monetary value at the time, but that doesn't change the fact that you stole it. We could have you arrested."

"You won't find it here or nowhere," Bridget declared.

"No, but we all heard you confess to taking it," Deborah continued.

"There's no proof," Bridget insisted.

"She's right," Daire said. "For all we know, her son took it and she's lying for him."

"I thought you were a Christian, Bridget," Paul spoke up in a sullen voice. "You always prayed with us at meals."

"Aye, and I prayed that God would provide for my son, and there was that bottle setting there with no one caring a whit for what happened to it."

"You can't buy hope," Susan said. "I'm an heiress. I can have all the stuff I like, but my heart is still lacking something I know only comes from God, if I can figure out how." She added the last bit under her breath.

Daire shot her a quick glance then returned his attention to Bridget. "At least let me talk to your son."

"I can't be doing that." Bridget's face worked, and tears brightened her eyes. "You'll be having him arrested if he has the goldfinch in his possession."

"I won't." Daire sighed. "Mrs. McCorkle, I just want my property back."

"Aye, and when you get it, my son will have naught."

"I can—" Daire stopped, and his features twisted as though he were in pain. "I can't make him promises, ma'am, but if you keep him from selling the goldfinch to Leonard Heath for a week, I'll work out a fair exchange for him."

"All right, then." Bridget folded her hands across her middle. "I'll be doing that—if it's not too late."

⸺

"I have to go home," Daire announced.

He stood on the walk in front of the Morris house with Susan, who still held the baby bundled in her shawl. The other Morrises had vanished inside the instant the front gate opened, leaving him alone with Susan.

He gazed down at her, his heart heavier than it should have been with the hope of retrieving the goldfinch before Heath still holding life.

"I don't have the resources to persuade Bridget's son to sell me the goldfinch," he explained, though his neck felt hot with the humiliation of admitting that he, a man of twenty-five, still depended on his family for his income. "I should have money. They've given me enough over the years. . . ."

"And mine is secured away from me, or I'd give it to you for being the cause of so much trouble for you and your family." Susan's eyes glowed in the dying light of the day. "I wanted to give it to this baby's father so he didn't have to abandon his son. If I—"

"I'll work for my family at anything and earn it back," Daire broke in. "It's beyond time I stopped being irresponsible and took my place in the family business."

"Even if you don't want that?"

"I want to be with my family. The city. . ." He gazed past her shoulder, away from the heart-melting sight of her cuddling an increasingly fussy baby. "I've done nothing but make mistakes here."

"Then—then you won't come back?" Her voice broke only a little, but from the corner of his eye, he caught the glint of a tear on her cheek.

"I can't."

One reason was that a mere five more minutes in her company and he would do something ungentlemanly and foolish, like kiss her right there in front of her family home and all the neighbors. In no way could he make that sort of a commitment. She didn't share his faith in God, and even if she found a relationship with the Lord, she had just reminded him that she was an heiress. If he married her, he would simply go from depending on his family for his daily bread to depending on his wife. He would never learn to make responsible decisions for himself.

"How will you get the goldfinch back from Mr. McCorkle if you stay away?" Susan asked.

"I'll send up one of my brothers, or even my grandfather." He managed a smile. "Grandfather is a formidable figure."

"Isn't that having your family help you out of a scrape again?"

Daire winced at the truth of her words.

"I can't help but think," Susan continued, shifting so he couldn't avoid meeting her gaze, "that if you're putting your hope for your future in God, you could find out what is right for your life no matter where you live, with or without your family to protect you."

He opened his mouth to object, and nothing emerged. Surely she misunderstood something. At the moment, he couldn't think what, though he wished to believe she was wrong.

"I'll ponder that," he compromised. "And what will you do with that baby?"

"I'll take care of him until someone can be found to do so. My family won't care. They love children, and all the women near Bridget's flat know I have him. Someone will send word if the father comes seeking him."

"I'll pray for you, Miss Susan." He laid his forefinger along the baby's smooth cheek. "And this one."

"Thank you. I'll practice praying by praying for you." She smiled, though more tears trickled down her face.

"Don't despair." Daire brushed them away. "God will show you what He wants for you."

"I already know," Susan said. "What I need from God is for Him to make the bankers give me control of my money." She turned her head and kissed his fingertips. "Good-bye, Daire Grassick. I won't give up looking for your goldfinch."

❧

"Nor will I give up on you," she whispered to his retreating figure.

With the baby fussing, she blinked tears from her eyes and headed for the house. Deborah had already prepared the family for the new arrival, and Momma had everything set up in the nursery.

"You can't keep him, though," she said. "You're too young and without a husband. It wouldn't look right."

"I know. He needs his father." Susan spooned mush into the baby's mouth. "His father needs him, too. I could see how much it hurt him to leave his son with me, a stranger, but he couldn't afford his flat and needed to work and—Momma?"

"Yes?" Momma paused at the nursery door.

"Do you think Daddy can tell me how I can break the trust Great-aunt Morris set up for my inheritance?"

"Of course he can. He's an excellent banker, for all his dreamy poet's heart." Her smile held tenderness. "Would you like me to send him in?"

"If he doesn't mind the baby."

"Your father mind? My dear, he loves babies. Have you never read the poems he's written about all of you as infants?"

"No." Susan bowed her head. "I've read very little of his poetry." She'd thought it merely a personal amusement, much like Gran drawing caricatures purely for her own enjoyment.

"I'll give you the notebook he wrote for you." Momma left Susan.

A few moments later, her father arrived and settled himself on a chair adjacent to Susan's. "You're doing a good thing there, Susan, taking in that poor orphaned child."

"It's only temporary, but someone needed to do it, and I was the only person who could. I have the resources to take care of him, at least for a while." She leaned toward her father. "I want more resources. There's a man named Leonard Heath who lures young men west with promises of land if they work for him for a while in his mines and on his railroad. But they never earn enough to get the land, or even to come back here, because they hardly get any wages. People here are finding out the truth of his plans, and they're wary of accepting them, but they don't have hope for anything else if there's no work on the docks." She paused for breath.

"I know of Heath. We can't seem to stop him, as much as we'd like to. He has some powerful friends in high places. But what does this have to do with your trust?"

"I want to break it. I want to start a mission that will help people resettle farther west, where there's land and work. I haven't quite thought of how I'll do this, but I want the money to try."

"Hmm." Her father tapped his toe on the carpeted floor. "You want to do something similar to Heath's work, but honestly."

"Yes." Susan patted the baby's back. "Is it possible?"

"Not unless you marry," he said. "I'll talk to your trustees tomorrow, and from what I recall, that is the only way you gain control of your money."

"Control if my husband allows me to spend it." Susan ground her teeth in frustration. "And what husband will want to spend it on other people?"

"The right one, my dear. The right one."

That right one was definitely not Daire Grassick. But, oh, how her heart hurt over his leaving.

Oddly, reading her father's poetry helped soothe her pain over Daire leaving. The verses weren't terribly good, as their meter was uneven and the rhymes often forced. Yet the sentiment and emotion behind each line told Susan that he didn't in the least ignore his children's presence. On the contrary, he loved every one of them and his grandchildren.

He's shy, she thought. *Like me.*

The baby cooed at the sound of her voice.

"You should be sleeping, young man."

He slept soon and woke hungry. Susan fed him, got herself ready for the day, and set out for the tenements. She didn't have more than her pin money to use to ease the plight of the people there, but she had time and willing hands. She used both for half of each day, watching children for weary mothers, cooking or fetching and carrying for infirm elderly persons, and always seeking Bridget McCorkle's son.

On the third day there, she learned that his name was Daniel, a good, hard-working young man, who wanted to marry the daughter of a ship's purser.

"He'll do anything to win her father's approval," gradually trusting ladies admitted.

"I understand," Susan said.

She had taken some foolish steps to win her family's attention, if not their approval, from buying the goldfinch to show them she understood pretty things, to dashing about the city with Daire and Deborah to find Sam. Deborah had gone along to make Gerrit jealous enough to propose at last, and Susan had lost her heart to Daire.

Gerrit proposed to Deborah after church on Wednesday night, and Susan was the first person to learn the happy news.

She hadn't been able to keep Daire in the city, but she had become friends with her sister and gained an understanding of her own abilities.

She couldn't sew or persuade people to donate money to good causes. She couldn't even use her own money to support those causes. But she could bring a smile to a weary woman's face by washing her clothes so she could rest, and she could sing small children to sleep. Her new charge went with her everywhere. She wanted to ensure the father would know where his son was so he could find him. In the meantime, she tried to find a family willing to take on another responsibility for the little bit of money she could give them from the allowance the bankers permitted. Thus far, everyone said his father's or mother's family should take on the responsibility of caring for the boy. So, each day, carrying the little one, whom she had taken to calling Frankie, she went home weary and often dirty, and so joyful it masked the hurt of Daire leaving.

Going to church on Sunday reminded her of being there with Daire and the sermon on the lost lamb. She sat in the pew, reading the previous week's lesson in Luke, and her heart opened to the fullness of understanding. She was like the lost lamb, and God cared so much about her, He had led her into the fold. "Please forgive me for not following You sooner," she prayed under her breath. "I accept You into my life."

She still wanted her family's approval. She still longed for a husband who would not want her inheritance to line his pockets, but to do good in the world. She prayed she would find the goldfinch so Daire would return and she could share her newfound faith with him. And she now knew God had been paying attention to her all along, that He was interested in even the least of her actions. As she hoped, He provided, for He was the source of all hope.

For the first time, she stood and sang the hymns with her heart, not caring if her voice soared above the others. She sang to the Lord, not to gain attention.

"What a blessing your singing was," an elderly lady told Susan as they exited the sanctuary. "Why have we never heard you sing before?"

"I never felt God's Spirit in my soul before." Susan wanted to skip out of the church and tell the whole world.

She settled for her family. "I finally understand," she announced at dinner. "God cares about me as much as anyone, and He will provide me with the right husband if I'm supposed to have one."

"We'll help introduce you to nice young men," Opal pronounced. "As soon as we find another maid for Momma."

"I did hope it would be that nice Grassick boy," Momma said. "I thought he showed some interest in you the other day when he was so distraught about you not being home."

"He wants his family more," Susan said, gazing at her plate. "He doesn't care for the city."

"Then he doesn't care enough about you to deserve you," Deborah declared. "We'll find someone else, now that you seem ready to marry."

"I'll wait." Susan cocked her head. "Frankie is crying. Please excuse me."

"What will you do with him?" Momma asked. "You can't keep him."

Susan stood. "I'm praying his father comes back."

The child's father came back that Thursday. He tracked Susan down in one of the courtyards, where she was reading the story of Noah to a group of children and mothers pretending not to listen.

"I'll be taking my son now." He held out his hands.

Trying not to feel a little resentment that he would just snatch Frankie away from her without a by-your-leave, since the child was his, Susan scrambled to her feet and scooped Frankie from his nest of blankets. "You found work?" The question was brazen, perhaps even rude, and she wanted to ensure the baby would be cared for.

"Aye, I'm going to sea." The way the young man drew his son against his chest brought tears to Susan's eyes, his love was so apparent.

Yet alarm tightened her chest. "He's too little to go to sea, sir."

"He won't. I'm marrying his mother's cousin before I ship out."

"Is she—can she. . . ?" Aware of their audience, Susan decided not to ask if the new wife was old enough to take care of the boy.

She twisted her hands in the apron she'd taken to wearing. "May I still call on him?"

"If you like." The young man's features softened. "I know I owe you for taking him in like you done."

"No sir, you don't. I was happy—"

"I don't take charity." His strong chin jutted forward. "I haven't the coin, but I have the information you're wanting."

"Information?" Susan held her breath, not daring to speculate or hope.

"Aye, I know where you can find Daniel McCorkle."

Chapter 13

I've failed." Daire faced his entire family for his confession. "I couldn't find the goldfinch, and by now, Leonard Heath has it." He made himself look his grandfather in the eye. "I'm sorry. I've helped that greedy, dishonest man destroy your life's work."

"I knew we never should have—"

"Jock," Jordan interrupted the youngest brother. "Leave off. Daire had a right to take the goldfinch."

"It's my fault for putting the formula in it in the first place." Maggie screwed up her face, and tears glistened in her eyes.

Maggie never cried. Daire remembered thinking that when Susan had burst into tears in her kitchen. Now Maggie held her serviette to her face and sniffed.

"Twice in one week," he muttered.

"Twice what?" Jordan asked.

"I've made a lady cry." Daire glanced toward his grandparents and parents. "Have you nothing to say to me? Will things be so bad that I can't beg you all to hire me on as an accountant or something menial like sweeping up the cullet?"

"You'd probably cut yourself on the cullet," Jock muttered.

Daire shot him an impatient glance. Only the most incompetent of people would cut themselves on the pieces of glass let to fall onto the glassworks floor as the glassblowers snipped and shaped the cooling glass.

"I've a great deal to say to you, lad," Grandfather spoke, his Scots burr thick. "You should not be making the ladies weep."

"What other lady?" Maggie demanded, her own tears drying in an instant.

"Well, um—" Daire squirmed on his dining room chair. His neck cloth felt too tight. "Miss Susan Morris, the young lady who bought the goldfinch from me."

"Why did you make her cry?" Grandmomma asked.

"I took her into the tenements." While the family drank tea or coffee, according to personal preference, and ate scones and other delicacies in the afternoon tea Grandmomma had taken to while in London seven years earlier, Daire recounted the tale of his days in Hudson City.

"And you just left her there?" Maggie cried. "Daire, you dolt, you nodcock, you—"

"That's enough," Father broke in, his voice quiet, firm. "Daire made a wise decision if the young lady doesn't know if she's a Christian or not."

"But what if she becomes one?" Maggie persisted. "He's thrown away someone who sounds perfectly lovely—"

"She's an heiress," Daire announced.

A moment of silence reigned over the table; then Jock said, "She can save the company after the queen sues us for breach of contract."

"What is wrong with being an heiress?" Grandmomma demanded.

She had been an heiress herself, a fact that stood in her and Grandfather's way of happiness for a while.

"I don't think—" Daire looked from Jock, to Jordan, to Maggie.

"We won't leave," Maggie declared. "We worried about you while you were gone, just as much as anyone else, so we have a right to know."

"I'll make Jock behave himself." Jordan shot a playful punch in his younger brother's direction. "Can you keep your trap shut?"

"I suppose." Jock sighed, but the glance he sent in Daire's direction held compassion. "I can make some guesses about our proud big brother."

"I'm not—" Daire blinked and began to turn his coffee cup around on its saucer. "It's more than pride."

"Is it?" Grandfather asked. "If the young lady were a Christian, would you still have left her behind?"

Daire stared at the whirling liquid in his cup until he thought his eyes would cross. In each shimmer of afternoon sunlight off the brew, he thought he saw Susan's face, her purplish blue eyes shimmering in the daylight—sparkling with joy. Sparkling with tears. Sparkling with an emotion he understood she directed at him.

"Does this heiress care for you?" Momma asked.

Daire nodded without looking up.

"Was she seeking the Lord," Grandfather inquired, "or was she more like Miss Heath?"

"She was nothing like Lucinda." Daire's head shot up. "Susan is lovely and sweet and kind and shy and—"

His family's laughter drowned out his acclaim of Susan's virtues.

"Then why didn't you make her an offer and bring her down here to meet us?" Jock demanded.

"Or invite us up to meet her?" Jordan added.

"Her family needs her, and I'm not sure of her faith, and—"

"You're thinking you have naught to offer her," Grandfather concluded.

"I don't even have my inheritance or share from the glassworks if the formula is truly lost," Daire confirmed.

"Is she interested in you?" Jock asked.

"I—yes." Daire welcomed the cool breeze through the open windows.

"And is it your connections to us or your money she's wanting?" Grandfather pressed.

"I—don't believe so." Daire spoke with caution, not certain what Grandfather intended.

"Then 'tis you that attracts her," Grandfather pressed.

"I have reason to believe so," Daire admitted in a tone that sounded hoarse. He swallowed a drink of coffee. "But it doesn't matter. She lives in the city, and I live down here. She wants to work with the poor in the city, and I want to remain here, where—where—"

No, he wouldn't admit that much in front of his siblings.

"Besides, none of it matters, now that I've lost the goldfinch."

Silence fell over the table, save for a bee that had flown through one of the windows and hovered over the jam pots, buzzing.

"If you had found the goldfinch," Father posed, "would you have considered pursuing a courtship of this young woman?"

"Yes," Daire responded without hesitation.

"Then that settles it." Grandfather snapped his handkerchief through the air and captured the bee against the tablecloth. "I created the goldfinch as a gift for the lady I love, not as a possession to cause strife and heartache in the family I love. Now 'tis coming between you and your brother and sister, and you and the lady you love, and you and God; we need to all confess that we've made an object too important to us."

"But the formula," Maggie burst out. "Grandfather, it's more than the goldfinch we're looking for. It's the formula."

"And the contract with Queen Victoria to always be able to produce her crystal," Jock added. "You know we will be ruined without it."

"And if we're putting our financial security above our happiness, or worse, our relationship with the Lord," Grandfather said in his sonorous voice, "then 'tis past time we gave it up."

Daire opened his mouth to argue. From the corners of his eyes, he saw his siblings and even his grandmother struggling with the same impulse. Momma and Father, like Grandfather, sat motionless with peaceful faces.

Mouth dry, Daire snatched up the handkerchief still trapping the bee and carried it to the window. Gently, he lowered the cloth over the sill and drew the fabric away. The bee lay on a rhododendron leaf for a moment as though stunned; then its wings fluttered and it soared toward the nearby rosebushes.

"Even the bees have a purpose in their lives," he murmured, more to himself than anyone. Then he turned his face up to the clear blue sky and spoke with more firmness. "My life was centered around proving myself good at something so you all would care about me, but I didn't succeed, and you all still care. Then I failed to get the goldfinch and formula back, and yet you continue to care, to love me. Now I just need to have something to do with my life, and if the glassworks will perhaps fail, you won't need me to keep the books and take orders, or even clean up cullet. I haven't been very good at getting through life on my own." He faced them. "Will you help me?"

"It's past time you asked, son," Father said. "What would you like help with? And I'll start by asking you what you've prayed for besides help with finding the goldfinch."

"I—well, I. . ." Daire held his father's gaze. "Nothing. I simply ran back to you all each time I didn't succeed at something."

"We're happy to have you home." Momma held her hands out to him. "But you've never found your niche here, which tells me you're supposed to be somewhere else."

"Not that we're telling you to leave again," Jock put in. "Not even me."

Daire's heart warmed and swelled until his chest tightened.

"You haven't the aptitude for the glassmaking or the farming," Grandfather pointed out. "So we've always thought the Lord had something else planned for you."

"*Therefore shall a man leave his father and his mother.*" Maggie quoted from Genesis in a whisper loud enough to be heard from a stage.

"We hoped you'd find it in your wanderings," Grandmomma said.

"But I never did." Daire met each of his family members' eyes. "My carelessness and wanderings cost this family dearly. How can God have a plan for me now?"

"He does," Grandfather said. "But you thought you failed us, so you've run back here to hide, but you won't be hiding from what the Lord wants for you and have the peace in your heart. Now, if you all will be excusing me, I am going to the glasshouse to mix the crystal formula as I recall it."

"Grandfather." Maggie leaped to her feet. "I'm certain you're adding too much quartz—" She dashed after her long-legged grandfather.

"So what do you plan to do, Daire?" Jock challenged.

Daire smiled. "A lot of praying."

And a lot of walking.

Summer's sticky heat hadn't yet descended upon southern New Jersey. Daire took advantage of the warm sunshine and coolness beneath the towering pine trees to walk and think. He tried to focus on praying, on asking God what he should do now. He found himself crying out in despair that the goldfinch had remained lost, that a man like Leonard Heath would prosper.

Even if Heath's prosperity at the expense of the Grassicks meant a better life for Bridget's son, Daire couldn't understand why God would allow the wicked to win. He fought against it.

And when he wasn't struggling to accept how things worked out, he too often thought of Susan. He prayed she found her relationship with God for which she had been seeking. He thought he should pray she found the right sort of husband so she could use her fortune for the good. The words refused to come to him. His mind—and his heart—would not wrap around the notion of Susan as another man's wife.

"If I had something to offer her"—he began his daily devotional a week after returning home, as he had begun it many other times—"I could—"

The sight of Jock and his fiancée, Violet, walking hand in hand toward him, changed the course of his words.

"I could marry Susan. If only I'd found the goldfinch."

Yet what would he have done if he had found it? It wouldn't make him talented at glassmaking or interested in farming. The search for it had taken him from his family, back to the city, where he freed his mind and heart of the Heaths' tug on him, met Susan, and saw a need to help the families in the tenements, do something in opposition to Heath's swindles. With money, he could do so much good, especially with a wife interested in the same.

Especially with a wife with an inheritance.

Daire shook his head, rejecting the notion. It would be wrong, would it not?

"Only if you do not love her," Grandfather assured him later, when Daire told him of his notion. "And if 'tis what the Lord wants for you, Miss Morris will be wanting the same, I'm thinking."

"And it will make up for the loss of the goldfinch and the formula," Daire added.

"Or 'tis the reason for the missing goldfinch," Grandfather suggested.

"I'd find comfort in knowing that." Daire studied his grandfather's craggy face. "How do I go back there, face her after I simply walked away? She'll think I only want to marry her because she's an heiress."

"Nay, lad, not if she, too, is seeking the Lord's will. But don't tarry. Take one of our horses."

Daire did tarry. He kept imagining Susan rejecting his suit. She would have no use for him, a man with no prospects except for a way to spend her money for her, however much good he intended. Staying home, making himself useful wherever he could, from cleaning out stables to indeed sweeping up cullet from the glassworks floor to packing fragile pieces of glass for shipping, was safer.

And wrong for him.

He knew this. For nearly ten years, he'd left the family every chance he found. Now he wanted to stay when his family encouraged him to go. He didn't want to fail again. At the same time, no success came from hiding away. Without trusting in God to direct his steps, he would never find the purpose in life for which he'd hoped for a decade.

The Thursday after he returned home, he woke and began to pack.

"I'm leaving tomorrow," he announced at breakfast.

The telegram arrived by suppertime:

FOUND BRIDGET'S SON.

Chapter 14

This is a wedding." Susan stared at the throng of people filling one of the tenement courtyards as she spoke to Deborah and Gerrit. "Frankie's father said I'd find Daniel McCorkle here."

"You will." Gerrit gestured above the heads of most of the crowd, using his height to advantage. "I believe Mr. McCorkle is the bridegroom. At least Bridget is standing beside the best-dressed man here, and a young lady is in a white dress and veil."

"But—" Susan blinked back tears.

If Daniel McCorkle was getting married already, he must have sold the goldfinch to Leonard Heath. The information from Frankie's father had come too late to help Daire.

And Daire wasn't there. She'd sent the telegram Thursday morning. This was Saturday afternoon, and she had received no response. He should have gotten there by now, if he were coming at all. Her heart ached with emptiness and now loss. Perhaps Daire not coming was for the best. Her telegram must have raised his hopes, and now the wedding would dash them again.

Unless, of course, he'd gone straight to Heath, or sent someone from his family straight to Heath, to negotiate for return of the goldfinch and formula. Perhaps the Grassicks could take legal action against Heath if they proved he had acquired the goldfinch and formula through illegal means.

"And that would get Mr. McCorkle arrested, since he stole the goldfinch," Susan mused aloud.

She doubted even Deborah and Gerrit could hear her above the fiddle music and cheers and shouts of friendly teasing erupting from the throng of merrymakers.

"His mother stole it," Deborah responded, apparently possessed of excellent hearing. "She'd be the one to be arrested."

"Her son knew it wasn't hers." Susan stood on tiptoe, craning her neck in an attempt to see the bride and groom.

She saw Daire Grassick instead. He stood on the other side of the courtyard, engaged in much the same activity as she was. For a moment, before Susan lost her balance, their eyes met, and he smiled.

Warmth flooded through her. She grasped Gerrit's arm for support on one side and Deborah's on the other. "He's here." Her voice squeaked, and she swallowed. "Daire is here."

"Where?" Deborah rose to her toes. "I don't see—ah. He's approaching the happy couple."

227

Susan didn't waste more time trying to stand on her toes. She pushed through the crowd, apologizing when she jostled others but not stopping until she, too, reached the bride, groom, and Bridget McCorkle.

Daniel looked like his mother, with heavy dark hair and eyes too brilliant to be a true black. Their smiles matched, too.

The smiles of all three persons died the instant Susan propelled her way into the group around the newlyweds.

"Miss Morris," Bridget grumbled. "Could you not stay away another day?"

"No, I—"

Daire strode into the circle. Bridget grasped her son's arm and tried to draw him away. The young man stood his ground, his gaze fixed on Daire.

Susan watched Daire, too, wondering what he would do or say, every muscle in her body tense.

"Mr. McCorkle." Daire held out his hand to the young man. "I see I am to offer you felicitations."

"Ye–es sir." Daniel McCorkle hesitated a moment then shook Daire's proffered hand. "Though I'm not sure—"

"Daire Grassick." Daire's smile set Susan's heart racing. "And this is your lovely bride?" He bowed to the fair young lady beside Daniel. "May the Lord bless your union."

"Thank you, sir." She bowed her head. "We are honored to have you here. My father—" Her gaze darted around the courtyard.

"He's gone for more lemons," Daniel assured her. "He'll be back." He turned his attention to Daire and Susan right behind him. "We have more guests than we expected."

"I'm sure they wish to give you a good send-off to—" Daire cocked his head, as though he listened to something far away. "Iowa, is it, that Heath has land?"

"I—I dunno, sir." Daniel shifted from one foot to the other. "I'm not going to farm."

"He's going aboard my father's ship." The bride raised her head and her whole face lit. "When Daniel promised to do that, Father gave us his blessing to marry, but we had to do so right away." Her porcelain fair features turned begonia pink. "Because they ship out in three days, that is."

"You do?" Daire's shoulders jerked as though someone had struck him between the shoulder blades.

Susan felt the same impact in her middle. She caught her breath and took a step forward. "What have you done with the goldfinch, then?" she demanded before she could stop herself. "We thought you were going to sell it to Mr. Heath in exchange for land out west."

"I couldn't." Daniel gazed down at his bride. "She. . .um. . . fell in love with it, and when her father said there was work aboard the ship he is with, I—I let her keep it as a wedding present."

"And now you'll be wanting it back, won't you, Mr. Grassick?" Bridget's words emerged more challenge than query.

"Oh no," the younger Mrs. McCorkle cried. "You cannot. Daniel said you sold it."

Daire remained silent for several moments. Though the fiddles crooned and many danced, others watched the group around the bride and groom. Susan's stomach clenched so hard she feared she'd be sick. She understood if Daire wanted the goldfinch back, but the bride looked so stricken, the notion of taking away her gift seemed cruel. Yet it had been stolen.

"Mr. McCorkle," Daire spoke at last, "did you truly give up the prospect of land of your own so that your wife could have the goldfinch bottle?"

"Aye sir." Daniel held his head at a proud angle. "When I learned how my mother got it, and how you needed it, I'd have given it back, but you were gone, and when Pearl wanted it so bad, I couldn't bring myself to give it even to Miss Susan. But we'll give it up to you now that you have come for it. It's only right."

"Though it's ever so pretty." Pearl looked about to cry.

Daire glanced around the encircling crowd. His lips tilted in a half smile when he met Susan's gaze upon him; then he settled his glance on Pearl. "Mrs. McCorkle, you may keep the goldfinch. It was created to be given to a loved one, and that's what's been done with it. But please allow me to extricate what is inside it."

"There's something inside it?" Pearl asked.

"A slip of paper precious only to a few," Daire answered.

"Like Heath." Daniel looked dismayed, as though regretting not seeking for something inside, then smiled. "You won't damage the bottle?"

"I wouldn't think for a moment of doing so." Daire nodded.

"So it's mine?" Pearl breathed. "Then you can have whatever's in it whenever you like."

"Right away," Daniel added.

"It can wait," Bridget declared.

Daire nodded. "Yes, it can wait until after the celebrations. I have other, more important matters to tend to now."

Nearly sagging with relief and joy, Susan stepped away from the circle around the bride and groom. They hugged Daire, along with Bridget, as though he were a member of the family. Since his arrival in the group, no one had noticed her. Once, this would have hurt her deeply, sent her scrambling for a way to get noticed. Now she simply smiled at the happy conclusion to Daire's situation and started back toward Deborah and Gerrit, with more courtesy this time.

"Thank You, Lord, for finding the goldfinch," she murmured beneath the noise of the crowd. "May Daire now find his purpose in—oh." A hand touched her arm, and she jumped, spun on her heel, and came face-to-face with Daire Grassick.

"I didn't mean to startle you." He gave her a tentative smile. "But you were running away."

"I wasn't running." Susan's voice sounded breathless to her ears. "I—you—I was thanking the Lord for making everything work out for you."

"He has indeed worked matters out for my family."

"Except you lost the goldfinch."

"I didn't lose it. I gave it away to someone who wanted it more than a secure future because her beloved gave it to her."

"I know, but—" Susan's throat closed, and her eyes burned. "Your family," she managed in a whisper.

"We'd already given it up as lost for good."

"You could have taken it back."

"No, I couldn't. My grandfather said the goldfinch had caused strife in the family, when it was to symbolize love and constancy, and we needed to be rid of it, give it up to the Lord." He tucked her hand into the crook of his elbow and turned toward the side of the courtyard. "Will you walk with me?"

"Deborah and Gerrit are here, too."

"I see them. They won't miss us for a bit." He turned his head to the left.

Deborah and Gerrit had joined those dancing to the lively music.

Susan laughed. "They look so happy. I expect theirs will be the next wedding I attend."

"Perhaps." Daire covered her hand with his free one and guided her through the throng to where a narrow street led out of the courtyard. "Perhaps not theirs, if I can change your mind."

"If you—" Susan stopped and faced him in the darkness. "What are you saying?"

"Too much, or perhaps just in the wrong order." He rested his hands on her shoulders. "Let me start with this: Susan Morris, I am not a man of many talents. I failed at farming and glassmaking and never trained for a profession, unlike the rest of my family. But I could have stayed there forever, even taken a wife there, and never wanted for anything."

"But you haven't?" Susan could hardly speak her chest felt so constricted.

"I was hiding there, hiding from my own fear of making more mistakes instead of trusting in the Lord to guide me. Your telegram guided me right back here." He moved his warm hands to cup the sides of her face. "I've known what I wanted for days now, but I was afraid." He laughed. "I'm still afraid."

"Of what?" she whispered.

"You're an heiress, Susan, and although I get a share of the profits from the family business quarterly, it's not anything like your inheritance, and that's why I left."

"You left because I'm an heiress?" Indignation loosened Susan's tongue. "If that isn't the most absurd thing I've ever heard. That money is to help me catch a husband, not lose me one. I mean—that is. . . Oh, dear. I've spoken out of turn."

"Not at all," Daire said.

Then he kissed her. Though the music behind them rose in a jig, on fiddles,

Susan thought it sounded more like a concerto with a full orchestra. She crushed Daire's neck cloth between her hands and would have sagged at the knees if Daire hadn't held her upright.

"I love you," he murmured with his lips a fraction of an inch from hers. "Will you be my wife?"

"Maybe."

"Maybe?" He jerked back. "You just let me kiss you."

"I suppose that was bad of me." Susan ducked her head, and her hair tumbled loose around her face and shoulders. "I've so been hoping you would, I forgot. You see, Daire—" She peered at him through the curtain of her hair. "I want to work with the people here, help young men like that baby's father and Daniel McCorkle and the young women, too, to find work and settle where they can have better lives. Do the things Heath promises to do but never does. I have the money, but only if I get married to a man who agrees to use it for this purpose." She tilted her head flirtatiously. "And I don't know where to find such a man."

"Minx." Daire laughed and kissed the tip of her nose. "You can stop searching if you're willing."

"I'm willing." She rested her head on his shoulder. "If you're asking me to marry you, then the answer is I will."

THE NEWCOMER

Dedication

To my nieces, who are precious to me.

Chapter 1

A flick of the turkey-feather brush dislodged dust, an invitation to a picnic, and a gray and silver–striped kitten from the parlor mantel. The invitation wedged itself in the fire screen, where it stuck out like a child's insolent tongue. The kitten displaced a picture of a solemn-faced couple in wedding garb.

Sneezing from the flying dust, Marigold McCorkle caught the picture before it smashed on the hearth. In the foyer, the kitten squacled then vanished into the library. For a moment, the dust whirled about in the afternoon sunshine, like a taunt, then settled over the carved mahogany mantel once again.

"That never happens when Mrs. Cromwell dusts." The observation came from nine-year-old Beryl Chambers. She stood in the parlor doorway, her long-fingered hands on her hips, and every aspect of her appearance—from the white straw hat perched atop her glossy, blond pigtails to her white dress banded with dove gray ribbons to her white button shoes—was in place, spotless, and unblemished.

In contrast, Marigold knew her flaming hair was bursting from its pins in a hundred directions. Her plain, gray dress bore the marks of stove blackening on one sleeve, and white was no longer a word one could apply to her apron.

"You should go slower," Beryl continued. "That way the feathers collect the dust instead of just making it fly around. Would you like my handkerchief?"

It, too, would be pristine.

Marigold sighed. "No, thank you. I need to go change my dress and wash a bit. Where's your sister?"

"Sulking in the garden." Beryl stuck her pert nose in the air. "She's such a baby."

"She's only six."

And worried about the new person about to spring upon her life.

"You need to be patient with her." Marigold dusted the silver picture frame with a clean corner of her apron and set it on the mantel beside the clock. That instrument ticked by the minutes in an ominous reminder that the train was due in less than an hour, and she'd better get herself up to her room and into clean clothes. Just because her original duties as the girls' nurserymaid had also turned into governess and housemaid since the death of their parents, didn't mean she could meet the new master of the house looking like a duster if someone turned her on her head.

"Is she ready for your uncle?" Marigold asked.

"No, she wouldn't let me help her, and Mrs. Cromwell is busy making dinner."

"Then will you please fetch her inside and send her up to the nursery?" Marigold let her gaze dance around the room in search of anything in need of dusting, polishing, straightening.

Every stick of furniture glowed with the patina of fine wood. The aroma of beeswax and lemon scented the air from the polishing, along with the fragrance of some late-blooming roses cut out of the garden and set in tall, crystal vases. White puff balls of hydrangeas appeared to float in their shimmering glass bowls set amid framed photographs, china figurines, and some small, wooden carvings that covered every available surface. Above her the ceiling fan spun in a lazy circle, the moving air countering the warmth of the August sunshine spilling in through draperies open to welcome home the new owner of the house.

"It will do," Marigold decided and headed for the doorway.

Beryl still stood there, her hands now clutched together at her waist.

"What is it, child?" Marigold asked.

"I'm not a child." Beryl's suddenly trembling lower lip belied her claim. "I'll be ten in another month."

"I beg your pardon. I'm more than twice your age, and my father still calls me 'child.' You, of course, are quite grown up and don't need me at all, but how may I help you?"

"It's Ruby." Beryl blinked her huge, blue eyes—eyes that looked a little glassy. "She's afraid Uncle Gordon isn't very nice."

So was Marigold. After all, how good could a man be when he took three months to come care for his orphaned nieces? For herself, she was prepared to heartily dislike him. Those three months of not responding to her pleading telegrams to return to Cape May, New Jersey, had cost her dearly.

She offered Beryl an encouraging smile she feared wouldn't ring true. "He's nice enough to come home, isn't he? And his telegram was kind."

No, kind wasn't the right word. Polite and promising generosity, yes. Considerate, barely. Kind? Only if implying he could make up for his long and unexplained absence by paying her extra wages was kind.

She clenched her fingers. A crack like a shot burst through the room. A sharp pain gouged Marigold's hand.

"Miss Marigold," Beryl cried, "you're bleeding!"

"I am?" Marigold glanced down to discover blood indeed trickling from her palm. She'd broken the handle of the feather duster, and the sharp ends of the split wood dug into her flesh. "I'd better go wash this. Will you please fetch Ruby upstairs? We can talk while I'm washing up and changing my dress."

"We can't talk about Ruby being scared." Beryl turned away. "It'll make her feel bad."

"Then we'll pretend we're talking about you."

Marigold wanted to hug the child, but Beryl would never tolerate a smudge or wrinkle to her appearance. She was already moving away, anyhow. As she reached the door, she slipped her hand into a tiny white pocketbook and withdrew what was, without a doubt now, a spotless, white handkerchief with a black border to remind everyone of her recent loss.

"Poor babies," Marigold murmured.

Her own eyes burning—possibly from the dust—she gathered up her skirt and raced up the steps. Fifty-three minutes were not enough to wash, change her dress, and do something reasonable with her hair, plus tidy Ruby.

"Please don't let anything else interfere," Marigold prayed, meaning she hoped Mrs. Cromwell, the cook and housekeeper, wouldn't request her assistance for anything.

Marigold darted into the room the girls' parents had converted to a nursery bathroom. She longed for a bath after cleaning all morning in the sticky, New Jersey, August heat. She settled for a wash in the deep bowl of the sink then pulled the remaining pins from her hair. It cascaded around her face and shoulders in carroty curls so tight most combs broke trying to make their way through. It would have to wait for renewed pinning until after she donned a clean dress and saw to Ruby.

Marigold's clothes lay on her bed in the room reserved for the governess, though she'd only been hired as a nursemaid fifteen months earlier. White muslin dotted with tiny violets fluttered over her head, sending her hair floating outward, then settled onto her petticoats. Twisting a bit, she managed to get the buttons into their holes, then reached for her buttonhook to remove the heavy black footgear she wore while doing housework and don the pretty white ones for dress apparel.

She'd gotten off the first pair and stood in her stocking feet, reaching for the second pair in her wardrobe, when Ruby scuffed through the bedroom door and Mrs. Cromwell called up the back steps for assistance lifting the roasting pan out of the oven.

"Now," the housekeeper emphasized.

Marigold eyed Ruby's smudged chin, grubby hands, and torn dress with its suspiciously squirming pocket. "If that's not the kitten in there, take it outside immediately. If it is, sit on the chair there and wait for me. I'll be back in a moment."

"It's Dahlia," Ruby mumbled. Her voice had grown too soft since her parents' death. "She was sitting on Daddy's desk, and he doesn't like her there."

"If you hold on to her, Dahlia is in good hands." Marigold tousled Ruby's golden hair, which would also need to be braided again, then dashed out the door and down the rear staircase to the kitchen.

"Do you have a clean apron? I don't want to soil this dress."

"You know where they are." Mrs. Cromwell pointed her salt-and-pepper bun toward the pantry door.

On a row of hooks, spotless aprons hung. Marigold snatched one down and yanked the strings so hard around her trim waist that one parted from the apron.

"I'll sew it back on," she said before the housekeeper could scold her.

"If you go more slowly," Mrs. Cromwell admonished, "that sort of thing won't happen." She gave the apron a narrow-eyed glance. "That was the one you mended last week."

So she didn't sew any better than she dusted.

Marigold sighed and, with the speed of a turtle crossing the road, removed another apron from a hook and tied it behind her.

"My roast is drying out." Mrs. Cromwell tapped the toe of her heavy brogan, shoes that reminded Marigold of her great-grandmother Bridget. "Can't be waiting all day."

"No ma'am." Marigold snatched up towels folded for the purpose of protecting one's hands from the heat and opened the oven door. Steam smelling of roasted beef, potatoes, carrots, and sweet onions billowed toward her. Her stomach growled. Her mouth watered. Her hair sprang into wilder curls, as it tumbled around her face, tickling her nose and tangling with her eyelashes.

She blew the hair out of her face and hefted the huge roasting pan onto the worktable, something Mrs. Cromwell was growing too frail to manage on her own. "Do you need anything else, ma'am?"

"No thank you, I can manage from here." Mrs. Cromwell frowned at Marigold. "But will you please tie your hair back before coming into my kitchen. As pretty as it is, we don't want to be eating it."

"Pretty?" Marigold laughed. "It's a fright, and you are a dear for saying otherwise." She kissed the old lady's wrinkled cheek then raced back up the steps.

"Slow down before you hurt yourself," Mrs. Cromwell called after her.

If only she had time to slow down. The train was due into the station in ten minutes. Even if Mr. Gordon Chambers disembarked last and waited for his luggage to be unloaded, experience with the train on a weekday, not as busy as the weekends, told Marigold he would arrive in half an hour at the most—and possibly less. Cape May just wasn't large enough for getting anywhere to take long.

Marigold charged into her bedroom to gather up Ruby and take her for a wash and change of clothes. But Ruby no longer perched on the desk chair. Nor did she appear to be anywhere in the room or the bathroom. Marigold glanced into the girls' room. No Ruby appeared there either, though her dress, matching Beryl's, lay across her pink gingham coverlet.

"Ruby, where are you?" Marigold called. "Where—"

A thud and a cry from the schoolroom on the other side of the bathroom interrupted the query.

Marigold sprinted in that direction. She burst through the doorway in time to find Ruby lying on the floor beside an overturned chair and Dahlia, the kitten, glaring down at the scene from atop the bookcase.

"Are you all right?" Marigold dropped to her knees beside Ruby.

Ruby nodded but didn't move.

"Where are you hurt?" Marigold touched the child's head, seeking lumps. "Look at me, baby."

Ruby looked at her and gasped for air.

"She's just winded." Beryl marched into the room, stood on tiptoe, and plucked the kitten from the shelf. "You should know better than to climb onto chairs."

"I—know." Ruby managed to wheeze. "She was—crying to get down."

"Next time," Marigold admonished, "you ask someone taller to get her down, all right?"

Ruby nodded.

"Good. Are you in pain?" Marigold debated whether to call for a doctor. "Can you get up on your own?"

Ruby nodded again.

"Then let's get you dressed and your hair combed." Marigold took the girl's soft little hands in hers, noting a long scratch on one of them. "And clean up that scrape."

"You need to let Dahlia go when she wants to go." Beryl sighed. "You never learn."

"Beryl," Marigold said, "please go downstairs and see if Mrs. Cromwell needs your help setting the table."

"She doesn't." Beryl selected a book from the shelf and perched on the window seat. "I already did it."

"At least one of us is competent," Marigold muttered. Aloud she said, "Come along, Ruby."

"Yes ma'am." Ruby sat up with no apparent difficulty.

Marigold helped her to her feet then led her into the bathroom to wash her up, then to the girls' room to change Ruby's dress. Her hair, like Beryl's, brushed out with barely a snarl to slow the progress. It waved so prettily, Marigold was half tempted to leave it flowing down Ruby's back. But Beryl insisted that they have their hair braided and wear white ribbons tied around the ends. So Marigold sat on the dressing table stool and began the tedious task she'd performed that morning—twisting the child's waist-length tresses into smooth, even plaits.

Throughout the process, Ruby stood perfectly still. Marigold would have been pleased at such compliance, except Ruby had fought having her hair tended to only three months ago, right up to the day her parents, full of life and laughter and love for their children and one another, went out sailing on one of the boats the Chambers Excursion and Sailing Company owned and returned when the tide washed their bodies ashore. Now Marigold wished Ruby would squirm and complain instead of playing like she was a breathing statue of a little girl.

Halfway through the second braid, Marigold remembered she was going to talk to the girls about not being frightened of their uncle. She supposed it was best. Just the sound of his name in her own head made her stomach curdle like cream left in the sun. Gordon. Too much like "gorgon," some mythological monster out of a fairy tale.

"Ouch!" Ruby exclaimed.

Marigold realized she'd tugged too hard on the child's hair while thinking of Gordon Chambers and his tardy arrival home.

"I'm sorry. Almost done here." Marigold picked up the second ribbon and tied it around the end of the pigtail. "You look lovely. Let's go show Beryl."

Hand in hand, Marigold and Ruby started for the schoolroom. Before they reached it, Beryl's voice reached them. "He's here."

"Already?" Marigold peeked at the clock hanging on the schoolroom wall.

Either the train arrived early or Mr. Gordon Chambers hadn't waited for his luggage.

Marigold's stomach felt as though it were wrapping itself around her sinking heart. In a few minutes, she would turn her charges over to a man who hadn't cared enough to come home in time for his twin brother's funeral, then waited another ten weeks to say whether he would return at all, and another two weeks to send a telegram announcing the train on which he would appear. As much as she wanted to get back to her own family in Hudson City, she hesitated at the top of the steps, each of her hands gripping that of one of the girls, her feet unwilling to carry her forward to open the front door to such a cold, indifferent man.

"These girls need lots of love, Lord," she mouthed toward the fanlight spreading its jewel-toned light over the foyer and steps. "They only have me, and I can't stay."

The doorbell chimed. It reverberated through Marigold's head like a hammer blow.

"Answer that." Mrs. Cromwell's voice drifted through the house.

"Follow me down," Marigold whispered. "And stand at the bottom of the steps and wait to be introduced. Remember to—"

The doorbell chimed twice in rapid succession.

"We know," Beryl said. "You'd better go."

"You don't want to get punished for making him wait," Ruby murmured.

No, it was Mr. Gordon Chambers who needed the chastisement for being late.

Marigold gripped the banister for support and ran down the carpeted steps and across the runner to the front door. Well-oiled, the bolt slid open without a sound. Marigold tugged the heavy portal open and stepped back to allow the man on the front porch to come inside.

Other than giving her a brusque nod, he didn't acknowledge her, but strode past to set his valise on the floor and crouch before the girls. "Beryl, Ruby, I'm your uncle Gordon and so very sorry it's taken me this long to get home." He spoke in a voice as warm and rich as lemon custard. "Will you forgive me now that I'm here to see to things?" He held out his hands—long-fingered hands like his brother's, like Beryl's, only his were bronzed and hard-looking.

The girls made no move to take his hands or even speak. Ruby stuck the first two fingers of her right hand into her mouth, and Beryl's right toe tapped against the carpet.

"It was inexcusable of me to stay away so long, wasn't it?" Mr. Chambers said.

Though Marigold only saw him in profile, she caught his smile and the way it creased the corner of his eye. Breath snagged in her throat. From the side, his resemblance to his brother made her blink. For a heartbeat, Gerald Chambers might have returned to them—but only for a heartbeat. A second glance showed Gordon's hair curled more, and his shoulders appeared broader, his arms more powerful.

Marigold inhaled to steady herself from the shock and switched her gaze to the girls. Their faces had paled, their eyes widened. Marigold half expected them to cry "Daddy," but they remained silent, motionless, possibly as stunned as she.

He took one of the girls' hands in each of his. "I'll make things as right for you as I can, I promise," he continued into the silence.

"You're not as handsome as Daddy," Beryl pronounced.

Marigold licked her dry lips. Beryl must prefer a more refined look. To Marigold, Gordon Chambers, at least in profile, outweighed his brother in attractiveness, at least to her, silly female that she was in that moment.

"Will you bring Mommy and Daddy back?" Ruby asked in her whispery voice.

"I wish I could, child." His voice roughened. "But since I can't, I'll make sure you have good people to take care of you."

Good people? Not him?

The doorbell announcing his arrival should have been an alarm.

Marigold clenched her teeth to keep herself from speaking out of turn.

Beryl stuck her pert little nose in the air. "We already have good people to take care of us, sir—Mrs. Cromwell and Miss Marigold."

"I see." Releasing the girls' hands, Mr. Chambers stood. "I know Mrs. Cromwell, but who is Miss Marigold?"

"She's right behind you," Beryl announced in a tone verging close enough to insolent that Marigold would have to talk to her about respect.

But not now. At that moment, she found herself receiving Gordon Chambers' full attention. Eyes the brown of root beer swept over her from head to foot, from her unbound mop of hair to her unshod feet.

"Miss Marigold, I presume?" he drawled.

"Yes." Marigold's voice sounded as whispery as Ruby's.

"Then I am making the right decision, and no one here should be in charge of these children for much longer."

Chapter 2

Gordon Chambers stared at the female in charge of his nieces and wondered how anyone thought her old enough, let alone responsible enough, to oversee the well-being of children whose parents were alive, let alone...dead.

His heart tripped over the last word, thoughts of the brother he hadn't seen in eleven years, the sister-in-law he'd never met. Careless actions had driven a continent-wide wedge between him and his family, and he wasn't prepared to let someone as young as he had been at that time remain in charge of Ruby and Beryl.

Which meant he couldn't go to Alaska as soon as he wanted.

He sighed. "You are Marigold—"

"McCorkle, yes. I came here fifteen months ago to be the girls' nurserymaid."

He expected her to bob a curtsy, as his nurserymaid had done with his parents when he was a boy. She remained upright and met his gaze with bold green eyes.

"I've also taken on some of the duties of a governess," she added with a hint of censure, "since they haven't been able to continue their summer lessons."

"What summer lessons—" He stopped. "We'll discuss that later." He glanced around. "Which room was prepared for me?"

"Your old room," Beryl spoke up. "Mommy left it just as it was so you'd come home."

Ruby pulled her fingers from her mouth. "Just like we left Mommy and Daddy's room just like it is so they'll come home."

Miss McCorkle cleared her throat. Gordon thought he understood why. His own neck tightened.

He swallowed. "Well, you see, I did come...back here. And I'm glad I'll have my room to go to." He tried to smile, though his lips felt stiff like the mouth on a mask. "Can someone bring me up hot water? From the smell of it, Mrs. Cromwell has dinner about ready, and I need to wash first."

"You don't need someone to bring up hot water," Beryl announced, her pert nose a bit elevated. "We have bathrooms."

"Hot water comes up from a reservoir in the kitchen," Miss McCorkle added.

"Thank you." He glanced at her, shuddered at her wild appearance, and picked up his valise. "I have a trunk back at the station. Will you send the coachman to fetch it?"

242

"We don't have a coachman no more," Ruby mumbled around the fingers in her mouth once again.

"Anymore," Beryl and Miss McCorkle said at the same time.

"That's right," Gordon said. "It's his day off, isn't it? That's why he couldn't come get me at the train station."

"No, that isn't why no one could come get you." Miss McCorkle's tone sounded as hard as railroad ties. "When Ruby said we don't have a coachman, she meant we don't have a coachman or any other staff except for Mrs. Cromwell and me."

"Why not?" He had to face her to see what her expression gave away beyond her words. "The last I knew, this house was overflowing with servants."

"It was until—" She glanced at the children. "Girls, go wash your hands and see if Mrs. Cromwell needs you to help her carry things into the dining room."

"Ruby can't carry anything." Beryl made a face. "She drops the plates and spills the water."

Miss McCorkle drew together brows as red as her hair. "Then help her sit in her chair and be quiet until we join you."

"But Uncle Gordon gives us orders now," Ruby protested in an undertone.

"I'm going to my room to make myself presentable for Mrs. Cromwell's dinner." Gordon smiled at the girls. "You may wait for me in the parlor, and Miss McCorkle can set the food on the table."

Beside him, the nurserymaid ground her teeth hard enough for him to hear it.

The girls shot her glances of triumph and strolled into the parlor.

"How dare you counter my directions." Her tone, though low, held so much fury Gordon expected sparks to fly from the ends of her hair. "I am their governess, and they need to view me as an authority."

"I am their uncle, and they need to view me as an authority." He made his own voice as cool as he could to emphasize her hot fury. "Since I am their legal guardian, I believe what I say has precedent over what you say."

"Since you couldn't be bothered to come home for months," she shot back, practically hissing, "you seem to have relinquished your right to barge in here and start telling them and me what to do."

"I couldn't get here faster."

"Or ensure that we had money for wages and other fees?"

"I didn't realize—"

"The only reason we have had food to eat and clothes the girls fit into is because their parents had good credit and the vendors knew they'd be paid eventually. The music teacher and others haven't been quite so accommodating, nor were servants."

"You're here."

"I"—she slapped her hands onto her hips—"cared too much about the girls to desert them in their time of need."

The twin daggers of her green eyes hit their target. Gordon's heart clenched. He flushed from his necktie to his hairline.

"We'll continue this discussion later." He bowed his head. "I seem to be in need of some information surrounding the deaths of my brother and sister-in-law."

"Indeed you are."

Her hauteur should have been the final straw of her ill-judged behaviors to compel him to dismiss her on the spot. Instead, he found the corners of his lips twitching. He suppressed the urge to grin at her insolence and gave her a brusque nod. "In the library after supper. I presume that hasn't changed?"

"No sir." She seemed to grow smaller before his eyes. Even her hair looked less like the ruffled flower for which she was named. "If I may, um, may have a few minutes to finish dressing?" Her face turned the color of a New Mexico sunset, clashing with her hair. "I mean, my hair." She yanked on a strand, straightening the curl. When she released it, the tendril coiled back like a watch spring.

"Please do." He headed for the steps before he gave into the temptation to see if he could make her hair spring back from his fingers, too. "I'd rather not have that mane end up in my soup."

Behind him, the front door closed with a bit more force than necessary. When he glanced over the railing, only a spark of carroty hair flashed by on the way to the kitchen and back steps. That door closed more gently than the street entrance, and Gordon stood alone at the head of the staircase.

The cavernous foyer yawned below him, rising two stories so that the fanlight window above the door spread out across from him, and a skylight glowed red and blue and green above him. The upstairs hallway stretched out like a road he knew would lead him away from where he wanted to be—east toward the sea, not west toward another ocean, snow, ice, gold.

Jaw tense, he stalked down the hallway to where his bedroom overlooked the back garden and the house next door. He could see the ocean from the back windows, too, the capricious, stormy Atlantic. How he'd wanted to sail on that ocean, lift the canvas to the wind and disappear without the noise and stench of the steam engines. He liked sails with their peace and struggle of man against nature, or man working with nature. He'd objected when their father began to get rid of the sailboats for their excursion company and replace them with the steam-powered vessels. Father had kept one sailboat until Gordon—

He slammed the door on that memory and opened his bedroom door. As Ruby had claimed, nothing had changed. Framed watercolors and photographs of sailboats lined the walls. Blue and white curtains fluttered at the open windows, wafting the scent of the sea around the spotlessly clean chamber. His model ships still graced the mantel, bedside table, and every other available surface.

"Welcome home," he said with a sardonic twist to his lips, setting his valise on the floor with a thud.

He opened the door that had been the dressing room he and his brother had shared, curious to know if his clothes had been kept, too. They hadn't. The large closet was indeed a bathroom now, complete with basin and tub. If the aroma of roast beef and tarts hadn't been climbing the back stairs to creep under his door, he would have taken advantage of the latter. Every muscle ached from days on the train. His stomach hurt worse, gnawing at his insides in demand of food.

He settled for a wash and change of shirt and necktie, a comb through his hair, and a touch of water to hold it in place off his face. Then he descended the steps, finding Beryl and Ruby perched side by side on the sofa, as though awaiting a photograph portrait to be taken—or sentencing.

He was going to sentence them.

Shaking off that ridiculous thought, he offered them a smile and held out his arms. "May I escort you lovely ladies to dinner?"

"It's more proper for you to escort Miss Marigold," Beryl said. "Since she's so old."

Gordon lowered his arms. "Miss McCorkle eats with us?"

"Of course." Ruby spoke around her fingers. "We're too little to eat alone."

"You're too little to eat alone." Beryl stuck her nose in the air. "I am quite capable of taking care of myself."

"But when your parents were—here. . ." Gordon glanced toward the patter of footfalls in the hallway, a click of heels.

"We ate in the nursery." Beryl narrowed her eyes at him. "Don't you know anything about children?"

"Apparently no more than you know of manners, Miss Beryl." Marigold strode into the room, her hair already beginning to slip from the knot on the back of her neck. "You know better than to talk to an adult that way. Now, apologize."

The girl's blue eyes clashed with the woman's green ones. Gordon expected to see sparks ignite in the middle. Beryl's mouth thinned. Marigold's grew thinner.

And Ruby began to cry. "Just say you're sorry, Beryl. I don't want Uncle Gordon to go away like Mommy and Daddy."

No sparks ignited from the older two females, but the younger one's words sent an arrow straight into Gordon's heart.

Apparently it struck Beryl, too, for she bowed her head. "I'm sorry," she mumbled.

"It's—" Gordon found his chest too tight for easy speech. "I accept your apology, Beryl. I should have realized you wouldn't normally eat in the dining room."

"And speaking of eating," Marigold said, "Mrs. Cromwell is waiting for us."

He wouldn't ask her why she wasn't helping the housekeeper serve. He'd already stepped into deep waters in this familiar yet unfamiliar household. Nor did he offer Marigold his arm. He simply stood back and gestured for the ladies to go ahead of him into the dining room.

It, too, had remained much the same, with the long french windows open to the veranda, filmy draperies floating on the sea breeze, and silver shining in the late afternoon sunshine. White linen gleamed like new snow. The chairs remained the heavy mahogany from his parents' day, but now the cushions were deep blue instead of red. Likewise, the velvet hangings on either side of the windows had been changed to blue.

Mrs. Cromwell trotted in from the kitchen, bearing a laden tray; she had changed more than anything he'd seen thus far. Her hair held far more silver than black, and her eyes reflected the milky cast of cataracts. Her shoulders stooped, and the food dishes appeared to weigh more than she did.

"My dear Mrs. Cromwell." Gordon stepped toward the woman who had sneaked him cookies when he was a lad, who had added an apple to his supper of bread and water when he'd been sent to his room without supper. "Mrs. Cromwell," he repeated, for lack of anything better coming to his lips.

Marigold turned from tucking a napkin into the neckline of Ruby's dress and stepped between Gordon and Mrs. Cromwell. "Let me take that." She removed the tray from the old lady's gnarled hands. "I'll make sure everyone gets everything, but go hug Mr. Chambers, as I know you're anxious to do."

"Hug him?" Mrs. Cromwell fixed her brown eyes on Gordon.

He wanted to squirm.

"I suppose all those apples I sent up to you spoiled you so much you forgot your duty to your family." She scowled. "What took you so long to get here?"

"Too many things to say without spoiling dinner." Gordon held out his arms.

Mrs. Cromwell embraced him then swung away, dabbing her apron to the corners of her eyes. "Come into the kitchen after dinner and tell me."

She beat a hasty retreat.

Gordon returned to the table and his wide-eyed nieces. "I thought she was old when I was your age."

"She's at least seventy-five now," Marigold said from where she dished up plates of food at the sideboard. "She wants to retire to Georgia with her sister."

"I can arrange for that." Gordon picked up his glass of lemonade and sipped. He hadn't tasted many lemons in his wanderings of the past eleven years. The sweet tartness triggered a hundred memories of picnics on the beach or aboard one of the boats.

"She can't go away," Ruby protested. "Who will cook for us?"

"He'll hire someone else." Beryl frowned at the plate Marigold slid before her. "I expect he'll hire lots of new servants now."

"I hope he doesn't expect me to cook." Marigold laughed as she set food before Ruby and him. "We'd be eating eggs and bread for every meal."

The girls made faces.

Gordon dropped his gaze to his plate. With each passing moment, his plan to leave seemed more and more difficult. But not impossible. He would have to find the girls a school quickly. A boarding school, perhaps in Philadelphia, someplace where they could remain on holidays, too, or find friends who would take them home.

"Will you ask the blessing, sir?" Marigold asked. "Before the food gets cold?"

"Of course." Gordon reached out a hand to each of his nieces. Two hands, less than half the size of his, tucked themselves into his palms like trusting kittens. For a moment, he couldn't speak, couldn't think of anything but these small charges, couldn't recall what one said in a blessing. No one in mining camps or aboard freighters asked the blessing over a meal. The silence grew, profound enough for the drone of bees outside the window to sound like distant engines and his stomach rumbling to resemble thunder.

"Thank You for Mr. Chambers's safe arrival," Miss Marigold murmured from the other side of Ruby.

"Yes." Gordon cleared his throat. "Thank You for a good journey and for the health of these children. Thank You for this meal we are about to partake and for the hands that prepared it. Amen."

"Amen." Beryl removed her hand from his.

"Thank You for the blackberry tarts." Ruby added her own blessing.

"You have to eat your green beans first," Beryl admonished.

"I will." Ruby picked up her fork and stabbed a mouthful of beans.

Smiling, Gordon tucked into the food himself. While the first savory bite of roast beef fairly melted on his tongue, he conjured questions he could ask the girls. He should get to know them, his last living relations.

Or maybe he shouldn't. If he was leaving in a week or two, why should he allow himself to get close to them?

He continued to eat in silence.

"Girls, tell your uncle what we've been reading." Marigold McCorkle wasn't eating. She perched on her chair, a forkful of potatoes balanced in her hand, and darted glances between Gordon and his nieces. "Tell him about reading *Little Women*."

"Beth didn't come back." Ruby's face screwed up. "Jo shouldn't have cut off her hair. Maybe Beth would have come back if she hadn't cut her hair."

"She couldn't come back," Beryl said with a twist of her lips. "She's dead like—"

"Beryl." Marigold's voice cut through Beryl's scornful response to her sister, though the nurserymaid never spoke above a murmur.

"Beth was sick," Beryl said in a gentler tone. "That's why she didn't come back."

"Mommy and Daddy weren't sick." Ruby smiled for the first time since Gordon's arrival. " 'Cause drowning isn't the same as being sick."

"No, it's not." Gordon looked to Marigold for help before he said more.

She caressed Ruby's cheek. "No, my dear, it's not the same. But your mother and father. . . Here, eat these lovely tomatoes. They're fresh out of the garden."

As delicious as the food was, Gordon had lost his appetite. He finished what remained on his plate, while allowing Marigold to direct the conversation around walks on the boardwalk, the pretty shells they'd found on the beach, the dolphins they'd spied from the lighthouse.

"And the nel—the. . .elephant!" Ruby cried. "I want to go inside the elephant."

"The elephant." Gordon laughed suddenly. "I remember drinking sodas at the top—"

"It's not safe now," Marigold cut in with such sharpness he jerked back in his chair.

"That's too bad." Gordon set his knife and fork on his plate in an X, rearranged them into a cross, then returned them to an X, watching Miss Marigold all the time. "What else has changed?"

"I wouldn't know." She held his gaze. "I've only lived here since a year ago May."

"May I be excused?" Beryl folded her napkin next to her plate. "I want to go read the next part of 'A Little Princess.'"

"Of course," Gordon said at the same time Marigold said, "Not until Ruby is finished eating."

"Those magazines with 'A Little Princess' in them have been around for over ten years," Marigold continued. "They can wait for another fifteen minutes."

"I want my blackberry tart." Ruby made a face and shoved the last green bean into her mouth.

Memory flashed into Gordon's head. Him as a boy, probably her age, aching for dessert, hating the vegetables on his plate. Both had become precious to him during his wanderings.

"You don't want your sweet?" he asked Beryl.

"No thank you." Beryl stood. "I don't like berries."

"Beryl, sit down," Marigold commanded.

"Uncle Gordon said I could leave." With that pronouncement, the girl stomped from the room.

Ruby's lower lip quivered. "Oh no, she's being naughty. Bad things happen to naughty girls."

"No, no they don't." Marigold slipped her arm around the child. "Why would you think that?"

"Why indeed?" Gordon scowled at the governess. "And Beryl isn't being naughty. I told her she could be excused. Now cheer up, or Mrs. Cromwell will think you don't like her cooking."

Ruby, however, looked pale and tense. She slipped out from under Marigold's arm and mumbled a request to be excused. "I need to be with Beryl."

"All right." Marigold looked pained.

Gordon stood. "I'll get the door for you." He opened the heavy panel, waited for Ruby to head up the stairs, then turned back to the nurserymaid. "You're right, Miss McCorkle. This upset to Ruby is a fine example why one of us has to be the authority around here, and, as their guardian, that is me."

"When you know nothing about them?" Marigold stood, her hands on her hips, her hair fanning out around her head like a lion's mane. "When I have risked my future happiness for them, you want me to step aside and tell them to listen to you and not me?"

"I haven't seen that you do such a fine job of it, madam." Gordon clasped his hands behind his back. "Beryl is insolent, and Ruby is anxious and seems to think her parents will come back. That looks like poor guidance to me."

"Poor guidance, Mr. Chambers, is leaving us in limbo for three months and making me stay here for three months longer than I ne–eeded to."

To his horror, her voice broke, her eyes sparkled extra bright, and her lower lip quivered.

He set his jaw against the lure of feminine tears. "If you should have left three months ago, madam, then don't let me keep you here. There's still enough daylight left for you to pack and reach your destination before dark."

Chapter 3

Marigold clapped her hands to her head, flattening out her hair as best she could. As though that would hold in the tidal wave of outrage surging up her throat like bile.

"Mr. Chambers," she said with exaggerated calm, "I would love to leave. I wanted to leave three months ago. I was planning on leaving the day after Ruby's birthday, but your brother and sister-in-law were killed, you didn't respond to the telegrams for weeks, and I wouldn't abandon the girls any more then than I will now, to see them dropped into a school and left thinking no one loves them."

"That won't happen for several weeks, perhaps months." Gordon Chambers began to pace along a line of roses woven into the carpet. "I will have to sell the business and get my brother's financial affairs in order. Selling the business this time of year may be difficult." He completed a circuit and began the walk again. "I'll have to speak with the lawyer. I'll have to find an appropriate school." He reached the far end of the room and faced Marigold, his eyes as cold as deep brown could be. "But I won't keep you here."

"You can't take care of the girls on your own. It'll take time to find an appropriate governess or nurserymaid, even if you can find one who is willing to work for only a month or two."

"Mrs. Cromwell—"

"Cannot take care of the house and oversee the girls' education and care," Marigold cut in.

Gordon narrowed his eyes. "Do you have no respect for others, Miss McCorkle?"

"Of course." He was going to dismiss her anyway, so she added, "When the person deserves it."

"I see." He crossed his arms over his broad chest and clamped his lips together, but one corner twitched suspiciously.

Marigold flung out her hands, sending what pins remained cascading onto the floor and her curls bounding about her head like corks on waves. "Mrs. Cromwell has already told me she will leave within a month of your arrival. She wants out of this climate before winter comes."

"Are you willing to stay until arrangements can be made?" Gordon asked.

"I'm willing, but I can't."

"Because you've decided to dislike me even before I arrived?"

"No, because I can't remain in this house alone without a respectable woman like Mrs. Cromwell here to lend propriety to the arrangement."

"Of course. I should have thought of that." A faint flush rose along his high cheekbones. "Then what do you suggest I do?"

"Stay, Mr. Chambers. Your nieces need you."

"I know nothing about children. I've lived aboard ships or in mining camps since I was eighteen years old."

"You can learn." Marigold's heart ached. Her passion for seeing their futures as secure as two orphaned girls' lives could be, she pressed on. "You can keep the business in the family for them to have a heritage, keep this house so they have something familiar on school holidays, give them Christmas and summers here, as they've always had." Her voice broke. "Give them as much of a family as possible so their lives aren't wholly empty of love."

"But I can't carry on my own life, make my own business and future, if I stay here, not that that's any of your business."

"No sir, it's not." Marigold clenched her hands at her sides to stop herself from throwing something across the room—preferably at his head. God wouldn't honor such behavior. Nor would He want her to spew out the words blazing on her tongue. God would want her to—what? Grovel so Gordon Chambers wouldn't send her away and make the girls lose one more person solid and secure in their lives?

She gritted her teeth until her jaw ached. Her chin felt like carved marble. She could barely open her lips to speak. "Mr. Chambers, if you can find a respectable woman to take Mrs. Cromwell's place, I will guard my tongue about my opinions and see to the girls' welfare until"—every word felt like she was having to expel a cannonball—"until you can make arrangements for them."

"That must have cost you a year's worth of your pride, Miss McCorkle." He grinned.

She flinched away from its charm and melting impact on her senses. And she kept silent.

"If I don't agree to your terms," Gordon continued, "do you have somewhere to go?"

"Yes sir, I do."

More than the girls had—a family, a sister getting married, an opportunity to mend the breach with Lucian, her supposed fiancé—if that were possible.

"Mrs. Cromwell wants to leave in a month?" Gordon persisted.

Marigold nodded. "Yes, that's when her sister leaves for Georgia. If she goes later, she'll have to travel all that way alone."

"Then that gives me four weeks to work things out, doesn't it?" He shoved his fingers into his thick, wavy dark hair. "Let us put our spat behind us and declare a truce, all right?"

"For the sake of the girls, yes." Marigold held out her hand to shake but couldn't help adding, "It gives me four weeks to make you see that abandoning the children is not a good decision."

He laughed out loud, a rich rumbling exclamation of mirth. Then he strode forward and clasped Marigold's hand with his warm, strong fingers.

She started as though she'd touched a live electrical wire. He snatched his hand away and rubbed it on the skirt of his coat. Without another word, he turned on his heel and stalked from the room.

Marigold perched on the edge of the nearest chair and stared out the window. She didn't know how she could like a thing about him, not his eyes, not his smile, and definitely not his touch. She should scrub her hand—erase the sensation of his strength, the kind of strength of a man who could pull a lady from danger and hold her in safety and security.

A lady? Didn't she mean two little girls who desperately needed a permanent home, something to depend on in a world that had gone topsy-turvy for them in a single clap of thunder and stroke of lightning?

Of course she did. She was merely tired and overwrought and thoroughly determined that nothing less than Gordon Chambers remaining in Cape May would satisfy her. Nothing else was the right decision. She would make him stay if she had to—had to. . .

She'd think of something.

Meanwhile, she had promised to help Mrs. Cromwell with the cleaning up so she could talk to Gordon Chambers herself. Then the girls would want a story before bedtime. Ruby would want her to hold hands until she slept. . . .

Feeling like the rag with which she was about to do dishes, Marigold stumbled into the kitchen. Mrs. Cromwell had put the extra food away, but pots, pans, and dishes littered the worktable. Through the open back door, Marigold caught a glimpse of the housekeeper talking with Gordon on the porch. They held glasses of lemonade, and a plate of ginger cookies rested on a table between them. Their voices carried into the house. Though the words remained indistinct, the tone spoke of affection, kindness, and sorrow.

Marigold rested one hand on the edge of the sink and closed her eyes. "God, please forgive me. I am still too selfish and wanting things the way I want them."

No sense of peace washed through her. She knew God didn't approve of her stiff-necked pride, her certainty that she knew what was best for everyone. Yet she couldn't help herself. Other people just made a mess of their lives. Mr. and Mrs. Chambers shouldn't have gone out in the boat that late May afternoon. Marigold had told them of the weather, had predicted a storm. She felt storms coming in the place where she'd broken her arm as a child.

Or rather, when one of the Grassick boys had pushed her out of a tree.

Thoughts of her childhood friends made her smile. They were scattered around the country now like she and her own siblings—attending college and work, military service, and positions at the Grassick Glassworks.

The glassworks, where she should be living with her husband, one of the glassblowers, and proudly displaying her inheritance passed down from a Grassick to her family nearly half a century earlier—the goldfinch bottle, the symbol of love, loyalty, constancy, and hope that had resided in her bedchamber at home since she and Lucian announced their engagement nearly a year and a half ago.

A lifetime ago.

She picked up a sturdy skillet and slammed it into the sink. Scrubbing away the remnants of food might help alleviate her annoyance at the man outside, whose rumbling laughter drifted in through the open door.

"That's right. Enjoy your homecoming that has cost me so much." She gritted her teeth to stop herself from growling like the kitten.

Suds lathering up her arms, she made herself sing, running through her favorite hymns. It helped keep her from dwelling on her anger with Gordon Chambers and pass the time through the onerous work of cleaning the kitchen.

"Hark! The herald angels sing—"

The rumbling laughter broke through Marigold's recital with such a blow she gasped, choked, and coughed.

"I didn't mean to scare you." Gordon Chambers touched her shoulder. "I wanted to find out who has the angelic voice in here."

"Angelic you think?" She set her soapy hands on her hips and frowned at him. "Are you in the habit of laughing at things you consider angelic?"

"No ma'am." He backed off as though frightened. "I was merely amused to hear Christmas carols in August."

"Christmas—oh." Her cheeks heated from more than the steaming water. "I was just singing the songs I can remember without the words in front of me."

"Please, don't let me stop you. I merely returned for more lemonade." He glanced at the icebox. "Where are the girls?"

"Playing in the schoolroom, from the sound of it." Marigold glanced upward, where a series of light thumps, creaks, and an occasional giggle drifted through the floorboards. "They're quite good about that, playing on their own, that is."

"Should I—um—take them some refreshment?"

"That's very thoughtful of you." Marigold dropped the last plate into the dishwater. "But I'll get them a snack when I'm done here. They'll be ready for bed by then."

When he neither moved nor spoke, she looked at him again, eyebrows raised.

"It's still light out. Isn't that too early for bed?" he asked.

"Not when you're six and nine."

"I didn't know." He swung toward the icebox. "How do we get more ice? This chunk looks nearly done."

"He comes by in the mornings and leaves it for us." She couldn't resist adding, "And I'm sure he'd like to be paid."

"As would you, I imagine."

"It won't go amiss," she hedged.

She didn't need the meager wages of a nurserymaid, but he didn't need to know that. In fact, she'd rather he didn't know that her family was probably as well-off or more so than the Chamberses. If he did, he'd ask too many questions. Marigold didn't want to answer questions about herself.

"I'll visit the bank tomorrow," Gordon said.

"Grand." Marigold lifted her now-red hands from the dishwater. "I'll see to the girls. If you wish to say good night to them, please do so."

"I'll think about it." He retrieved the pitcher of lemonade from the icebox and retreated to the porch.

He didn't come up to wish the girls good night. Though Marigold read them a second story, much to Ruby's delight, she heard no sound of footfalls on the steps leading to the top floor and nursery.

"I told you he doesn't want us," Beryl pronounced in the middle of *Cinderella*.

"He's probably weary from his journey." Although she was no doubt telling the truth of this, Marigold felt like a liar making excuses for the girls' unfeeling uncle.

In her own room, adjacent to the one the girls shared, she sank onto her knees and tried to pray for an extra helping of grace. A half hour later, cramped from remaining in the same position, she rose and readied herself for sleep. She knew God possessed it but wasn't certain He would give her the amount of forgiveness needed to cover Gordon Chambers.

Chapter 4

Gordon escaped from the house at what he hoped was an early enough hour to avoid sharing breakfast with his nieces and their nursemaid, especially the nursemaid. No one had made him feel guilty with a look since the last time he'd seen his father. And the last thing he wanted right now was a reminder of the parent who had driven him from the house and ensured Gordon wouldn't want to return.

None of them, apparently, had planned on Gordon needing to return.

But there he was, striding along the quiet street and headed toward the sea. Sunlight spilled through the branches of the trees, and a cool breeze off the sea stirred air that would later become oppressively hot and humid except near the water. The aromas of hot dog and sweetmeat vendors didn't yet invade the fresh air along the boardwalk. With the tide coming in, only the sea itself scented the morning.

Gordon paused at the edge of the sand and gazed toward the rising sun. As yet uninhabited by too many people in bathing costumes or women in hats so wide they surely limited the wearer's sight, the beach formed the perfect view for a postcard. Gordon wished he owned a camera so he could capture this moment. It would better serve his memories of this place he should think of as home than the stormy winter day and voices shouting louder than thunder that plagued his dreams.

"Life here wasn't all strife and sorrow," he told a passing flock of seagulls.

They screeched at him, as though condemning him for not tossing them any bread.

"I'll remember tomorrow," he promised.

A pity his life had been full of promises he intended to carry out tomorrow. Tomorrow he would make a fortune on his own. Tomorrow he would return and show that fortune to his brother to prove he wasn't a ne'er-do-well. Tomorrow he would remedy the financial problems plaguing his nieces and their household.

He set his jaw. "Today, I'll go to the bank. No, I'll go to the boathouse."

The latter was closer. There, from a neat, whitewashed building set at the end of a pier near Second Street, visitors to Cape May had been able to take excursions around the cape and into Delaware Bay for thirty years. Gordon's father had started the business when he grew weary of being a naval captain during the Civil War and then a merchantman captain. He'd made a lot of money doing both and found the peaceful seaside town of Cape May perfect for his young family and business dedicated to bringing people enjoyment in one of

God's greatest creations—the ocean. The early boats had all been sailing vessels. By the time Gordon left home, all were powered by steam, noisier, but able to go regardless of the winds and with fewer crew members.

As a boy, Gordon loved watching the dolphins in the bay and the occasional pods of whales. Now the temptation to take out one of the craft bobbing at anchor and keep sailing until he could see neither land nor mankind quickened his pace. The realization that no one would yet be at work slowed it again.

"That should change," he mused aloud. "If sightseers could view the sunrise from the sea—"

He cut himself off. His father had severed him from the business because of one youthful prank, and if the old man hadn't wanted his younger son involved, then Gordon would sell it. Two little girls couldn't manage things. They would need a trusted manager for that.

As they'd needed for the past three months.

Gordon paused to gaze into the rising sun again, in an attempt to recapture his earlier peace. But others now invaded the quiet early morning. A man with a camera set upon a tripod perched at the edge of the tide line. Three elderly ladies in straw bonnets dug about in the sand with sticks. Seeking treasure or pretty shells?

Gordon started to smile at the memory of how the smallest find felt like the discovery of Blackbeard's gold. He raised a hand and opened his mouth to wish the ladies good luck.

"Uncle Gordon! Uncle Gordon!" The chorus of childish voices rang on the breeze. "Uncle, wait!"

Not waiting would be churlish. Plastering a smile on his face, Gordon faced his nieces and their governess.

The girls wore identical white dresses with black ribbon trim, a concession to their mourning. Ribbons fluttered from their white straw hats, and they carried miniature parasols with ruffled edges. With their golden curls and blue eyes, they could pose in front of the ocean for the photographer and make his picture perfect.

Miss Marigold was another matter. Her gray frock bore not a bit of trimming. If not for her vivid hair beneath a plain hat, she would have blended into the weathered boards upon which she strode. But the hair, as he was growing accustomed to seeing, sprang out behind her as though it wanted to go in different directions than the head to which the curls were attached.

And so did he. Though his lips twitched into a reluctant smile—or perhaps because of the urge to grin, even laugh at Marigold McCorkle—Gordon wanted to head in another direction than one that would bring him into greater proximity with the uppity woman.

"You're out early," he greeted them instead. "It's a wonder you had time for breakfast."

"She always makes us eat breakfast." Ruby stuck her fingers in her mouth.

Gordon reached out his hand and tugged them free. "I thought only babies sucked on their fingers."

"She is a baby." Beryl tossed her head. Her hat ribbons fluttered like small birds. "She started doing that after Mommy and Daddy. . ." Her lower lip quivered before she finished her sentence. Hauteur left her face.

"They went away." Ruby stared at her fingers, still resting in Gordon's hand. "Mommy promised me a new doll last time I stopped sucking my fingers. Do you think"—she glanced from Gordon to Marigold, her eyes sparkling—"if I stop this time, Mommy and Daddy will come home?"

"They can't." Beryl's voice was flat.

Gordon's heart felt flattened.

Marigold yanked a handkerchief from her pocketbook and dabbed at the corners of her pretty green eyes. "I'm sorry, Ruby, sweetheart." She coughed. "Your mommy and daddy went to heaven and can't come back. Remember what the pastor said?"

"Yes." Ruby nodded, started to stick her fingers into her mouth again, then curled her tiny hand around Gordon's fingers instead. "Will you go for our walk with us?"

"We can return if we're disturbing you, Mr. Chambers," Marigold said. "I didn't realize—we like to come out early before it's too crowded and hot down here."

"My own thoughts." As much as he wanted to tell them he was heading to the boathouse, where he doubted they'd be welcome, Gordon shrugged. "It's a public walkway. If you wish to keep going, I won't stop you."

Not exactly gracious.

His conscience stinging him, and Ruby's small hand in his, prompted him to add, "Of course I'll join you."

"Thank you." Ruby tugged on his hand and started skipping down the walkway.

Marigold didn't hold her back. "That's thoughtful of you." She flashed him a smile warm enough to make the August sun feel inadequate.

Beryl said nothing, but her solemn little face brightened as she trotted along, twirling her parasol.

"We're going to look for dolphins," Ruby announced. "I saw one the day Mommy and Daddy went away and wondered why he didn't find them. Miss Marigold says dolphins are intell–intell—" She ended on a sigh.

"Intelligent?" Gordon suggested.

"Yes, it means smart." Ruby grinned up at him, showing that she was missing one of her incisors.

Suddenly, Gordon remembered losing one of his own teeth around her age.

"Did you put that tooth under your pillow when you lost it?" he asked.

"I did." Ruby changed from a skip to a hop. The heels of her shoes clattered on the walk. "And I got a penny there instead the next day."

"She's getting rich." Marigold laughed. "Three pennies since April."

"I got a whole dime once." Gordon gazed into the distance, a distance beyond the visible world around them. "It was just what I needed to buy the sails for my model ship."

All three females stopped to gaze at him as though he'd grown two heads or sprouted wings.

"You made all those model ships?" Marigold asked.

"I haven't always been a grumpy old man." He feigned indignation.

The little girls giggled.

The grown-up lady colored something akin to her hair. "I only meant—I thought they were given to you. They're so. . . good."

"I've always loved the sea."

"But you were in New Mexico." Miss Marigold still looked bewildered. "There's no sea there."

"I've been to sea. I've been on land." He shrugged. "Wherever my fortunes or misfortunes have taken me."

"Do you have a fortune?" Ruby asked. "Or a misfortune?"

"Ruby, I don't think that's a polite question." Miss Marigold took Ruby's hand in hers. "We should be going home and not asking your uncle impertinent questions."

"If he had a fortune," Beryl spoke up, "he wouldn't want to be going off to Alaska for gold."

"How did you know—" Gordon caught himself too late.

He had all the females' undivided attention once again and felt his own face heating from more than the early sunshine could be causing.

"I heard him talking to Mrs. Cromwell last evening." Beryl twirled her parasol in everyone's faces before tilting it back over her shoulder. "The nursery windows are right over the back porch, you know."

"I'd forgotten." Gordon thinned his lips. "I'll have to find a better place to talk in the future."

"We heard the gardener kissing one of the maids there," Ruby announced. "So don't kiss anyone there, either."

"All right." Marigold, though blushing, barely managed to suppress her laughter. "We need to get to your lessons."

"But you said we can go to the lighthouse," Beryl protested.

Gordon glanced down to the point of land jutting out between the Atlantic and the entrance to Delaware Bay. A lighthouse soared into the sky, its lamp appearing darkened in the daylight but ready to glow as soon as dusk fell to warn ships away from the cape or lead them toward the safety of the bay and harbor.

"It won't be open for visitors now," Gordon murmured. "Maybe later. . ."

He'd loved that lighthouse as a boy, all the way up to the day he left. Since then, he'd seen dozens more around the world, taller, fancier lighthouses. None had said home—

He slammed the door on that memory, too.

"I need to get down to the boathouse." His tone was deliberately brusque. "I expect someone will be there soon."

"The first excursion starts at eight o'clock," Beryl informed him. "That's in another forty-five minutes, so someone had better be there."

"We haven't been since the accident." Marigold sidled closer to him to speak in an undertone. "Maybe you can take the girls out on one of the boats so they don't become afraid of the water. It would be a pity for the owners of a boating company to fear water."

"But they won't be—" Gordon glanced at the children, realized that little ones did have big ears, and nodded. "We'll see what happens during my visit."

"Your visit?" Ruby snatched at his hand again. "I thought you were here to live."

"I can't—" He gazed into her guileless blue eyes, and what he couldn't do was say he was leaving as soon as he could.

In that moment, he understood why Marigold McCorkle had stayed behind, even when she wanted to leave. Abandoning these children would be downright cruel, if a body let them grow fond of him. Or if he grew fond of them.

"He has to find gold." Beryl engendered the last word with scorn, as though it were a foul substance.

"Beryl," Marigold spoke with gentle firmness, "remember what Proverbs says about mockers."

"I wasn't—" Beryl sighed. "I'm sorry. I guess we should go home now. It's getting hot."

It wasn't, but her pale cheeks had turned scarlet.

"I'll see the three of you at lunch." Gordon offered them a bow.

The girls dropped curtsies then gave Marigold their hands and headed back toward the residential part of town.

Gordon watched the trio until a growing crowd of people swallowed them up in a froth of pale gowns and fussy parasols. Even then, he didn't move until someone bumped him and apologized profusely.

"All this camera equipment—" The photographer from the beach turned pale. "Gerald, I thought you were—that is. . ."

"I'm Gordon Chambers." Gordon's shoulders stiffened. "Gerald's brother."

The man laughed, and his color returned to normal. "Cole Ambrose, local photographer and friend of your brother. I'd shake your hand if mine weren't so full."

Gordon shifted from one foot to the other. "Wayfarer and black sheep of the family."

Ambrose laughed, a rich "haw-haw" that boomed across the sand like breakers. "Never heard your brother say that about you—the black sheep part. All Gerald ever said was you liked to wander and had seen most of the world."

"I don't think 'most' is accurate." Gordon smelled smoke and wondered if it was coming from the boat engines firing up. The rumble of powerful motors told him he was right and gave him a good excuse to extricate himself from the stranger's clutches.

Except he felt oddly reluctant to do so. This man, with his broad smile and bright hazel eyes, demonstrated such warmth, leaving him standing on the boardwalk with his arms full of camera equipment would have been worse than rude.

And Gordon wanted to know more of what his brother hadn't said against him. "I have seen a good part of the world, though," Gordon added.

"Oh, I want to do that, take pictures of lions in Africa and elephants in India." Ambrose laughed. "But the Lord's seen fit to keep me here taking pictures of sunrises in New Jersey."

"There was an elephant here once, wasn't there?" Gordon scanned the horizon and found the joy of his youth, a wood and tin elephant, rising seventy feet in the distance.

Ambrose grimaced. "It's an eyesore now and is scheduled to be demolished any day. No one could make money off of that monstrosity. But I got pictures of it in its glory days. And pictures from the top of it. What a pleasure. Happy to show them to you. Stop by my studio anytime."

"Thank you. I just might do that." That was the polite thing to say, yet Gordon thought he just might.

The girls would enjoy—

No, he mustn't take them on outings. They might grow to care for him, and he. . .

Already cared for them. How could he not? Ruby, so young and needing of attention and reassurance; Beryl, trying to be older than she was and so haughty. Marigold. . .

"Can you manage all that equipment all the way back to town?" Gordon found himself asking.

"Do it all the time. My wife says it keeps me from getting fat from her cooking." Ambrose nodded as though reaching a conclusion. "Now that you're here, we'll have you over for dinner."

"I won't be here for long," Gordon admitted.

A flash of disappointment crossed Ambrose's face. "Then we'll make it sooner than later. Have a blessed day."

His stride jaunty despite his heavy equipment, he trotted toward town.

Gordon watched him for a few moments; then, feeling as though his morning had been spent seeing others walk away from him, he spun on his heel and marched to the boathouse.

Two of the small steam-powered boats bobbed and smoked along the dock. A couple dozen people in hats and carrying hampers of food stood in line, where two pretty young women in garb resembling sailor costumes with skirts instead of trousers stood taking tickets.

Gordon nodded to them then entered the office.

The instant he opened the door, the smell of paper and ink overwhelmed the odors of smoke and sea. Dust motes danced in shafts of sunlight streaming through windows that could stand to be washed, and piles of ledgers covered every surface.

Behind these piles, two clerks bent over open account books and a third counted money at a till.

The money man glanced up. "Tickets are sold out—" Like Cole Ambrose, the man paled.

"Gordon Chambers," he said with haste. "Mr. Gerald Chambers's brother and now his daughters' guardian."

Much to his bewilderment still.

"Of course. Of course." The man nodded like a marionette with a broken string. "The resemblance. . . Well sir, it's extraordinary."

"Of course it is." Gordon managed a stiff-lipped smile. "We were twins."

"I see. I see." The man glanced toward each of the clerks, who stared openly at Gordon. "You'll be wanting to talk to Mr. Randall. He's the manager."

"Yes I would. Is he in?"

"He is. He is."

Without being told, one of the as-yet-silent clerks scrambled off his stool and retreated to the back of the office and knocked on a door. A high, thin voice commanded him to enter. Moments later, he emerged and beckoned Gordon forward. "Mr. Randall will see you, sir."

Gordon wound his way between tall desks and overflowing shelves until he reached the rear office. A reedy man stood behind a massive desk nearly bare of papers and books—but not of dust.

Didn't they ever clean?

Gordon stifled a sneeze and held out his hand. "Gordon Chambers."

"Lawrence Randall. So pleased you could finally join us." Randall shook Gordon's hand. "Dockerty, fetch us some coffee."

The clerk departed. Courtesies were exchanged as to the weather and journeys and the wellness of one another's families. Then the coffee arrived, rich and piping hot, and the two men got to work.

"Do you know anything about accounting ledgers?" Randall asked.

"I was the supercargo on a merchantman for two years."

"That'll do."

They bent their heads over the latest figures, the busiest summer months and the months since Gerald's death. Gordon added figures in his head, as he'd always done, and found the accounting of receipts and expenditures meticulously recorded.

"It appears you've done well by the business," Gordon said after two hours of too much coffee and too many numbers. "I appreciate your time." He rose. "In a few days, I'd like to go out on a couple of the boats, if that's possible."

"Of course we'll make room for you, sir." Randall shook Gordon's hand in farewell. "We're full-up about a week in advance, so you'll have to wait and see if someone doesn't show up or cancels. Don't like to overcrowd the boats, you know."

"I do know. Send word if you have a cancellation. And I'll be taking the girls and their governess out on the water as soon as you have openings for four."

"We'll try." Randall's long, narrow face grew even longer. "Mr. Chambers never took his family aboard the public excursion boats, since they had the family one. But that's gone." He sighed. "We all told him not to go out that day, but he saw that pod of dolphins and wanted to show his wife."

"Interesting." Gordon had never known his brother, older by thirty minutes, to be impulsive like that. "A tragic mistake."

Wanting no more talk of Gerald, he beat a hasty retreat and headed back along the boardwalk at a brisk pace—or tried to. He hadn't gone more than a dozen feet before an older gentleman in clean but ragged clothes stepped in front of him, barring his path.

"Are you Gordon Chambers?" the man asked.

"I am." Gordon frowned. "What do you—"

"Dennis Tripp." The gentleman held out his hand.

Gordon didn't take it. "How may I help you?"

"It's not how you may help me, sir," Tripp announced, "it's how I may help you."

"Oh?" Gordon glanced from side to side, deciding which way to take to evade the man.

Tripp caught hold of his arm. "You've got to listen to me, sir." He spoke in a whispering rush.

"Why?" Gordon removed the hand with gentle firmness.

He'd met such men all over the world, those not quite right in their heads, wanting to predict doom and gloom and the end of the world. Most of them wanted money. Gordon had brought none of the latter with him.

"You want to save lives," Tripp said. "And you won't—"

"Good day, Mr. Tripp." Gordon skirted the man and continued walking.

Tripp fell into step beside him. "I'm not a madman, Mr. Chambers. I'm telling you the truth. If you listen to Lawrence Randall about how well the business is doing, people will die on one of those boats one of these days."

Gordon skidded to a halt and glared at the man. "I'd be careful about spouting that kind of nonsense, Mr. Tripp. If you drive business away, you can expect serious legal trouble."

"It's worth the risk." Tripp clasped his hands before him as though he were praying. "I worked for the Chambers Excursion and Sailing Company until a month ago. When I discovered Randall and his minions were dishonest and confronted him, he dismissed me."

A disgruntled employee.

With a sigh, Gordon stopped. "All right, let's have this out here and now.

Randall dismissed you, so you want to get even with him."

"No sir. He's a nice man and a fair manager."Tripp's gray eyes looked straight into Gordon's. "But he's dishonest, sir. He shows expenses for boats being repaired, but there haven't been any repairs made on those boats all season."

Chapter 5

Marigold decided to let Gordon see to the girls' dinner. Though he'd tried to hide it, she'd noticed the softening of his hard features in response to Ruby's eagerness and Beryl's condescension. He had even smiled once or twice, and little gold lights, rather like trapped sunbeams, had danced in his eyes. If the girls won him over, perhaps he wouldn't leave.

"And you can?" She scowled at her reflection in a silver bowl that stood on the foyer table.

When the Chamberses had been alive, that bowl overflowed with invitations to dinners and picnics, fishing excursions for Mr. Chambers, and shopping outings for Mrs. Chambers. Now its spotless surface, gleaming without so much as a speck of paper, let alone a letter from Lucian in response to the three letters a week she'd been sending him, left a lump of lead deep in Marigold's belly. A house that once rang with laughter was now far too quiet.

"Yes," she whispered, "I can leave."

But to what? She'd told Gordon Chambers she had somewhere to go. She did. At least she had a home with loving parents and a sister she got along with like a cherished friend. That sister, however, was getting married in two—

"Yoicks." Marigold's hands flew to her hair, pressing it flat.

She needed to tell Gordon Chambers immediately that she would have to be gone for a few days. Well. Perhaps she should stay home then, mend her fences with Lucian, force Gordon Chambers to stay with his nieces.

Mending matters with her fiancé should be a priority. She supposed he had reason to be distraught when she'd made the girls her priority and postponed her wedding from the end of June until the beginning of October. She was distraught. She wouldn't be the first McCorkle daughter to marry. She wouldn't get to keep the family heirloom that was still hers, since she was the first sister to become engaged—if she could still consider herself engaged. Thanks to her father's machinations in sending her off to be a servant for a year—to remind her of her family roots, to remind her she was not the gilded social princess she'd been acting like, much to her shame—and now her loyalty to Ruby and Beryl, she had probably lost that privilege unless something changed between her and Lucian soon—like receiving a letter from him saying he regretted his harsh words back in June—Marigold's plain, shy sister, Rose, would bear the honor of displaying the goldfinch bottle in her home.

Thanks to Gordon Chambers, too.

Hearing him in the library, Marigold continued through the foyer and down the short hall leading to the book-lined room. The door stood half open, framing him in an oblong of dark wood, with a backdrop of light from the windows. His back was to her—a long, straight back topped by broad, sturdy shoulders. At that moment, those shoulders were bent just a little, as though they bore a burden too heavy even for them, and his head was bowed, either in prayer or over some object he held.

As quietly as she could, Marigold slipped away. She could wait to tell him she was leaving for home in two weeks. If ever a man appeared as though he needed a few minutes alone, Gordon Chambers did in that glimpse through the half-open door.

For the first time since Gordon Chambers walked into his brother's house, Marigold considered his feelings in all of this. He'd lost his only brother, his twin. He had the responsibility of two little girls, though he was a bachelor who had lived on ships or in mining camps for nearly twelve years, and his personal plans had been interrupted. Even if he didn't intend to stow the girls in a boarding school like horses kept along a family's travel routes then ride off for the far-flung wilds of Alaska, his burdens must be numerous. He had to take care of the business for one thing. Surely he knew nothing of ledgers and balance sheets, supplies and boat repairs.

Well, maybe he knew about boats. But the rest? Marigold expected she knew more of accounting than Gordon Chambers did. She'd helped her father in their business during her summers away from school. She could add numbers faster in her head than someone with one of those new adding machines.

And as for his knowledge of children? Of course he had little. Yet he possessed something better than experience in taking care of little ones.

Kindness.

The way he'd treated his nieces since his arrival demonstrated that, for all his neglect of the past three months, the man's heart held tenderness for the little girls he'd never seen before.

"So how could he abandon them so abruptly?" Marigold slapped her fist into the palm of her other hand and headed up the steps.

At that moment, she was abandoning the girls for too long. She'd come downstairs to fetch Beryl's book left in the front parlor and gotten distracted by the lack of mail. That wouldn't do. The girls needed to keep up with their lessons, even if they weren't in school. Beryl sailed through her arithmetic, but Ruby needed a great deal of assistance with learning addition and subtraction, especially subtraction.

Gathering up the skirt of the gray gown, she detested every morning she donned it to play nursemaid, as it made her skin too pale, Marigold raced up the steps to the schoolroom. Her feet pounded a little too loudly on the treads, and both girls greeted her in the corridor with censorious expressions.

"You aren't supposed to run in the house, Miss Marigold," Ruby chided.

"Do you have to write an essay about not running in the house?" Beryl asked. "You made me do that the last time I ran up the steps."

"You're right, I did." Marigold rested a hand on each girl's shoulder and turned them to their work. "And I will do so, too."

"Why were you gone for so long?" Ruby plopped down in her miniature chair before the low table. "I thought maybe you got lost."

"She wouldn't get lost in the house." Beryl remained standing, her hands on her nonexistent hips. "Where's my book?"

Marigold caught her breath. "Your book. I forgot it."

Beryl sighed.

"I'll get it for you when we go downstairs for lunch." Marigold gestured to the other small chair at the table. "Sit down. We need to finish the math."

"I finished mine." Ruby held up her slate. "Beryl says I got two of them wrong, but I don't think so."

"Of course you don't think so." Beryl settled onto her chair and took Ruby's slate. "You wouldn't put down wrong answers if you thought they were wrong."

Marigold couldn't argue with that logic. But she couldn't let Beryl ridicule her younger sister, whose lower lip was trembling.

"Beryl, I will be the judge of Ruby's work. You need to be a little older to teach school."

"And get your answers all right all the time," Ruby added.

"No one is perfect." Marigold perched on the edge of an adult-sized chair and suppressed a sigh.

Perhaps she didn't know any more about children than did Gordon Chambers.

"Except for Jesus," she pointed out. "He was perfect."

"Can we read another Bible story after arithmetic?" Ruby asked.

"Yes." Marigold balanced Ruby's slate on her knees and examined the sums. She did indeed have two problems wrong. The same kind of problems.

She was transposing numbers, writing eighteen instead of eighty-one and seventy-two instead of twenty-seven. The problem of nine. Too difficult for her, or a common difficulty with numbers that flipped around too easily?

Her grip tightened on the slate, and her jaw ached. She wasn't a teacher. She never intended to be a teacher. She wanted to be a wife, a mother, an artist good enough to draw designs for her husband's glasswork.

Instead, she was sitting in a stifling schoolroom smelling of chalk dust and cleaning polish. She was teaching two little girls who weren't her own, however much she cared about them. She'd stayed because their uncle couldn't be bothered to come home in a timely manner, demonstrating he didn't care about them, no matter how kind he'd been that morning.

"Miss Marigold?" Ruby's squeaky voice cut through Marigold's anger. "Are you going to cry?"

"Not now." Marigold made herself smile as she erased the two wrong numbers. "Let's start over with these two numbers. Beryl, you may go get your book and read until we're finished."

"May I sit on the window seat?" Beryl asked.

"Yes, you may." Marigold slipped to her knees so she was eye level with Ruby. "I think if you write down every number, you can keep them straight. . . ."

She and Ruby worked through the math problems until the child got all her answers right. Then the three of them went onto the back porch, where a cool breeze off the ocean rustled through the leaves of the sycamores shading the backyard. Marigold read from the book of Acts of the Apostles, where Paul is shipwrecked. She loved these times of reading scripture to the children. Ruby listened without sucking on her fingers, and Beryl made no derisive comments.

After a few minutes, Mrs. Cromwell joined them. When Marigold finished reading, they enjoyed lunch in the kitchen then returned to the schoolroom for reading lessons. Both girls liked books and read well according to their ages, and the time passed quickly.

Free to help Mrs. Cromwell with housework while the children played, Marigold allowed herself a sigh of relief, took the back steps two at a time, and missed the last step.

~

Gordon caught the nursemaid's shoulders an instant before she slammed into him. Her nose connected with his chest, despite his efforts, and she reared back, one hand cupping the appendage.

"So solly," she mumbled from behind her hand. "I never expected—I shouldn't have been going so fast."

"Are you all right?" He tugged at her wrist to remove her hand and inspect the damage.

A slightly red, tip-tilted nose emerged. For a heartbeat, he experienced an odd urge to kiss it and make it better. But she was his nieces' governess, not one of them. A man didn't kiss the nose of a serving maid, even if she neither acted like nor, come to that, looked like anyone who had previously worked in the Chambers household.

Except for one, dear, sweet Louisa—

He jerked his hand away. "No blood, no damage."

"No sir." She tucked her hair behind her ears, dislodging a pin. "Oh dear." She stooped to retrieve it.

He stooped to retrieve it.

Their heads collided.

"I'm so sorry." She dropped onto the top step and buried her face in her hands. Her ridiculous hair tumbled and bobbed around her face. Her shoulders shook.

Gordon rocked back on his heels. "You aren't. . ." He cleared his throat. "This is nothing to cry about, Miss McCorkle."

"Not crying." She lifted her head. Although tears starred her lashes, her eyes danced with merriment. "I didn't know butting heads was literal."

"Nor I." Gordon's lips twitched into a full smile. His cheeks felt stiff and unnatural, bunched up and creased from the grin. Yet how did a body look at the absurd excuse for a governess or nursemaid and not come close to laughing aloud? "But what are we about to butt heads on, miss?"

Marigold sobered. "I was intending to speak to you about the girls sometime today, but this is when I usually help Mrs. Cromwell clean the house."

"Clean? What needs to be cleaned?" Gordon stood and offered Marigold his hand to help her rise.

She possessed rather elegant hands, slim and narrow with long, straight fingers. They were hands that should gleam white and feel as smooth as silk, but they held a hint of redness in their rough texture. Perhaps the abrasiveness against his own work-hardened hands explained the odd tingle he experienced as she rested her fingers in his palm and surged to her feet. A tingle and warmth. His mind conjured a fuse smoldering before it burst into flame and ignited the gunpowder that would blast another pile of rock apart to expose the precious metal inside.

He jerked away from her. "I have an appointment with the banker and my brother's attorney in a few minutes." He spoke with too much sharpness to dispel the ludicrous image from his brain. "We'll have to talk about the girls tomorrow. I'll know more of their financial situation at that time."

"But I want you to start overseeing their dinner instead of me." Marigold looked directly into his eyes. "They need to be with family now that they have one."

"I am hardly family." The image had exploded inside him, leaving the familiar hole that talk of family opened in his heart.

"You're their uncle."

"My brother was complicit in our father turning me out. That isn't family to me."

"Your brother made you their guardian in his will."

"He had little choice."

"He could have—" She snapped her lips shut like a clamshell closing around its inhabitant.

Gordon narrowed his eyes. "Who else?"

"No one is better than family. Now, if you'll excuse me, there's laundry to do." She started to push past him.

He stepped in front of the door to the kitchen. "You didn't answer my question, Miss McCorkle."

"No sir." She lowered her gaze to somewhere below his chin, as he was used to servants doing. "What Mr. Gerald Chambers decided to do with his daughters upon his and his wife's death is none of my concern. But I do need to tell you that I must be gone for several days in two weeks' time." Her words tumbled out in a rush as though she expected him to interrupt her. "My sister is getting married, and I am in the wedding, so you cannot leave then. I will send the girls down to dinner at six o'clock." Speech delivered, she stepped around him and slipped into the kitchen full of the aroma of roasting chicken.

"I'm not sure I'll be back—" The door swung shut on his protest.

He knew he should open the door again and dismiss her on the spot. If she wanted to be at her sister's wedding, he would give her plenty of time to get there.

But of course he wouldn't do that. No, he couldn't do that. He needed her here and she knew it. She knew it enough to take advantage of the truth and say whatever she liked, daring him to send her packing, as she deserved.

He supposed he could find another female to look after the girls, perhaps not keep them up with their schoolwork, if they even needed to in August, but make certain they were looked after and dressed neatly and washed behind their ears, all those minute details of children's lives, whatever they were. But he needed someone to care for them in a different way, the way Miss Marigold McCorkle cared for them—with love. He certainly wasn't capable of doing so to these offspring of his brother, who now possessed the inheritance that should have been at least half his.

All right, he would give Marigold her way. He would oversee the girls' dinner. He would stay until after she returned from her sister's wedding. He would stay until after the business sold.

If the business sold.

Thoughts of Dennis Tripp and his accusations replaced thoughts of Marigold McCorkle, keeping Gordon's mind occupied all the way to the bank.

The attorney met him there. With a clerk writing notes and dispensing various documents, Gordon spent two hours in the overcrowded office, with too much furniture and a ceiling fan that moved the air too slowly to do more than waft the odor of the macassar oil slicking back the banker's thinning hair into Gordon's face. He found himself growing drowsy as the attorney droned on; then the banker took his turn, then the attorney again. In the end, he learned exactly what he expected to learn—his brother had done well. Despite the financial panic of a half dozen years earlier, his brother had grown their father's investments. The excursion boat company prospered in the months it was open, even managing to take a few tours out in finer weather throughout the year. Gerald had expanded the boats to making emergency runs across Delaware Bay to Philadelphia for another profit source.

"Have you heard anything about a man named Dennis Tripp?" Gordon asked.

Both men shook their heads.

"He seems to be a disgruntled employee—former employee," Gordon explained. "He accosted me on the boardwalk this morning and told me that the manager is cheating the business by making false accounting entries about repairs."

"I wouldn't believe Tripp," the attorney said. "Lawrence Randall has been a faithful employee for nearly eight years."

"But feel free to look into the matter yourself, if you like," the banker added. "I can arrange to hire some accountants."

"No thank you, I'll do it myself." Gordon noted the time. "I need to leave soon, but first, is it all right if I sell the boating business? And invest the money for the girls, of course."

The banker and attorney exchanged glances.

The latter cleared his throat. "I must not have made myself clear, Mr. Chambers. You can do whatever you like with the boating business. Your brother left it to you."

Chapter 6

Marigold set her only good hat atop hair she had pomaded into submission and began to tilt the brim first one way then the other.

"Miss Marigold," Beryl called from the doorway, "we're going to be late for church if you don't hurry."

"Why are you taking so long?" Ruby asked from around her fingers.

"She wants to look nice for Uncle Gordon." Beryl giggled.

Marigold jammed the hat pin so hard it went through her pile of hair and pricked her scalp. She flinched. It served her right. Of course she was primping for Gordon Chambers, which was the most ridiculous action in the world. She was simply tired of him looking at her as though he didn't see her.

And no wonder. In her plain gray dresses, she looked dowdy and unattractive. She looked like what she was supposed to be—a servant. Only in her Sunday dress, one of the two gowns fit for church Father had allowed her to bring with her to Cape May—as part of her lesson in humility—did she deserve any notice. This Sunday she'd chosen the vivid green muslin that spread over her petticoats in rows of ruffles edged with fine ivory embroidery. Matching green ribbons trailed from her hat brim and down her back.

"I can't go to church in my cleaning dresses," Marigold told the girls in defense of her finery. "I never have before."

"But you never changed your hat ribbons before." Beryl tilted her head to one side. "You look like a Christmas tree."

Ruby giggled.

So did Marigold. "Thank you for keeping me humble, child."

"What's humble?" Ruby asked.

"Hmm. Not proud." Marigold tried to think of a better explanation. Something she wasn't, her father would say. Fifteen months in servitude hadn't changed that, as he'd intended.

"It means not putting yourself above others," Marigold concluded.

"If humble means wearing ugly dresses," Ruby said, "then I don't want to be humble."

"Humble is in your heart," Beryl said. "You can be prideful in an ugly dress. Like Miss Marigold."

"Maybe I will get taken down a peg or ten," Marigold grumbled then laughed. "All right, girls, I'm ready for church."

But not for the sight of Gordon Chambers in a fine new suit in a cream color that set off his tanned skin and dark hair. His image literally drove the air from her lungs. She gripped the newel post and tried to look past one of his broad shoulders, with a firm reminder that she was supposed to marry another man—someday.

Not that he'd written in response to her many letters.

"What a blessed man I am to have all these charming females to accompany me." Gordon smiled at his nieces and then Marigold.

Stomach suddenly queasy, Marigold made herself release the banister and glide forward. "We are all ready. Is Mrs. Cromwell coming today?"

"I'm right here, Marigold." The older woman stood beside Gordon.

Yoicks, she'd been there all along.

"Well, then, let's be on our way." Marigold offered a vapid smile all around.

She took hold of Ruby's and Beryl's hands and preceded Gordon and Mrs. Cromwell out the front door. The church stood only a few blocks away, so walking in the morning coolness proved easy and convenient. Others also walked: older husbands and wives arm in arm, mothers and fathers with flocks of small children, a few young people strolling in pairs. They greeted Marigold and the girls and cast curious or surprised glances at Gordon, who followed the younger women with Mrs. Cromwell on his arm.

He was such a gentleman. Despite a dozen years living in less than genteel locations, he must have learned a great deal as a young man, for Marigold could not fault his manners. He treated his nieces like princesses and Mrs. Cromwell like the loyal family retainer she was—with dignity and respect. For whatever reason he had left home and been reluctant to return, it surely wasn't because he lacked goodness in his heart.

Yet something tragic must have driven him away, kept him away, made him reluctant to return or stay. Occasionally, over the past week, she'd caught glimpses of pain on his face as he glanced at a photograph of his brother or parents, a tightening of his mouth at quiet intervals of the day.

Marigold he avoided, ignored, or simply pretended did not exist. She wasn't a lady to him. She wasn't a relative. She wasn't a loyal family retainer. She wasn't a pretty girl. She wasn't even a girl anymore at twenty-five.

Papa, you might get your wish after all about me learning humility.

Especially if silence continued from Lucian and Gordon Chambers persisted in ignoring her. But no, Lucian would come around once she told him she was coming home for good soon, and Gordon should ignore her. She worked for him.

She shouldn't think about him. This was a time for worship, for thanking God for all He had done for her, like bringing Gordon to them at last, and for learning how to live her life better.

She held the girls' gloved hands more tightly and led them up the steps of the church. The pastor greeted them. Many other little girls spoke to Beryl and Ruby. They were with their parents, who nodded at Marigold, started to speak, then stopped, eyes widening.

"It's my uncle Gordon," Ruby announced to the foyer at large. "He's come back after a long time, so I think Mommy and Daddy will, too."

The foyer fell silent. A handful of women drew handkerchiefs from their pocketbooks and dabbed at their eyes. Men cleared their throats and kept their gazes on a point behind Marigold—Gordon, she presumed.

He stepped forward and took Ruby's hand in his. "Your mommy and daddy won't be coming back here to Cape May like I did, sweetheart, but if you keep trusting in Jesus, you can go to them when it's your time to do so."

A collective sigh nearly slammed the door. Marigold's own heart felt squeezed. She didn't blame the females in the room who gazed at Gordon Chambers as though he were the most important man alive. At that moment, in that church entryway, he was.

"But I want to see them now," Ruby protested amid a rising wave of murmuring voices.

"Be quiet." Beryl cast her little sister a scornful glance. "You sound like a spoiled baby."

"And you sound unkind," Marigold whispered to Beryl. "Let your uncle take care of Ruby."

"But she gets all his attention acting so silly." Beryl stuck out her lower lip.

"She doesn't do it on purpose."

At least Marigold didn't think Ruby was playacting to get her uncle's attention.

"She's still sad about your mother and father."

"I am, too." Tears started in Beryl's eyes. "But I know what dead means, and so does she."

"I'm not sure she does." Marigold squeezed Beryl's hand and tugged her forward, into the throng now surrounding Gordon and Ruby.

Mrs. Cromwell had slipped away to join her sister and some other older ladies.

"I'm a lot older than she is, and I don't know how sad she is," Marigold added.

She had grown fond of her employers over the year she lived with them, but they were employers, not friends, not people with whom she socialized, except on those rare occasions when someone who knew her family happened to be in Cape May and invited her, too. It was awkward, but Mr. and Mrs. Chambers were so gracious that they'd never asked her not to accept invitations, though Gerald Chambers had done business with Marigold's father and agreed to hire his wayward, prideful daughter for a year.

Though the Chamberses knew Marigold was supposed to remember she came from folks who knew life serving the wealthy, not being served, they encouraged her to go to parties. Marigold wearing the same dresses to every occasion was her humiliation. Katherine Chambers, who had been married at eighteen and a mother by nineteen, had worried about Marigold being in her twenties and barely engaged, had tried to give her gowns. Marigold had refused and accepted the scornful glances of ladies recognizing a dress thrice worn. Marigold did have a fiancé. Lucian proposed to her in March of 1898 and received her father's permission. Albeit his reluctant, hesitant permission. Marigold had gotten her pride from somewhere, and Father wanted more for her than a glassblower's apprentice, however talented.

She wondered if Father hoped the marriage plans would end with the year-long separation. He never said so, but perhaps he had asked the Chamberses to find her another beau, see that she married someone more suitable in his eyes. If they held that responsibility, they should have lived so Marigold could be married now, perhaps on her way to being a mother.

The flash of annoyance took Marigold's breath away. She hadn't realized she could be angry with two people who weren't alive. She hadn't realized she was angry at all. She loved Ruby and Beryl. She wanted to see them happy and settled before she started her new life with Lucian.

At the moment, she wanted to see them settled for the service. The swirl of people around Gordon and Ruby seemed likely to make that impossible. With a sinking sensation in her middle, she glanced from Gordon, his head visible above a garden of ladies' hats, to Beryl then back again.

"Go join your uncle, Beryl," Marigold said on a sigh. "I'll sit somewhere else today. Be sure to say excuse me if you have to go between two people."

Beryl gave her a pointed look and slipped away.

Marigold followed the crowd into the sanctuary, as she must today and every Sunday Gordon Chambers remained in Cape May. Marigold couldn't sit with him and the children. It wouldn't look right. When Mr. and Mrs. Chambers had been alive, Marigold had joined the family. That was expected. She was there to see to the children's needs. But a single female and single man could not share a pew without arousing gossip, harmful gossip with Marigold living in the house, however good a job Mrs. Cromwell performed as a chaperone.

Longing to be home with her family and friends, Marigold slipped into a pew near the back. She must remember that this was a time of worship, not socializing. She didn't need to have loved ones around her to pray and sing hymns and listen to the sermon. In an hour and a half, she would rejoin the girls for the walk home, for their Sunday dinner, for quiet activity reading or playing the piano.

Presently she felt lost in a church she'd attended for over a year. No one was unfriendly. They simply weren't cordial beyond an initial nod and acknowledgment of her presence. She was a nursemaid, a temporary fixture, as was more than half the congregation. Most of them remained in Cape May for no more than the hot summer months.

She'd worn her second prettiest dress and gone to the trouble of changing the ribbons on her hat for nothing. God didn't care what she looked like.

Hot in the layers of ruffles, Marigold nearly fell asleep during the sermon.

Although she managed to stay awake, she couldn't keep her mind on the thread of the pastor's subject. She heard her father instead, reminding her of vanity, of pride, her overabundance of both.

When the service ended, she made herself remain seated, her hands clasped in her lap, until nearly everyone else had filed out. Gordon and the girls passed by early in the recessional. Ruby waved, but Beryl pulled her along; two attractive young women in pastel gowns and blond curls followed so closely behind that Marigold couldn't have stepped out of her pew if she'd been standing.

Gordon Chambers, the Pied Piper of Cape May.

Smiling, Marigold slipped into the aisle and exited the church.

"Miss McCorkle?"

Marigold turned at the sound of her name. "Mr. Tripp?"

She knew the man as a regular attendee of the church, but he'd never approached her before.

He gave her a courtly bow then stepped closer than strictly necessary for polite conversation. "I apologize for waylaying you, but I am concerned about the Chambers Excursion and Sailing Company. I approached Mr. Chambers, but he hasn't heeded my warning."

"Warning?" Marigold looked into the man's gentle gray eyes and frowned. "What are you talking about?"

"I warned him about Mr. Randall claiming he's repairing the boats but not doing it. When I approached him about it, he dismissed me."

"I see."

"No, I don't think you do. I'm not a disgruntled employee seeking revenge. I care about people's lives."

He looked sincere—and worried.

"I don't have any influence over Mr. Chambers. I'm nothing more than an employee myself."

And not a highly regarded one.

"But I'll try to see if he's doing anything, Mr. Tripp."

"Thank you." His smile lit his haggard face.

Insides uneasy, Marigold scanned the crowd for the family. Because of his height, she spotted Gordon straightaway. He stood on the front walk talking with a middle-aged couple Marigold recognized with an uplifting of her heart and a hastening of her steps.

"Mr. and Mrs. Morris!" The cry left her lips before she could stop herself.

They, Gordon, and too many congregants turned to stare at her.

Her cheeks heated. "I beg your pardon." She skidded to a halt a yard from the group. "I was just so happy to see you. . . ."

"No pardon necessary." Paul Morris took Marigold's hands in his and squeezed them between his strong fingers.

His wife kissed Marigold on the cheek. "You look lovely, child. We're staying only three houses from the Chambers's place, so you must come visit."

"I will if I can." Marigold glanced at Gordon.

"I believe you're entitled to time off." He looked half amused and half bemused.

"Then come down whenever you can. We'll catch you up on all the news of home. But now we must rush off." Mrs. Morris, petite and with more silver in her hair than gilt, turned back to Gordon and the girls. "We'll expect you next Saturday night then, Mr. Chambers. And when my great-nieces and nephews come to visit next week," she added to the girls, "you all must come down to play. There are quite a lot of them, you know, so you ought to find one of them you like." She squeezed Marigold's hand. "I'll talk to you later, my dear."

Leaving the girls and Marigold smiling, the Morrises bade good day and headed down the sidewalk.

"They're nice," Ruby announced around her fingers.

"Their great-nieces are all Ruby's age. The only person my age is a boy." Beryl swept toward the sidewalk with the air of a grande dame wearing a ball gown.

Gordon met Marigold's eyes, and they shared a smile that made a butterfly take off in her belly.

"How long before she changes her mind about that?" he asked.

"Four or five years?"

Marigold wasn't about to admit she never went through a time when she didn't think boys were great companions. She'd been nearly as good at baseball as any of the Morris or Grassick boys.

"How do you know the Morrises?" Gordon asked Marigold as he steered Ruby after Beryl. "Do they come to Cape May every year?"

"Yes, but I grew up knowing them. That is. . ." Marigold took a risky plunge. "My great-grandmother worked for Paul Morris's parents."

It was strictly the truth, just not all of the truth.

"Interesting." The look Gordon Chambers gave her, his dark brows arched over those deep eyes, told Marigold he knew she wasn't telling him everything.

But he *was* looking at her.

"Is it all right if I call on them?" she asked.

"Of course. Whenever you like. Mrs. Cromwell can watch after the girls some, too."

"Or you could."

"I already do." His voice turned dry. "And speaking of Mrs. Cromwell, where is she?"

"She always goes to her sister's house on Sunday afternoons. Didn't she tell you?"

"No. Um, what do we do for dinner?"

"I cook." Marigold laughed at the shock on his face. "I was teasing about the bread and eggs. I'm rather good at it, I'll have you know."

"Not in that, I hope." Though the look he gave her barely touched on her

276

hat, then face, then gown, a tingling warmth in her tummy warned her to watch her step.

She hovered close to the edge of being disloyal to Lucian.

As soon as they reached home, she changed back into one of her gray gowns. The girls pulled pinafores over their good dresses and went into the garden to sit beneath the trees, Beryl with a book and Ruby with her slate and colored chalks. Where Gordon slunk off to Marigold neither knew nor cared—or so she told herself. She needed to cook.

She knew how to make exactly two meals well, besides bread and eggs, which he would learn if he were around many more Sundays. Today it would be roast beef with carrots, potatoes, and onions. She also made passable biscuits. Fresh blueberries would serve for dessert.

By the time the girls and their uncle seated themselves at the dining table, Marigold was hot and perspiring, with her hair either in tight corkscrews or as fuzzy as mohair. But the vegetables were tender, the meat juicy, and the biscuits flaky.

"Enjoy yourselves." She set the dishes on the table in front of Gordon. "I'll start washing up."

"You aren't going to eat?" Gordon asked.

He apparently wouldn't dream of inviting her to join them, and she wouldn't invite herself and risk being rebuffed.

She smiled. "When I finish cooking, I have no interest in eating. I'll make a sandwich out of the leftover meat."

"What if we eat it all?" Ruby giggled.

"We can't eat that much." Beryl gave the roast a disdainful glance.

"We'll try not to." Gordon reached out his hands to the girls. "Shall we bless this meal?"

Dismissed without the words, Marigold retreated to the kitchen then continued to the relative coolness on the back porch. A few minutes in the shade and breeze wouldn't hurt anyone. She flopped onto the steps and fanned herself with the hem of her apron. She must talk to Gordon about Dennis Tripp's admonition concerning the boats. It was likely nothing. Gerald Chambers had trusted Lawrence Randall, his manager, implicitly, allowing him the primary operation of the business. In fact, the late Mr. Chambers had rarely gone to the company's office. He didn't seem to like it much.

So Mr. Tripp could be right. Gordon, of course, wouldn't want anything to do with it if he wanted to move on as fast as he could. . . .

Well, he just couldn't move on, whatever his reasons. She would stop him somehow. Leaving the girls without family was wrong and—

"Marigold?" Mrs. Morris called from the back gate. "Is that you?"

"It is." Marigold descended the steps and crossed the lawn to greet the older lady over the wicket. "What brings you down the alley?"

"I was taking the shortcut from visiting some friends down the way." The older lady's bright blue eyes scanned Marigold from head to foot, growing troubled as they did so. "My dear, why do you continue this masquerade? Your father only required a year of service for you."

"I couldn't abandon the children. They're so...lost without their parents, and their uncle—" Marigold's hands tightened on the top bar of the gate.

"But you put these children before your marriage. Are you sure that was the right choice?"

"Would leaving them to no familiar faces except for Mrs. Cromwell's been the right choice?"

"They have an uncle."

"Who couldn't be bothered to come home." The gate bar creaked.

Mrs. Morris laid her hand, soft in its silk glove, atop Marigold's. "If you'd told him what you had to sacrifice, perhaps he would have come sooner."

"I wasn't sacrificing really." Marigold gazed past Mrs. Morris to the glint of the sea. "This is a grand place to spend the summer, as you know. And I love the girls."

"But you made a promise to Lucian."

"Lucian," Marigold enunciated, her chin lifted, "needs to understand about patience and giving if he wants to marry me."

"Yes. Yes, he must." Mrs. Morris frowned. "Perhaps that's why. . . Has he written to you?"

"Not in weeks."

And that letter had been impatient and demanding.

"Well, it doesn't matter now." Mrs. Morris's brow still lay in deep furrows. "I've come to tell you that he is sailing into town with my daughter and son-in-law tomorrow."

Chapter 7

By Monday morning, Gordon knew his idea of leaving within two weeks was ridiculous. He still didn't know if he gave any credence to Dennis Tripp's warning, but before putting the business up for sale, even if he trusted an agent to oversee the particulars, Gordon couldn't hire an agent without being certain the business was sound.

The problem he was encountering lay in finding the discrepancies in Lawrence Randall's bookkeeping. Twice he presented himself at the boating office. Both times Randall was out, either on one of the excursion boats, according to the clerks, or at the bank. They didn't feel right giving him the ledgers without asking Mr. Randall which ones were the right ones.

"That is the one for this year," one of the mousy little men clarified. "Since Mr. Chambers has been gone. The other Mr. Chambers, that is."

The third time, that Monday morning, when Mr. Randall just happened to be absent, Gordon made his way to the attorney's office to ask what recourse he could take.

"You have a right to the books, of course." The rather youthful-looking Mr. Phillips, attorney-at-law, drew off his spectacles, making him look even younger. "Just take whichever ones you like. Randall has no right to stop you. But the real problem you're facing is that you can't sell the business until the will is probated."

"Probated? I thought—" Gordon subsided onto a chair he'd refused to take a few minutes earlier. "I thought that had already been done."

"No, it'll take a few more months to go through the court. Your long absence slowed matters. I thought you would know this." Phillips raised his eyebrows.

Gordon resisted the urge to squirm like a schoolboy caught not knowing his lessons. "I've never inherited anything before."

"Of course. Then let me explain."

Gordon listened and wondered if he would get to Alaska before the great glaciers melted. Or before he melted from the heat.

At last freed, he returned to the house to find a stack of invitations awaiting him in a silver bowl that resided on the foyer table. Apparently mindful that he was in mourning for his brother, none of the invitations were objectionable, being quiet and small affairs, but Gordon cringed at the idea of accepting any of them. They would first gasp at his resemblance to Gerald, as many had done in church. They would then ask about what he'd been doing for the past dozen years, why he had gone away, what he would be doing now, why he had stayed away for months after his brother's death—all questions too painful to think about, let alone discuss. Besides that, single young women would swarm around him, an affluent eligible bachelor in their eyes, and he would want to head for the nearest boat and out to sea.

He'd felt that way in church: stifled, hemmed in, trapped. He wanted to forget about his life in Cape May, not recall every childhood memory. He certainly didn't want to get into a young lady's clutches simply by being too polite to her.

He didn't want to encounter anyone who might know why he'd been asked to leave home and been cut out of his father's will. At the same time, he couldn't ignore the invitations. Good manners had been drilled into his head deeply enough he hadn't lost them in the roughest of living conditions. He'd enjoyed comfort from the knowledge he wasn't shaming his mother's teachings, even if his father thought him a failure as a good and obedient son.

He spread the invitations out on the table. He needed advice on which ones he absolutely could not reject and which ones he could get away with declining. Perhaps Marigold—

No, the less time spent with that minx the better. She was a bold piece, brazen in her manner toward him. She acted as though she didn't care in the least whether she pleased him.

No, on second thought, she wasn't acting. She didn't care if she pleased him or not.

A reluctant smile tugged at his lips. Odd for a nursemaid—but refreshing amid fawning females. Even the men seemed to want to see him happy. And now the hostesses had left their mark in the form of too many invitations for a man who preferred to spend his days alone.

Alone was safer.

With a flick of his wrist, he sent the invitations flying into a disorderly pile and turned from the table.

"You can't ignore them, you know—sir." Marigold came around the end of the staircase, a stack of clean rags over one arm, a pot of something reeking of lemon and beeswax clutched in her other hand. She wore another one of those hideous gray dresses, and an enormous white kerchief nearly covered her hair.

His fingers twitched, and he clasped his hands behind his back to stop himself from snatching the cloth from her hair. The action would not only be rude and obtrusive, it was an absurd idea. She should keep that mop covered all the time if that's what it took to control the wild red mass.

"Mr. and Mrs. Morris invited you personally yesterday," Marigold continued, "so ignoring them would be unconscionable."

"Thank you for your advice." He didn't keep the edge of sarcasm from his tone. "I was brought up in a barn, you know."

"I know no such thing. But you have been away from civilization for a while."

"And would like to be away from it again, if it's all as vapid as this." He

280

waved one hand at the invitations.

"The Morrises aren't vapid. They're smart and amusing and love the Lord." She began to polish the newel post, turning her profile to him. "And one of Mr. Morris's sisters is married to a Grassick."

"Is that supposed to impress me?"

"No, not if you don't know who they are. I'm sorry to interfere." Her voice sounded suddenly thick.

"Miss Marigold?" Gordon stepped closer to her before he realized his intention. "Is something the matter?"

She shook her head. A red curl popped out from under the kerchief.

He touched a fingertip to the tear tracing down her cheek. "Then the polish is too strong and making your eyes water."

"No, I—it doesn't concern you. Excuse me, please. This banister gets terribly dusty with the windows open." Wafting the nose-tickling scent of lemon behind her, she plowed up the steps, her head bowed, her face hidden.

Gordon watched her for several moments, seeking words to make her come back, while wondering why he should care. He couldn't befriend her. He didn't dare. Even if a friendship between master and employee was appropriate, which it wasn't, he was no good as a friend, as a brother, son, uncle. . . .

He returned to the table, gathered up the invitations, and carried them into the library. Of the twelve, he accepted three. The dinner party at the home of Mr. and Mrs. Paul Morris was the first one—on Saturday. The other two were invitations to nights of music. He loved music, and all he'd heard since returning to Cape May, other than the hymns in church, were his nieces' painful renditions on the piano and Marigold singing Christmas carols in August.

They were young. They would learn. He suspected Miss Marigold wasn't the best of music teachers. All the more reason to find them a school.

With that in mind, he accepted a fourth invitation, to a luncheon with just men, business associates of his brother and people he'd been introduced to at church. Reintroduced to. Some of them probably had daughters in school, judging from their ages. He could talk to them about where to send the girls.

He needed to talk with them about something. Long social conversations weren't among his talents. Talking to anyone for more than half an hour hadn't been part of his life for so long that dinners with his nieces left him feeling exhausted. After an initial shyness, they'd begun to ask him questions and wouldn't settle for the concise responses he gave adults.

❧

"No, Uncle Gordon, tell us how you got back on the ship after you fell in the water," Beryl insisted.

"Did you do something bad?" Ruby asked. "Is that why God made you fall?"

"God didn't make me fall, child." Gordon gazed at the little girl, wondering how she got such a notion. "I made myself fall by not putting away the rope I'd been splicing together. I tripped over it and. . . *Splash!*"

"But how did you get back aboard?" Beryl persisted.

"Someone saw me fall and sent me a line." Gordon grimaced at the memory. "It's a good thing the water was calm."

"Because you were naughty?" Ruby asked.

Beryl cast her a glance of annoyance. "People don't drown because they're naughty."

"But—"

"Mommy and Daddy weren't bad," Beryl continued with dogged ruthlessness.

Gordon flinched. Perhaps he hadn't chosen a good story. Next time—

He couldn't think about next time. Ruby had begun to cry.

"Not again," Beryl groaned, but her own eyes shimmered with tears.

Marigold! Gordon cried silently.

As though she heard him anyway, she swept through the door leading into the kitchen, dressed in a plain but attractive dress of white with little pink flowers on it, and dropped to her knees beside Ruby. "It's all right, baby. No one's been naughty."

"I was," Ruby wailed. "I left my doll outside in the rain."

Over Ruby's shoulder, Gordon met Marigold's eyes. She looked as bewildered as he felt.

They hadn't had rain in the week he'd been back in Cape May.

"Your doll is in your room." Beryl pushed her plate aside. "I would like dessert, please. Mrs. Cromwell said we have ice cream."

"We have to go get it. Would you like that, Ruby?" Marigold tugged one of the girl's pigtails.

Ruby blinked away her tears. "I like strawberry ice cream. But I only get it if I'm good."

"You're good." Marigold rose, holding Ruby's hand. "You even got your arithmetic right today. Are you going with us, Mr. Chambers?"

"I think I must."

He didn't want to. In the cool of early evening, the streets would be crowded with vacationers swarming toward ice cream shops and soda fountains for refreshing treats after dinner or on their way home from the beach. But he felt responsible for Ruby's bout of tears and thought the least he could do was take her for ice cream.

Alone.

"You don't need to come with us, Miss Marigold," he said.

Her face tightened, whether with annoyance, anger, or hurt he couldn't tell, for she smiled immediately. "I wasn't going to go with you, Mr. Chambers. I have. . . I have a guest calling tonight."

"Indeed?" Gordon raised his eyebrows in query.

Marigold turned to the children. "Go wash your hands, girls."

A note had arrived from Mrs. Morris in the middle of the afternoon, warning Marigold that Lucian had reached Cape May. A message from him had arrived shortly afterward with the information that he would call upon her that evening after supper. An appeal to Mrs. Cromwell's kindness had arranged the ice cream expedition.

"It's about time you saw that young man you've moped over for the past year," the older lady had declared.

So Marigold donned a dress suitable for everyday wear, a step above her gray maid's dress, and paced from the library to the music room to the front parlor, waiting, praying, willing Lucian to call before Gordon Chambers and the girls returned. And waiting... And waiting...

Mrs. Cromwell had cleared away the supper dishes and gone to her room by the time a rap sounded on the back door. Marigold flew down the hall, through the baize-covered door and through the spotless kitchen.

Spotless except for the puddle of water where the icebox pan had overflowed. Her right foot landed in the pool and slipped. She flung out her arms for balance, dislodged a copper pan hanging on the wall, and slammed her shoulder into the door. The pan flew across the room with a resounding clang, and her cry of pain accompanied the thud of her body striking wood.

"Marigold?" Lucian called through the portal. "Is that you?" He opened the door, and she tumbled into his arms.

"So sorry." She clung to him, his sturdy shoulders, his arms wiry with tensile strength. She smiled up into his handsome face and waited for the rush of warmth she'd always experienced when near him, the thrill of being in his presence.

The only heat she experienced was a flush of embarrassment for her clumsy introduction to a man she hadn't seen since his last visit in June, the day he'd arrived to persuade her to leave, to go ahead with their wedding regardless of the inconvenience to the girls.

The day he'd suggested she take off her engagement ring until she had her priorities straightened out.

She rubbed her bare finger and scanned him for the lump of a ring box in his pocket. Seeing nothing, feeling a little unwell, she said, "I expected you at the front door."

"I wasn't aware servants could receive callers in the front." The merest hint of a sneer curled his upper lip.

"It would be all right here. Mr. Chambers isn't strict or all that formal."

"Humph." He laid his hands on her shoulders and set her from him. "What was all that racket?"

"Just me being a bit clumsy." Marigold shrugged. "Shall we go onto the porch? No one else is home except for Mrs. Cromwell, and she's in her room. Would you like some lemonade?"

"No thank you, I won't be here long."

"No?" Marigold gripped the edge of the door to support her now wobbly knees. "Do you—do you have another engagement?"

"I may." He turned and strode to one of the wrought iron chairs scattered around the wide veranda. "It all depends on your answers."

"Well, since I haven't heard the questions, I guess I can't give you those answers, can I?" Marigold didn't intend the note of asperity that slipped out.

At the moment, with Lucian showing no affection toward her, she felt no inclination to take back the words or apologize for the tone.

Lucian laughed as though she'd made a joke. "Let's be comfortable so I can ask them." He turned one of the chairs so she faced the sliver of ocean visible between the neighboring houses.

She settled herself and waited for him to sit.

He didn't. He leaned against the white-painted railing and faced her. Evening light gleamed in his blond hair. His countenance lay in shadow. "When are you coming home?" he demanded.

"When things are settled here." Marigold clasped her hands hard enough to hurt her fingers. "I think Mr. Chambers will hire someone else, but it takes time. Perhaps October?" She hated the uncertainty in her voice, the queasiness in her stomach. "I know it's a long time, but—"

"It's too long. We were supposed to be married at the end of June. Do you know how embarrassing it is for me to have to tell people my fiancée thinks more of some children than me?"

"Perhaps as embarrassing as it is for me to keep telling my friends I never hear from you."

"I have work in Salem County to keep me busy."

"And so do I."

"You don't need to. Your father said a year away to make sure I—" He snapped his teeth together and paced to the end of the porch and back, his hands clasped behind his back.

Marigold stared at him, her ears buzzing. "To make sure you what?"

"Never mind." He bit out the words like someone eating a distasteful dish. "You were sent here to these business associates of your father because you needed to be reminded of your humble roots before marrying a mere glassblower." Now the bitterness rang as loud and clear as the crickets in the grass chirped with the advent of sunset.

Head spinning, Marigold rose and approached him. "Lucian, it's not like that at all. I got above myself, was mean to my sister, was too proud of marrying—"

"So you could get the goldfinch first." Now the sneer was more than a hint. "I'd say your father is the one who needs to remember his humble roots, far more humble than the original Grassicks."

"No one looks down at even apprentice glassblowers now, Lucian. You're artists, as well as artisans. Half the Grassick family are glassblowers. You can't think my father. . . ."

Apparently that was exactly what he thought.

Marigold held out her hands to him. "My dear, yes, my father sent me here to learn humility—"

"To get you away from me—"

"And I just can't leave these children—"

"Who are more important than I am."

"No no, Mr. Chambers wants me to leave." Marigold swallowed against a rising lump in her throat, took a deep breath against the band that seemed to tighten around her chest. "I'll be home for Rose's wedding. I–I'll stay home then."

"Do what you like." Lucian strode to the porch steps. With his back to her, he added, "I just came calling tonight to tell you I'm seeing someone else."

∼≈∼

With two clean hands in his, Gordon walked to the nearest ice cream parlor amid a throng of other families bent on the same enjoyment. Though many people smiled at him and nodded, he knew none of them, and they seemed not to know Gerald. None of them spoke to him.

Strawberry ice cream for Ruby and vanilla for Beryl obtained and consumed, Gordon took two sticky hands in his and returned home. Ruby chattered the whole way, as though she'd never shed a tear in her life.

Beryl said little beyond thanking him for the dessert. He wondered if he'd said something to upset her now. But when they reached the house, she ran halfway up the steps then turned around and blew him a kiss. "You're a good uncle," she announced, "even if you took too long to get here and want to leave us again."

"You can't leave," Ruby wailed.

At that moment, with her big blue eyes gazing into his, he thought she was right.

"We won't worry about that now, Ruby." He patted her head. "Go on up and get your hands washed before you stain your dress."

"All right." She, too, blew him a kiss and raced up the steps like an awkward colt.

Out of sight, the girls grew out of mind, or at least sentimental feeling. His brother might have made Gordon their guardian because he was their only living relative, but Gerald wouldn't want Gordon to raise them. Gerald had known his brother seemed only to hurt those he cared about, whatever his good intentions.

Gordon supposed Marigold McCorkle could stay on and see to the majority of their upbringing. That wasn't unusual. Perhaps it was even better than sending them to a school. But that meant he would have to stay, and Alaska called. Gold called. The wild aloneness called. A man could think in air that fresh and clean and devoid of people. He didn't want to worry about anyone else's troubles. His own had consumed him long enough. Right now, working out if anything was wrong with the business consumed him.

Wednesday morning he went down to the boathouse and inspected the crafts bobbing at their moorings along the pier. All appeared clean and shiny. Paint gleamed white; the names in gold leaf caught the sun and the eye. Brass shimmered. But fresh paint was easily applied and could merely be an illusion of good repair.

Yet why should he believe this Dennis Tripp, a man dismissed from his job, over a longtime and reliable employee like Lawrence Randall? The answer was simple—he shouldn't. Tripp merely wanted revenge against the man who'd sent him packing. Still. . .

Gordon knocked on the office door then pushed it open.

"Mr. Chambers." The clerks greeted him cheerfully. "We have your ledgers ready for you."

"Well, uh, thank you." Gordon felt a flush of embarrassment for his doubt of the manager creeping up his neck. "That's thoughtful of you."

"It's not a problem, sir. Do you want someone to carry them back to the house for you?"

"No thank you, I can manage." He lifted the stack of account books from the clerk's arms. "I'll bring them back as soon as possible."

"No hurry." The clerk smiled.

So did his companions.

Gordon frowned on his way out the door. Though fifty pounds of ledgers filled his arms, uneasiness nagged at his middle. Yes, Randall had voluntarily given up the books, yet not wanting them back immediately struck a discordant note in Gordon's mind. This made no sense. An accountant should want the books back immediately. He should need them to refer back to and add on to, as the business was still open and current—

Ah, that was it. Gordon hadn't received the current books.

Jaw set, he marched the rest of the way home and slammed the books onto the desk. A gasp caught his attention. Marigold, her hair restrained by a lacy cap—that would have looked better on Mrs. Cromwell—and wearing a gown that made her skin look the color of a fish's belly, knelt in front of one of the bookcases, a heavy tome in her hands.

"Did I startle you?" he asked.

"Yes." She rose. "I didn't expect you to slam those books down."

"I didn't slam—" He stopped and scowled.

He didn't need to explain or apologize for his actions. It was his house until the girls turned twenty-one. This was his office and his desk. Females wanted to interfere, introduce themselves into a man's life even when he didn't need one, and make him feel as if he'd done something wrong because he made a little noise.

He glanced at her book. "Isn't Elizabeth Gaskell's work a little old for my nieces?"

"It's not for your nieces. It's for me." That said, she turned on her heel and stalked from the room.

Gordon stared at her. He'd never met such an uppity female, not even in the West, where women tended to have freer spirits than in the East. She had no right—

Well, he'd just dismiss her. Finding someone else to look after the girls was going to be difficult and cause yet more delays, but Marigold McCorkle had to go. He wanted a female who moved around unobtrusively like Mrs. Cromwell, one whose company he could seek out if he wanted it.

Which he wouldn't. He never sought out anyone's company. He had in the past and caused too much trouble.

Shoving the ledgers to one end of the desk, Gordon rounded the massive structure and dropped into a chair. He found paper and a fountain pen in one of the drawers. After filling the pen, he composed an advertisement for the local paper. He also found the name of an employment bureau among some of the household books stashed in the desk. That might be easier than advertising. They would be able to send qualified candidates without him having to interview a dozen females to discover if they were suitable to care for his nieces. Perhaps he should ask the pastor.

Messages to the agency and pastor composed, Gordon pulled the top book from the stack of ledgers and began to work. He worked until his eyes burned and his stomach growled. Somewhere in the house, a clock chimed just once. He didn't know if that meant a half hour or one o'clock. As if in response, the library door swung open and the smell of mushroom soup preceded Marigold into the room.

"I brought you your lunch." She set the tray on a table before the empty fireplace. "Would you like coffee afterward?"

"I would, thank you." Gordon rose.

Marigold started for the door.

"Miss Marigold?"

She stopped, didn't turn, but tilted her head in a listening attitude.

"Why are you wearing that cap all of a sudden?" he demanded.

Her hands flew to the unbecoming headgear. "Mrs. Chambers had all of us wear caps to keep our hair out of the food and from falling over the house. I stopped after she. . . It's hot and I hate it, but it's disrespectful not to wear it."

"And when"—he closed the distance between them—"did you start worrying about being disrespectful?"

She raised her gaze to his, and he flinched at the sadness that clouded their bright color. "Since I realized that perhaps I'm better off staying here with the girls than going. . .home. Now, if you'll excuse me, I'll fetch that coffee."

Before he thought up an appropriate response, she whisked from the room, the full skirt of her dress lingering behind her like the tail of a gray mouse.

Not that anything about Marigold was mousy. She could wear all the gray dresses and caps she liked. A girl with her demeanor could never come across as timid.

Gordon found himself smiling as he carried his lunch to the desk and continued running his own calculations through the books. A few more hours of the work, and he wasn't smiling at all. The walls closed in on him. The air stifled him. He yawned and longed for a long ride in the open, or perhaps a sail across the bay and back.

He would take one, a moonlight sail. Someone should have a boat he could rent.

Hearing the girls playing the piano, he made his way to the music room and tapped on the door.

"Uncle Gordon." Ruby slid off the bench and raced to hug him. "I haven't seen you all day."

"I've been busy."

And he shouldn't feel a pang of guilt.

"And now I'm going to leave for a few hours," he told her.

"You're not dressed for a dinner party," Beryl pronounced.

"I'm going sailing." He addressed this to Marigold, who stood behind the piano.

"Sailing?" Ruby clutched his hand. "You can't go sailing, Uncle Gordon. I was naughty today."

Chapter 8

Marigold stood at the front parlor window and pounded her fists against her legs. She should have been down on her knees praying for her soul, for forgiveness, for the ability to like Mr. Gordon Chambers. But at that moment, watching him stride toward the house at nearly two o'clock in the morning, she wanted to yank open the front door and shove him down the steps.

"If you want to be alone," she mouthed to the fluid shadow of the man, "then leave. Give us access to money this time, and we'll do just fine without you."

If Mrs. Cromwell weren't so determined to leave New Jersey for a warmer climate, Marigold would have said that. Now she had no reason to go home. Lucian had betrayed her. He hadn't waited as he promised. Going home meant facing people's pity, the kind of sympathy she'd witnessed in Mrs. Morris's eyes.

Except Marigold had to go home for her sister's wedding. The pity would be rampant there. She was the daughter who'd gotten engaged first. She should have wed before Rose. She should have the family heirloom now residing in her dresser at home. But because of the man now climbing the front steps, Marigold was a spinster too angry to sleep or pray or even speak to the man.

"But you could have stayed home for Ruby's sake." She ground her teeth and drew into the shadows of the parlor so he didn't catch a glimpse of her and feel inclined to speak. At the moment, she intended to practice the premise that if she could say nothing nice, she should keep her mouth shut. Let Ruby make him feel his guilt.

Not that the child had been able to when he announced he was leaving. She'd started crying too hard to have any of her words coherent. When Gordon tried to comfort her, she'd turned her face away from him and reached for Marigold. She caught a glimpse of hurt in his eyes—or thought she did. The fact that he'd simply said, "I'll be late," and departed made Marigold doubt her own judgment in what she'd witnessed of his expression.

After a few moments of Ruby crying, Beryl announced, "She's afraid of water."

"And Uncle Gordon's going on the water," Ruby said through hiccups.

"He'll be all right." Marigold made the promise, knowing too late what would follow.

"Mommy and Daddy weren't." Ruby stopped crying but grew quiet and ate little dinner.

Afterward, Marigold took her into the garden to play with Dahlia, the kitten, and a ball of yarn. When both child and kitten flopped onto the grass exhausted, Marigold settled beside them and asked why Ruby told Uncle Gordon not to leave because she'd been naughty.

"You weren't even naughty," Marigold concluded. "All you did was drop your slate and break it. We'll get you another one."

"But you told me to be careful and I wasn't." Ruby played with the kitten's pointed ears.

Marigold tugged one of Ruby's pigtails. "I know. But it was an accident."

"But what if Uncle Gordon has an accident?"

He'll deserve it. Marigold asked for immediate forgiveness for such an uncharitable thought. She didn't need to concern herself about him except where his actions affected the girls.

"What does breaking your slate have to do with your uncle having an accident?" Marigold asked.

Ruby shook her head and didn't answer. She probably didn't know any more than Marigold did. Yet somewhere in the child's head, she connected the two.

Ruby could be a little naughty. Beryl might have a rough tongue on her, but she never got herself dirty, did all her lessons with care and precision, and did what she was told. Ruby, on the other hand, got restless and fidgeted, didn't always obey, and got dirty just looking at the yard. She was a sweet and precious child, though. So was Beryl. How Gordon Chambers could dismiss them—

Marigold waited for his footfalls to grow silent on the steps then the upper floor before she slipped down the hallway to the back stairs and on up to the nursery wing at the rear of the house. In the morning she could reassure the girls that their uncle was all right.

~~≈~~

Except, in the morning, because she'd waited up half the night, Marigold didn't wake up. Two hours past her usual waking time, she roused to the girls giggling in the schoolroom and the smell of coffee. Snatching up her dressing gown, she stumbled through the doorway.

Breakfast lay spread out on the worktable. Her breakfast of toast, eggs, coffee, and an apple.

"Mrs. Cromwell helped us," Ruby announced.

"Uncle Gordon thought you might be ill." Beryl tilted her head to one side and inspected Marigold's face. "Do you have a cold? Your eyes are kind of puffy."

"Not enough sleep." Marigold hugged the girls. "And look at the two of you all dressed. Did Mrs. Cromwell help you?"

"We helped ourselves." Beryl picked up the coffeepot. "I'll pour. It's too hot for babies like Ruby."

"I'm not a baby."

"You cry like one." Beryl sent a jet of dark brown liquid arcing into the cup as though she did it every day.

290

"Very good." Marigold applauded.

"I buttered your toast." Ruby held up the plate—and sent eggs sliding down the front of her pinafore.

"You are such a slob!" Beryl cried.

"I didn't mean to." Ruby's eyes grew huge with tears.

"I told you to leave it—"

"You leave it, Beryl." Marigold took the plate from Ruby before any more harm occurred. "Ruby, you need to be more careful, you know that. And, Beryl, don't ever call your sister names again."

"She needs to read the Bible about love," Ruby declared.

Marigold managed not to smile. "And you need to read about forgiveness."

Her own words sent a stab of pain through her conscience. Ruby wasn't the only one who needed to read about forgiving one another. Marigold had a lot of people to forgive—Gordon, Lucian, the young lady who had accepted Lucian's advances. . . .

"After I eat this delicious breakfast," Marigold said, "we'll go outside and read, all right?"

"Uncle Gordon went down to the beach," Beryl announced. "I want to go. We never go with you."

"It's too crowded right now." Marigold grimaced over the notion of keeping track of the girls amid the hundreds, perhaps thousands, of people on holiday.

"Then let's go to the lighthouse," Beryl persisted. "You said we could go."

"So I did." Marigold perched on her chair and picked up the coffee cup. "Ruby, change into a clean pinafore and fetch your bonnets. I'll be ready in a trice."

She was, wearing one of her cotton day dresses instead of the ugly gray things. The lighthouse was one of their favorite places. As little as she was, Ruby managed all the steps to the top then stood in awe of the panorama of sky and sea spread out below.

On top of the world like that, Marigold gloried in the beauty of the Lord's creation and managed to push thoughts of Lucian and the upcoming humiliation of her sister's wedding aside. Change seemed possible amid light and beauty. Lucian would see her and remember that he made a promise to her. Despite the harsh words they had exchanged over the back gate, they would mend their fences at the wedding.

She supposed she should mend her fences with her employer, but he seemed preoccupied with ledgers and sailing and business meetings. She supposed she should be pleased that he seemed to be making friends with gentlemen in Cape May. Perhaps they would convince him to stay. Yet the more time he spent with others, the less he spent with his nieces, and that she couldn't abide. Her conscience pricked her a bit over that last. She should care about Gordon leaving for the girls' sake, not her own. They needed him if they couldn't have her.

She supposed something rang falsely in that thought, too, but found herself too preoccupied about the upcoming party to think about it. Gordon didn't know she was invited, and she didn't want to tell him. He might forbid her to go, and she didn't want another reason to find him annoying.

Sometimes she found his presence in the house an irritation. She no longer felt free to play. The Chamberses had asked her to play, but Gordon closed the library door every time his nieces began work on their scales and simple melodies. Marigold didn't know if their beginner efforts bothered him or if he didn't appreciate music. She didn't want to find out, so she avoided one of her pleasures in life—playing the piano.

One more way he had harmed her life.

"I should play in the hope it annoys him," she grumbled as she sorted through music. "Something loud and obtrusive."

No no, she shouldn't think that way. God wouldn't want her to be mean.

"But, God, I can't forgive him for the harm his actions have caused me. What if Lucian is seriously attached to this niece of Mrs. Morris? What if—"

She made herself think of the flashes of pain she'd seen on Gordon's face when the past came up through conversation, a photograph, or an old landmark. He might have good reason for staying away, and she should have compassion.

But to go home without a fiancé stung without having yet done it.

She managed not to think about Lucian when teaching the girls, when reading, when concentrating on her anger with Gordon Chambers. Dressing for a dinner party, the first one she'd dressed for since the Chambers's deaths. Her thoughts turned to the one her parents held to announce her engagement to Lucian.

Thirty people had been present, and she'd embarrassed her sister, who was not yet engaged, despite being two years older. Rose and Marigold had argued bitterly afterward, Rose in tears, Marigold angry with herself and unable to change anything—without humiliating herself. When she couldn't bring herself to apologize, because every time she looked at the goldfinch residing on her dressing table, the words stuck in her throat, Father had sent her into service with the Chamberses, his business associates.

If Father hadn't done that, Lucian wouldn't have betrayed her with some distant Grassick cousin.

Surely Marigold could change that. Surely marriage to her would benefit him more than to a girl he couldn't know well, since he'd only worked at the glassworks for a few months. If Father. . .

But Lucian thought Father wanted an excuse to send her away, keep her isolated from him until he moved south to Salem County. Whoever was right, Marigold faced questions and sympathy and the pain of seeing her sister marry first.

She mustn't cry. Crying would make her eyes red, which would not look at all attractive. And Marigold wanted to look attractive. For no good reason other than feminine vanity, she wanted Gordon Chambers to faint with shock when he saw her walk into the Morrises' parlor.

Except he wasn't in the parlor when Marigold arrived. A dozen other people were, including the bespectacled Mr. Phillips, the Chamberses' attorney. He raised his eyebrows at Marigold in her blue silk gown, as did a few others who recognized her, but when Mrs. Morris introduced her as "a friend from home," people treated her like the guest she was, out of politeness to the Morrises, if nothing else.

Mr. Phillips gravitated to her side and brought her a glass of lemonade, then offered to escort her into dinner. Then he asked about her family.

"You know," Marigold said.

"Of course. I wouldn't have let you and the old housekeeper remain in that house alone with the children without looking into your background. You could have stolen all the silver and left the children on their own."

"I'm happy to know someone was looking out for them." Marigold curled her lip. "Unlike—ah, and here he is."

Gordon, looking rather splendid in a black broadcloth suit and shimmering white shirt, strode into the parlor and straight up to Mrs. Morris. Only the low rumble of his voice reached Marigold's ears, but she guessed what he was saying—apologies for being late.

"He had to buy a new suit," Phillips murmured.

Marigold glanced at the attorney in time to see his upper lip curl.

"You don't like him," she whispered.

He shook his head. "He was irresponsible for taking so long to get here and irresponsible for wanting to leave again. But my mother tells me I shouldn't be so hard on him. He had reason for wanting to leave Cape May."

Marigold started to ask what, realized it was gossip, and compressed her lips. If Gordon wanted her to know, he would tell her. She would not lower herself to asking.

"You are such a fine girl." Phillips took her hand in his and tucked it into the crook of his elbow. "You won't talk about your employer."

"No sir."

"But you don't like him." Phillips started to lead her across the room.

Her skirt brushed against the scented geraniums trailing their velvety leaves from pots along the baseboard. Their lemony freshness scented the air, mingling with hair pomades and perfume. Perhaps she should see about obtaining some geraniums for the Chambers—

"You don't need to acknowledge that," Phillips was saying. "Your eyes give you away."

"Then I should keep them downcast if they're conveying those kinds of messages."

She did dislike him. She had every reason to. He was inconsiderate and selfish. Just look how late he'd been to a party.

"Where are you taking me?" she asked the attorney.

"To meet the town's newest bachelor." Phillips laughed.

It couldn't be avoided. With only a dozen guests, Gordon would notice her sooner than later.

He noticed her when she and Phillips were still a half dozen feet away. His root beer–colored eyes widened enough for her to catch the golden lights in them.

"Mr. Chambers," Phillips called, "let me present Miss Marigold McCorkle."

"We've met." Gordon's bow was stiff, his expression too blank.

Marigold almost felt sorry for him. Almost. Mostly, she wanted to laugh.

She dropped him a curtsy. "Yes, indeed we have, Mr. Chambers. Wasn't it kind of the Morrises to invite both of us?"

"Very. . .democratic of them." Gordon glanced to Phillips. "Things have changed since I was here last."

"Not all that much," Phillips began.

Before he could elaborate, Mrs. Morris invited everyone to move to the dining room.

Gordon sat at the far end of the long table from Marigold. She sat next to Mrs. Morris on one side and Mr. Phillips on the other. Both kept her entertained. The food slid past her palate on a variety of textures, spices, and categories—poultry, fish, beef; consommé, creamed vegetables, salad; trifle, cake, chocolates. She'd forgotten that life at the Chambers household had grown austere in comparison. They had enough to eat, but it was plain, unimaginative, prepared by an excellent cook of everyday dishes. The chef had gone with the other servants. By the time Mrs. Morris led the ladies from the dining room to freshen up in the upstairs chambers, Marigold decided she preferred simple meals on a daily basis. Her corset felt like it was about to cut her in half if she so much as breathed too deeply.

She felt rather unwell and out of place among women who hired nursery-maids. They didn't entertain them.

"I should leave," she whispered to Mrs. Morris. "Before the men come in. I shouldn't have come."

Mrs. Morris looked pensive for a moment. "Do you truly care what Mr. Chambers thinks of you being here?"

"He wasn't happy to see me here. I shouldn't have come."

She'd come to tweak his nose, to annoy him. It was an unwise decision.

"I don't want him to know who I am," she explained.

"But he needs to, child. You need to go home."

Marigold's overly full stomach dropped to the bottom of her belly. "Is that why you invited me? You want Mr. Chambers to realize I shouldn't be working for him and dismiss me?"

Even before Mrs. Morris answered in the affirmative, Marigold knew the old family friend had betrayed her.

⌒

Gordon wasn't annoyed so much as confused by Marigold's presence at the

Morrises'. Before he'd left Cape May, he'd learned in no uncertain terms that those who employed did not fraternize with those they employed. America might be the land of opportunity, but that meant that servants could become employers, if they chose. He hadn't accepted that as a youth, who saw a damsel in distress, a maidservant damsel, and charged to the rescue—and caused trouble.

He always caused trouble when he took the time to care about someone.

Gordon didn't think social mores had changed in Cape May over the past dozen years, yet Marigold stood chattering away with the attorney, dressed in a gown every bit as pretty and fine as those of the other women in the room, and being treated like a special guest. No wonder she didn't care what she said to him, if she had friends like the Morrises.

And why would a nurserymaid have friends like the Morrises? It had to be more than the explanation of her grandmother working for Paul Morris's family decades ago.

Gordon intended to ask her the first opportunity he received. He intended to walk her home. It was only half a block, so he didn't know how much of an answer he would receive, but he would invoke his authority over her as her employer.

The notion unsettled him. He'd never been anyone's employer. He didn't like being anyone's employer. He never rebuked Marigold for her bold speech, because he'd lived in the West too long to remember that things were different in the East.

So he would ask Mr. Morris.

Gordon opened his mouth to pose the question, but music began to drift from the parlor, a piano played with a light and skillful touch.

"Ah," Mr. Morris said with a satisfied smile, "my wife has persuaded Marigold to play for us."

Gordon followed the other men into the room then stood in the doorway and stared regardless of the rudeness of doing so. Marigold perched on the stool, her gown billowing around her, her hair subdued to a rich auburn in the gaslight. She held her back straight but not rigid, and music flowed from her fingertips as though it came directly from her instead of the instrument.

In that moment, he understood why he endured her boldness. He knew why he smiled even when she made him angry.

He was fast on his way to falling in love with her.

The realization set his resolve to end matters that night. He couldn't have her under his roof under the circumstances. He couldn't risk hurting her. If it meant he had to take the first applicant who approached the door, he would see Marigold gone the following day. Women never failed to complicate his life beyond patience. He was certain God had shown him he should be alone. How else had he eluded the clutches of dozens of females in the past dozen years? God had protected him and kept directing him onward, to where few people lived, especially not females, with their troubles.

And their deceptions.

He found himself seated on a sofa with Mrs. Morris while he listened to Marigold play. Most people talked. Gordon listened, enthralled, enchanted, sick with a knot forming in his middle.

"Who is she?" he asked at last.

"Marigold McCorkle." Mrs. Morris smiled. "Do you know the story of the goldfinch bottle?"

"I don't think so. Should I have?"

"Perhaps not. It's a tale of faithfulness and giving up what's too important to us for our hearts to serve God." Mrs. Morris settled back against the hard pink and white–striped cushions. "About ninety years ago, a young Scots glassblower made a goldfinch bottle for his fiancée. That man was Colin Grassick, and he married the owner of the glassworks that employed him."

"Grassick." A bell rang in Gordon's head. "Your husband's sister is married to a Grassick."

"Yes, Colin Grassick's grandson. Because of youthful indiscretions, he lost the goldfinch. It was starting to be passed on to the eldest son."

Gordon rested his elbow on the arm of the sofa and hoped the warmth of the room and his full stomach wouldn't send him to sleep over a tale he didn't understand why he should know.

"My husband's sister helped Daire Grassick find the goldfinch," Mrs. Morris continued, "and throughout it all, Daire learned that it was just too important to him and his family, so he gave it to the son of the Morrises' maid. That gift and help from the Grassicks gave the McCorkles the push they needed to better their lives. They're quite prosperous, and both of their daughters have graduated from Vassar."

Gordon jerked upright. "Marigold? I mean, Miss McCorkle?"

Mrs. Morris smiled and nodded. "And now she's inherited the goldfinch. At least she did. There weren't any males in her generation, so her father decided it would go to the first daughter to marry."

"Miss McCorkle is getting married?" Gordon felt like the fish from dinner had come alive and begun to swim about in his belly at this news.

"Not any longer. When you took so long to arrive, her fiancé broke off the engagement."

Chapter 9

Marigold glanced from Gordon's proffered arm to her gloved hand to the tips of her white shoes peeking from beneath the bottom ruffle on her gown. "I'm quite all right walking on my own, thank you."

"A gentleman offers a lady his arm when escorting her, Miss McCorkle." Gordon's tone was as grim as his expression.

Marigold let her gaze stray to Mrs. Morris. The older lady smiled and nodded.

Marigold ground her teeth and rested her fingertips on the sleeve of Gordon's coat.

She'd taken Mr. Phillips' arm without a moment's hesitation, and he'd been nearly a stranger until that night. She knew Gordon Chambers. She should welcome his courtesy for the half-block stroll home.

Or perhaps she welcomed it too much. She was supposed to be in mourning for her lost fiancé, not liking the feel of the strong arm beneath her hand. Her heart was supposed to be breaking, not her person tingling, as though she anticipated a run straight across hot sand to dive into cold water.

Her face stiff, as though she'd spent too much time in frigid temperatures, Marigold bade her host and hostess good night and allowed Gordon to lead her from the house. To call his pace leisurely would exaggerate the speed. He crept down the sidewalk like a man three times his age. And he said nothing past the first house. Quiet filled the night, save for the distant rumble of carriage wheels and the whisper of the ocean breeze through the trees.

Wanting to burst into raucous singing, Marigold tossed out a question in front of the second house they passed. "So what did Mrs. Morris tell you about me?"

"Why," he demanded, as he stopped and faced her, "didn't you tell me what you lost by staying with my nieces when I delayed so long getting here?"

"Why did you take so long getting here?"

"That doesn't concern you."

"Apparently it does, since you just asked me why I didn't tell you about my canceled wedding."

"I—" He set his mouth in a thin line then sighed. "You're right. I caused the difficulty. That gives you a measure of a right to know. But. . .it's difficult."

She said nothing. She didn't move.

That one corner of his mouth twitched. "You're stubborn, aren't you?"

She remained still.

297

"I honestly didn't get the telegram for nearly a month. Then. . ." He looked away. "I did have some business matters to settle before I left New Mexico, but, yes, mostly it was because my brother's death grieved me, and I couldn't face the idea of coming back here, facing this place without him. Not particularly manly of me, is it?"

"I think that took about as much courage as a man can have to admit."

She thought a great deal more, too. Nothing she would share with him— her shame for being so annoyed with him, her softening heart toward him. Too softening.

She needed to be away, to be home with her family, seeing Lucian when he returned for visits, mending matters, restoring her relationships. She couldn't begin to have a regard for a man who wanted nothing more than to abandon people he should love.

Yet now she understood he just might have a reason.

"We can't undo the past," she said. "So no sense in worrying over it."

"I feel responsible for the damage I caused you with my thoughtlessness. I didn't think. . . . I didn't realize. . . ."

"If Lucian's love is so weak," Marigold said with more bravado than she felt, "he isn't—I'm better off. . . ." She blinked to clear her vision. "What's done is done."

"Perhaps not. You said you were to be in your sister's wedding. Are you not going home for it within the week?"

"Yes, but I don't know how you would manage, you and Mrs. Cromwell. Ruby's so worried lately whenever anyone leaves her, and if I go home. . ." She turned away and folded her arms across her middle to hold in a sudden stab of pain that bore no resemblance to physical discomfort.

Her discomfort lay in her heart, in her spirit, in her soul.

"You can't stay here just because Ruby doesn't want you to go away, Miss McCorkle."

Miss McCorkle. Somehow his using her surname instead of "Miss Marigold" hurt. Though only a foot of warm night air swirled between them, it felt like a wall, or a hurricane blowing her out of Cape May.

"You can't stay." Gordon's voice hardened. "I cannot continue to have a lady from your family acting as my nieces' nurserymaid."

"You're—you're dismissing me?" Marigold's eyes widened. "You're not just telling me to go home for my sister's wedding? You're telling me to go home—forever?"

Poultry and pie warred in her belly. Her throat burned. In a moment she was going to be sick right there in front of an elegant mansion.

She swallowed and plunged on. "You take three months to get here. You give no explanation as to why. You make me postpone my wedding until my fiancé gives up on me, until my charges are convinced I am the only constant left in their lives, until I have to bear the shame of—you're dismissing me because I'm not in need of this position? Why you, you—"

He laid his forefinger across her lips. "Careful, or you'll give me more cause to dismiss you."

For a full minute, they stood motionless in the center of the sidewalk, his finger burning against her mouth, her heart racing. Her lips moved; she thought to protest. She realized she had just kissed his hand. She jerked away and spun on her heel. Skirts crushed between her shaking fingers, she ran away from him. Her heels clattered on the sidewalk. Her breath rasped in her throat, from panting or sobs, she neither knew nor cared. Getting away was what mattered, far away, secluded in her room, where she could cry all she liked and no one would have to know.

She not only had to face the humiliation of going home to see her sister married, she had to face seeing her unfaithful fiancé with another woman, face the moment when she would be expected to hand the goldfinch over to her sister, and now to confess she had been dismissed from her position because her family had pulled themselves out of poverty—because she was arrogant and insolent to her employer.

Because she'd kissed his hand.

Surely dying was easier than enduring such humiliation.

She didn't reach her room before the floodgates opened and tears spilled down her face. Sobbing, she dropped onto a chair in the kitchen and rested her head on her folded arms. Life had been going so well for her. She had graduated from college; she, a female, had a better education than anyone in her family. She was engaged to a handsome and talented man, engaged before her sister. She would receive the goldfinch to pass along to her children. Yes, Father had sent her into service, but she loved the girls, and the Chambers family had told her again and again she was indispensable. When Gerald and Katherine Chambers died, Mrs. Cromwell begged Marigold to stay. The lawyer and banker sent her letters begging her to stay. She was needed, important.

Now she was nothing but a passably pretty spinster with no prospects.

Her gut tightened. Her chest tightened. She felt as though someone had lit Independence Day fireworks inside her, and they were about to blow up.

She wanted to rush upstairs and start packing. If she slipped away early enough, she could catch the train without seeing Gordon Chambers another time. He could send her wages to her. Perhaps, if she went quietly, he would write her a reference so she could find other work, perhaps work that would take her west to someplace out of the way.

Like Gordon Chambers wanted?

For the first time since hearing of the prodigal Chambers brother, Marigold understood the lure of open spaces without man to interfere in one's life. It would be refreshing, not in the least judgmental—

Lonely.

The fireworks exploded, leaving Marigold hollow inside; a gaping wound of loneliness filled in the space where her heart had been at the notion of going day after day without people around her to love and need her. She was so fond of the girls.

She loved the girls so much; she couldn't run away from them. She couldn't leave them at all. Yes, she had to go to her sister's wedding, endure the stares, the whispers, the pitying glances, but she must return, must persuade Gordon that he couldn't do without her.

She must make herself indispensable yet again.

During a restless night, in which she slept little and paced her room a great deal, she figured out a small action she could take to help him.

He needed to be certain that Lawrence Randall was honest, despite that single warning by the former employee. He had good reason to wonder. Dennis Tripp was a Christian man. Quiet and devout, he never missed church, praised God for having a purpose even after he lost his position, always helped those in need despite his own meager income.

She would take a page from his book, so to speak, and would go over the ledgers she'd seen on Gordon's desk. He might have been a supercargo for a merchantman, but Marigold could wave her degree and course work in math from Vassar and all the accounting she had done for her father's business interests.

Before dawn on Monday morning, she washed, dressed, and slipped downstairs. With a cup of tea at her elbow, she began to go through the ledgers. The oldest one lay open on Gordon's desk. A glance said it was all right and that his calculations added up with the numbers in the book. Marigold decided to recheck his calculations. And he was correct. Everything added up. The only odd thing she noticed, something Gordon couldn't know, was a number of names of employees she didn't recognize. Not that she would know everyone in Cape May with so many people coming to the town for the summer work. Still, apparently Dennis Tripp wasn't the only employee who had lost his position soon after Gerald Chambers's death. She should point this out to Gordon: How many names had been rubbed out and added in elsewhere so that following the thread of who worked when grew bewildering, even for her. First, she would look into it herself.

She rose from the desk, slipped upstairs to ensure that the girls still slept and to collect her hat, then left the house. The back gate led her into the alley. From there, she cut through other backstreets to keep her off the boardwalk as long as possible. In minutes, she stood outside the boathouse ready to pounce upon—or at the least, enter with—the first employee to reach the office and unlock the door.

She leaned against the portal and studied the boats bobbing on the ebb tide. Mist blurred their outlines, making them look like crafts floating out of dreams. Despite the warmth of the morning, Marigold shivered. On just such a day, the Chamberses went for a sail and returned on the tide after a sudden, violent storm, their boat wrecked, their bodies battered and bruised.

Marigold prayed the fog didn't portend another storm but merely a rain shower later that might break the stale humidity of the air. If the fog continued, the excursions would be canceled and the boathouse empty of all but employees.

And if Dennis Tripp was correct, she could be in danger.

"Ha," Marigold laughed aloud. She was being fanciful, ridiculous. Nonetheless, she wondered if she should leave, point out the changed employees to Gordon, and go about the business for which she had been hired—tending to the girls.

Hands tucked under her arms, she turned from the doorway. A shadow moved across the sand, his features indistinct in the murky light. He headed straight for the office. Keys already jingled in his hand. She couldn't leave without him seeing her. So she waited, waited until he drew near enough for her to recognize him as one of the clerks. Good. Mr. Randall would be harder to persuade.

"I've come to find out about the influx of new employees here—for Mr. Chambers, of course." She spoke a little too loudly, quickly, to take the man by surprise. "You have records on these men, of course."

He jumped and dropped the keys.

Marigold retrieved them. "Allow me, sir." She fitted the brass key into the lock. It turned as though recently oiled—without sound or hitch.

"Miss, I can't allow you—" The clerk snatched for the keys.

"Of course you can." Marigold pushed open the door. "I'm on an errand for Mr. Chambers, the owner." She scanned the room that never seemed to change. Dusty ledgers, inkstand desks, boxes of tickets. "Where can I find the most recent list of employees and when it changed?"

"You can't until Mr. Randall returns." The clerk wrung his hands. "Please, no one is supposed to be in here. I could lose my position."

"I won't tell if you don't. Where's Mr. Randall?"

"Sleeping, like decent folks still are."

Marigold raised her eyebrows. "Are you saying you're not decent? If so, perhaps Mr. Chambers shouldn't employ you."

"Of course I'm decent." The clerk's flush glowed even in the dim light. "I am at work, as some of us should be."

"I'm working, too." Marigold smiled. "For Mr. Chambers. Those lists, please." She tucked the keys into her pocket and held out her hand.

"Miss, er—I don't know of any lists or change of employees, Miss McCorkle."

"Of course you do, Mr. Pollock. You've worked here for twenty years, I understand. Where are the lists? Or don't you keep clear records of who works here and who doesn't?"

"Of course we have clear records of employees. They're in Mr. Randall's office. So you see, I can't get them for you."

"Huh." Marigold sidled past him and approached Randall's office door.

Pollock scampered behind. "You cannot—"

Marigold twisted the knob. Locked. She drew out the keys. Pollock snatched for them.

"You wouldn't harm a lady, would you, Mr. Pollock?"

"You're a maid, not a lady."

"Mr. Chambers would disagree with you on that score." She fitted another key into the lock. Nothing. She tried a third key.

Click.

"Very good." She pushed open the door.

Air smelling of tobacco and spirits smacked her in the face. She wrinkled her nose and headed for the dim shadow of the desk. Six books lay upon it.

Mr. Pollock charged forward and set himself between Marigold and the desk. "You cannot. We could both lose our positions."

"I have nothing to lose, so do, please, step aside." She strode around him, certain he wouldn't outright lay hands on her. "And I'll ensure that if Mr. Randall dismisses you that Mr. Chambers hires you back, unless you're up to skulduggery here, of course."

"Nothing of the kind, Miss McCorkle."

The clerk's lower lip stuck out and quivered like a child's.

Marigold nearly backed down, but the man's odd actions set the hairs on the back of her neck to prickling. She slipped around the desk and flipped open the top ledger at random; then she ruffled through some pages while the clerk spluttered and backed away. It didn't look the same as the ones in Gordon's office. It was far neater.

She snatched up both stacks of books. "Good day, Mr. Pollock. If Mr. Randall has any questions, he can come to the Chambers house." Before the man decided to tackle her for the heavy volumes, Marigold trotted out the door.

"Miss," Pollock called after her. "The keys."

"Send someone for them," she shouted back. "My hands are full."

By the time she was halfway back to the Chambers house, her conscience pricked her as badly as her hackles. She shouldn't have taken advantage of the old man if he was innocent of any wrongdoing. He probably did need his position, and Randall was likely to dismiss him. Somehow, though, she would make things right. Gordon would make things right. He was the owner of the business, not Lawrence Randall. As for the keys, Pollock wouldn't need them for a while. She would take them back later.

Despite telling herself nothing permanently bad would happen from her actions, she lugged her burden with a heavy heart. Perhaps this wasn't the kind of "indispensable" Gordon would like. Perhaps he would prefer to see to matters himself.

Except he hadn't seen to them very well himself.

Mouth set, mind prepared for any kind of argument from Gordon Chambers, Marigold strode into the house.

Mrs. Cromwell stood at the stove frying eggs. She gasped at the sight of Marigold. "What are you doing with those books this early and in this fog?"

"I got them for Mr. Chambers." Marigold continued through the kitchen and into the library.

To her relief, Gordon was nowhere around. She set the ledgers on the desk then raced upstairs. Though beginning to stir, the girls still slept. Marigold removed her hat and washed dust from the ledgers off her hands before she returned to the girls' room and touched their shoulders to wake them up.

"No walk today," she explained. "It's too foggy and may rain soon."

"Can we draw pictures?" Ruby asked.

"*May* we? Yes."

"Big ones." Beryl sat up, rubbing her eyes. "I want to draw big pictures if we can't go outside."

So Marigold worked out how they could create large pictures. After the girls ate breakfast, she glued several sheets of drawing paper together and hung them on the schoolroom wall low enough for Ruby to reach the top edge. Armed with colored chalks, the girls set to work. Marigold slipped downstairs in time to find Gordon entering the library. She paused in the doorway, not certain if she should tell him about the ledgers or let him discover them himself.

He could hardly miss them. They took up half the desk. Still, he didn't go to the desk immediately. He drew back the draperies from the windows to reveal rain-streaked glass. For a moment, he bowed his head, his shoulders slumped. Not a good time to intrude on his privacy.

Marigold started to turn away.

"Wait!" he called to her.

She waited.

"Where are the girls?" he asked.

"In the schoolroom, drawing."

"They're all right alone?"

Marigold laughed. "Of course. They're six and nine years old, not six and nine months old."

"I didn't know. . . ." He sighed. "Please come in."

Slowly, Marigold faced him. His eyes looked shadowed. Lines radiated from the corners of his mouth, and his jaw sported a lump of bunched muscle.

So he hadn't been sleeping any better than she had.

"Miss McCorkle. Please sit down. We need to talk about replacing you."

Marigold remained standing. "I won't talk about replacing me. If you insist on doing so, then you will do so, but you've already told me to go, so I have nothing to lose by disobeying you."

He narrowed his eyes. "I feel like a fool for not realizing all along you weren't a regular serving girl. You have too much pride."

"That's precisely why I'm a serving girl. My father thought I needed to be humbled a bit."

"It didn't work, apparently," came his dry response.

A reluctant smile tugged at her lips. "Not particularly. But right now—" Her throat closed. Her eyes blurred.

"Are you all right?" He took a step toward her.

She nodded.

"Good." He strolled across the room and started around the desk. "After your sister's wedding—what's this?" He looked down at the ledgers.

"The ledgers Mr. Randall should have given you."

Marigold's tone held a hard edge that kept the tears at bay. "You didn't notice because you started with the oldest ones, but these are newer."

Gordon stared at her. "Dare I ask how you got these?"

"I walked in and took them. It's not Mr. Pollock's fault if Randall dismisses him."

"I see." He flipped open the first book. "Why did you bring these?"

"You need them. If Mr. Tripp is telling lies about the business, then he needs to be proven wrong, or he'll ruin it. If Mr. Randall is in the wrong, then he needs to be stopped."

"Yes, that's why I'm going through the books, but why did you. . .involve yourself?"

"I like numbers." She squared her shoulders. "I worked for my father for years and often found errors—" She lowered her gaze. "I'm boasting, aren't I?"

"Yes." He coughed. "And it may have gotten you into a pickle. If you like numbers so much, then perhaps you should be the one going through the ledgers, not I."

"I already have. The names of employees—skippers on the boats, deckhands, and so on—confused me, so I got these from Randall."

"He gave them to you?" Gordon looked dubious.

Marigold shrugged. "No one stopped me from taking them."

"I see." He tightened the corners of his lips, but one corner twitched suspiciously. "You don't want to continue with dusty old books, though."

"It's such a rainy day, and the temperature is dropping, so going through books is a perfect way to pass the time when the girls don't need me."

"I thought females read novels on cold, rainy days."

"No sir. I'd rather read Adam Smith."

"*Wealth of Nations?*" He shuddered. "I think I'd prefer to read a novel." He smiled.

Marigold smiled. "Let me see if the girls are all right, then I'll get to work."

The girls were happily coloring in leaves on the trees they'd drawn leaning so far over a body of water they looked about to topple into the stream at any moment.

"You should make their reflection in the water," Marigold suggested. "Now, if you need me, I'll be in the library."

The girls scarcely acknowledged her presence as they proceeded to discuss and squabble, in a friendly way, whether the trees' reflection would show in their water.

Marigold returned to the library, pulled a ledger from the stack, and settled in front of the hearth. When the air grew chilly and damp, Gordon built a fire. Mrs. Cromwell brought in hot tea and cookies. Marigold thought as she drank her tea and nibbled the cinnamon and sugar pastries. She focused on her work, seeking discrepancies. She hoped she would find them. One more way she would be indispensable. Gordon would tell her to return after the wedding. If things didn't work out with Lucian, she could tell everyone that she was needed on Cape May, needed for two orphaned girls whose uncle didn't care enough to stay among civilized people—

She stopped thinking in that direction. Numbers first. Numbers that worked out with revolting accuracy and neatness throughout the day—with one exception.

"It's odd that Leonard Pollock's name never appears in here," she told Gordon. "I know he works there. I talked to him when I took the rest of the ledgers."

"Do you recognize any of the names?" he asked.

Marigold shook her head. "I've never heard of any of these people, and you'd think that I would have after a year in Cape May. For local people, it's a small town."

"Could my brother have brought in outsiders?"

"Ye–es." Marigold began to ponder the name differences, but when Ruby called for her, she spent the rest of the afternoon helping the girls finish their drawing and then practicing the piano.

At dinnertime, she went into the kitchen and helped Mrs. Cromwell prepare the meal and set the table.

"You shouldn't be in the library alone with Mr. Gordon," the older woman admonished. "It doesn't look right."

"He hasn't been in there a great deal of the time," Marigold pointed out. "But he might be this evening."

"Then you should go up to the schoolroom."

"I'd rather keep working."

"So Mr. Gordon can leave us sooner?"

"So I can find something wrong, and he'll have to stay." The instant she spoke, Marigold wished she had bitten off her tongue rather than speak. "I mean. . . I didn't intend. . ."

"You spoke your mind." Mrs. Cromwell patted her arm. "That's all right. None of us wants him to leave these little girls."

"But you want to leave."

Mrs. Cromwell sighed. "No, I don't want to. I'll worry about them every day if I don't pray hard for them, and even then probably will, but I need to retire, child. I'm getting too old to handle this much work, and the winters are hard on my old bones."

"I understand. My great-grandmother had to move down to Georgia a few years ago for the same reason. I miss her."

"Then you go down and visit her. Family is important."

"I know. But right now. . ." Marigold twisted the dish towel so hard it began to tear.

Not even to this dear lady could she admit that her family only reminded her of how she wasn't going to have a husband and children of her own. She was expected to stand up there with the other bridesmaids and smile and pretend she was happy for Rose.

She was, of course. She simply couldn't help thinking how awful it was going to be to have to endure others' pity, especially when her parents would expect her to hand over the goldfinch to Rose.

It's only a thing, she reminded herself. It was a piece of glass. An old and beautiful piece of glass.

With a whole lot of meaning behind it—love and constancy, sacrifice and the strength of knowing one was not alone.

But she was alone now and didn't deserve the bird. She hadn't been able to keep her fiancé interested in her. She was better off without him. He didn't have a constant heart. But her heart ached with emptiness. Where now would she find someone she could marry so she wouldn't end up a spinster living with her parents even more years than she had already, watching Rose so happy and raising children?

A tray of hot coffee in her hands, Marigold returned to the library, to Gordon Chambers, a man who needed to learn he shouldn't be alone.

Chapter 10

Gordon didn't know how to tell Marigold to stop working on the ledgers. The grandfather clock in the foyer had long since chimed eleven o'clock. Mrs. Cromwell nodded in the chair she had settled by the door so she could chaperone. And Gordon could scarcely see numbers for the grit in his eyes.

Marigold, on the other hand, chewed on the end of a pencil while working out numbers on one of several sheets of paper, her face intent behind curls that had escaped their pins hours ago. She seemed impervious to the hour or the fact that she'd been working over the books for three hours without so much as moving from her chair.

More loudly than necessary, Gordon rose, stretched, and gathered up the tray of hot chocolate Mrs. Cromwell had made for them an hour earlier. With a flick of his finger, he sent a spoon cascading onto the marble hearth. It landed with a ring of fine silver on stone.

Marigold jumped and looked up. "Oh yes, let me help with that." She set the books aside and reached for the spoon.

Gordon reached for the spoon.

Their heads collided.

"I think we've done this before." He rubbed his scalp.

She pressed a hand to her head. "I am so sorry. Are you all right?"

"I am. You have a great deal of padding on your head."

"I have what?" She stared at him with wide, green eyes.

He grinned despite his fatigue and did what he'd wanted to do for weeks—pull one of her curls. "Your hair cushioned the blow."

"Oh, this." She grimaced. "Do you know a hundred years ago women cut their hair short? I think that would have been wonderfully freeing."

"I like it as it is."

He hadn't intended to say anything. He thought he considered her hair a disaster. Yet it was so vibrant, so full of energy and life—like her—he couldn't imagine her with sleek, obedient tresses.

He tucked his hands behind his back to stop himself from touching one of those silky curls again, burying his fingers in it and drawing her face to his, kissing her—

A man who wanted open space and peace didn't find himself attracted to a female who was anything but peaceful. A man who feared the harm he brought those with whom he grew close, those he loved, didn't dare take a wife, start a family.

Care for his orphaned nieces.

Yet leaving seemed more difficult with every person he met, every moment he spent with the girls, every time he looked at Marigold.

He scrambled to his feet. "It's late. Mrs. Cromwell needs her rest, even if you don't."

"Of course." She masked it quickly, but he caught the flash of hurt on her face. "I can finish up this work in the next two days, before I leave." She bowed her head and scrambled to her feet. "I am sorry, Mrs. Cromwell. Why don't you stay in bed and sleep late tomorrow? I'll make breakfast."

"Can you make a decent breakfast, too?" Gordon asked.

"Of course." Marigold picked up the serving tray and trotted from the room.

Gordon went to the housekeeper and took her hands. "Let me help you up, madam."

"Watch out for that young lady." She smiled as she stood, her joints popping. "She's trying to impress you for a reason."

"She knows better than to set her cap for me. She just doesn't want to go home without a fiancé. Rather humiliating, I'd think."

"Even more so if you knew what her sister looks like."

"Pretty?"

"Plain as skim milk, but she has the sweetest nature a body can possess this side of heaven. And her fiancé is one of the best-looking young men these old eyes have ever seen." She chuckled.

Gordon frowned. "You know the family?"

"Her sister came down to introduce Marigold to her fiancé last September."

"So my brother knew Marigold—I mean, Miss McCorkle—when he hired her?"

"Not Marigold, but her father."

"Why didn't you tell me?"

"Marigold asked me not to." Mrs. Cromwell stifled a yawn. "As to why Gerald hired her, you'll have to ask her."

No, he didn't. The less he knew of her the better. In fact, avoiding her until she departed would be an excellent idea.

An idea he carried out over the next two days. He knew she worked on the ledgers when not with the girls, so he stayed away. He went fishing one day and climbed to the top of the lighthouse another morning. One day he simply walked, pausing at the derelict structure that had been a man's dream of entertainment—the wood and tin elephant. Standing seventy feet high, it had allowed people to climb inside the huge legs and sit down to enjoy ice cream. One could climb to the top and look out to sea. Now it was an eyesore, a blot on the lovely city, and someone had been commissioned to tear it down.

He'd gained his love for being alone at the top of that elephant. He would pay a dime for the privilege of standing on the elephant's back, above most people, and gaze out to sea, dreaming of what lay beyond the horizon.

He'd taken Louisa there once on her afternoon off. She'd been so pretty; even her plain dress looked finer than those of the society ladies around them. Was she still pretty, or had those fine looks and that sweet nature gotten her further in life? She'd wanted so much more than she had, and he—

"Why are you staring at that, Uncle Gordon?" Ruby asked beside him.

Gordon glanced down. If they'd greeted him, he hadn't heard. "I liked to climb up there when I was a young man."

"It's ugly," Beryl pronounced. "Why would you want to climb it?"

"It wasn't ugly then. Well. . ." He grinned. "I suppose it was, but it has steps inside, and one can see a long way from the top. There was even an ice cream parlor inside."

"I wish there was now." Ruby stuck her fingers in her mouth.

In silence, Marigold tugged them out again. She looked tired, with shadows beneath her eyes and a pallor to her skin.

"Isn't it late in the day for one of your walks?" he asked.

"We need new shoes," Ruby said.

"I need new shoes." Beryl grimaced at her tiny black boots. "These are getting too small, but Ruby can wear them. They're hardly worn at all."

"I want new shoes, not your old ones. Mommy doesn't make me have old shoes."

"Mommy isn't here anymore, and Miss Marigold likes to practice economies." Beryl cast Marigold an approving glance. "We probably aren't as rich as we used to be."

"You are quite well off," Gordon said, "but that doesn't mean you should spend irresponsibly. There are a lot of people in this world who need things."

"Like Miss Marigold." Ruby stuck her fingers in her mouth then took them out again before continuing. "She needs a husband."

"I think it's time to go." Marigold clasped Ruby's hand. "Come along, Beryl."

The girls protested. Gordon told them to go. Marigold didn't look at him.

Go, indeed. Having her around, knowing she was in his house under what amounted to false pretenses, made him too uncomfortable.

He stayed away for several more hours, wandering along the beach. When the sun began to vanish behind the houses, he returned via the backstreets.

And found his nieces playing with the kitten in the yard.

"Shouldn't you be ready for bed by now?" he asked.

"Miss Marigold sent us outside to play." Ruby stuck her fingers in her mouth.

Beryl gave her a reproachful look. "You and the cat were getting in her way while she was fixing dinner."

"Why is she fixing dinner?" Gordon glanced to the house just as a billow of smoke sailed out the back door. "Stay here," he commanded.

He raced for the house. Smoke filled the kitchen, so thick he could scarcely see. Instantly, he began to cough. The kitchen reeked of burning chicken and onions.

Covering his nose and mouth with one arm, he darted to the stove. No flames on the top, only a pan smoking enough to send signals to Philadelphia. It snapped and sizzled and glowed like metal in a forge.

He snatched up a dish towel and wrapped it around his hand. Holding his breath, he carried the smoking and hissing mess outside. "Stay out of my way, girls," he called, unable to see them through the steam rising before him.

He carried the pan to the gravel of the alley and set it down where it could do no harm, except cause a bit of stink.

"Eeew." Beryl appeared beside him, holding her nose. "That's awful. What is it?"

"Dinner, I'm afraid." Gordon spun on his heel and headed for the house. "Where's Mrs. Cromwell—and Marigold?"

Mrs. Cromwell was nowhere in sight, but now that the smoke had cleared a bit, Gordon noticed Marigold sitting at the kitchen table, her head down on her folded arms.

He touched her shoulder. "Are you all right?"

She didn't respond or budge.

"Marigold?" His heart began to race until he felt breathless. "Marigold." He shook her.

She jumped. Her head slammed back against his belt buckle. "Ouch." She rubbed the back of her head. "What did you hit me with?"

"You hit your head on me." Still feeling as though he'd run a race, Gordon backed away from her. "You fell asleep and burned dinner."

"I did?" She blinked up at him then glanced around. Her nose wrinkled. "Oh dear. Oh dear. Oh dear." Rubbing her eyes, she stumbled to her feet. "So very sorry. I'll think up something else to make."

"Where's Mrs. Cromwell?" Gordon averted his gaze from the sight of Marigold's tumbled hair and sleep-misty eyes.

In that moment, she appeared too soft and pretty for his comfort.

"She's visiting her sister," Marigold said, "to try to persuade her to stay here a bit longer, so I offered to make dinner. But I was up late with the ledgers. They're almost done—and—"

"You're done with them. I shouldn't be allowing you to do my work for me."

"But I love numbers."

"Then do numbers for your father. My business affairs are my concern." Realizing his tone and words were too harsh, he added, "I am grateful for all the work you've done, Miss McCorkle, and it's past time you left for Hudson City and home. Surely your family wants you."

"Yes, but. . ." She bowed her head. "I'll go pack my things after dinner."

"You can go now. I'll take the girls to a restaurant. They're both old enough to behave in public."

"But they'll need their dresses changed and—no, I'll make dinner. I–I'm supposed to be a maidservant. And I need—" She gazed at him with pleading eyes. "I need to come back, Mr. Chambers. I can't stay home, and you need me here."

"You'll be gone for a week." Gordon made himself speak with an authoritative edge to his voice. "By the end of that time, I'll have hired someone to replace you."

"I see. Then I'll pack all my things."

If she'd cried, he might not have cared so much that his harshness hurt her. Females used tears too recklessly. He'd been duped by feminine tears as a young man, lured by the sympathy they evoked in him into being foolish and hurtful to others.

He wanted to reach out to her, assure her that he appreciated the work she'd done for him. Before he found the right words, she had slipped out of the kitchen and headed up the back stairs. Her footfalls echoed on the bare, wooden treads.

The next day, when she had taken a carriage to the train station, he still heard the echo of her flying heels beating against the steps. Each beat slammed into his heart, echoing in the hollowness there.

He wondered why he'd let her go and how he could get her back.

❧

Marigold walked into a household of organized chaos. Gifts filled every available surface in the front parlor. The aromas of roasting meats and baking cakes wafted from the kitchen, and bits of ribbon and fabric created a silky layer to the carpet of hallway and steps. From the second floor, laughter drifted like the fall of ribbon scraps. Laughter overflowing with joy. Rose, ecstatic with her future settled and her wedding in two days' time.

Her luggage resting where the driver of the carriage from the train station had left it, in a meager pile in the foyer, Marigold began to gather up ribbons as she mounted the steps toward the laughter, toward the joy, toward the acknowledgment that she was not the one to star in this performance.

Not only that, but she wasn't welcome back to Cape May. Gordon had made that clear. He didn't need her. For all her sleepless nights, she couldn't reconcile the two sets of ledgers in any way that said Randall and his clerks had done anything wrong but change employees and keep a sloppy set of books. Dennis Tripp must have been mistaken or was trying to get even with the man who had dismissed him, a fact that saddened Marigold. She'd thought Mr. Tripp was a good, Christian man who wouldn't indulge in petty revenge.

Yet why would a man try to take revenge in a way that could so easily be proven wrong?

Simply because it couldn't easily be proven right or wrong. For all her skill as a bookkeeper, she had found no conclusive evidence of wrongdoing.

Marigold paused at the top of the steps to gather up a scrap of veiling. Bridal veiling. Rose would be so pretty behind the gauzy fabric, her freckles dimmed, her pale lashes unimportant, her hair, even more orange red than Marigold's, hidden. Her sweet smile would shine through, and Adam would see only the beautiful person Rose was inside her skin, not the plain and painfully shy girl with the ability to paint birds in such detail they looked like they would fly off the page.

Birds like the goldfinch.

Marigold swiveled on her heel to change course from her trajectory toward the laughter to plod toward her own room. It would be ready for her, aired and cleaned, as she would share it with cousins visiting from out West for the wedding. Before she announced to her sister that she was home, Marigold needed to collect the family heirloom that now belonged to Rose, the sister no one thought would marry.

The door to Marigold's room stood open. Grass green carpet shone with recent cleaning, and a window stood open to catch the breezes off the river. Scents of late roses and recently cut grass floated through the window like welcome guests at the door, the summer smells she'd grown up with, had inhaled while holding the goldfinch and dreaming of the man she would marry.

Lucian fulfilled all her childish imaginings—tall and handsome, ambitious and skilled, and professing a faith in the Lord. Now that she was home for good, perhaps she could change his mind, renew their relationship. She had no other commitments in her life. She'd loved Lucian for years, prayed for several to have him notice her among all other girls. Finally he had—until she was no longer in sight. So now that she was, though, he was in Salem County working except for a few visits home. This wedding, when he would be home for the celebration of his friend, was her only chance to convince him he'd made a mistake in breaking things off with her. He was simply piqued at her long absence, her change of plans. She would humble herself and be compliant now. But even if she were successful in restoring her love life, it was too late for her to keep the goldfinch. By rights, Rose should already have it in her room.

Marigold paused before her dressing table and lifted the goldfinch bottle from its secure resting place before the mirror. Hands shaking only a little, she held up the ornament. Afternoon sunshine gleamed in the fragile amber glass, depicting each fine detail Colin Grassick had etched in hot glass ninety years earlier, a gift for the lady he loved. His son had given it to the lady he loved, and his son would have done likewise, but he'd made mistakes as a young man and lost the goldfinch. It came into the hands of Marigold's grandfather. Daire Grassick had told her grandfather, a poor Irish immigrant, to keep the goldfinch.

For Marigold's grandfather, the bird symbolized generosity and trust. He and Daire Grassick became friends. Through that friendship, the McCorkles prospered.

To Marigold, the goldfinch symbolized how far a body could change, from her grandparents being so poor they lived in one room to her and Rose growing up in a house, which, if not a mansion, was larger than four people needed, and attending private schools and college. She and Lucian should be living in a fine house in Salem County near the glassworks, where she would have displayed the goldfinch on the parlor mantel, letting everyone know how she was connected to the Grassicks from many years back. The Grassicks, after all, displayed photographs of the goldfinch in their house and the glassworks. She, Marigold McCorkle—

She located the special box for the goldfinch and tucked the glass bird into its layers of cotton wool. She'd been so proud of her family for owning this bit of glass that she wanted to be the one to carry it on to her own children.

Maybe if she could win Lucian back, no one would expect her to give up the glass. After all, she'd postponed her wedding for a noble cause. But she would make the gesture of giving it to Rose. Their parents would be proud of their elder daughter for understanding the new tradition they began when they'd only produced daughters.

Smile affixed to her face, Marigold held the box aloft like a holy grail and headed down the corridor to Rose's room, from which the laughter and chatter rippled like reflected sunlight on waves.

It ceased the instant Marigold appeared in the doorway. Rose, three of her friends, and Momma swung away from a pile of beautiful dresses and undergarments spread across the bed. Rose's trousseau, of course. No, the dresses were all alike. They must be bridesmaid dresses.

Marigold's head lightened. She clutched at the door frame. Of course she was in the wedding. Rose's sister was expected to stand up with her. Stand up in front of everyone, a bridesmaid instead of a bride.

"When did you get home?" Momma asked, smiling and striding across the floor to hug her daughter. "You look exhausted."

"I was up late packing." Marigold made herself return her mother's smile, and her sister's, and those of the friends in the room, as though she didn't have a care in the world. "I'm home for good."

"Eeee!" Rose squealed. She bounded off the end of the bed and dashed forward.

"Careful." Marigold held the wooden box over her head. "I brought this to you." She looked past her sister's shoulder. "It's yours."

"The goldfinch!" Rose's gray-green eyes widened then began to sparkle with tears. "Oh, Mari, it should be yours, not mine."

Marigold's lips felt stiff. "You're the first one to marry, and this was created for the lady Colin Grassick loved. So it's yours."

"But you'll get married." Rose exchanged a glance with Momma.

"Someday," one of Rose's friends murmured.

"God knows my future." Marigold's face felt hot.

"Take it, Rose." Marigold held out the box.

"But—"

"Take it," the Marsh sisters overrode Rose's protest.

Rose took the box, her face pink with pleasure, her eyes bright with tears but dancing. "I never thought I'd marry, let alone first."

"So," Marigold said with too much briskness, "what can I do to help?"

Nothing, apparently. Momma, Rose, friends, and cousins had taken charge of all the wedding preparations from finding housing for the guests coming from long distances, to cooking, to decorating the church for the ceremony and the yard for the reception. Marigold did have to have her bridesmaid dress, purchased in the event she could participate, altered because she'd lost weight sometime in the past year.

It was a bright blue silk confection that brought out the green of her eyes when she took off the hat that matched. But she wouldn't. This was Rose's day to shine.

And shine she did. No stunning white gown sewn with seed pearls and handmade lace compared to the glow of joy radiating from every fiber of Rose's being. Her face, her eyes, even her hair shimmered with a sparkle that brought tears of joy to Marigold's eyes. She was so happy for her sister.

She wanted that joy for herself.

Pleasure in Rose's happiness held Marigold up throughout the day in which she had nothing to do but watch others work. After fifteen months of rarely sitting down except to read to the children or mend, idleness made her want to run up and down the steps for exercise. But she didn't want to disturb her carefully coiffed hair, the dress, or the masses of flowers. . . .

She'd wanted her bridesmaids to wear rich rose pink. Roses bloomed in June.

And dreams died.

No, she mustn't feel sorry for herself. Tears would ruin her face and her dress and Rose's joy.

"It's time to go," Momma called from the foyer.

Carriages decorated with white satin ribbons stood waiting in front of the house to take them to the church. Momma, Father, and Rose climbed into the first one. Marigold joined the bridesmaids in the second one. Whips cracked. The horses tugged the vehicles forward and through the streets to the church, its bell announcing the happy occasion.

"Lucian's here," Priscilla pointed out.

Marigold tried not to look or ask.

"He's with Carrie Grassick," Priscilla added. "Look." She pointed out the window.

Carrie, like all the Grassicks, was lovely, with her smooth black hair and brilliant green eyes, fair skin, and willowy figure. Like everyone else still outside the church, she and Lucian turned toward the carriages. Her left hand rested on Lucian's arm.

Even from twenty feet away, Marigold couldn't miss the sunlight sparkling off the diamond ring displayed outside Carrie's glove.

Chapter 11

The knock sounded on the front door too early for a social call. Gordon rose from behind the desk now void of ledgers, of business correspondences, or invitations. Only a map of Alaska spread out before him so he could dream over its mountains and uninhabited spaces. He should answer the door. Mrs. Cromwell was busy helping the girls dress for the day, and the new nurserymaid applicant was due to arrive at eleven o'clock.

"And if she's arrived at eight o'clock instead," Gordon grumbled, "I'll send her packing. I won't have a female around who can't listen to instructions."

Jaw set, he yanked open the door.

"Good morning," Marigold said with too bright a smile to be anything but forced and brittle.

"What are you doing here?" he demanded.

"You advertised for a nurserymaid. I thought I'd apply for the position." The smile cracked, and her lower lip quivered. "I don't have anything else to do."

"I'm fairly certain that the position's been filled."

And his heart shouldn't be leaping about like a fish joyous to find a multitude of flies skimming over the surface of its pond, without a one being attached to a hook.

Or was it?

Gordon looked at Marigold's face, the eyes shadowed, the skin pale, her hair in disarray. In the morning sunshine, she glowed like a precious statue, beautiful and rare.

And the hook drove deep, its barbed end driving deep into his heart.

"Come in," he said.

Go away! his heart shouted. *For your own sake, go!*

He stepped back and allowed her to enter. She carried only a small valise.

"Your luggage?" he asked. "Or is this a brief visit?"

"I never even unpacked and brought a few more things." She set down the valise as though it weighed more than she did. "It's at the station. I walked here."

"After you must have traveled all night." Gordon clasped his hands behind his back to stop himself from reaching out and embracing her. He shouldn't be happy to see her. He'd told her to go. He'd told her to resume her normal life so he could resume his without her standing about, judging him on his actions.

Yet there she stood, fatigued, a little grubby, smelling of coal smoke from the train and the coffee staining the front of her ugly gray gown.

Marigolds should never be gray. They should never droop with tiredness.

Their eyes shouldn't convey sorrow, nor their lips curve any way but upward.

His fingers twitched with the urge to tug a corner of her mouth upward until she smiled again. Or if he kissed her. . .

He curled his hands in on themselves to make them behave. She was a maidservant in his home.

No, she wasn't. She was a young lady with no business standing in his foyer. And he had no business being so happy to see her, to feel like a prayer he hadn't uttered had been answered.

"I've made arrangements to borrow the Morrises' coachman when necessary, so I will send him for your trunk."

"Then I may stay?" Her face lit with that smile he so wanted to see. Her curls bounced. "Thank you. It's only been three days, but. . .Mr. Chambers, I didn't have anywhere else to go."

"Your family didn't want you?" He let all his incredulity at that ring through.

"No. I mean yes. That is—"

"Miss Marigold!" Ruby's cry rang loudly enough to be heard all the way to the beach. Her footfalls thundered down the steps.

Gordon stepped out of the way just in time to avoid being bowled over as his niece charged for Marigold, arms outstretched. Marigold dropped to her knees in time to catch the child in full flight.

"You came back." Ruby wrapped her arms around Marigold's neck. "I told Beryl you would. She said you wouldn't 'cause you were going to a wedding and would get engaged again, but I said you'd come back 'cause you promised never to leave us alone."

"She didn't leave us alone." With more dignity, but considerable speed, Beryl descended the steps. "Uncle Gordon is here."

"Yes, but he doesn't have time for us and doesn't help me with my arithmetic or piano." Ruby shot Gordon a glare that stung. "He wants us to go away to school."

"A school will have more girls your age and better teachers than I am." Marigold released Ruby to hug Beryl. "Don't you want that?"

"I have to stay here for Mommy and Daddy." Ruby stuck her fingers in her mouth.

Beryl sighed and pulled them out again. "You'll be here until you die, too."

Marigold laughed. "I've missed you." She cast Gordon a sidelong glance. "All of you. It makes me happier than I've been since I left."

"The wedding?" He began to inquire.

"Have you girls gone for a walk yet?" Marigold broke in. "I hope not. I missed the sea."

"We haven't done anything since you left," Beryl announced. "Uncle Gordon is too busy trying to get rid of us, and Mrs. Cromwell is too busy interviewing people for your position."

"Oh, of course she is." Dismay tightened Marigold's face. She glanced at Gordon. "I'm intruding, aren't I? You've likely found someone."

Gordon opened his mouth to repeat that he was fairly certain he would offer the job to the woman coming in three hours, but the words wouldn't come. "I have an interview or two with candidates Mrs. Cromwell finds acceptable."

"What's 'acceptable'?" Ruby asked.

"Good enough." Marigold tugged on one of the child's braids. "Like your hair isn't. It looks as bad as mine."

"She doesn't have a stain on her dress," Beryl pointed out. "You do."

"Oh, dear." Marigold flushed nearly as red as her hair. "Should I go change?"

"You look like you should rest." Gordon wanted her out of his vicinity before he hugged her like the girls and told her how much he'd missed her, too. The house no longer echoed as though empty of even the children. It rang with Marigold's sparkling voice, vibrated with her energy. "I'm leaving for the boathouse."

"You found something?" Marigold gave him her full attention.

"No, I have a potential buyer and need to inspect the boats before I can think of selling."

"You're going to sell the boats?" Beryl asked.

"As soon as I can."

"Can we go out on them before you do?" Beryl persisted.

"No." Ruby backed to the steps, her fingers in her mouth. "No no no. I won't. I can't—"

"Ruby." Gordon and Marigold reached the child at the same time.

Gordon crouched before her and took her hands in his. "Sweetheart, the boats won't hurt you."

"They hurt Mommy and Daddy. They went away because of the boat."

"No, Ruby." Gordon caught a tear on her cheek with the knuckle of one hand. "The storm made the boat go down. It was a squall that took them by surprise."

"Mr. Tripp told them not to go out," Beryl announced.

Gordon swung around to face her, nearly losing his balance. "What do you mean? I thought he'd been dismissed."

"He got dismissed a few weeks later," Marigold said.

Gordon's stomach twisted. "I'm not sure I like the sound of this."

"The ledgers—"

"Not in front of the children." Gordon cut off Marigold's question.

Beryl scowled at him. "People never say interesting things in front of us. You'd think we're babies."

"We don't want to say anything bad if it isn't true." Gordon tried to smile at her. "Let's talk about taking that boat ride soon. Right now I have business to conduct, and Miss Marigold needs a nap. Where's Mrs. Cromwell?"

"She's in the kitchen," Beryl answered.

"She said she needs a cup of tea after getting us ready." Ruby giggled. "She wants me to dress just like Beryl, but she has new shoes and I don't."

"And your hair won't stay braided." Beryl tossed her head. "Mine never comes undone."

"Pride goeth before a fall, Beryl," Marigold said, then grimaced and raised a hand to her eyes. "I do believe I will take that nap."

"Did you leave right after the wedding?" Gordon couldn't stop himself from asking.

She nodded. "I left as soon as my sister and her new husband departed for their wedding journey. I couldn't. . . stay." She yawned, perhaps the reason for the hitch in her voice, but Gordon didn't think so.

With all his heart, he wanted to know what was wrong, why she looked so sad, why she had come back when he'd said he didn't want her there, why home had become so onerous to her. He opened his mouth to ask her to take some refreshment in the library before she went to her room, a room still ready for her, but snapped his lips together without speaking.

Concern for others led to trouble. He was better off alone and praying for them.

"I'll be on my way," he said and swung toward the door. "I must be back by eleven."

"When is the boat trip?" Beryl asked.

"There's room for us on a boat tomorrow." He tossed the answer over his shoulder. "We'll go tomorrow."

"No." Ruby's protest was the last thing he heard as the front door clicked shut behind him.

He wished his heart would click shut with so little effort. For ten years, he'd managed to keep the door on caring too much for others firmly closed, usually locked. If he saw others in trouble, he prayed for them and moved on. He did not get involved. Doing so had cost him too much in the past. Yet his niece's fear of going on the water disturbed him. Marigold's reappearance and obvious unhappiness tore at him.

"God, I need to get away sooner than later."

A passerby on the sidewalk gave him an odd look. Gordon smiled. He must remember that he was in the middle of a town, a small town bursting at the seams with summer visitors. Praying out loud wasn't an option for him.

Nor was a peaceful walk. He passed too many people. Most of them knew him by now, or knew who he was. He passed the eyesore of the derelict elephant and wished he could still climb to the top. Even with others there, he had felt alone when he gazed out to sea, imagined sailing over the horizon.

He'd sailed over that horizon and back again. He'd climbed over the mountains and back again. Alaska was the closest thing to a frontier left for him to discover. It was the last place where he had a chance to build his own fortune, to prove to his father that he would amount to something.

He'd done a poor job of it so far. Every penny he'd earned had gone into his next excursion. The sale of the boating business would go into his next excursion. This time he wouldn't fail. He would be properly equipped. He'd planned.

And his brother's death had interrupted those plans. Marigold threatened to interrupt those plans.

He stopped in the middle of the boardwalk and stared out to sea, wondering where such a notion had come from. Marigold might help him make his escape. He could trust her. If she truly had nowhere else to go, she could stay at the house once he left. He could hire a companion for her to make things respectable. They could keep the house for the girls; the girls would have a place to return for holidays and someone who loved them with whom they could stay.

Excited with his idea, Gordon hastened his steps to the boathouse, secured a place for them on the boat for the following day, and headed home to talk to Marigold about her future.

About her present. As much as he told himself he needed to know because what had happened at home impacted her ability to continue working for him, he admitted to himself that he wanted to know because some of her sunshine had clouded.

His wanting to know was good reason for him to be gone as soon as possible.

Piano scales and the aroma of baking gingerbread greeted him when he entered the house. Moments later the applicant arrived, fresh-faced, cheerful, and far too young.

"I'm sorry," he told her, "I need someone more. . .matronly."

The young woman glanced at Mrs. Cromwell, who had joined him for the interview. She shook her head. Neither female knew what Gordon wanted in a woman he hired. He didn't either, not until he talked to Marigold.

Once the girl left, he followed his ears to the sound of the piano and found Marigold presiding over Ruby's practice.

"Miss McCorkle?" he asked.

She glanced up.

Ruby slid off the stool and raced across the room. "I can do two octaves without making a mistake. Do you want to hear?"

"Of course I do." He couldn't say anything else.

Ruby demonstrated her growing skill. Then Beryl showed him how she had improved, playing a simple piece.

"Now you play, Miss Marigold," the girls urged.

Gordon didn't encourage it. Nor did he discourage it. Marigold's playing was worth listening to. By the time she finished the sonata, Mrs. Cromwell entered with milk for the girls and coffee for the adults, gingerbread and cookies for everyone.

So the day went. Every time he tried to talk to Marigold, she vanished behind the girls' needs to eat, to practice, to go play with the cat in the yard. Not until after supper, when the girls settled down to read or draw on their own in the parlor, did he track her down in the kitchen, where she was washing dishes.

"Why did you come back?" he asked without the preamble of social niceties.

She rinsed a plate before setting it in the rack to dry and turning to face him. "My father doesn't need me working in the business. He's an exporter, you see, which is how I met my fiancé—my former fiancé. I'm afraid he thinks I'll fall for someone else, who–who's unsuitable. I find my mother's charity work tedious, and—and—" She snapped her teeth together and returned to the washing up.

"And?" Gordon prompted.

"I'm back. That's what matters. If you don't want me to stay, I won't, of course, but those little girls need someone who loves them, and I love them."

"I know you do."

And he loved her. He loved her so much he knew he should send her away before he hurt her, before she buried herself in Cape May and never found someone who wanted to love her.

He didn't want to love her, didn't want to face the pain and grief of being pushed aside for someone with better prospects, for a man worthy of her generous heart and loving spirit.

"You can stay." Huskiness invaded his voice. "Tomorrow we'll take the girls out on one of the excursion boats."

"Ruby's scared." Marigold glanced at him, her eyes clouded.

"I know. It's the best way to get her over her fear. And she must. She can't go through life being afraid of boats."

"Unless she wants to move to Kansas or something." Marigold smiled.

"Even so. . . If she's too frightened, we'll come back."

"It's because of her parents, you know." Marigold began to wash dishes again, her hands nearly elbow-deep in sudsy water. "She can't accept that they won't come back. I don't know how to fix that for her."

"Time, I think. But perhaps going on the water will help her understand. . . something." Not wanting to leave, despite his business with Marigold concluded, Gordon picked up a dish towel and began to dry the stacked plates. "So tell me about the wedding."

"Rose was beautiful. My mother had everything planned to perfection. Everyone asked me why I—" She ducked her head. Curls cascaded across her cheek.

"Why you gave up your marriage plans for near strangers?"

"I wasn't the one who gave them up."

"If he wouldn't wait for you, then he doesn't deserve you."

"That's what my sister said. But when he arrived at the wedding with—I told them I was committed to the girls here. And Lucian—" She heaved a sigh. "I didn't want to stay any longer than I had to. I missed everyone here so much, and the river isn't nearly as nice as the ocean."

"Would you like to stay on even after I leave?" Gordon asked.

She jumped, sending a glass plopping into the water with a spray of suds that soaked the front of her gown.

He smiled. "I didn't mean to startle you. I'm only thinking about this, but if you really have nowhere to go, I can hire a companion for you if you'll stay on and manage the house. It will give the girls somewhere to go on school holidays."

"They'd rather come home to you, Mr. Chambers. They need their family."

"Odd you would say that when you have chosen to leave yours."

"Yes, well, staying where everyone knows me was too—" She sighed. "I'll go back if you choose to stay here."

"I can't stay." He stacked several plates before he admitted, "This isn't my house. It's my father's. He tossed me out of it and wouldn't welcome me back if he were still alive. I'll return to stay when I can buy a house of my own."

"Hmm." She collected a pan from the top of the stove and dunked it into the dishwater. "I can't imagine any father tossing his son out of his house forever. Nothing is that bad."

"I ruined someone else's life, hurt the family's reputation. . . . He was justified in his actions. Even Gerald sided with him." He lifted the stack of plates and carried them to their cupboard before he said too much, before she asked him to say more.

She didn't ask him anything. When he returned with a dry dish towel, she tilted her head to one side and smiled up at him. "I'll tell you about my father sending me packing if you'll share your story."

Chapter 12

Marigold didn't know what possessed her to make such a personal suggestion to her employer. Yet he didn't feel like her employer, standing there with a dish towel over his arm and his shirt cuffs wet. He looked like something she had never envisioned Lucian being—a spouse who was a companion, not just a vague figure across the breakfast table.

The revelation struck her like a rolling pin between the shoulder blades, and she blurted out, "I never loved him."

Gordon dropped the glass he was drying. He dove for the shining fragments. Marigold dove for the pieces. Their heads collided.

"Oof." Marigold jerked back, slipped in a patch of water, and landed on her seat.

"I am so sorry." That treacherous corner of his mouth twitching, Gordon leaned down and offered his hands. "Are you all right?"

"I think so." She tried to get her feet under her. Her heels tangled in her skirts, and she moved no further than her knees.

"Here." Gordon clasped her by the waist and lifted her to her feet—and didn't let go.

She knew she should tell him she was all right, that he could release her without worrying she would fall again. She wanted to tell him she would go to her room now and not bring up anything personal.

She looked into his deep brown eyes, saw the sparkle even in the murky gaslight of the kitchen, and lowered her lashes, ready, willing, perhaps too eager, and not caring in that moment when his lips met hers.

The contact lasted no more than a heartbeat. It was the best moment in the past year and a half of Marigold's life. She wanted to run off to her room, write the moment down, savor every detail of his tender expression, his scent of sunshine and lemons, his lips as gentle as a summer breeze, though they flooded her with a hurricane gale of longing.

"I. . .suppose that was completely inappropriate." His voice emerged as though he spoke from a dry throat. "You work for me."

"I can leave your employment."

"You just lost your fiancé."

"He never should have been my fiancé." She spoke in a breathless rush, trying to get everything out before he walked away. "He wasn't in love with me, or he'd have waited for me, instead of getting himself engaged to one of the Grassick girls. And I couldn't have loved him, or I wouldn't—"

No, she wouldn't humiliate herself by admitting she loved him until he told her he felt more than an attraction for her. One humiliation at the hands of a male was quite enough for one summer.

"Have just let you kiss me," she concluded.

"Perhaps not." His smile was gentle, his fingers against her cheek gentler. "Now I understand why you came back. Facing that kind of humiliation must have been difficult for a proud lady like you. But I can't let you hurt yourself by entangling yourself in my life. Kissing you was. . .wonderful. Believe me. I'd do it again in a moment if I thought it would benefit either of us. But it won't, Marigold. It was an error in judgment, and I'm too good at making errors in judgment to be responsible for anyone other than myself."

"No no, I don't believe that. You knew you had to stay here longer than you thought."

"But stayed away too long."

"You—"

"Hush." He pressed his finger to her lips. "I won't let you make an error in judgment either. And saying things to me right now will likely be just that."

She wanted to argue with him further but feared he was right if that concerned how she felt about him.

Or maybe just thought she felt about him.

Yet because she cared, however deeply that caring ran, she couldn't bear the pain flickering in his eyes, the pain of his words, claiming he made poor judgments. She wanted, needed, to say something to ease that burden.

She took a deep breath. "Perhaps you depend on yourself instead of the Lord for your decisions, and that's why you think they go awry."

"My relationship with the Lord is my concern." His face tightened. "Go to your room, Miss McCorkle. I'll finish clearing up in here."

"But—"

"Go, or I'll consider the worst of my choices has been to allow you to stay a minute after I got here." He smiled without humor. "Which it probably was."

"Gor—" With an effort, Marigold closed her mouth, turned on her heel, and raced up to her room.

For solace, she pushed aside the latter part of their encounter and concentrated on those moments of closeness. He'd kissed her.

Lucian had kissed her, too. They'd been engaged. She'd liked it.

When Gordon kissed her, she'd loved it. Because she loved him? She thought she did. She figured she had for most of the nearly four weeks she'd known him, if that was possible. At least for the past few days. At least since he'd opened the door to her and welcomed her back with a look she could only describe as joyous.

Because he loved her, too?

How she wanted to think so but dared not. She must keep herself aloof, protect her pride, protect her soul. She would become the perfect maidservant, beginning with having the girls ready for the boating excursion the following morning.

~

But the next morning, Ruby was missing. Marigold slipped into the girls' room to wake them up and found no child in the second bed.

"When did Ruby get up?" Marigold demanded of Beryl.

"Dunno." Beryl yawned and rubbed her eyes. "Sleeping."

"Perhaps she went downstairs." Marigold rushed down to the kitchen. "Is Ruby here?"

Mrs. Cromwell turned from the stove. "I haven't seen her this morning. Maybe she's with Mr. Gordon."

"Where's he?"

"In his library."

Marigold darted through the door separating the kitchen from the rest of the house and charged into the library. "Where's Ruby?"

Gordon dropped his coffee cup, spilling brown liquid across his desk and a map.

"I'm so sorry." Marigold made the apology in a breathless rush. "Ruby isn't in her bed, and Mrs. Cromwell hasn't seen her."

Before she finished speaking, Gordon was on his feet and reaching for the coat hanging on the back of his chair. "Finish searching the house. I'll look outside. If she's not there, I'll go to the Morrises' and get help."

Ruby wasn't inside. Beryl, Mrs. Cromwell, and Marigold searched from the attic to the cellar and found no sign of the little girl.

"She never goes anywhere alone." Trying not to cry, Marigold stood on the front porch and insisted her brain work on a solution. "She knows better."

"It's my fault," Beryl said and burst into tears.

"What do you mean?" Marigold put her arms around the child. "How can this be your fault?"

Beryl shook her head, sobbing. "I called her a baby for being afraid to go on the boat. I said—I said if—if we were nicer children, Uncle Gordon wouldn't go away. And. . .I'm so sorry."

"Why did you say those things to her, Beryl?" Marigold sat back on her haunches and looked into the girl's face. "Why were you so mean to her?"

"Because—because. . ." Beryl looked away. "She never liked the boats and keeps me from going on them."

"I see." At least Marigold thought she understood. "Well, Beryl, now none of us can go because Ruby isn't here."

Beryl bowed her head and scuffed at the floorboards with the toe of her shoe. "She's probably in the elephant."

"You know? You've known all along?" Marigold shot to her feet, her hands crushing fistfuls of her skirt. "Why didn't you tell us? Never mind that now. We'll talk about it later. Go to your room and stay there."

"You're angry with me." Beryl recommenced crying.

"Yes Beryl, I am. But right now, finding your sister is more important."

"But she's the one who's naughty."

"You're both naughty." Marigold spun on her heel and raced for the sidewalk.

The elephant, old and rickety, must be dangerous. Signs told people to stay away. It smelled of rotting lumber and rusting metal. Rats probably lived inside the enormous legs, and if Ruby tried to climb the steps, she was likely to fall through a disintegrating board and break something vital.

Marigold ran. She held her skirts as high as the tops of her shoes to keep herself from tripping on them. She passed people she knew and gawking strangers, ice cream sellers and barking dogs. She ran toward the blot on the Cape May landscape and ignored shouts for her to stop, calls of her name, warnings to slow down.

She started calling Ruby's name the minute the elephant heaved into view. And she kept running toward the beast, past signs that warned people away, past the signs that had once advertised on the monstrous sides. She hollered for Ruby until her throat hurt.

At the door to one of the elephant's legs, she stopped. Her heart raced. Her breath rasped in her throat.

The door stood open.

She laid her hand on the frame.

"You can't go in there, miss." A brawny workman shoved between Marigold and the door. "It's dangerous."

"I know." She bent double against a stitch in her side. "Little girl... Lost... Think—inside..."

The man murmured something that sounded like a prayer.

A prayer!

Marigold leaned against the elephant's scarred side and closed her eyes. She hadn't stopped to pray. She'd determined to find Ruby on her own.

"Please, God, help me find her," she whispered into her hands. "I need to—"

"I'll go look, miss." The workman pushed the door open further. "What's her name?"

"Ruby. She's only six."

"Too young to be on her own." He gave Marigold a censorious glance.

She frowned at him. "I didn't let her be on her own. She slipped out of the house without us knowing."

"Huh." Mouth set as though he were eating limes, the workman tramped into the elephant.

His footfalls rang hollowly. His voice sounded as though he called into a bucket. The silence in response sounded even louder.

"Ruby." Marigold stepped to the doorway of the elephant. The stench of mildew and rot assailed her nostrils. "I'm here. Don't be frightened."

She wanted to promise the child that she wouldn't have to go out on a boat. But Marigold couldn't make that kind of promise. It was up to Gordon, and he believed she should go out on the water to get over her fear. He said that way worked the best. He'd said it as though he knew what he was talking about.

She couldn't imagine Gordon Chambers afraid of anything. He was too big, too strong, too sure of what he wanted. Or didn't want—her.

"Ruby," the workman called.

"Please, Ruby, answer if you're here," Marigold reiterated.

No small voice responded. The workman's boots tramped back down the steps. The gunshot crack of a splintering tread ricocheted off the walls. The workman muttered something and leaped to the bottom of the steps.

"She's not here, miss," he told Marigold.

She resisted the urge to wipe a cobweb from his hat brim and crossed her arms over her chest. "You're sure? You looked everywhere? What about the other legs, the trunk, the top?"

"She's not here." The workman moved forward, compelling Marigold to step back. "I didn't see any footprints in the dirt."

"I see. Well then, thank you for looking." Marigold turned away and plowed through the small crowd staring toward the elephant. Her heart ached. She pounded one fist into the other. "God, why do I keep failing? Why do I keep losing? Why do I—"

She heard herself, heard one word repeated again and again: *I. . .I. . .I. . .*

She stumbled to a halt on the pavement and leaned against a lamppost, her knees too weak to support her, her pride enough to keep her from sinking to the ground in front of all the holidaymakers. She tried to think. Her head whirled. Sun and sound intensified until the brightness and volume of shouting youths, shrieking children, and chattering adults would explode like dynamite inside her head.

"Marigold—that is, Miss McCorkle?" Gordon Chambers touched her arm. "Are you all right?"

"No. Yes. I—"

There was that word again, selfish, self-centered, prideful.

God, how far do I need to fall?

She raised her gaze to Gordon's face, her vision blurred. "We have to find Ruby. Beryl said she'd be in the elephant, but she's not there."

"You didn't go in, did you?" Gordon looked alarmed.

Marigold shook her head.

"Good. It can't be safe. But how do you know she's not there?"

"A workman came around and looked for me." Marigold wiped her eyes on her sleeve. "But now where do we go?"

"Where else does she like to be?" Gordon asked.

"The lighthouse?"

They turned toward the towering structure at the point of the cape, where it guided ships to a safe passage into Delaware Bay.

"I don't like it, but there are always so many visitors there she would be safe." Gordon rubbed his temples as though his head hurt. "Shall we go look?"

"Yes please." Without thinking, Marigold tucked her hand into the crook of his arm as they headed for the lighthouse at a trot. "We have gone there twice. She likes looking out to sea to find dolphins."

"I used to do that as a youth, too. I missed the dolphins once I left here. Of course I saw them on my travels, but somehow seeing them from the lighthouse was more enjoyable. Maybe because I saw them from so far away no one on land could see them yet. It was like being first."

"You love it here, don't you?" Marigold spoke so softly, she doubted he heard her over the boisterous visitors surrounding them. He said nothing for several blocks, then without warning, he covered her hand with his and inclined his head.

"Then why leave?" She spoke in a low voice, afraid to speak louder for fear of breaking the contact between them.

Which meant she should break it. She should not be loving the sensation of Gordon Chambers, her employer, cradling her fingers between his large palm and muscled forearm. Not wishing he would kiss her again.

Once more, he remained silent and without expression for so long she thought he hadn't heard her. Then he gestured toward the boathouse, where visitors lined up to board the excursion boats. "It has to do with a boat. And me being young and impulsive and stupid and wanting my own way—like too many youths with more money than sense and discipline." He grimaced. "I had free rein of the boats that weren't being used at the time. Gerald and I always understood that I'd get the boathouse, and he'd get the real estate business. My father was clear that's how he'd divide up the inheritance. And it would have been all right if—"

"Mr. Chambers?" The voice rang over roar of surf and shouts of merrymakers on the beach.

Marigold and Gordon stopped, turned to the shouting man.

Dennis Tripp charged up to them then stood gasping for air, his hands on the threadbare thighs of his trousers.

"What is it?" Gordon demanded. "Speak now. We don't have time. My niece is missing."

"I know where she is." Tripp straightened. "I was looking for coins on the beach—" His face flushed at this admission of his poverty. "I saw her on one of the boats. I thought she must be with you, but you're here."

"She couldn't have," Gordon declared.

"She wouldn't have," Marigold said at the same time.

Tripp looked frustrated. "Why would I lie to you?"

"You lied to me about the ledgers," Gordon pointed out. "You claimed Randall was cheating me, but neither Miss McCorkle nor I found anything wrong with them."

"Look again." Tripp's face tightened as though he were about to cry. "They're in code or something. I know the boats are in ill repair. But after you get your niece back."

"And how do I do that?" Gordon sounded belligerent.

Marigold understood why—worry and frustration. Not a single boat remained at the jetty.

"Find a way. That entire operation should be shut down until the boats are inspected." Tripp turned away. "But you don't have to believe me. I just pray no one gets hurt, someone like your niece, until you do."

He stalked off and vanished into the crowd.

Marigold looked up at Gordon. "We must find someone with a boat to help us find her. Someone else will lend us a craft, I'm sure."

"I am, too, but we have no idea which way to look or for which craft." A muscle in his jaw bunched. "The man couldn't bother to tell us."

"Or we were rude to him and sent him away before we asked."

"He should have—" Gordon sighed. "You're right. Let's find him and ask. He can't have gone far."

But he had gone somewhere. They searched for ten minutes without spotting a little man with ragged clothes and a sad yet peaceful expression.

"He's just a troublemaker," Gordon grumbled. "Now we've wasted time when we should have been hunting for Ruby."

Movement on the water caught Marigold's attention. "One of the boats is coming back in."

Without another word, they raced for the jetty and the docking excursion boat. Laughing, chattering families poured over the gangway and onto dry land. From snatches of conversation, they'd seen only one dolphin, but it was amazing to people who didn't live near the sea.

The instant the last passenger disembarked, Gordon, with Marigold behind, leaped aboard the boat and grabbed one of the crewmen. "I'm looking for my niece. She's a little girl—"

"You're going to have to get a ticket to get aboard, sir." The crewman was polite but firm. "I don't give out information—"

Gordon grasped the man's shoulder. "My niece is only six and may have sneaked aboard."

"No little girls, sir. Now, if you don't get off this boat, I'll have to call the police—"

"I own this boat." Gordon shook the man.

"Get your hands off of me." The crewman punched Gordon in the middle. "I know the owner, and it's not you."

Gordon barely flinched from the blow, but he removed his hand from the man's shoulder, though curled it into a fist. "If you want to keep your position," he said in a deadly quiet voice, "you will answer my question. I don't know who you think owns this company, but I am Gordon Chambers, and the court will inform you that I own it by inheritance."

"I–I'm sorry." The man backed up, his hands in front of him. "I thought—we all thought—I'll get the skipper." He spun on his heel and charged aft.

Marigold touched Gordon's arm. "Are you all right?"

"Physically, yes. Otherwise—" He faced her abruptly. "Who does he think owns this company?"

"I don't know." Marigold felt sick, not from the gentle rise and fall of the deck as the tide sloshed against the pier, but from the apprehension that Dennis Tripp was right and something was terribly wrong besides Ruby going missing, and not taking him seriously enough was the worst judgment either she or Gordon had made.

Chapter 13

Gordon grasped Marigold's arm. "Stop anyone else from coming aboard. I'll find the skipper myself."

"What are we going to do?" She looked pale, frightened.

"Find Ruby if she is aboard one of these boats."

"I think she is. I think Mr. Tripp's right."

"I agree. That crewman should have known who owns this company. That tells me something is not right here." He released Marigold. "Let's hope Tripp's not right about the poor repairs."

Gordon should have taken an active role in the business instead of planning to leave as soon as possible. He should have been more responsible toward others, toward his nieces.

Yet once again, he wasn't thinking and was taking actions that hurt those he cared about, like seeking a school for the girls, like kissing Marigold.

He'd thought going through the ledgers would be enough, but of course it wasn't. He should have known that as soon as Marigold pointed out the name discrepancies. But he couldn't be bothered with details, because they got in the way of his plans to sell the business as soon as the court had probated Gerald's will and gave him the go-ahead.

"God, please let Ruby and the boat be all right. Or let her be on land somewhere safe."

He reached the pilothouse, where the skipper of the craft and crewmen stood at the wheel, talking in low voices. They turned on Gordon, their faces tight.

"I'm Gordon Chambers, the owner of this boating business," Gordon said. "We are going to go on your usual route and find the other boats in the event my niece is aboard one of them."

"I can't do that without Mr. Randall's permission, sir." The skipper spoke with more respect than the crewman had, but his bearded jaw was set in a pugnacious line.

"Mr. Randall isn't aboard. I am." Gordon glanced through the window and saw Marigold disappear into the cabin.

Seeking Ruby? Of course she would, bless her.

"Mr. Randall won't object, Captain," Gordon said with as much pleasantry as he could conjure. "Even if he does, I am in a position to ensure nothing happens to your position."

"But I don't know you." The skipper glanced toward shore.

330

Several people who looked like passengers lined up at the foot of the gangway. Lawrence Randall was pushing through them.

Gordon stepped in front of the skipper again. "You don't recognize my resemblance to my brother?"

"Why should I?"

"Because he owned—"

"We'll ask Mr. Randall now," the crewman said and shoved past Gordon.

He followed, along with the skipper. Marigold was nowhere around.

"Sir," the skipper called to Randall, "this man insists I take the boat out to look for his niece."

"Then, by all means, do it." Randall smiled ingratiatingly. "Of course, we'll disappoint a number of people, which won't do the business any good, but it's his company to ruin if he doesn't want to sell it for much."

A bell louder than any ship's timer boomed in Gordon's head. He frowned at the company manager. "Would you like to buy it, Mr. Randall?"

"Beyond my price." Waving, Randall headed down the gangway and began speaking to the waiting passengers.

"What are you waiting for?" Gordon asked the skipper. "Take this boat on the tour the rest take. We'll try to intercept them and see if my niece is aboard."

"If she ain't aboard this one," the crewman grumbled. "People who can't take care of their families. . ."

Apparently thinking better of whatever he'd been about to say, he turned away and followed the skipper back to the pilothouse.

Gordon began to hunt around chairs and tables set out on deck. They all looked well, painted with bright, white paint and clean. The deck, too, seemed to have been painted recently. Brass on railings and the cabin door gleamed in the sunlight.

Surely Tripp was wrong.

Gordon opened the door to the cabin. It resembled a luxurious parlor, with velvet-covered sofas and chairs set in groupings around the chamber. The windows could have been cleaner, and he caught one or two worn places on the cushions; however, keeping windows clean on a vessel and repairing furniture used as much as this was, was nearly impossible.

Calmed by the outwardly good appearance of the craft, as well as the familiar *chug-chug-chug* of the engine, Gordon headed out the forward end of the cabin in search of Ruby, in search of Marigold.

He heard her scream a moment after the boat left the wharf.

"Marigold?" His heart raced faster than the screw pushing the boat forward. "Marigold, where are you?"

"Here." Her voice was faint, muffled. "I'm. . .fine."

The hitch in her voice told him she wasn't quite telling the truth.

He followed the sound until he saw a companionway leading below. Nothing should be down there but a small cabin, perhaps, for the crew, the engine room, and a hold full of fuel.

And Marigold. She sat on the next to the bottom step, her foot caught in a hole in the bottom tread.

"I'm a bit clumsy, as you know." She smiled up at him, but the whiteness of her face betrayed pain.

"My dear girl." Gordon moved past her with care, testing each step to ensure it could hold his weight. "How did this happen?"

"I was just coming down here, and all looked well. . . ."

It did. Like on the deck, the paint appeared fresh. But the board beneath was rotten.

The icy waters of the North Atlantic seemed to flow through Gordon's veins. Sick to his stomach, he knelt at Marigold's feet and worked her foot from the hole. Thanks to the high top of her shoe, she hadn't cut it, but her gasp of pain and his probing fingers told him the ankle was swelling.

"I think a sprain," he said. "I'll have to carry you up."

"You can't. And if Ruby's here. . ."

"I'll find her when I get you settled."

"I'm too heavy."

"No, you're not." Before she could argue further, Gordon scooped her into his arms and headed up the way he had come.

She remained stiff in his hold until they reached the top. Then she relaxed against him, her head lolling on his shoulder, one of her arms encircling his neck.

She wasn't a burden at all. He liked his arms around her. With her face so close to his, the yearning to kiss her nearly left him breathless.

His guilt stopped him. He had caused this, just as he had caused many of Louisa's troubles. He hadn't wanted anything to be wrong with the company—so selling it would be easy and quick—so he'd ignored the warnings.

"I'm so sorry, my dear." He brushed his lips across her brow. "So very sorry."

"I'm all right. I'm sure Ruby is all right. Now, put me down and go look for her."

"In here." He carried her into the cabin and set her on a sofa. "You may wish to remove your shoe in case your ankle swells more. Even if they are as ugly as your gray dresses, you don't want to ruin good shoes."

She laughed, brushed his hair off his forehead, and kissed his cheek. "Don't blame yourself for this."

"How can I not?" He turned and left as quickly as he could.

Hunting through every recess of the vessel, annoying two more crewmen down in the engine room, he sought for other signs of decay covered over with fresh paint. He found none. That didn't mean other problems didn't exist, problems he should have found.

"God, where did I go wrong?"

With no sign of Ruby aboard, he returned to the deck. He saw Marigold through the cabin window, wanted to go to her, but didn't dare. She deserved better than a man like this Lucian, who had jilted her because she'd asked him to wait, for a good reason, and she deserved better than a Gordon Chambers, who wanted things the way he wanted them—a life free of commitments, free of responsibility. . . .

"I'm despicable, Lord. I deserved to be rejected by my father."

Yet God was a father who hadn't rejected him for his shortcomings, for going his own way. Gordon paid lip service to being a Christian, yet how often had he asked God what he should do? Not when he tried to help Louisa and caused disaster. Not when he'd invested years of savings in a mine that had been paid out years earlier. Not when he'd returned to Cape May determined to leave as soon as possible so he could try to make another fortune and prove his father wrong to predict he'd come to no good.

He gripped the rail and gazed out across Delaware Bay. Vessels from the smallest of fishing boats to oceangoing liners scattered across the crystal blue waters. Smoke from engines drifted into the cloudless sky, and sometimes a burst of laughter mingled with the rumble of engines. It was a familiar scene, one that had told him he wanted to own this company when his father allowed it. Gerald had known it, had tried to keep their father from sending Gordon away permanently. And in the end, he'd done what he could to make things right.

"And I was going to destroy it by neglecting it and your children."

The scene blurred before Gordon's eyes. He was even hurting Gerald after his brother was gone from this earth.

"Lord, I can't go on like this. Please, show me what to do. Please—"

A shout rose from the bow. Gordon spun toward it and saw a crewman waving his arms and pointing. Ahead of them and to the starboard two or three points off the bow, a vessel similar to theirs wallowed in the glassy waters of the bay.

"She's sinking!" the man shouted. "We've gotta get alongside her."

This was God's answer—that his neglect, his desire to be away from Cape May, might cause the deaths of the fifty people aboard the other vessel?

"It can't be worse," he cried aloud.

But it could, for clinging to the rail between two elderly ladies, her pinafore already soaking wet, stood Ruby.

Chapter 14

A rowboat. A dinghy." Gordon glanced around the deck as he shouted. He saw neither craft.

"A line. Where's there a line?"

With a rope, he could possibly climb across, secure the line and. . .

No, if the other boat went down too quickly, they risked dragging this vessel down, too. He would have to swim, risk getting sucked under with the other boat, but possibly save Ruby and a few other people. He could throw chairs overboard for people to grab. Chairs would float.

He raced to the main deck and the furniture.

"Gordon." Marigold grasped his arm.

He turned. "I'm going overboard to help."

"No, you're not." Grimacing with pain, she held on to him with both hands. "It's too dangerous."

"I can't let Ruby drown, not like my brother. If I'd been here—"

"You couldn't have saved them."

"But I can save Ruby." He tried to pull free without hurting her, but her grip was fierce.

"Wait, Gordon. Look."

Across the gap of a hundred yards of water between his vessel and the one sinking in the bay, a dozen small boats had converged. Men, women, and a few youths swarmed around the foundering craft and aided the passengers in climbing over the railings and into safety.

"If I'd lost Ruby—" He stopped himself, his eyes widening. "Bring them here." He meant to shout the words. His voice emerged choked. His eyes blurred.

The boatmen seemed to understand anyway. They pulled toward his boat, where the crew gathered to receive wet, frightened, sobbing passengers onto the sun-drenched deck. Though her ankle had to pain her, Marigold worked alongside them. She must have hugged every lady and child lifted aboard.

Joining the efforts, Gordon wanted to hug her. Her dress was torn and sodden, her hair whipped around her face in a frizzy mass of fire, and her skin was beginning to turn pink from too much sun, but she was the most beautiful woman he had ever seen.

He reached her side just as Ruby came over the rail on the shoulders of a burly fisherman.

"Uncle Gordon." The child launched herself into his arms and clung. "I was naughty, and the boat was going to go down to the bottom. I almost made everyone drown like Mommy and Daddy."

"No, child, no." He held her close. "It wasn't your fault. It was mine. I've been a selfish, bitter fool."

Ruby stopped sobbing long enough to ask, "What's 'bitter'?"

"Something nasty." He started to turn to Marigold again, but Dennis Tripp emerged from the crowd and stalked up to him.

"I told you. Those boats need work. Randall claims it was done, but he's a liar, and I won't mince words over it."

"Yes." Gordon met the man's gaze without flinching. "But the fault lies with me. I was too anxious to sell to look into matters carefully. If anyone was hurt, it's my fault."

"None of the boats should go out again until they're fully inspected," Tripp pronounced.

"They won't." Gordon glanced toward shore, knowing he said good-bye to his grubstake for a head start in Alaska. "I'm shutting the business down until we know all is well and safe. Can you—will you see to it, Mr. Tripp?"

"I'd be honored, sir." Tripp's face flushed as he ducked his head. "With the Lord's help, we'll set all to rights."

"Yes, with the Lord's help."

Past Tripp's shoulder, Gordon saw Marigold's face, her widened eyes, her mouth forming an O. He thought it was of approval. He hoped it was of approval as he added, "With the Lord's help and the help of those He has sent to be a part of my life."

In his arms, Ruby shivered but seemed to have stopped sobbing.

"We'll get you home as soon as we land," he told her.

Still carrying Ruby, he walked among the passengers, listening to their complaints, their praise, their anger. He blamed none of them for their outrage.

"You'll get your money back," he assured him. "I can't promise you more than that right now, as I'm closing the company until we're certain the boats are safe."

A few people protested that.

"Accidents happen, sir," one youth said. "And this was a great adventure."

"It could have been a great tragedy."

Ruby, sodden in his arms, was testimony to that.

As much as he wanted to rush straight home, he waited on deck with the skippers and crew from both boats while the passengers disembarked. When they were gone, he addressed his employees.

"Gentlemen, I want every excursion boat secured upon its return. A thorough inspection of each boat will be conducted, and proper repairs will be made before I will allow them to sail again. Passengers who've paid for canceled excursions will be refunded."

A murmur rose among the crewmen. They needed their jobs.

Ruby shivered in his arms. "I need to get my niece home, but I will return with further instructions. Dennis Tripp is in charge in my absence."

He nearly forgot about Marigold, until he heard a rustle behind him and turned to see her leaning against the rail, her face pinched with pain.

She smiled at him with tight lips. "Know anyone who can carry me?"

"I can. No one else here looks strong enough to carry you." He called to one of the dispersing crewmen. When the young man stopped and turned back, Gordon said, "I need your help with the young lady. Please carry my niece."

"I'm too big for you to carry," Marigold protested.

"No, you're not." Slowly, reluctantly, Gordon placed Ruby in the sailor's arms. The young man held her as though she were fragile, his face growing tender.

Ruby whimpered in objection.

"Miss Marigold hurt her ankle," Gordon told Ruby. "She can't walk."

"Your niece is safe with me, sir." The crewman stood motionless while Gordon scooped Marigold into his arms.

"You can't walk six blocks with me." She tried to squirm free.

"You can't walk six feet; now be quiet." Gordon strode down the gangway, his precious burden slumped against his shoulder.

Burden. That's what he'd thought of his nieces and any idea of a wife—burdens to be avoided. He couldn't drop a burden he didn't carry. Yet, as he walked beside the young man carrying Ruby, Gordon experienced no fear that he would drop Marigold. She felt light, though she wasn't a small woman.

Could he possibly. . . ? Did he dare. . . ?

Beryl, Mrs. Cromwell, and Mrs. Morris sat on the front porch. The older women rose as the odd procession came around the corner.

Beryl leaped all five steps in a bound and raced to greet them. "You found her. Ruby, you are in trouble. Why are you wet? Why is Uncle Gordon carrying Miss Marigold?"

Ruby turned her face into the young man's shoulder and didn't answer.

"Did you go to the elephant like you said you would?" Beryl persisted.

"Later." Marigold leaned out of Gordon's hold and caught hold of Beryl's hand. "She's frightened and cold. I'll talk to her later. That is, your uncle will talk to her later." She glanced at him. "I don't have the authority to question Ruby. Not now, when I've failed her."

"How?" Gordon adjusted his hold on her so she couldn't slip away from him.

"I ignored the way Beryl talks to her. We sisters aren't always kind to each other. The things I said to Rose shame me."

"But they're in the past." Gordon smiled at her then turned to Mrs. Cromwell. "Will you be so kind as to run a hot bath for Ruby? I'm afraid Marigold can't climb the steps." To the crewman, he added, "Thank you for your help. You did admirable work today. I won't forget it."

"Please don't, sir. If you close the excursion company, we'll all be out of work. It's hard enough to find here in the winter."

Gordon sighed. "We'll see what condition things truly are in. But I'll do what I can for all of you."

The young man set Ruby on the porch, bade good-bye, and fairly raced down the street.

"Come along, Ruby, precious," Mrs. Cromwell said.

"Bring Marigold into the parlor," Mrs. Morris suggested. "We can have the doctor in to look at them both, and you can tell me what happened."

Gordon started up the steps. Seeing Beryl standing by the door, he said, "Go help Mrs. Cromwell with Ruby."

"I'm not a nurserymaid."

"Beryl," Gordon's voice cracked across the child's protest, "you are in enough trouble without talking back to me."

"I'm in trouble?" Beryl stared at him. "Why am I in trouble? I've stayed home all along like I'm supposed to."

Gordon glared at her. "You know what you did, so don't play innocent with me. We'll talk about your unkindness later. Now go up to your room and help Mrs. Cromwell."

"Yes sir." Head bowed, Beryl dragged her feet on her way into the house.

"Don't be mad at Beryl," Ruby said. "She doesn't mean to be mean."

"I did mean it." Beryl spun around at the foot of the steps, her face contorted with an effort not to shed the tears in her eyes. "I meant everything I said, but then you really were gone, and I was scared, and then I didn't mean all those things I said to you."

"You didn't?" Ruby reached out her arms to Beryl. "I love you, Beryl."

"I love you, too." Beryl ran back to the porch and hugged her younger sister. "We have to get along. We won't have anyone else once Uncle Gordon goes away."

"And he'll go away now, too, because I was bad." Ruby began to cry. "Just like Mommy and Daddy went away because I was naughty."

~∕∕∕~

Dressed alike in white frocks, Ruby and Beryl sat on the parlor sofa and wore similar expressions of apprehension and contrition. Marigold—attired in one of the gray gowns Gordon wanted to ask the laundry to burn next time they went out for cleaning—sat between the girls, one hand on either thin shoulder, her face set, as though she were angry or distressed.

Gordon's own insides squeezed and softened. Seeing them after the past hour he'd spent working out what to do with the business felt like the first cool, sweet drink of water after months of brackish ship's fare. He could drink in the sight of them for hours, days, years.

He shook his head to clear it of such nonsense. He didn't want or need any more time with them than necessary. The girls needed playmates their own age and a female who could teach them things girls needed to learn, and Marigold needed to find a worthy man and set up her own household. He was a loner, who, at that moment, couldn't talk himself into staying alone.

"May I come in?" he asked.

The girls nodded. Marigold gave him a smile.

"How's the ankle?" he asked, then realized asking about a lady's limb was indelicate.

Marigold grimaced. "Sprained. I can't walk on it for days."

"You mean you'll have to let others do for you?" Gordon couldn't stop himself from grinning.

"Yes, a maidservant who can't serve." Her eyes twinkled. "Maybe I should go home."

"Do you want to?" His alarm startled him.

Her, too, for her eyes widened, and her lips parted without a sound emerging.

"It's all right if you do," he added more calmly.

"I don't want to leave the girls right now."

Right now. That meant one day she would leave the girls, leave him.

Gordon pulled up a footstool and sat facing the ladies. "Well then, let's get this over with." He focused his attention on Ruby. "Why did you run away this morning?"

"I dunno." She popped her fingers into her mouth then yanked them out again, squared her shoulders, and looked him in the eye. "I don't want to be afraid of the water and be a baby."

"So you stowed away on a boat to prove you're not afraid?" Gordon questioned with an effort around the unfortunate tendency of his lips twitching. "You didn't think that was naughty?"

"Yes, it was naughty." She hung her head. "And now you're going to go away again because I was naughty like when Mommy and Daddy went away."

"Died," Beryl interjected.

Ruby nodded. "Yes, died."

A strangled sound from Marigold drew Gordon's attention to her. She held her hand to her lips, and tears filled her bright eyes. Ruby's words sank in, and his own throat tightened.

"What does you being naughty and your parents' accident have to do with each other?" Gordon made himself ask.

Ruby started to cry, harsh, racking sobs. "Because I was always naughty."

Gordon crouched before her.

He removed his handkerchief from his pocket and began to wipe her cheeks. "Of course you were naughty. Children are naughty. Adults are naughty."

"But I made Mommy and Daddy go away," Ruby wailed. "Forever."

Gordon glanced at Marigold for help in understanding what Ruby was talking about. Marigold shook her head.

"How could you make them go away forever?" Gordon asked.

Ruby took his handkerchief and cried into it.

"She left her doll out in the rain the day before, and that day she broke Daddy's picture of Mommy," Beryl said. "Daddy yelled at her and sent her to her room. Mommy said it wasn't a good picture and she didn't like it anyway and—" her lower lip quivered—"they started to argue."

"They weren't arguing when they left." Marigold spoke up for the first time. "They looked quite happy with one another when they greeted me on their way out."

"You told me to stay in the nursery," Ruby said. "But I sneaked down to Mommy and Daddy's room to look at their pretty things."

Beryl slumped in her chair. "I didn't try to stop her. I wanted her to get into trouble because—because everyone thinks I have to be a good example to her, and they thought every time she did something wrong it was my fault. Mommy told me I should have gotten Ruby's doll from the lawn if I knew it was there. But this time it wasn't my fault. It was hers."

"I know," Ruby wailed.

"No, I didn't mean that. Oh Ruby." Beryl slid from the sofa and wrapped one arm around her sister's shoulders. "I didn't mean Mommy and Daddy going away. I mean I didn't have anything to do with it. You got into trouble all by yourself, like this morning."

"And now Uncle Gordon will go away forever," Ruby sobbed.

Gordon had gone days without speaking to another soul. He didn't mind the silence or his lack of facility with words—until there in the parlor with his niece. He looked to Marigold for help. She always seemed to have a great deal to say. But she shook her head and refused to meet his eyes.

He cleared his throat. He needed to speak. Ruby was his responsibility. He couldn't depend on anyone else to heal her heart, as much as he wanted to remain aloof, remote, out of trouble with his heart.

"I was going to go away even before I met you, Ruby," he began. "If—I mean, when I leave, it will have nothing to do with you being naughty."

"What if I'm especially good?" Ruby peeked at him above the broad handkerchief. "Will you stay? You know, if I don't suck my fingers and I'm not afraid of water?"

"And if I stop being mean to Ruby and calling her a baby and things like that?" Beryl added.

"I. . .um. . ." Gordon glanced around the room, as though an easy answer would spring forth from one of the dozens of books lining the walls. "I prefer to be alone."

"Why?" the girls asked.

"So I don't hurt people who love me." He spoke the truth for the first time to anyone, yet the confusion and sadness on his nieces' faces told him he was hurting them by planning to leave.

"I'm not leaving right away," he concluded.

"Then we can pers—pers—get you to stay?" Ruby asked, her eyes brightening.

"If I stay," Gordon said, "it won't be because you're naughty or good. It will be because—because—"

"Maybe God wants you to stay," Beryl suggested.

"He's certainly seen to it your inheritance is worthless for now," Marigold murmured.

Minx. She was a proud, wild-haired, outspoken minx.

And if he stayed, it was because he was in love with her.

"Let's pray and see what God tells us." Gordon rose. "I have to take care of the business right now, make sure my orders are being carried out, and reassure the workers they'll be paid. While I'm gone, I want you girls to come up with all the reasons why you should never leave the house without permission."

"But I didn't—" Beryl clapped her hand over her mouth. "I'll write them down."

"Good girl." Gordon tugged a pigtail on each girl. "Keep close watch on them. I shouldn't be long."

"Where are you going?" Marigold asked.

Minx indeed. No employee should ask that of her employer.

"I'm going to the boathouse to dismiss Lawrence Randall and ensure none of those boats go out again until I'm satisfied they're all seaworthy."

"That'll take months," Marigold said, her eyes narrowed.

"Months," he agreed. "But if he'll stay on, I'm hiring Dennis Tripp to oversee the operation. Do you know an honest bookkeeper? I suspect those clerks knew what Randall was up to and helped him cover up his accounting."

"I might," Marigold said and grinned.

"I'd have mutiny if I hired a female accountant," he said, grinning himself, though he felt foolish.

Chapter 15

A week later, when Marigold heard Gordon return to the house, she descended the steps, albeit still stiffly, to find him. The girls were working on their math, though giggling far more than the assignment warranted. She did nothing to stop the hilarity. Hearing them laugh, like little girls should, eased a burden from her heart.

Gordon had eased a burden from the girls' hearts—for the time being. If he departed, he would hurt them nearly as deeply as had the death of their parents, convincing them their naughtiness—far milder than the pranks Marigold had gotten into as a girl—had caused the losses in their lives.

She found Gordon in the library. He stood at the window, his back to the room, his shoulders slumped, his head bowed, as she had seen him too often before. His knuckles gleamed white he gripped the windowsill so tightly.

Marigold hesitated in the doorway then marched up to him and laid one of her hands over his. "What's happened?"

"I'm just feeling guilty about all the trouble with the excursion company. Dennis is doing well getting matters under way, and Randall didn't steal all the money." He snorted. "I suppose he had a certain honor. He only took the money he claimed he was spending on repairs."

"And no one's found him?" Marigold knew the answer.

"Not yet, but I expect they will. The West isn't as easy to hide in as it once was. We were even getting telephones in some places."

"Civilization has its advantages." She tried to smile.

Talk of civilization reminded her of how much he wanted away from it.

"I've come up with a way to set up the ledgers for the company," she said.

"And I suppose I will have to abide by them, or you'll badger me to death." His smile took the sting from his words.

It removed any protective coating from her heart that might have remained.

"I am a bit of a managing female except that I—" She bit her lower lip and closed her eyes.

An endless succession of *I*s floated across the inside of her eyelids then settled onto her shoulders like a leaden cloak.

"I'm not very good at managing anything," she concluded in a whisper.

"You've done remarkably well, considering the circumstances my selfishness left you in." Gordon faced her and touched her cheek with the tips of his fingers, a caress as light as a breeze, as powerful as a hurricane.

She jumped, and their gazes collided. The tenderness she saw in his smashed

341

the last vestiges of her pride.

"How can you think well of me?" Her voice emerged in a whisper. "I missed that the ledgers were in code. Your nieces have been so unhappy they misbehave when they used to be good children. I embarrassed you in front of neighbors. Then I sprained my ankle when you needed me most. And now—"

Now, the worst humiliation would be to tell him she was in love with him and not mourning her fiancé at all.

God, what are You trying to tell me?

But of course she knew the answer to that. She wasn't supposed to be the one who solved everyone's problems. She was supposed to depend on the Lord to solve them.

She backed away from Gordon, far enough away he couldn't reach out to her. Far enough away she couldn't catch his scent of sun-dried linens and a lemony soap. She would have to leave the room to be far enough away not to look into his dark but sparkling eyes.

"I shouldn't have come back," she said. "I should have stayed in Hudson City with my family and faced the fact that God's plan for my life isn't to make everything right for others. You have to make them right for yourself."

"I don't want you to leave," Gordon said. "I need you to stay and be as managing as you like."

"So you can leave as quickly as possible? I can't let you—"

Gordon started to laugh. Marigold glared at him for a moment; then as the reality of her words sank in, she laughed, too.

"So if I leave, I'm forcing you to stay." She stifled another fit of giggles, and unsuccessfully tried to stifle a different kind of fit—a wish to fling her arms around Gordon and tell him to laugh again so she could see his eyes dance.

She reached out to him instead, though she had stepped too far away to touch him. "Why do you want to leave us—I mean your family? Surely the past is behind you, whatever made you leave in the first place."

"I had hopes that it was." He began to pace around the library, laying a hand on his desk then his other hand on a vase sporting a spray of marigolds atop the mantel. "My father sent me away because I was so selfish I tended to hurt others without realizing it or, too often, caring that I had. The last straw—" He faced her. "Marigold, will you walk down to the boathouse with me? Is your ankle up to it?"

She would have walked to New York City on her sprained ankle if he asked her.

"Yes. But the girls—"

"Without the girls. Mrs. Cromwell can watch them. I need to get some supplies ordered for Dennis. . .and other things."

"All right. I'll be back in five minutes."

"Make that at least a quarter hour."

"It won't take me that long to tell Mrs. Cromwell we're stepping out and to get a hat."

"But it will take you that long to change out of that ugly dress."

She stared at him. "You don't like my dress?"

"I detest it." One corner of his mouth tilted up. "In fact, as your employer and your friend, I'm requesting you never wear it again."

And his friend.

The words lent wings to Marigold's feet. She raced into the kitchen to tell Mrs. Cromwell she would be gone with Mr. Chambers for a while, then charged up to her room to yank off the ugly dress. Buttons flew in all directions. She let them fly. The gown would make excellent rags for cleaning brass.

Beryl came in while Marigold was struggling to button up the back of a muslin gown sprigged with tiny purple flowers. "Are you angry, Miss Marigold? We're being good."

"You're being angels." Marigold hugged the child. "And, no, I'm not angry. I'm going for a walk and need something nicer to wear is all."

"Can we go, too?" Ruby asked from the doorway.

"Not this time. It's business."

"You look too happy for business," Ruby observed.

Beryl tilted her head to one side. "Are you going alone?"

"No." Her cheeks warm, Marigold plopped a hat onto her head and skewered it into place with a pearl-headed pin. Curls tumbled over her ears, but she left them alone.

Her fifteen minutes were up.

"If you're finished with your arithmetic," she told the children, "you may play in the yard or read out there, but I want you outdoors for a little while. Mrs. Cromwell will give you some lemonade."

"Is Uncle Gordon going with you?" Ruby persisted.

"We're going down to the boathouse."

"I want to come," Ruby said.

"Not this time. We need to talk about grown-up business."

Not the business Marigold thought they should talk about, the business she wanted to talk about—why she wanted him to stay. He would have to figure that out on his own. She wasn't laying her pride on the line with a man again.

She descended the steps and joined Gordon on the front porch. She didn't need to ask if her gown was acceptable; his glance said it all.

He offered her his arm. "Let's walk. I want to talk to you."

"About me leaving your employment? About you hiring me to do your bookkeeping instead of—"

"About me."

She winced. She would have to add *me* to all the *I* pronouns that pricked her conscience with their implication of self-centered behavior and thinking.

"I need to tell you why I left Cape May." Gordon set out at a leisurely pace that didn't strain her ankle. "Then you can decide...."

He didn't say what he thought she could decide. She didn't ask. She waited for him to speak.

"I thought I was helping. . .someone." He passed the walkway leading to the boathouse and directed their steps to the boardwalk. "It was a young lady. Well, most considered her a maidservant, not a lady, but she was soft-spoken and polite and—she acted like a lady."

"Unlike me." Marigold tried to ease the tension she felt radiating through his fingers.

He smiled faintly. "As to the soft-spoken part, yes, different from you, but you're a lady, Marigold. Never doubt that."

"Thank you. Go on if you must."

"I must. You need to understand why I found coming back so difficult, why being here has been difficult for me."

"You owe me no explanations."

He covered her hand where it rested on his forearm. "Don't I? I thought. . . Perhaps I was wrong. I don't trust my own judgment much, and it's difficult learning to rely on the Lord to direct me."

"I do understand." She smiled. "I'm better at directing the Lord. But go on. Tell me about this lady." And let her heart break if he'd been hopelessly in love, if he still loved.

They strolled along in silence for several moments, with the sea and sun spread out beside them in blue and gold splendor. Then Gordon took a deep breath and began. "She worked for us. She was a maid. She was a fine girl, but her brother wasn't a good man. He kept coming around and stealing her wages and trying to get her to make more by dishonest means like stealing from us. But he stole from us, and she was going to be arrested. My father didn't tolerate rule breaking of any kind."

"Oh no, that's so unfair."

"It happens too often, you know. I had a bit of a soft heart for her. No, it was more than that. I'd fallen for her prettiness, her sweetness, though my father always warned us not even to make friends with the maids, for the sake of propriety and, I suppose, because he didn't think they were good wife prospects."

"My great-grandmother was a maid. And I—"

"Have never been a maid, whatever work you've done." He smiled down at her and laced his fingers through hers. "But Louisa was. I bought her ice cream a time or two and some chocolates. It was all innocent from beginning to end. I was barely eighteen and she the same." He fell silent, his face pensive.

Marigold's gut tightened with the realization that he recalled another maid, another female, one who had indeed held his heart even a little.

Another stab to her pride that he would think of another female with such depth while he was with her.

She remained silent, waiting for him to continue speaking.

"I helped her escape from being arrested," he said abruptly.

"You did? Gordon—I mean, Mr. Chambers, that was very bad of you."

"I didn't think she'd go free if they arrested her, so I used my position as heir apparent to the boating business to take out one of the boats. I got her aboard without anyone knowing and intended to sail her across the Delaware Bay to Philadelphia. She could have gotten a train to anywhere from there, gone out West, and found a new life without anyone knowing the better for it." He sighed and turned his face to the sea. "But I failed. It was the only sailboat we had, and I capsized it. She couldn't swim."

Marigold stumbled. "She didn't—didn't—"

"No, she didn't drown. I got her to shore, but we were alone for a long time until someone rescued us, and on top of being accused of stealing, her reputation was further ruined. And it was my fault."

"But your intentions were good." Marigold's heart ached for the kindhearted boy.

"My intentions were selfish, Marigold." And his tone was harsh. "My father had often accused me of not ever thinking of others, so I wanted to prove I did. Except I really didn't. I did it for my own reasons and harmed her in the end."

"What reasons?"

"That I was man enough to take care of myself and others—that I deserved to run the excursion company. . . I'm not certain I know any longer."

"But—" Marigold stopped and instead of pressing him further, inquired, "What happened to her?"

"My father dropped the charges against her so I wouldn't be complicit in her crime; then he found her work in another city. He didn't tell me where."

"Then she got away from her brother."

"She did, but she also got stuck right back into a situation where something similar could happen to her. And the new people knew her background, so I doubt it was comfortable for her."

"You don't know?"

"No."

"But—" Marigold stopped again, words failing her except for the next question she didn't think she should ask.

They had reached the lighthouse. Gordon stopped and leaned against its white-painted wall, away from the door where people streamed in and out.

"My father said I'd abused my position of authority with the company to do harm, not good, and disinherited me. I thought my brother, my twin, would support me. He sided with Father, called me a fool. An irresponsible fool." He looked away toward a flock of seagulls diving for food on the sand. "Gerald was a good man, but he was business-minded like Father, and that scandal was bound to hurt some of his connections. So I left the next day and never came home again."

"Why?" Marigold could hold back no longer. "I don't mean why would your father do that? I expect he'd get over his anger and change his will back, unless he was a tyrant, so why did you leave and never come home? Didn't you miss your family? Didn't you miss having a home and friends and the same church every Sunday?"

"Every single day. But every time I let myself be too friendly with someone, I seemed to interfere somehow, making matters worse. I decided that I'm better off alone."

"Because you can't fix everyone's problems either?" Marigold grinned at him. He grinned back.

Marigold wanted to hold the moment, but she needed to hear everything from him, from past actions to future plans. "So you were afraid to come home for three months, even though you were needed here."

"Yes, but now I see that I have to let the Lord guide me through, to take the risk with His help. If I leave now, I'll hurt the girls and those depending on me for work at the excursion company, and I want to stay, especially if—but I cost you your fiancé, your wedding, your inheritance."

"Yes, to the inheritance, but it's just a piece of glass. A glass with sentiment and meaning behind it, but a piece of glass—nothing more." Marigold smiled. "And as for the fiancé, I'd say your delay saved me. If he couldn't wait for me for a little while longer, how much could he have loved me? That's a marriage I didn't need."

"You believe that? I mean—" He stared down at the toes of his shoes, up to the top of the lighthouse's flame—nearly invisible in the daylight—and not quite into her eyes. "Your heart isn't broken?"

"On the contrary." Marigold's heart raced like a colt in a derby. She now knew what she needed to say, but if she was wrong, if his feelings for her didn't run deeply, she would face the worst humiliation of her life. Without the risk to her pride, though, she would gain nothing.

She started to take his hands again then stepped closer and rested her hands on his broad shoulders. "Gordon, in these past weeks, I've come to realize that I—that I—" Her throat went so dry she could scarcely talk. "I convinced myself that I loved Lucian because I wanted to get married and he offered that to me. But when I met you, something happened to me. I stopped thinking about him, even before I knew there was no hope of getting him back, and. . . . Trying to persuade you to stay wasn't wholly for the sake of the girls. And coming back here after my sister's wedding wasn't all because I didn't like the humiliation of everyone knowing I'd been abandoned. Even though that was part of it." She laughed. "If my father wanted to teach me humility, he should have just bribed Lucian to jilt me publicly, instead of making me work for a year. But I'm glad he did. I found you here. If you leave for Alaska, I'll probably follow you."

"Marigold, are you saying—" The afternoon sunshine lit his features as though the lighthouse flame burned from within him. He clasped her shoulders then cupped her face in his hands. "Are you saying you care for me?"

"I'm saying that I love you." Words tumbled from her lips. "It's all right if you don't love me, too. I just had to tell you so you wouldn't think your staying away had hurt me or ruined my future somehow. But don't think you're hurting me if you don't feel the same—"

He pressed his forefinger to her lips. "Marigold, please be quiet." He replaced his finger with his mouth, kissing her longer, more deeply than he had before. Long enough to draw a crowd of appreciative onlookers. Long enough for Marigold to grow too breathless to even think of speaking. And amid the cheers and congratulations of the vacationers, Gordon raised his head for the moment it took him to say, "I love you, too."

Epilogue

Marigold and Gordon waited nearly eight months to marry—eight months in which they worked long days and into a few evenings to restore the business. As Gordon's bookkeeper and not his nieces' nursemaid, Marigold moved down the street to the Morris house, where one of their widowed cousins lived with her for propriety. So close to Gordon and the girls, Marigold managed to spend a great deal of time at their house, trying—and often succeeding—not to interfere with the girls' governess and Mrs. Cromwell's replacement.

Though Marigold worked with Gordon, she didn't see that much of him during the day. She spent her days in Randall's old office unraveling the man's ledgers and setting up a new bookkeeping system. Gordon worked with Dennis Tripp and some other employees, inspecting and repairing the boats and converting two of them into craft able to carry supplies across the bay, to increase the company's productivity even more than Gerald had begun to do.

By Easter the books were in order and two reliable clerks were hired to replace the ones who had disappeared along with Lawrence Randall, who had yet to be found. So Marigold went home to plan her wedding.

The weeks dragged by without Gordon, without Ruby and Beryl, without daily work. But at last, her family in tow, Marigold returned to Cape May to discover Gordon had conspired with her mother about one wedding arrangement.

"We're getting married on a boat?" Marigold exclaimed.

"Unless you object." Gordon held her hands as though never intending to let them go. "I'm sure I can talk the pastor into letting us have the church, but your mother and I have made all the arrangements."

"I don't object." Gazing into his root beer–colored eyes, Marigold feared she would agree to anything he said. "I'm just surprised. It's so. . .romantic."

"We're getting dozens and dozens of roses in." Ruby scampered into the library, braids escaping from their pink ribbons.

Beryl followed, neat and clean in her sky blue dress. "Not dozens and dozens. Well, maybe." She grinned.

"Roses?" Marigold shuddered. "But—"

"White ones," he assured her, "so they don't rival your hair."

348

Marigold laughed and hugged him.

"Tomorrow," he assured her, setting her from him with gentle firmness. "After tomorrow, we don't have to say good night and part."

"Tomorrow won't come fast enough."

But her mother and sister made plans that would hasten the time. She needed one more fitting for her dress. She needed to wash her hair so it had time to dry before bed. She had gifts to unwrap.

"Shouldn't Gordon be with me? And the girls wanted to be with me for the present-opening," she protested as they set her down amid her bridesmaids and a pile of packages tied up with white satin bows.

"Not for these." The bridesmaids, friends from college, giggled.

Marigold blushed, guessing that the parcels held delicate undergarments. She opened each box, sighed over the fine silks and intricate lace, then tried to rise, suddenly desperate for sleep to bring the next day faster.

"One more." Rose, not in the wedding because she was expecting her first child, sank to her knees before Marigold. "This is from me."

"But you and Adam already gave me that lovely tea service," Marigold protested.

"Yes, from Adam and me. This is just from me." Rose set a small box on Marigold's lap but didn't let go of it.

A rustling filled the room; then silence followed. Marigold glanced up to see the last of her friends whisking away.

"Why are they leaving?" Marigold asked, her stomach suddenly uneasy.

Rose smiled. "Because I asked them to. This is special. Between us."

Marigold's heart skipped a beat. "You're my sister, my best friend. I don't need more from you than that."

"I know, but you gave me so much. You sacrificed so much last year, staying here to take care of the girls, losing Lucian."

"No loss."

Lucian had broken his engagement to the Grassick girl and left New Jersey for parts unknown. He'd proven Father to be right in thinking that young man had too little of a sense of responsibility to be a good spouse.

"Maybe he wasn't a good catch," Rose said, "but it hurt you to see me marry first."

"I deserved it after being so awful to you."

"You were awful, but it's forgiven. I forgave you a long time before I even met Adam. Our friendship is too important for me to hold a grudge."

"Thank you. That's the most precious gift you could give me."

"Then let me seal it with this." Rose pushed the box more firmly into Marigold's hands.

"If you insist." She peeled back the wrapping.

Even before she opened the lid, she knew what the box contained.

It was the glass goldfinch, once again a gift of love and constancy.

A Letter to Our Readers

Dear Readers:

In order that we might better contribute to your reading enjoyment, we would appreciate you taking a few minutes to respond to the following questions. When completed, please return to the following: Fiction Editor, Barbour Publishing, Inc., P.O. Box 719, Uhrichsville, OH 44683.

1. Did you enjoy reading *Jersey Brides* by Laurie Alice Eakes?
   ❏ Very much. I would like to see more books like this.
   ❏ Moderately—I would have enjoyed it more if _____
   _____
   _____

2. What influenced your decision to purchase this book? (Check those that apply.)
   ❏ Cover   ❏ Back cover copy   ❏ Title   ❏ Price
   ❏ Friends   ❏ Publicity   ❏ Other

3. Which story was your favorite?
   ❏ *The Glassblower*   ❏ *The Newcomer*
   ❏ *The Heiress*

4. Please check your age range:
   ❏ Under 18   ❏ 18–24   ❏ 25–34
   ❏ 35–45   ❏ 46–55   ❏ Over 55

5. How many hours per week do you read? _____

Name _____

Occupation _____

Address _____

City_____ State_____ Zip_____

E-mail _____